Archie

Love Showdown

WHO WILL ARCHIE CHOOSE?

Archie & Friends All-Stars Vol. 18: Archie: Love Showdown
Published by Archie Comic Publications, Inc.
325 Fayette Avenue, Mamaroneck, NY 10543-2318.

ISBN: 978-1-936975-21-1

Printed in USA.

PUBLISHER/CO-CEO:
Jonathan Goldwater
CO-CEO: Nancy Silberkleit
PRESIDENT: Mike Pellerito
CO-PRESIDENT/EDITOR-IN-CHIEF:
Victor Gorelick
**SENIOR VICE PRESIDENT, SALES &
BUSINESS DEVELOPMENT:** Jim Sokolowski
**SENIOR VICE PRESIDENT, PUBLISHING &
OPERATIONS:** Harold Buchholz
EXECUTIVE DIRECTOR OF EDITORIAL:
Paul Kaminski
BOOK DESIGN: Duncan McLachlan
PRODUCTION MANAGER: Stephen Oswald
PRODUCTION: Kari Silbergleit,
Rosario "Tito" Peña
PRODUCTION INTERNS:
Michael Crowe, Josh Kirschenbaum
EDITORIAL ASSISTANT/PROOFREADER:
Jamie Lee Rotante
SPECIAL THANKS TO Paul Castiglia

Story:

Dan Parent, Bill Golliher, George Gladir

Pencils:

Dan DeCarlo, Dan Parent,
Stan Goldberg,
Doug Crane

Inks:

Henry Scarpelli,
Ken Selig, Alison Flood,
Mike Esposito,
Jon D'Agostino,
Bob Smith,
James DeCarlo

Letters:

Bill Yoshida,
Vickie Williams,
Jon D'Agostino

Colors:

Barry Grossman,
Rosario "Tito" Peña

Table of Contents

Chapter One

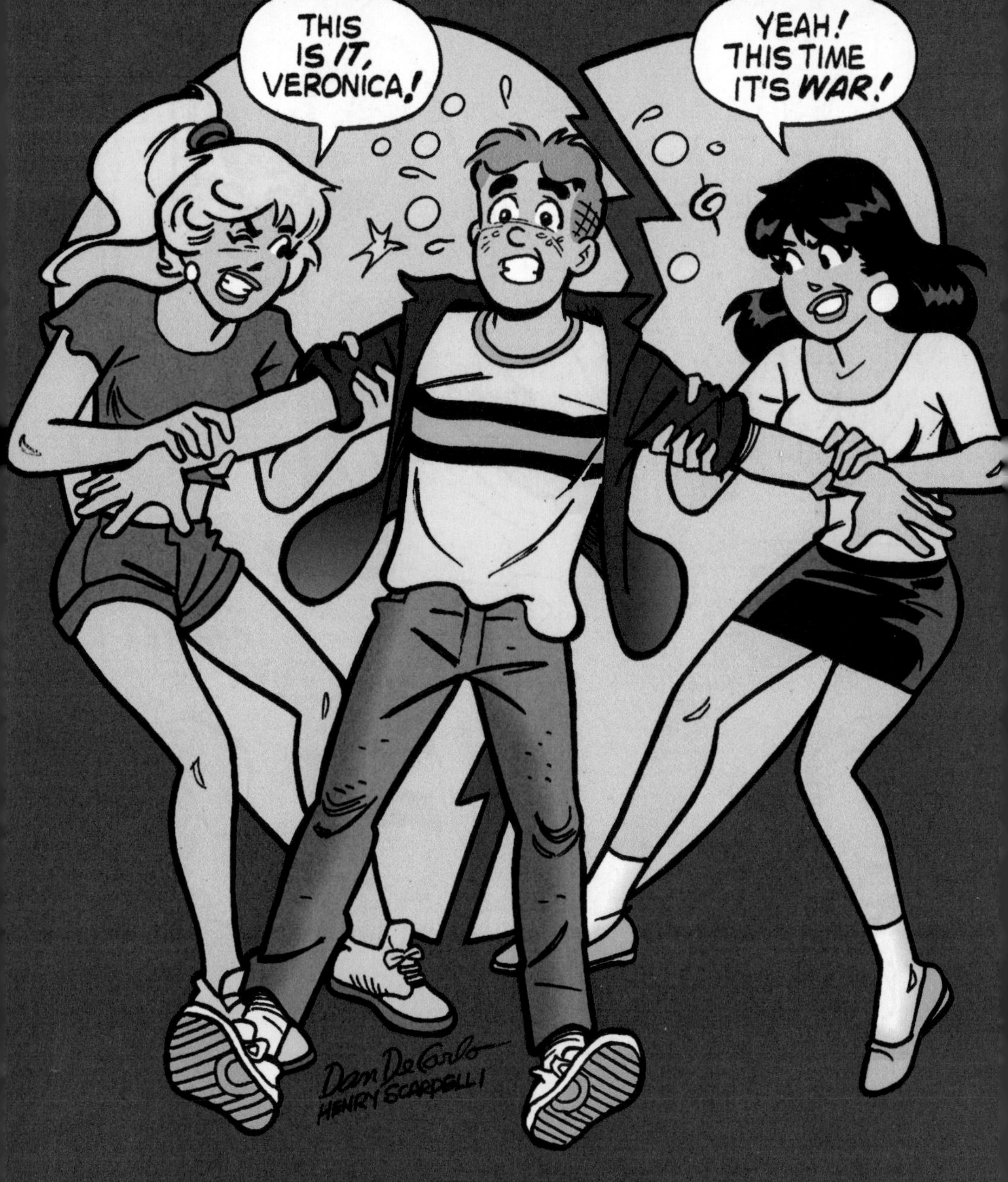
THIS IS IT, VERONICA!
YEAH! THIS TIME IT'S WAR!
Dan DeCarlo
HENRY SCARPELLI

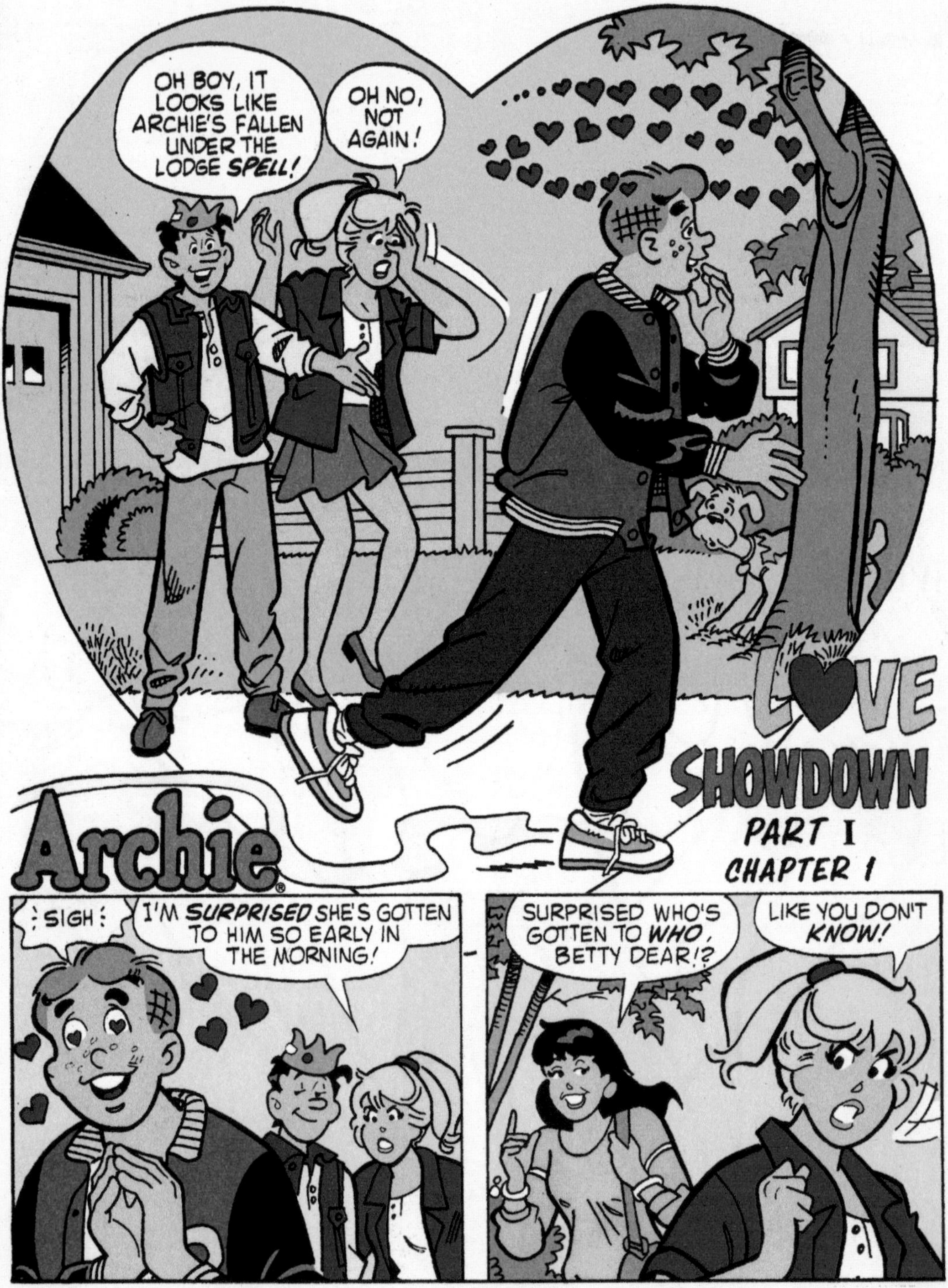
OH BOY, IT LOOKS LIKE ARCHIE'S FALLEN UNDER THE LODGE SPELL!
OH NO, NOT AGAIN!
LOVE SHOWDOWN
PART I
CHAPTER 1
Archie
SIGH
I'M SURPRISED SHE'S GOTTEN TO HIM SO EARLY IN THE MORNING!
SURPRISED WHO'S GOTTEN TO WHO, BETTY DEAR!?
LIKE YOU DON'T KNOW!

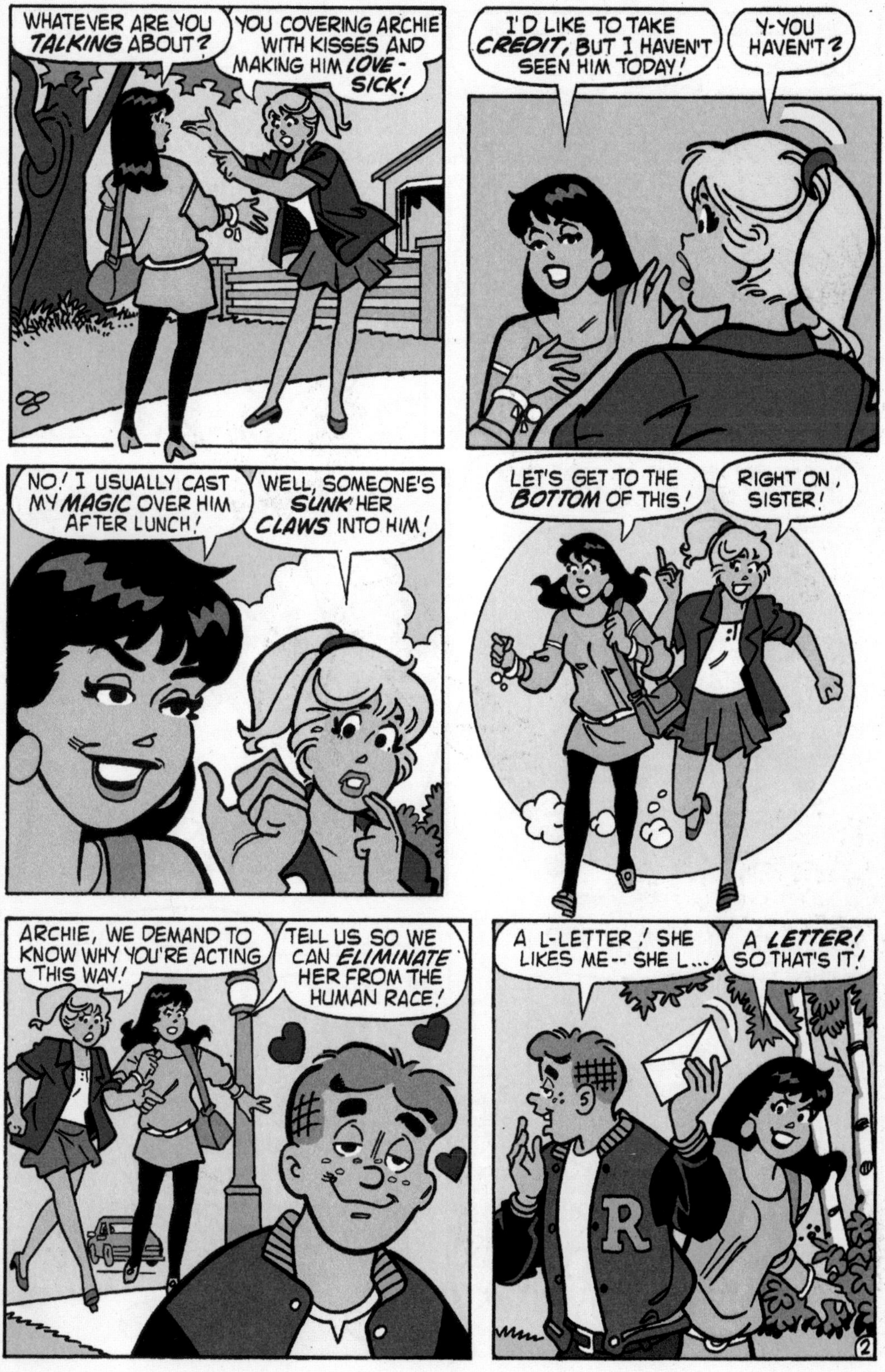
WHATEVER ARE YOU *TALKING* ABOUT?
YOU COVERING ARCHIE WITH KISSES AND MAKING HIM *LOVE-SICK*!
I'D LIKE TO TAKE *CREDIT*, BUT I HAVEN'T SEEN HIM TODAY!
Y-YOU HAVEN'T?
NO! I USUALLY CAST MY *MAGIC* OVER HIM AFTER LUNCH!
WELL, SOMEONE'S *SUNK* HER *CLAWS* INTO HIM!
LET'S GET TO THE *BOTTOM* OF THIS!
RIGHT ON, SISTER!
ARCHIE, WE DEMAND TO KNOW WHY YOU'RE ACTING THIS WAY!
TELL US SO WE CAN *ELIMINATE* HER FROM THE HUMAN RACE!
A L-LETTER! SHE LIKES ME-- SHE L...
A *LETTER*! SO THAT'S IT!
2

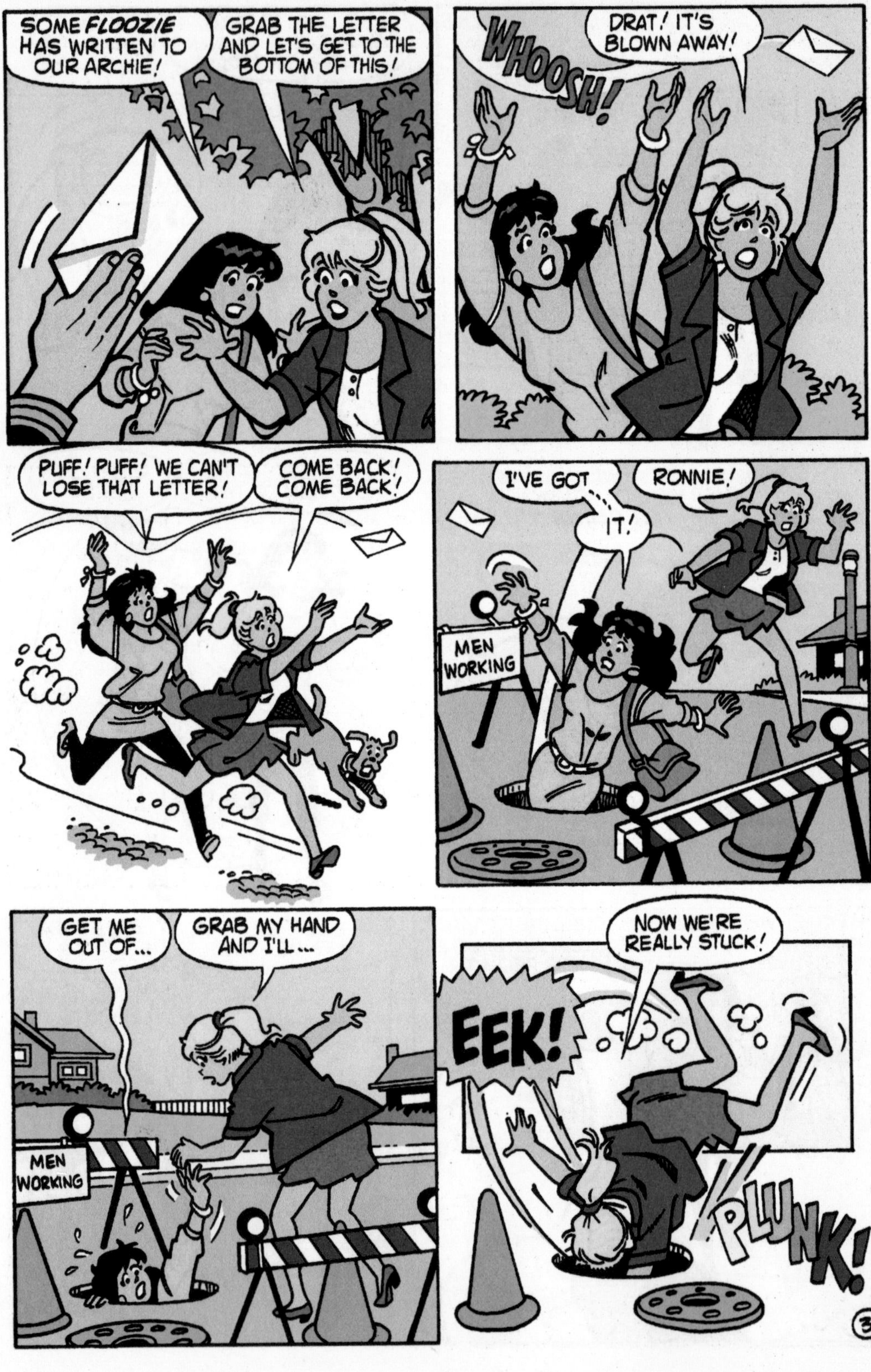
SOME FLOOZIE HAS WRITTEN TO OUR ARCHIE!
GRAB THE LETTER AND LET'S GET TO THE BOTTOM OF THIS!
WHOOSH!
DRAT! IT'S BLOWN AWAY!
PUFF! PUFF! WE CAN'T LOSE THAT LETTER!
COME BACK! COME BACK!
I'VE GOT
IT!
RONNIE!
MEN WORKING
GET ME OUT OF...
GRAB MY HAND AND I'LL...
MEN WORKING
EEK!
NOW WE'RE REALLY STUCK!
PLUNK!
3

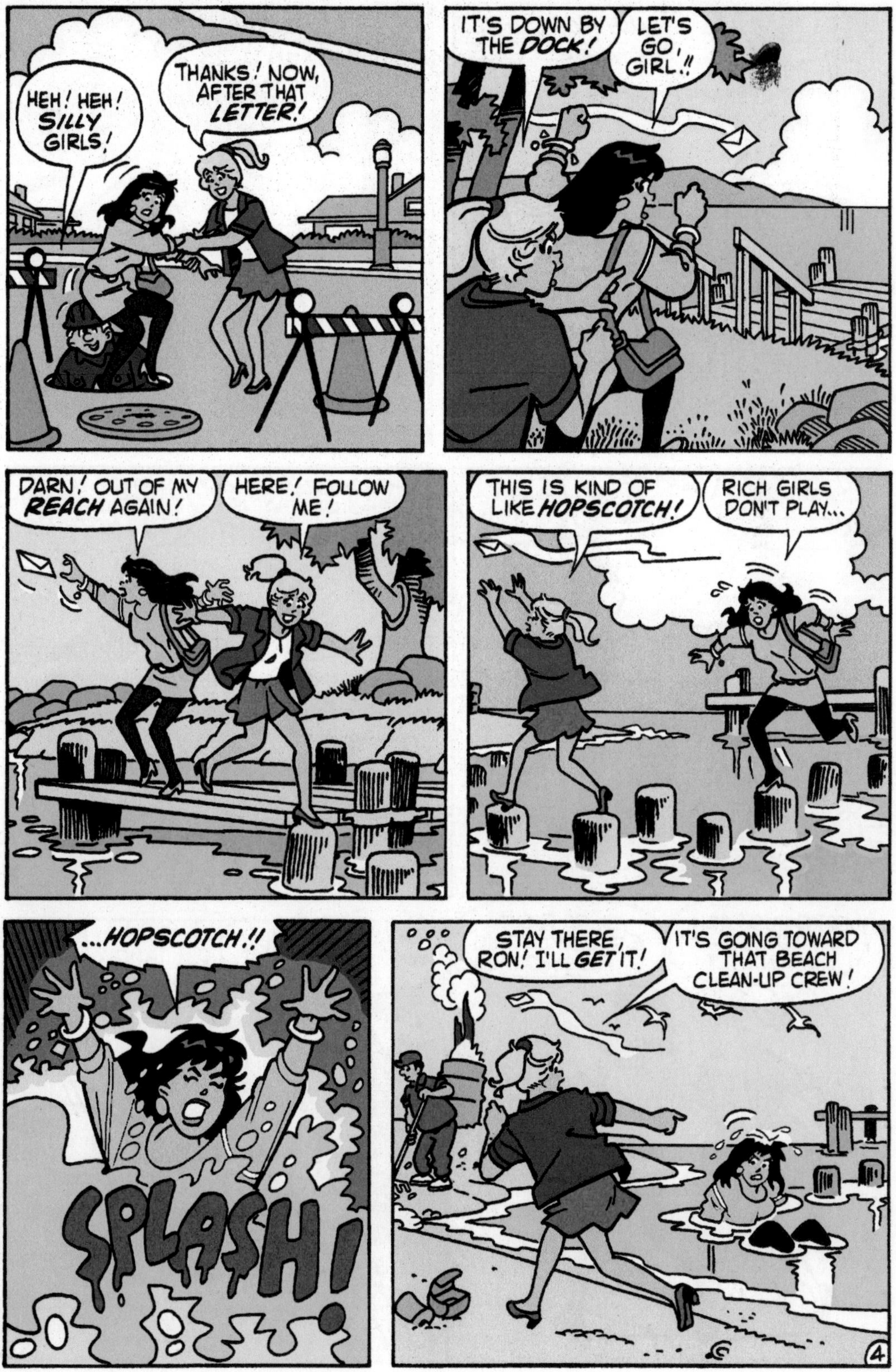
HEH! HEH! SILLY GIRLS!
THANKS! NOW, AFTER THAT LETTER!
IT'S DOWN BY THE DOCK!
LET'S GO, GIRL!!
DARN! OUT OF MY REACH AGAIN!
HERE! FOLLOW ME!
THIS IS KIND OF LIKE HOPSCOTCH!
RICH GIRLS DON'T PLAY...
...HOPSCOTCH!!
SPLASH!
STAY THERE, RON! I'LL GET IT!
IT'S GOING TOWARD THAT BEACH CLEAN-UP CREW!
4

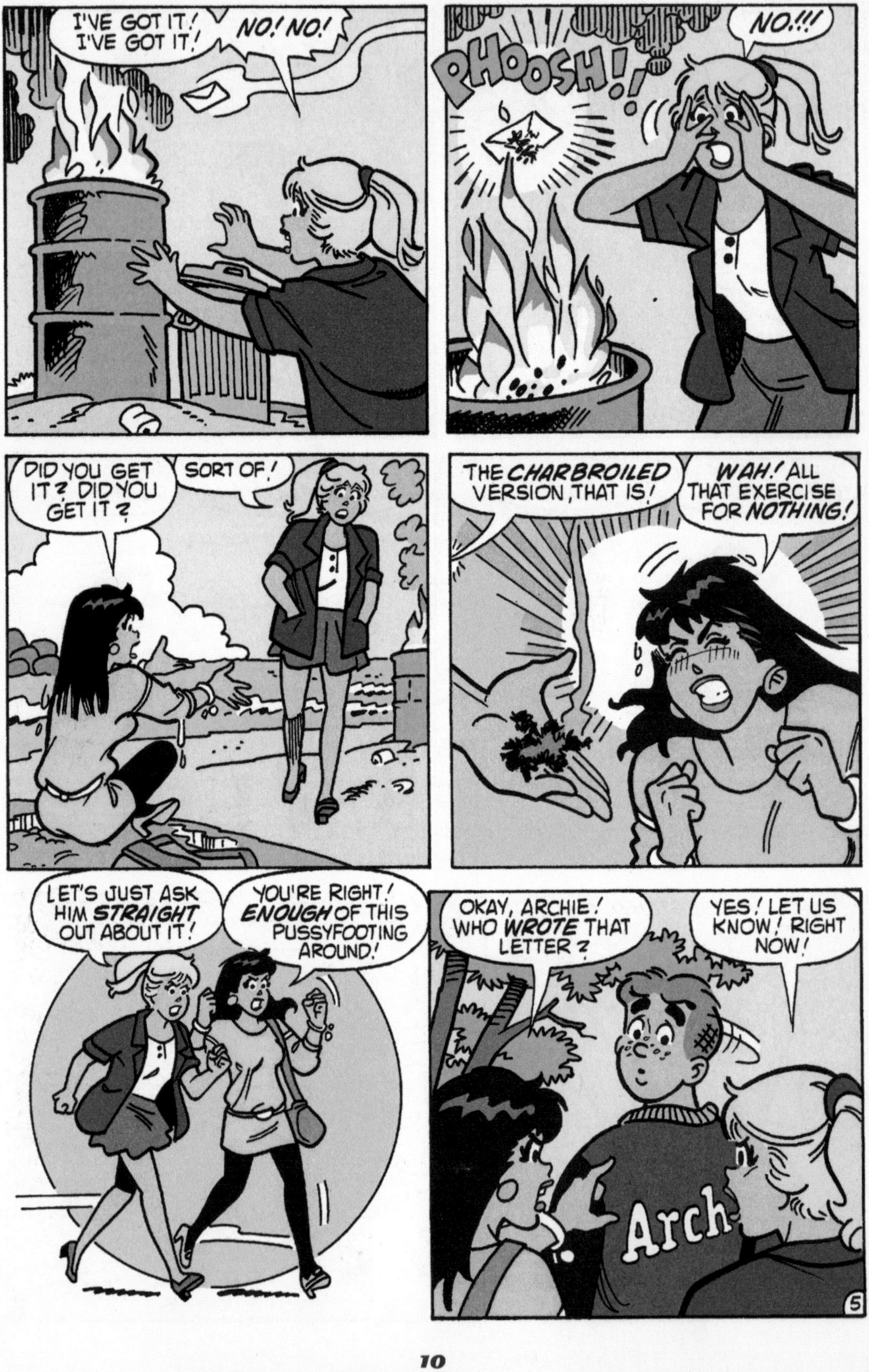
I'VE GOT IT! I'VE GOT IT!
NO! NO!
PHOOSH!
NO!!!
DID YOU GET IT? DID YOU GET IT?
SORT OF!
THE CHARBROILED VERSION, THAT IS!
WAH! ALL THAT EXERCISE FOR NOTHING!
LET'S JUST ASK HIM STRAIGHT OUT ABOUT IT!
YOU'RE RIGHT! ENOUGH OF THIS PUSSYFOOTING AROUND!
OKAY, ARCHIE! WHO WROTE THAT LETTER?
YES! LET US KNOW! RIGHT NOW!
Arch
5

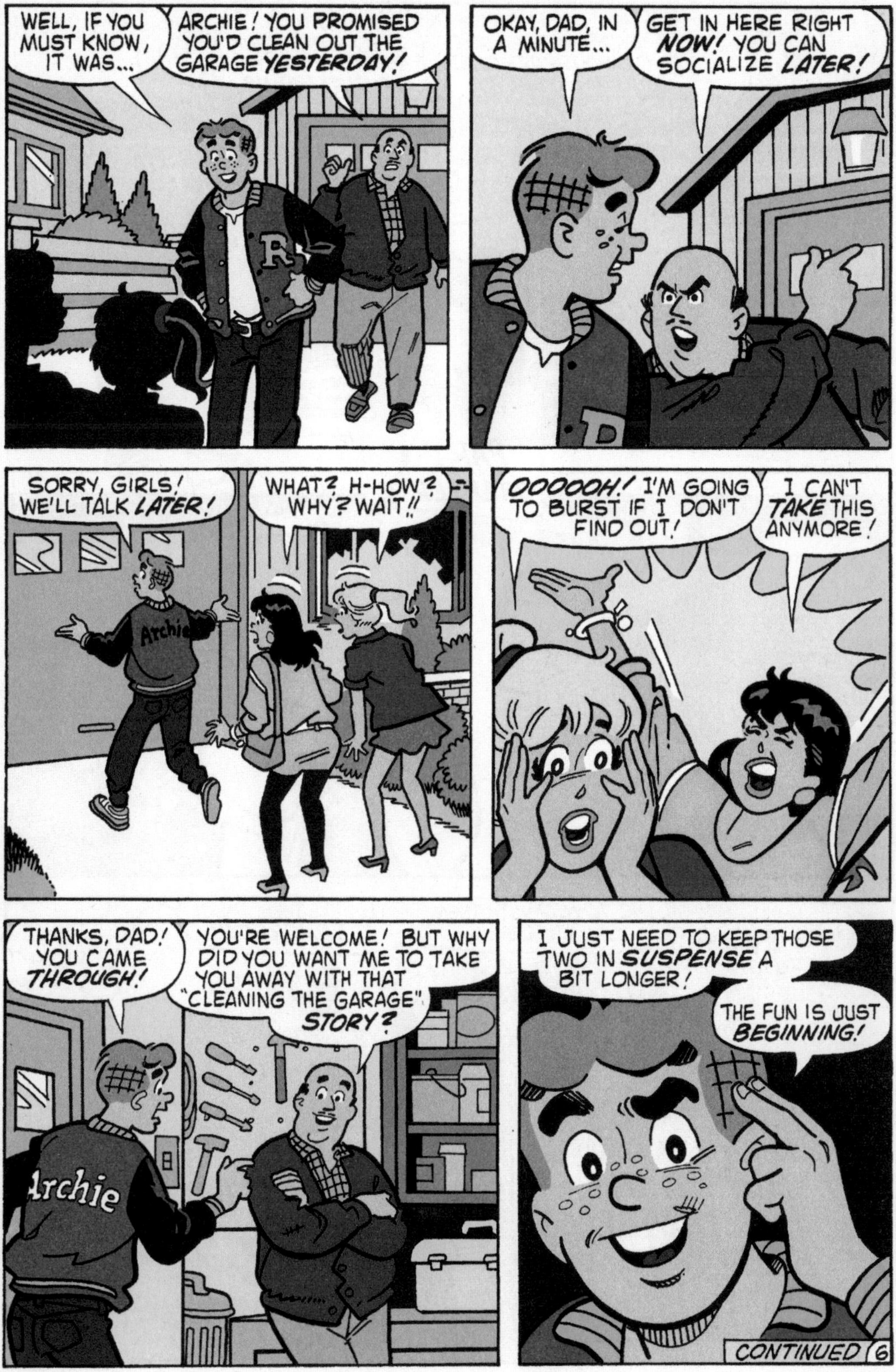
WELL, IF YOU MUST KNOW, IT WAS...
ARCHIE! YOU PROMISED YOU'D CLEAN OUT THE GARAGE *YESTERDAY*!
OKAY, DAD, IN A MINUTE...
GET IN HERE RIGHT *NOW!* YOU CAN SOCIALIZE *LATER*!
SORRY, GIRLS! WE'LL TALK *LATER*!
WHAT? H-HOW? WHY? WAIT!!
OOOOOOH! I'M GOING TO BURST IF I DON'T FIND OUT!
I CAN'T *TAKE* THIS ANYMORE!
THANKS, DAD! YOU CAME *THROUGH*!
YOU'RE WELCOME! BUT WHY DID YOU WANT ME TO TAKE YOU AWAY WITH THAT "CLEANING THE GARAGE" *STORY?*
I JUST NEED TO KEEP THOSE TWO IN *SUSPENSE* A BIT LONGER!
THE FUN IS JUST *BEGINNING!*
CONTINUED 6

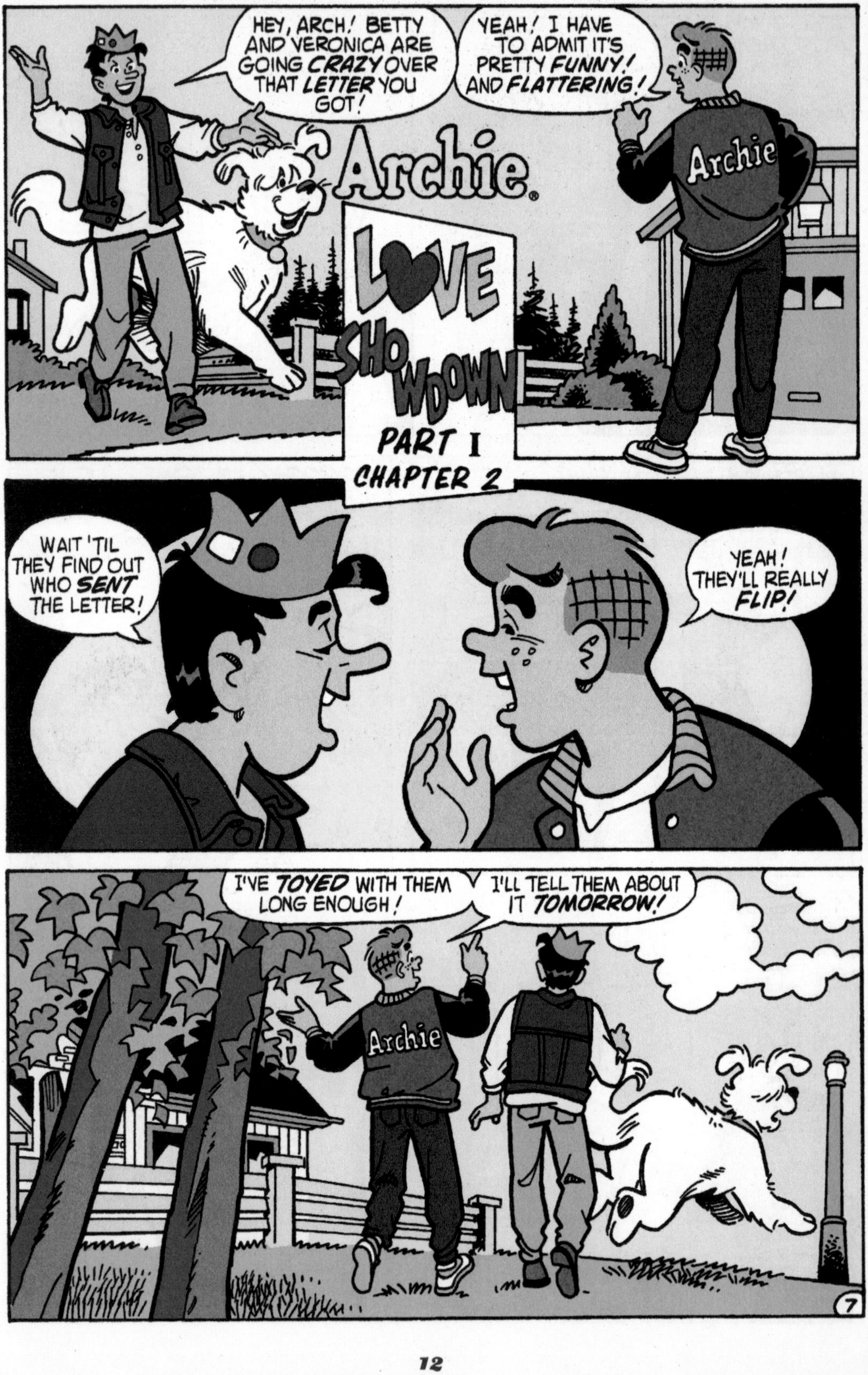
HEY, ARCH! BETTY AND VERONICA ARE GOING CRAZY OVER THAT LETTER YOU GOT!
YEAH! I HAVE TO ADMIT IT'S PRETTY FUNNY! AND FLATTERING!
Archie
Archie
LOVE SHOWDOWN
PART I
CHAPTER 2
WAIT 'TIL THEY FIND OUT WHO SENT THE LETTER!
YEAH! THEY'LL REALLY FLIP!
I'VE TOYED WITH THEM LONG ENOUGH!
I'LL TELL THEM ABOUT IT TOMORROW!
Archie
7

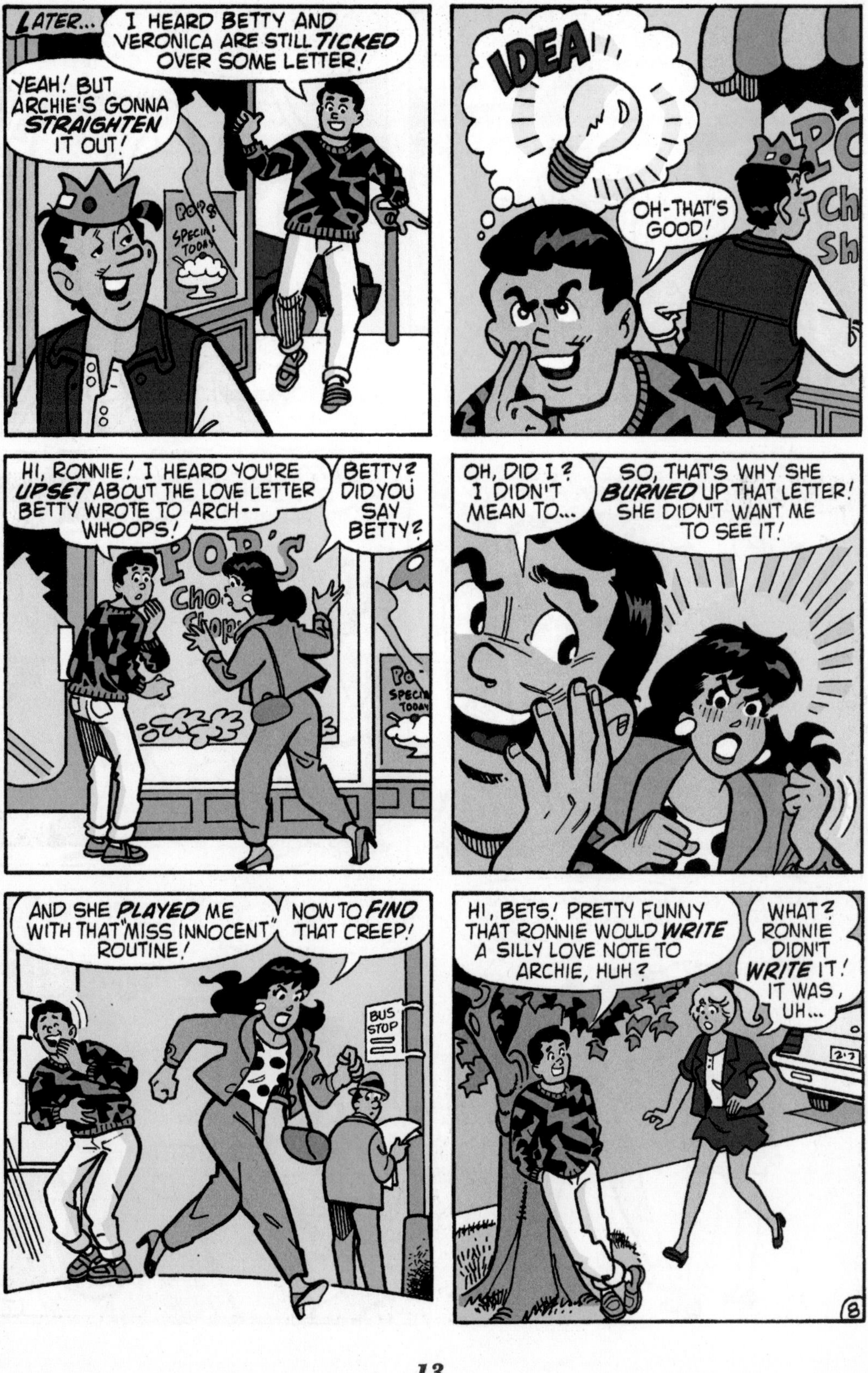
LATER...
I HEARD BETTY AND VERONICA ARE STILL TICKED OVER SOME LETTER!
YEAH! BUT ARCHIE'S GONNA STRAIGHTEN IT OUT!
IDEA
OH-THAT'S GOOD!
HI, RONNIE! I HEARD YOU'RE UPSET ABOUT THE LOVE LETTER BETTY WROTE TO ARCH-- WHOOPS!
BETTY? DID YOU SAY BETTY?
OH, DID I? I DIDN'T MEAN TO...
SO, THAT'S WHY SHE BURNED UP THAT LETTER! SHE DIDN'T WANT ME TO SEE IT!
AND SHE PLAYED ME WITH THAT "MISS INNOCENT" ROUTINE!
NOW TO FIND THAT CREEP!
BUS STOP
HI, BETS! PRETTY FUNNY THAT RONNIE WOULD WRITE A SILLY LOVE NOTE TO ARCHIE, HUH?
WHAT? RONNIE DIDN'T WRITE IT! IT WAS, UH...
8

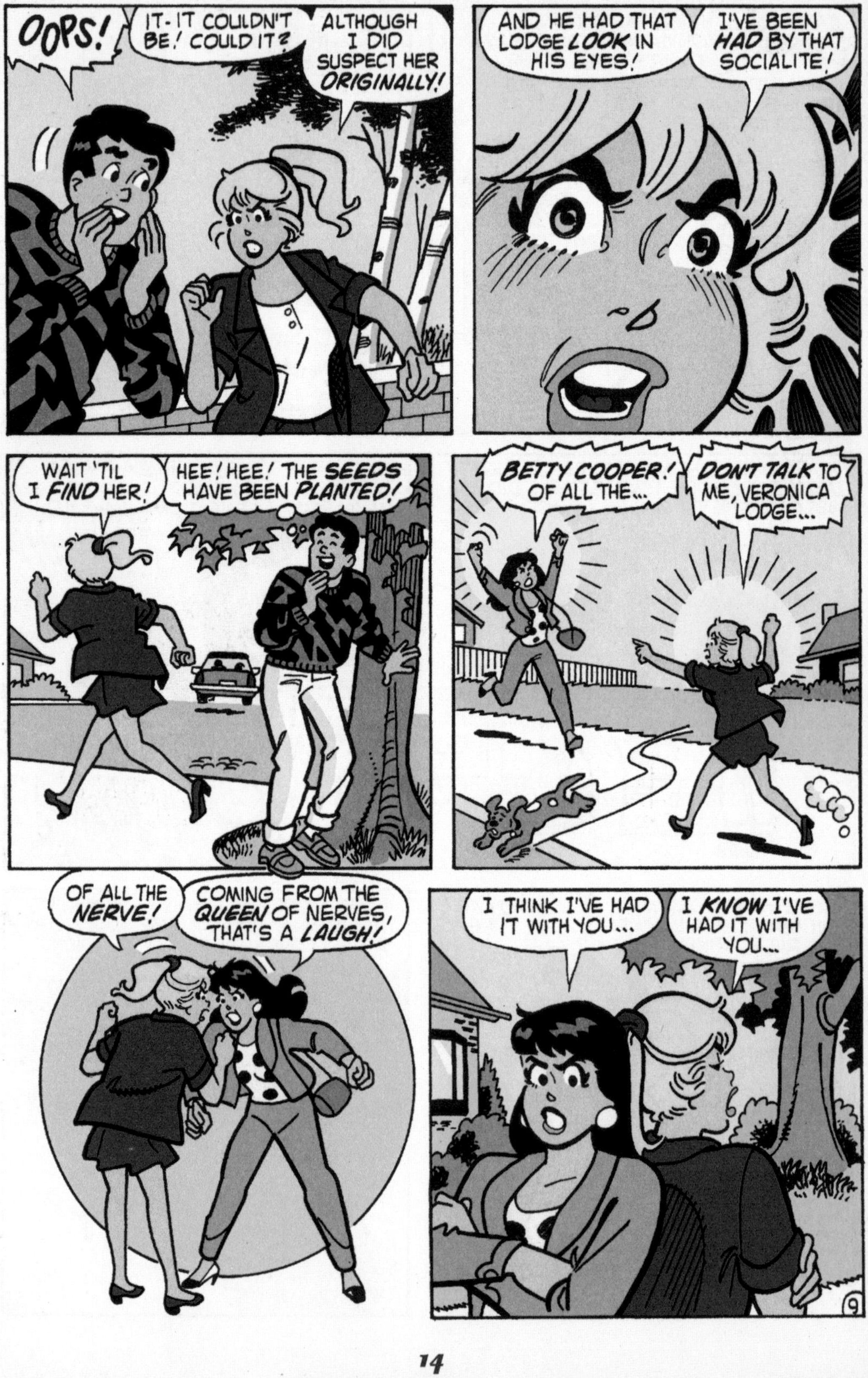
OOPS!
IT- IT COULDN'T BE! COULD IT?
ALTHOUGH I DID SUSPECT HER ORIGINALLY!
AND HE HAD THAT LODGE LOOK IN HIS EYES!
I'VE BEEN HAD BY THAT SOCIALITE!
WAIT 'TIL I FIND HER!
HEE! HEE! THE SEEDS HAVE BEEN PLANTED!
BETTY COOPER! OF ALL THE...
DON'T TALK TO ME, VERONICA LODGE...
OF ALL THE NERVE!
COMING FROM THE QUEEN OF NERVES, THAT'S A LAUGH!
I THINK I'VE HAD IT WITH YOU...
I KNOW I'VE HAD IT WITH YOU...
9

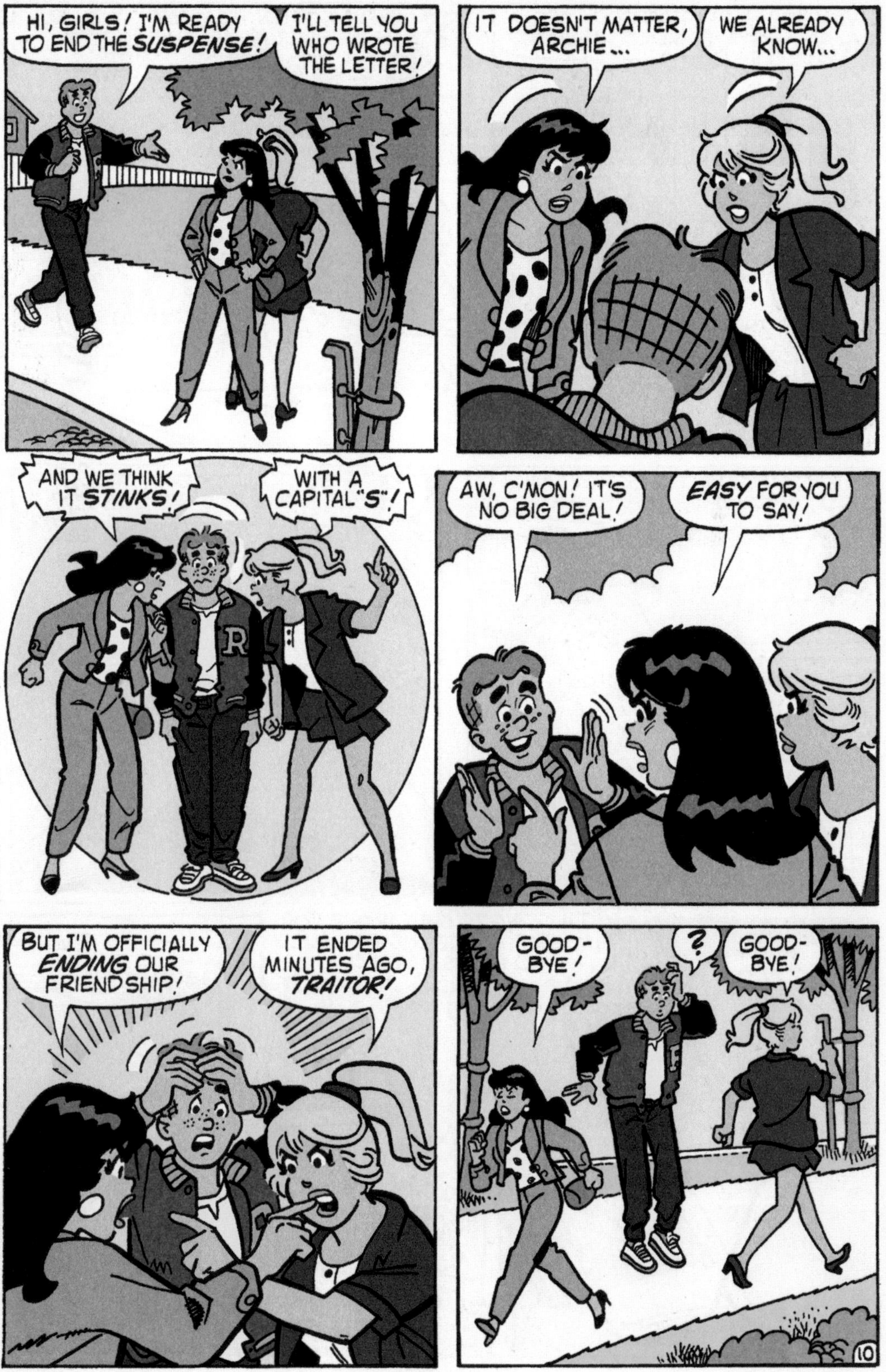
HI, GIRLS! I'M READY TO END THE SUSPENSE!
I'LL TELL YOU WHO WROTE THE LETTER!
IT DOESN'T MATTER, ARCHIE...
WE ALREADY KNOW...
AND WE THINK IT STINKS!
WITH A CAPITAL "S"!
AW, C'MON! IT'S NO BIG DEAL!
EASY FOR YOU TO SAY!
BUT I'M OFFICIALLY ENDING OUR FRIENDSHIP!
IT ENDED MINUTES AGO, TRAITOR!
GOOD-BYE!
?
GOOD-BYE!
10

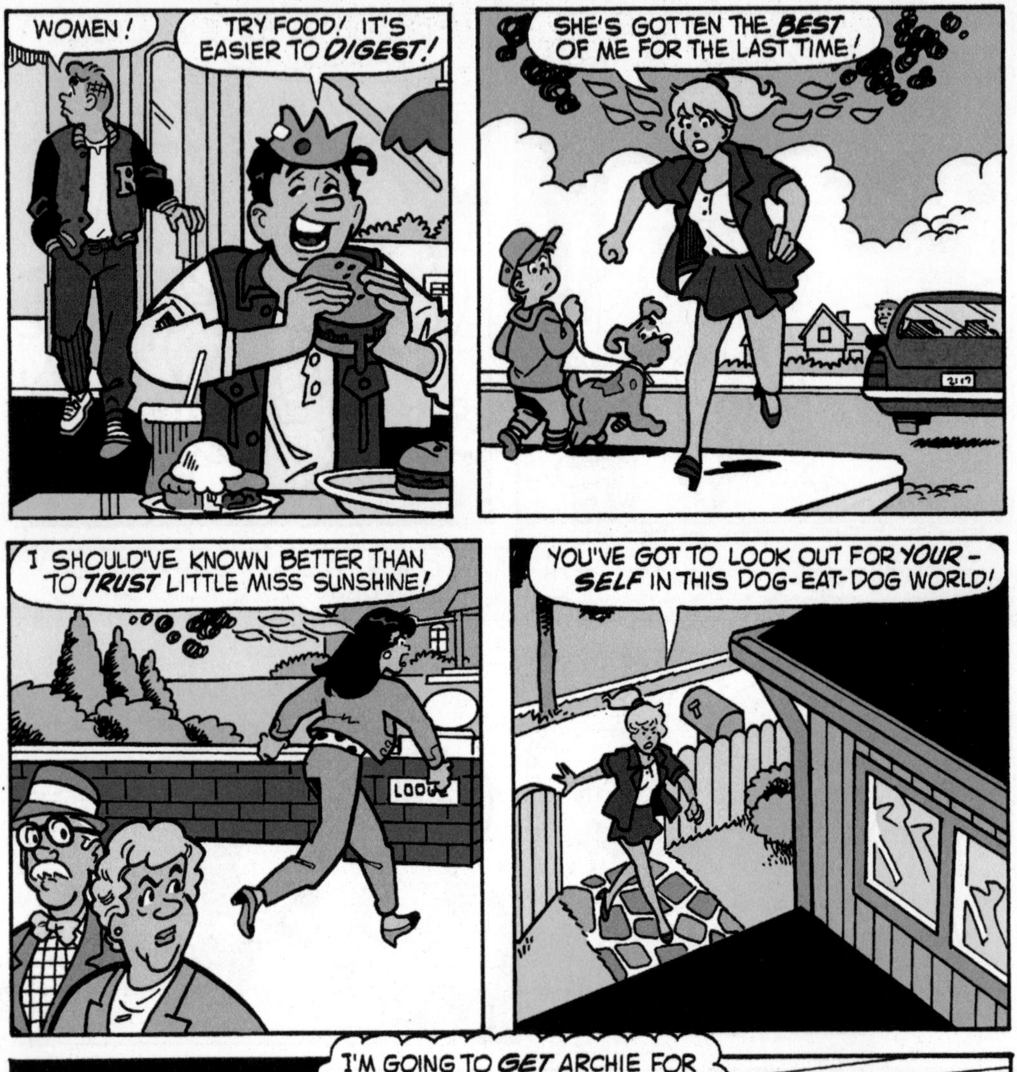
WOMEN!
TRY FOOD! IT'S EASIER TO DIGEST!
SHE'S GOTTEN THE BEST OF ME FOR THE LAST TIME!
I SHOULD'VE KNOWN BETTER THAN TO TRUST LITTLE MISS SUNSHINE!
YOU'VE GOT TO LOOK OUT FOR YOURSELF IN THIS DOG-EAT-DOG WORLD!
I'M GOING TO GET ARCHIE FOR MYSELF-- ONCE AND FOR ALL... NO HOLDS BARRED!
THE LOVE SHOWDOWN CONTINUES NEXT!
NOT THE END

Chapter Two

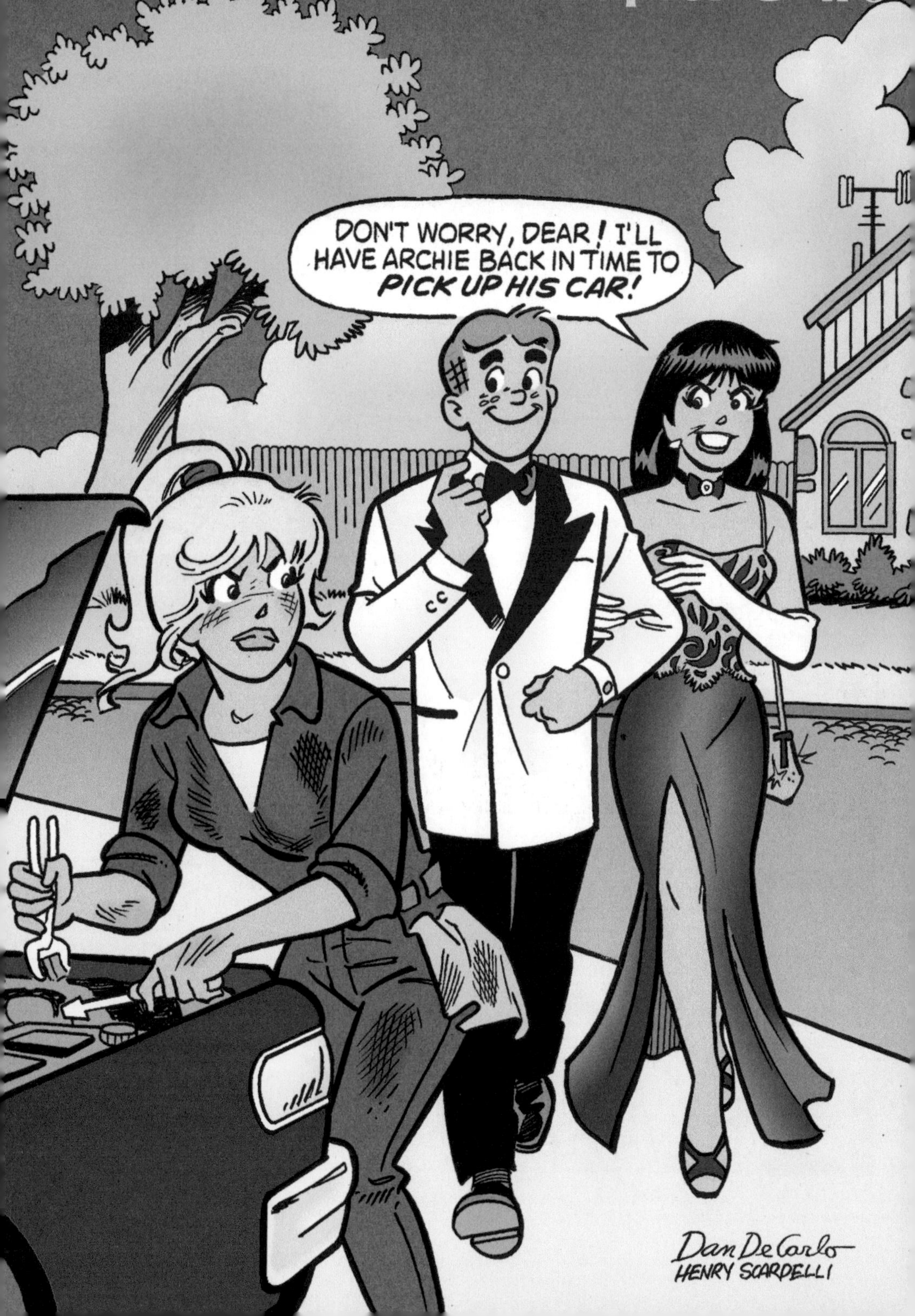
DON'T WORRY, DEAR! I'LL HAVE ARCHIE BACK IN TIME TO PICK UP HIS CAR!
Dan DeCarlo
HENRY SCARPELLI

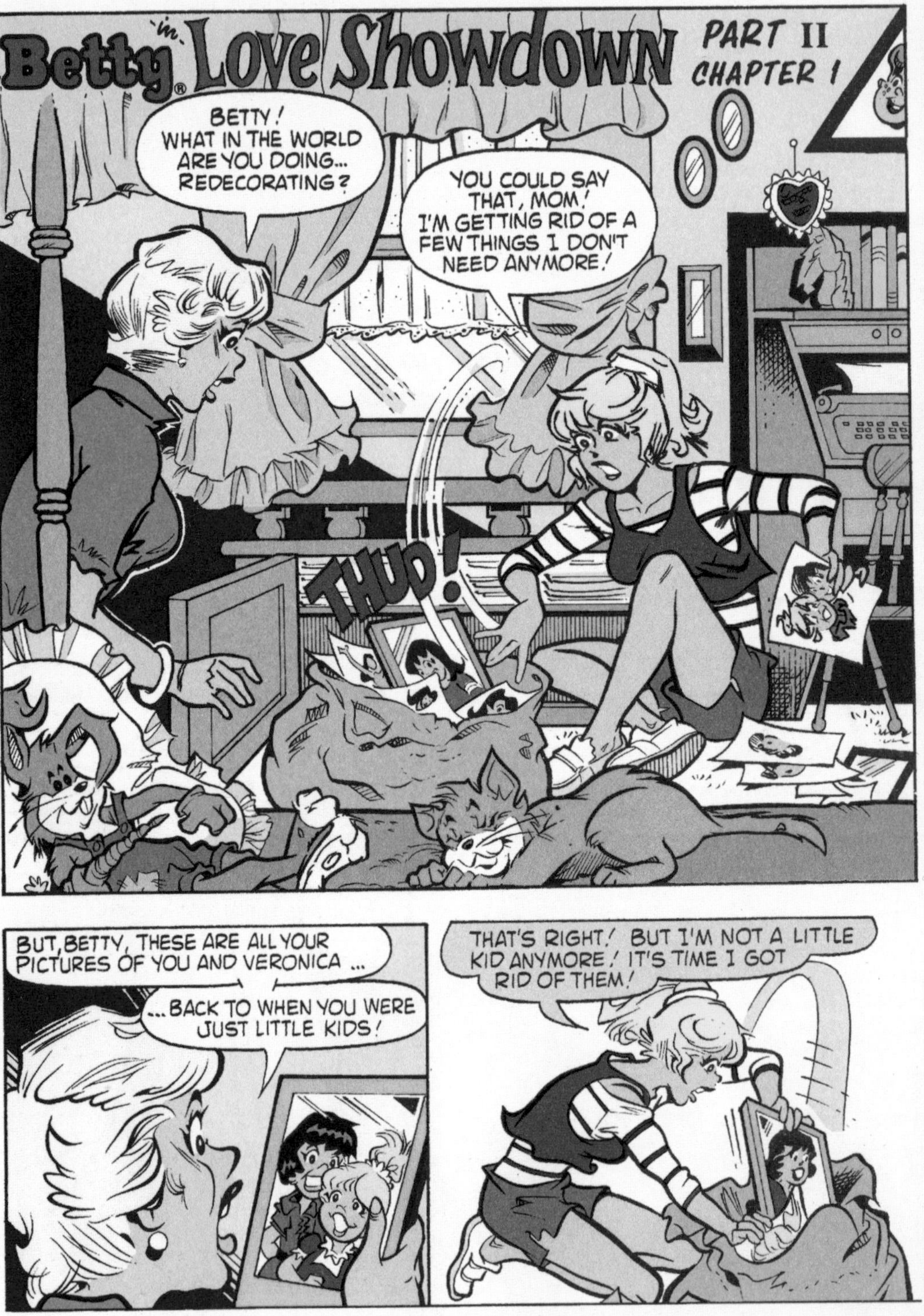
Betty in Love Showdown
PART II CHAPTER 1
BETTY! WHAT IN THE WORLD ARE YOU DOING... REDECORATING?
YOU COULD SAY THAT, MOM! I'M GETTING RID OF A FEW THINGS I DON'T NEED ANYMORE!
THUD!
BUT, BETTY, THESE ARE ALL YOUR PICTURES OF YOU AND VERONICA ...
... BACK TO WHEN YOU WERE JUST LITTLE KIDS!
THAT'S RIGHT! BUT I'M NOT A LITTLE KID ANYMORE! IT'S TIME I GOT RID OF THEM!

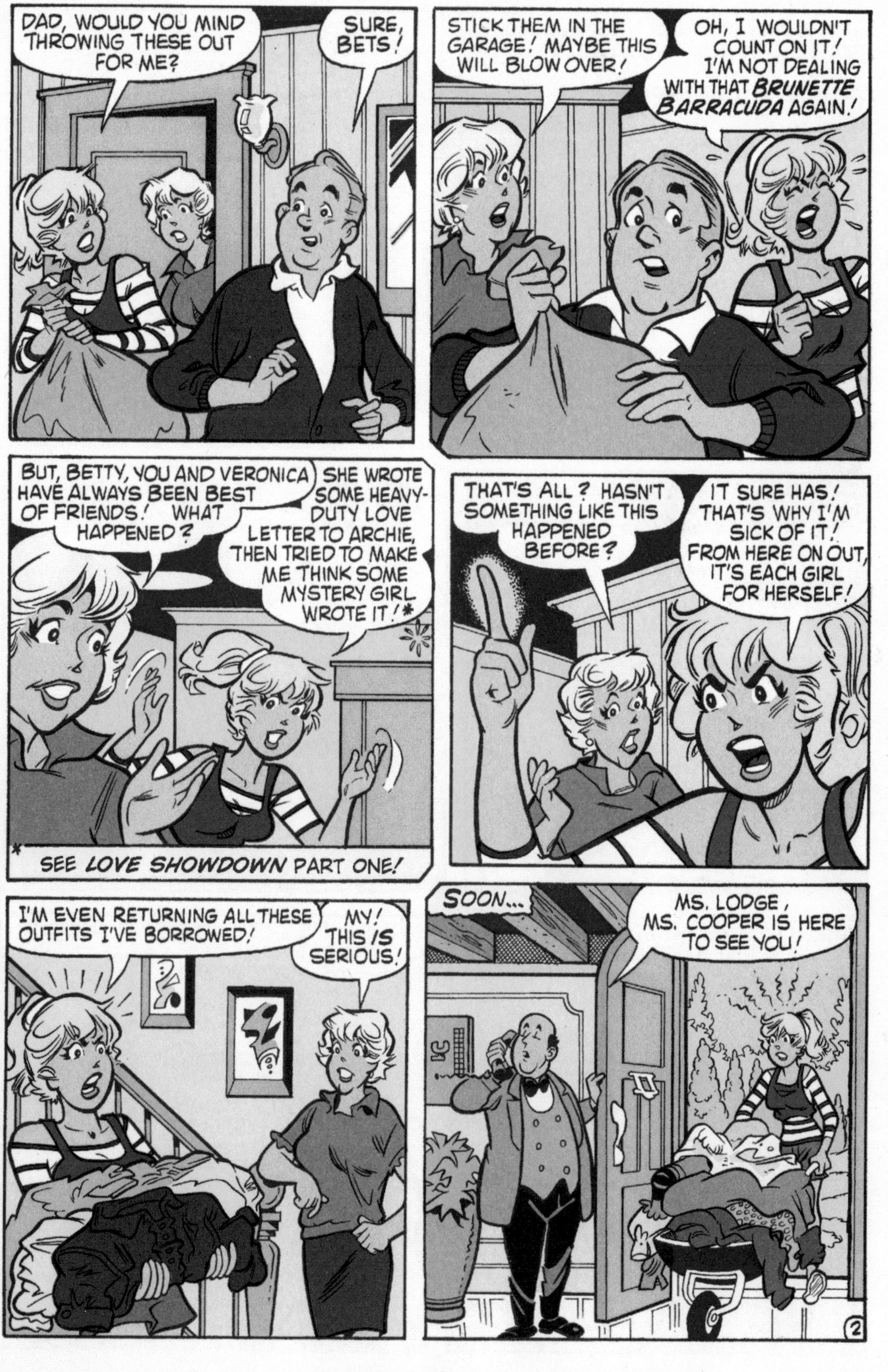
DAD, WOULD YOU MIND THROWING THESE OUT FOR ME?
SURE, BETS!
STICK THEM IN THE GARAGE! MAYBE THIS WILL BLOW OVER!
OH, I WOULDN'T COUNT ON IT! I'M NOT DEALING WITH THAT BRUNETTE BARRACUDA AGAIN!
BUT, BETTY, YOU AND VERONICA HAVE ALWAYS BEEN BEST OF FRIENDS! WHAT HAPPENED?
SHE WROTE SOME HEAVY-DUTY LOVE LETTER TO ARCHIE, THEN TRIED TO MAKE ME THINK SOME MYSTERY GIRL WROTE IT!*
* SEE LOVE SHOWDOWN PART ONE!
THAT'S ALL? HASN'T SOMETHING LIKE THIS HAPPENED BEFORE?
IT SURE HAS! THAT'S WHY I'M SICK OF IT! FROM HERE ON OUT, IT'S EACH GIRL FOR HERSELF!
I'M EVEN RETURNING ALL THESE OUTFITS I'VE BORROWED!
MY! THIS IS SERIOUS!
SOON...
MS. LODGE, MS. COOPER IS HERE TO SEE YOU!
2

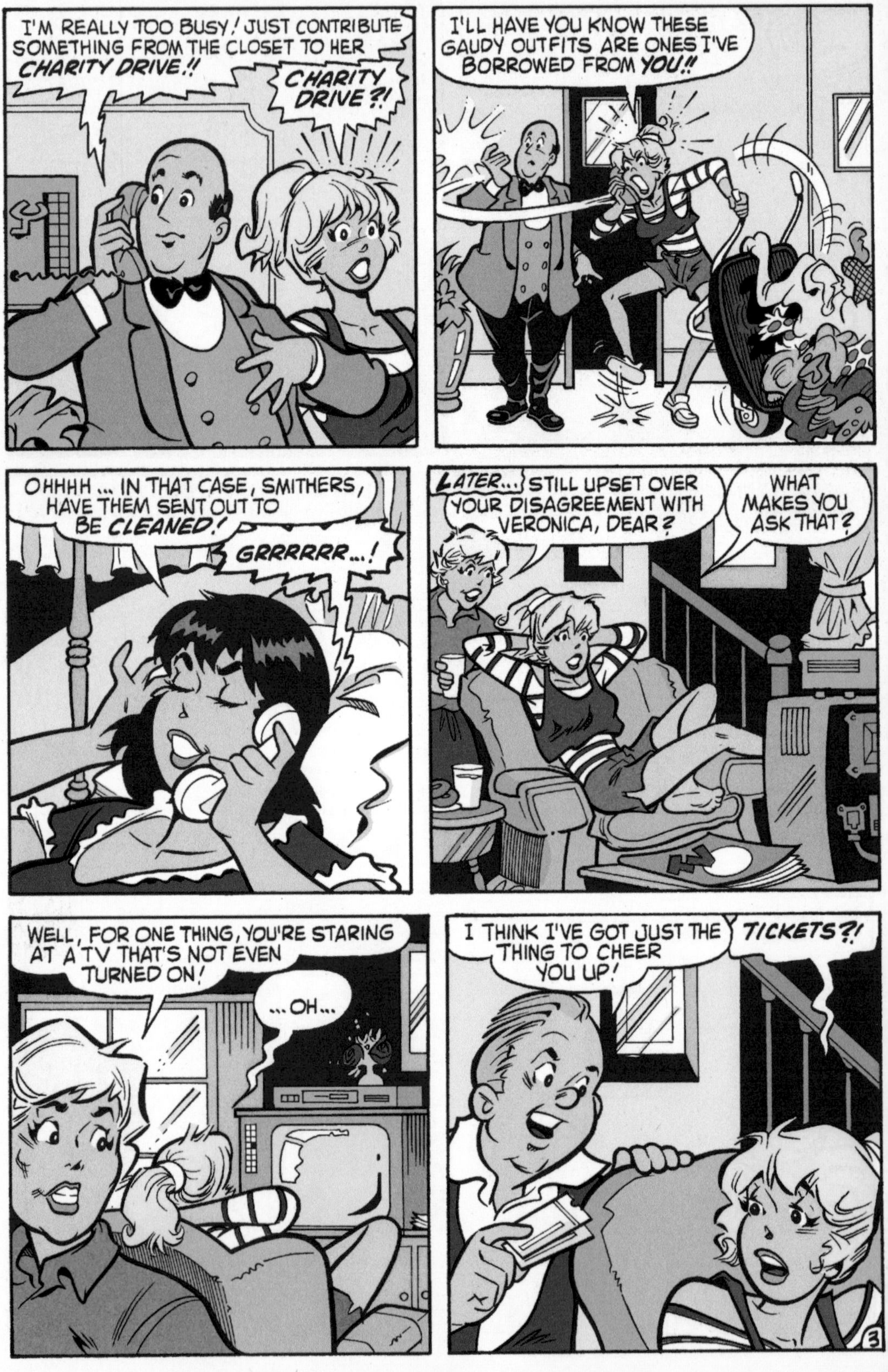
I'M REALLY TOO BUSY! JUST CONTRIBUTE SOMETHING FROM THE CLOSET TO HER CHARITY DRIVE!!
CHARITY DRIVE?!
I'LL HAVE YOU KNOW THESE GAUDY OUTFITS ARE ONES I'VE BORROWED FROM YOU!!
OHHHH ... IN THAT CASE, SMITHERS, HAVE THEM SENT OUT TO BE CLEANED!
GRRRRRR...!
LATER...
STILL UPSET OVER YOUR DISAGREEMENT WITH VERONICA, DEAR?
WHAT MAKES YOU ASK THAT?
WELL, FOR ONE THING, YOU'RE STARING AT A TV THAT'S NOT EVEN TURNED ON!
...OH...
I THINK I'VE GOT JUST THE THING TO CHEER YOU UP!
TICKETS?!
3

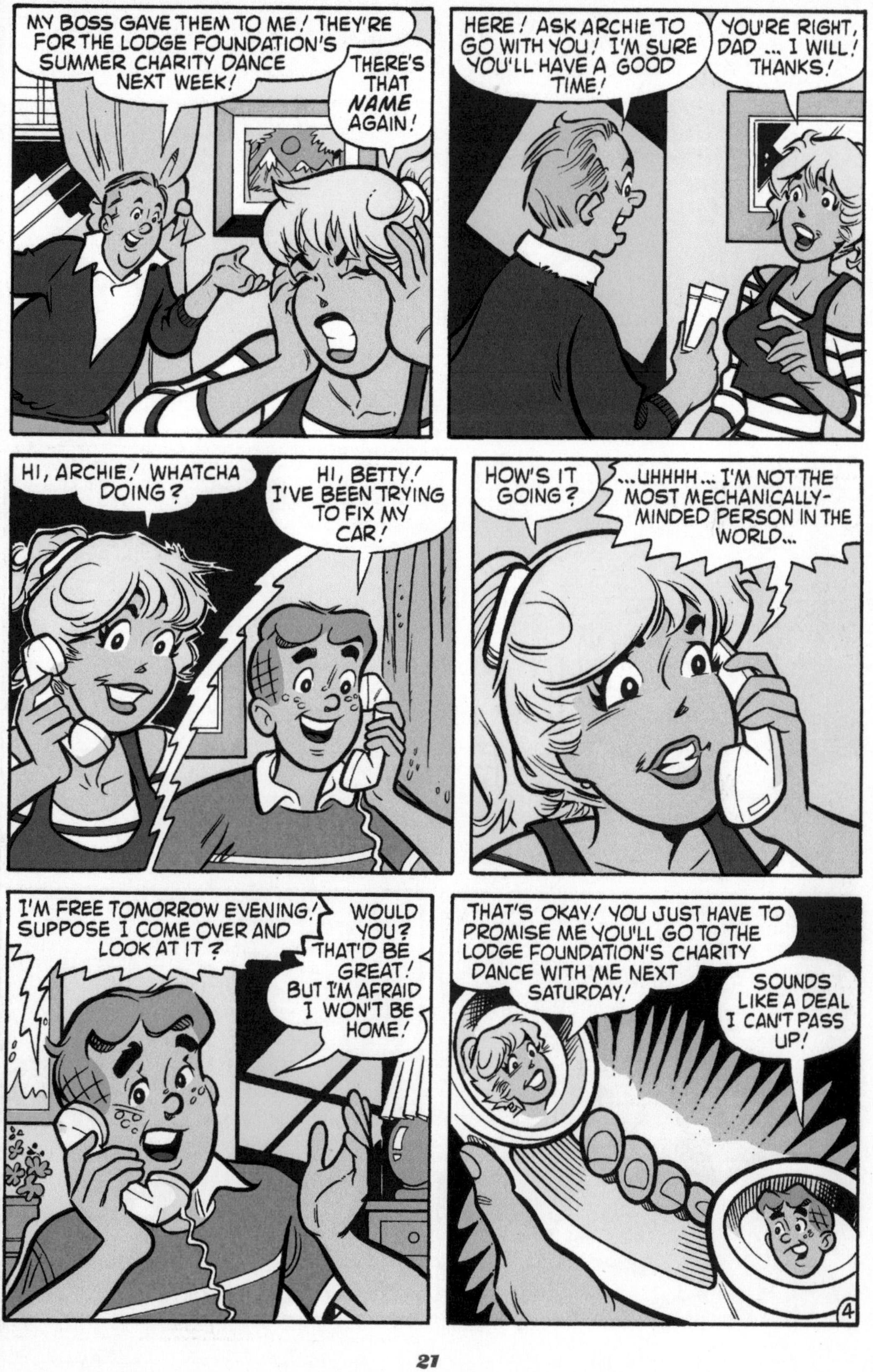
MY BOSS GAVE THEM TO ME! THEY'RE FOR THE LODGE FOUNDATION'S SUMMER CHARITY DANCE NEXT WEEK!
THERE'S THAT NAME AGAIN!
HERE! ASK ARCHIE TO GO WITH YOU! I'M SURE YOU'LL HAVE A GOOD TIME!
YOU'RE RIGHT, DAD ... I WILL! THANKS!
HI, ARCHIE! WHATCHA DOING?
HI, BETTY! I'VE BEEN TRYING TO FIX MY CAR!
HOW'S IT GOING?
...UHHHH... I'M NOT THE MOST MECHANICALLY-MINDED PERSON IN THE WORLD...
I'M FREE TOMORROW EVENING! SUPPOSE I COME OVER AND LOOK AT IT?
WOULD YOU? THAT'D BE GREAT! BUT I'M AFRAID I WON'T BE HOME!
THAT'S OKAY! YOU JUST HAVE TO PROMISE ME YOU'LL GO TO THE LODGE FOUNDATION'S CHARITY DANCE WITH ME NEXT SATURDAY!
SOUNDS LIKE A DEAL I CAN'T PASS UP!
4

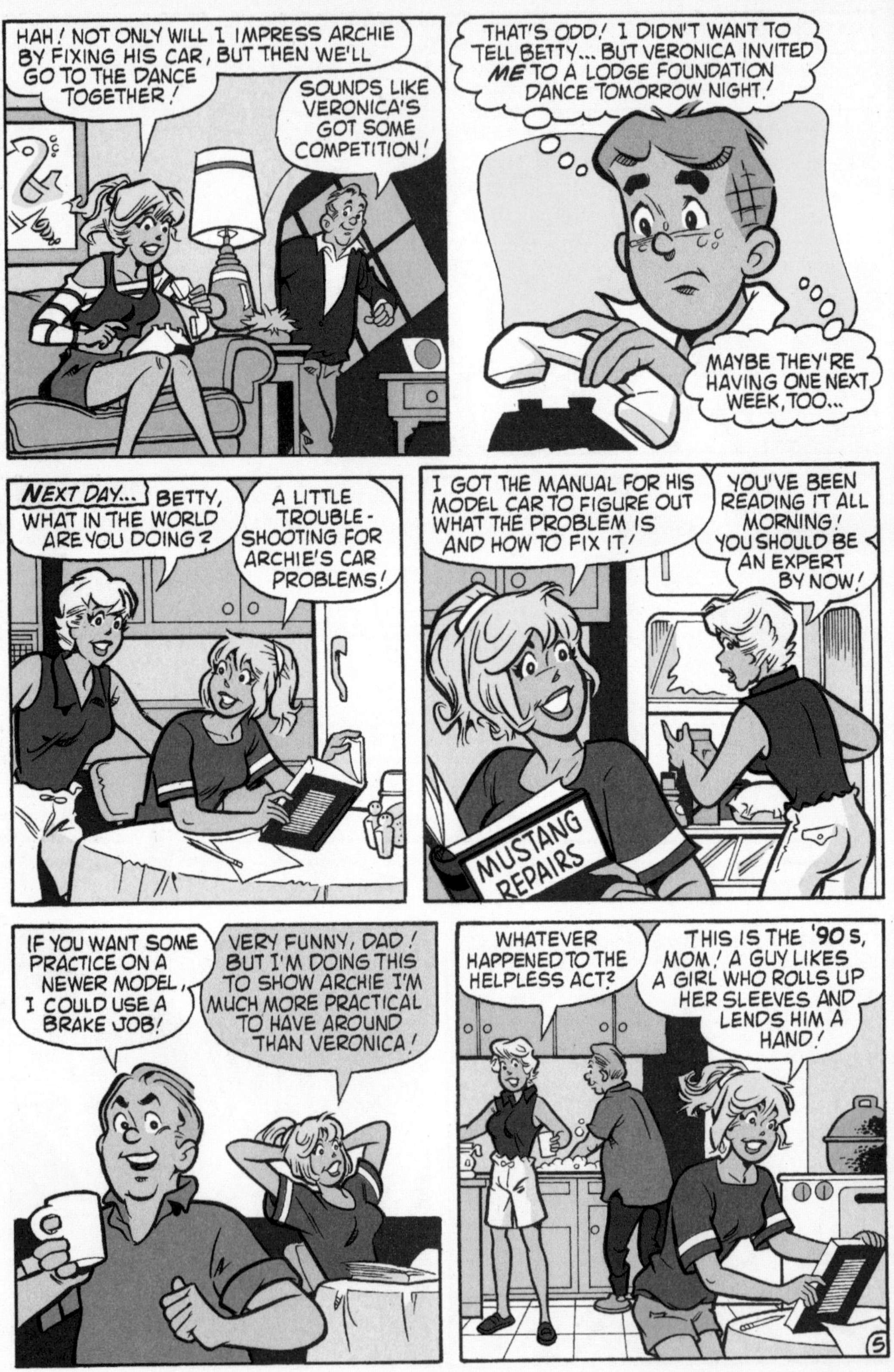
HAH! NOT ONLY WILL I IMPRESS ARCHIE BY FIXING HIS CAR, BUT THEN WE'LL GO TO THE DANCE TOGETHER!
SOUNDS LIKE VERONICA'S GOT SOME COMPETITION!
THAT'S ODD! I DIDN'T WANT TO TELL BETTY... BUT VERONICA INVITED ME TO A LODGE FOUNDATION DANCE TOMORROW NIGHT!
MAYBE THEY'RE HAVING ONE NEXT WEEK, TOO...
NEXT DAY...
BETTY, WHAT IN THE WORLD ARE YOU DOING?
A LITTLE TROUBLE-SHOOTING FOR ARCHIE'S CAR PROBLEMS!
I GOT THE MANUAL FOR HIS MODEL CAR TO FIGURE OUT WHAT THE PROBLEM IS AND HOW TO FIX IT!
YOU'VE BEEN READING IT ALL MORNING! YOU SHOULD BE AN EXPERT BY NOW!
MUSTANG REPAIRS
IF YOU WANT SOME PRACTICE ON A NEWER MODEL, I COULD USE A BRAKE JOB!
VERY FUNNY, DAD! BUT I'M DOING THIS TO SHOW ARCHIE I'M MUCH MORE PRACTICAL TO HAVE AROUND THAN VERONICA!
WHATEVER HAPPENED TO THE HELPLESS ACT?
THIS IS THE '90s, MOM! A GUY LIKES A GIRL WHO ROLLS UP HER SLEEVES AND LENDS HIM A HAND!
5

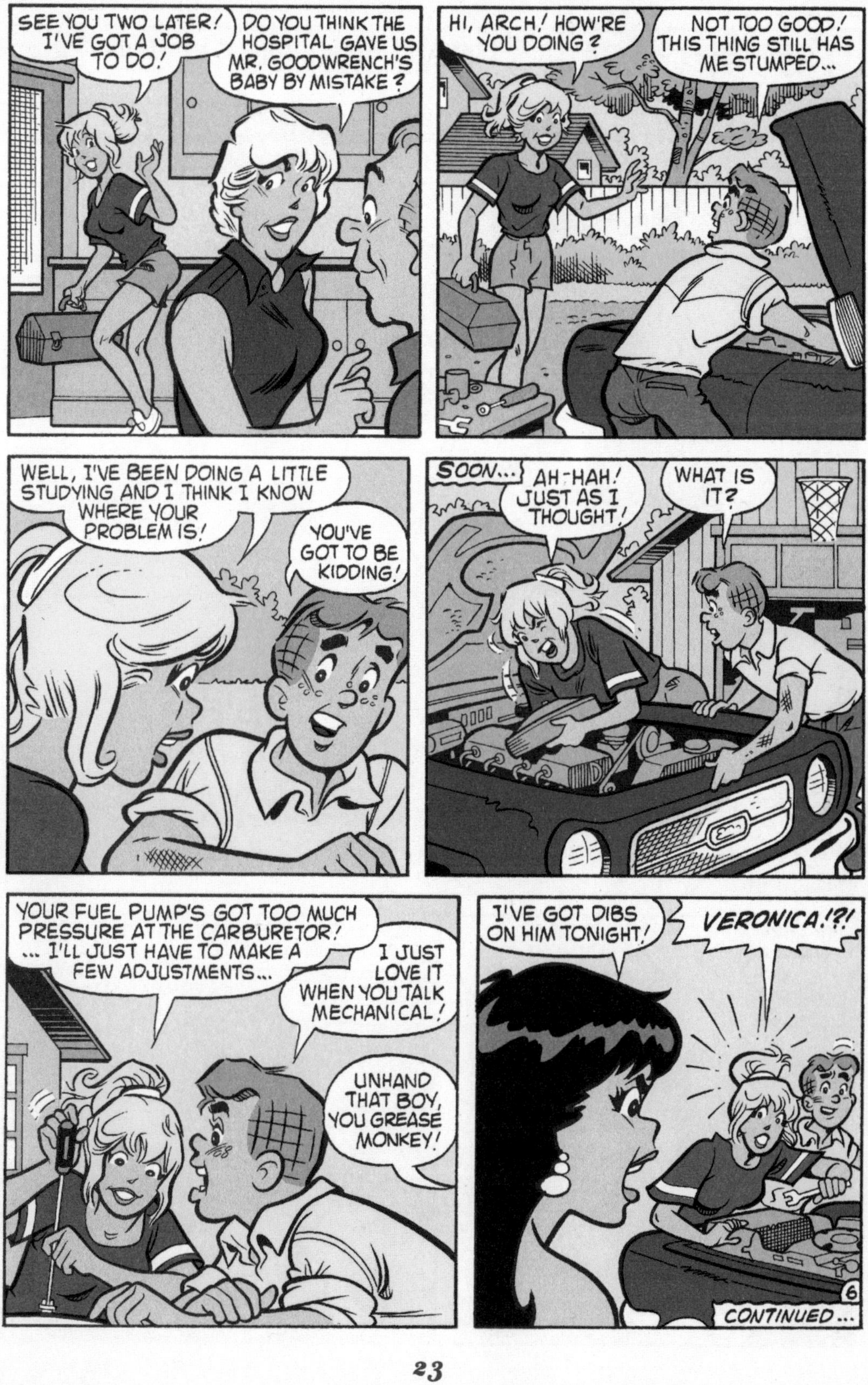
SEE YOU TWO LATER! I'VE GOT A JOB TO DO!
DO YOU THINK THE HOSPITAL GAVE US MR. GOODWRENCH'S BABY BY MISTAKE?
HI, ARCH! HOW'RE YOU DOING?
NOT TOO GOOD! THIS THING STILL HAS ME STUMPED...
WELL, I'VE BEEN DOING A LITTLE STUDYING AND I THINK I KNOW WHERE YOUR PROBLEM IS!
YOU'VE GOT TO BE KIDDING!
SOON...
AH-HAH! JUST AS I THOUGHT!
WHAT IS IT?
YOUR FUEL PUMP'S GOT TOO MUCH PRESSURE AT THE CARBURETOR! ... I'LL JUST HAVE TO MAKE A FEW ADJUSTMENTS...
I JUST LOVE IT WHEN YOU TALK MECHANICAL!
UNHAND THAT BOY, YOU GREASE MONKEY!
I'VE GOT DIBS ON HIM TONIGHT!
VERONICA!?!
6
CONTINUED...

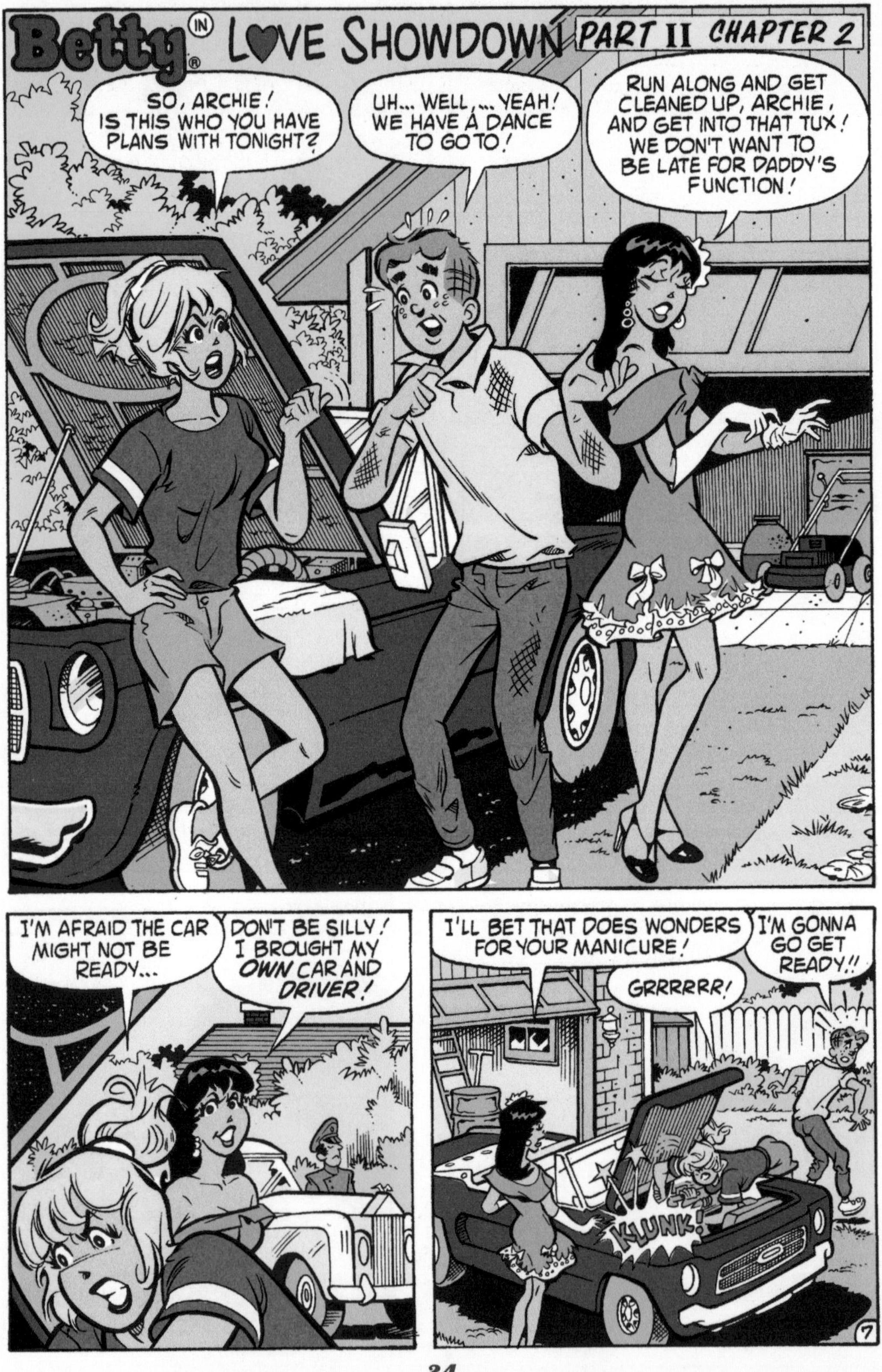
Betty IN LOVE SHOWDOWN PART II CHAPTER 2
SO, ARCHIE! IS THIS WHO YOU HAVE PLANS WITH TONIGHT?
UH... WELL, ... YEAH! WE HAVE A DANCE TO GO TO!
RUN ALONG AND GET CLEANED UP, ARCHIE, AND GET INTO THAT TUX! WE DON'T WANT TO BE LATE FOR DADDY'S FUNCTION!
I'M AFRAID THE CAR MIGHT NOT BE READY...
DON'T BE SILLY! I BROUGHT MY OWN CAR AND DRIVER!
I'LL BET THAT DOES WONDERS FOR YOUR MANICURE!
GRRRRRR!
I'M GONNA GO GET READY!!
KLUNK!
7

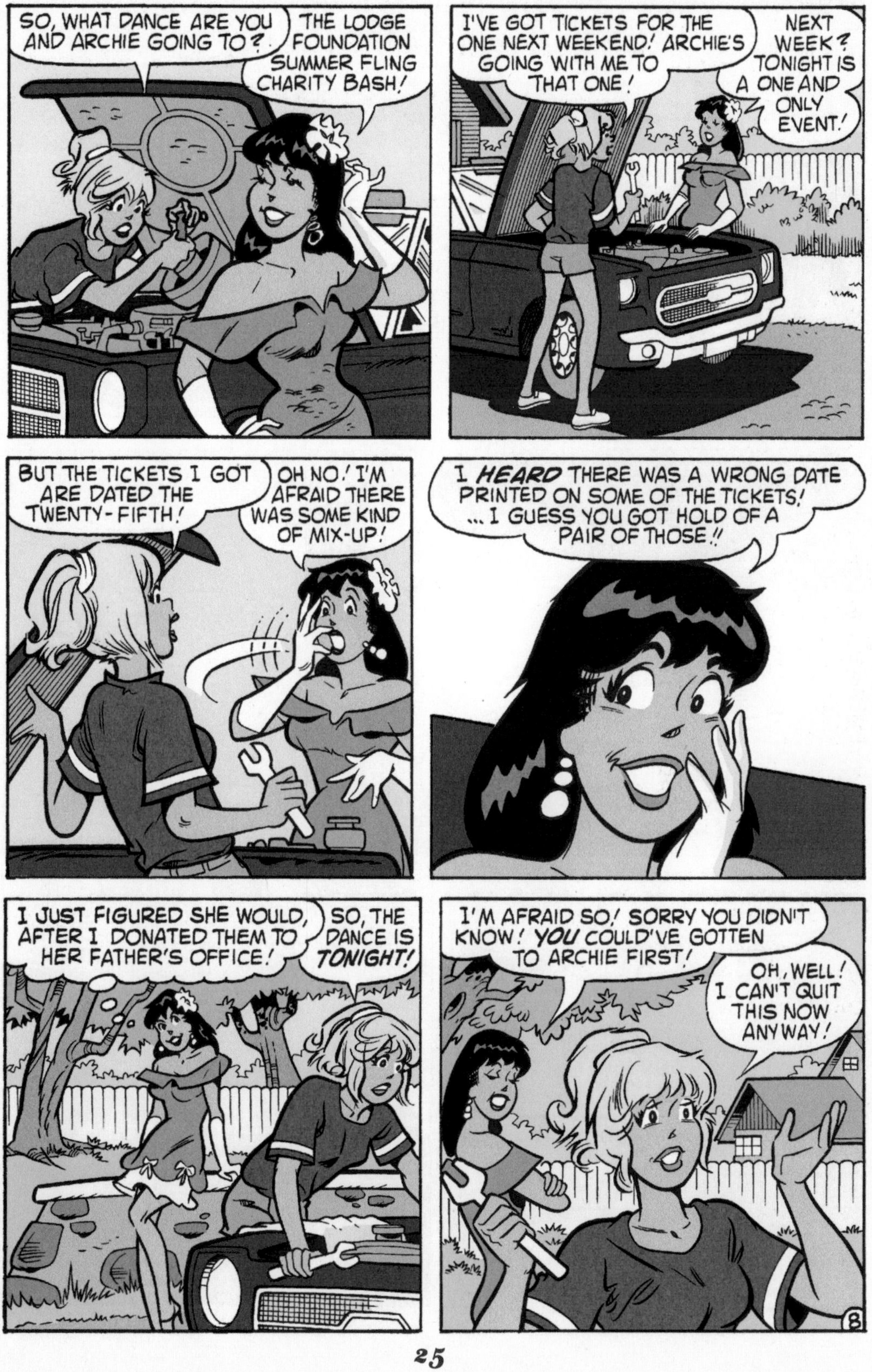
SO, WHAT DANCE ARE YOU AND ARCHIE GOING TO?
THE LODGE FOUNDATION SUMMER FLING CHARITY BASH!
I'VE GOT TICKETS FOR THE ONE NEXT WEEKEND! ARCHIE'S GOING WITH ME TO THAT ONE!
NEXT WEEK? TONIGHT IS A ONE AND ONLY EVENT!
BUT THE TICKETS I GOT ARE DATED THE TWENTY-FIFTH!
OH NO! I'M AFRAID THERE WAS SOME KIND OF MIX-UP!
I *HEARD* THERE WAS A WRONG DATE PRINTED ON SOME OF THE TICKETS! ... I GUESS YOU GOT HOLD OF A PAIR OF THOSE!!
I JUST FIGURED SHE WOULD, AFTER I DONATED THEM TO HER FATHER'S OFFICE!
SO, THE DANCE IS *TONIGHT!*
I'M AFRAID SO! SORRY YOU DIDN'T KNOW! *YOU* COULD'VE GOTTEN TO ARCHIE FIRST!
OH, WELL! I CAN'T QUIT THIS NOW ANYWAY!
8

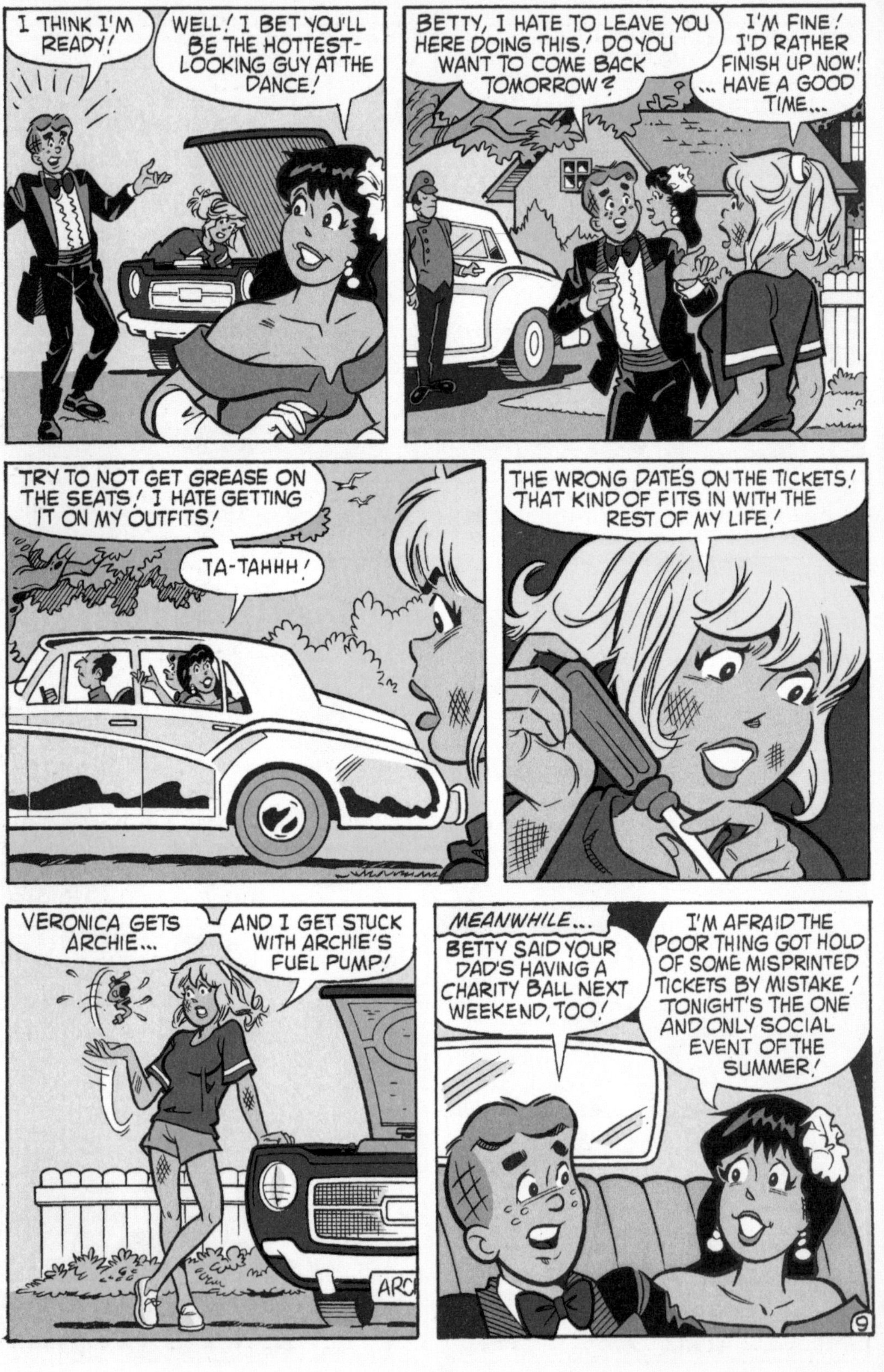
I THINK I'M READY!
WELL! I BET YOU'LL BE THE HOTTEST-LOOKING GUY AT THE DANCE!
BETTY, I HATE TO LEAVE YOU HERE DOING THIS! DO YOU WANT TO COME BACK TOMORROW?
I'M FINE! I'D RATHER FINISH UP NOW! ... HAVE A GOOD TIME...
TRY TO NOT GET GREASE ON THE SEATS! I HATE GETTING IT ON MY OUTFITS!
TA-TAHHH!
THE WRONG DATE'S ON THE TICKETS! THAT KIND OF FITS IN WITH THE REST OF MY LIFE!
VERONICA GETS ARCHIE...
AND I GET STUCK WITH ARCHIE'S FUEL PUMP!
MEANWHILE...
BETTY SAID YOUR DAD'S HAVING A CHARITY BALL NEXT WEEKEND, TOO!
I'M AFRAID THE POOR THING GOT HOLD OF SOME MISPRINTED TICKETS BY MISTAKE! TONIGHT'S THE ONE AND ONLY SOCIAL EVENT OF THE SUMMER!
9

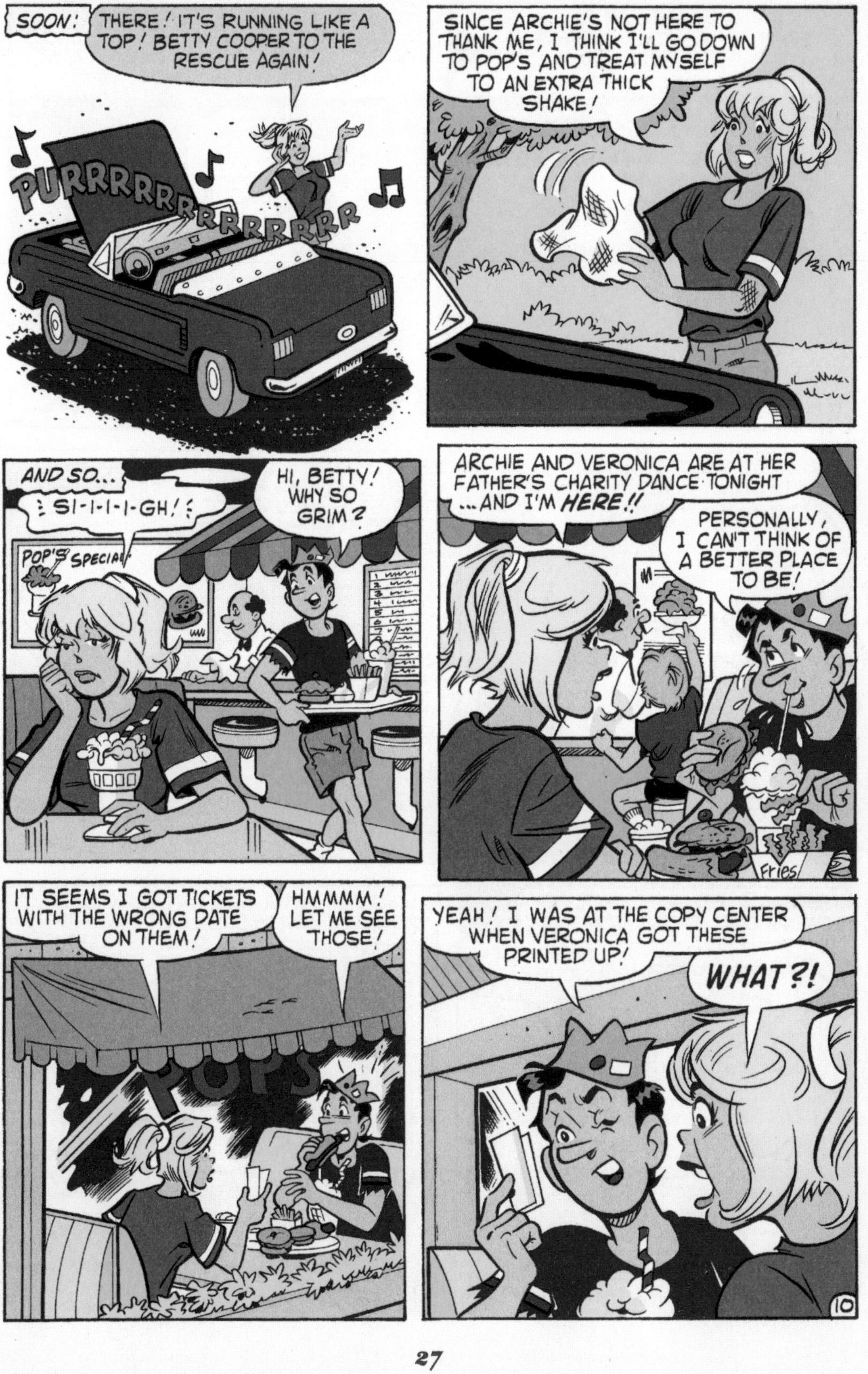
SOON!
THERE! IT'S RUNNING LIKE A TOP! BETTY COOPER TO THE RESCUE AGAIN!
PURRRRRRRRRRRRRRR
SINCE ARCHIE'S NOT HERE TO THANK ME, I THINK I'LL GO DOWN TO POP'S AND TREAT MYSELF TO AN EXTRA THICK SHAKE!
AND SO...
SI-I-I-I-GH!
HI, BETTY! WHY SO GRIM?
POP'S SPECIAL
ARCHIE AND VERONICA ARE AT HER FATHER'S CHARITY DANCE TONIGHT ...AND I'M HERE!!
PERSONALLY, I CAN'T THINK OF A BETTER PLACE TO BE!
Fries
IT SEEMS I GOT TICKETS WITH THE WRONG DATE ON THEM!
HMMMM! LET ME SEE THOSE!
POP'S
YEAH! I WAS AT THE COPY CENTER WHEN VERONICA GOT THESE PRINTED UP!
WHAT?!
10

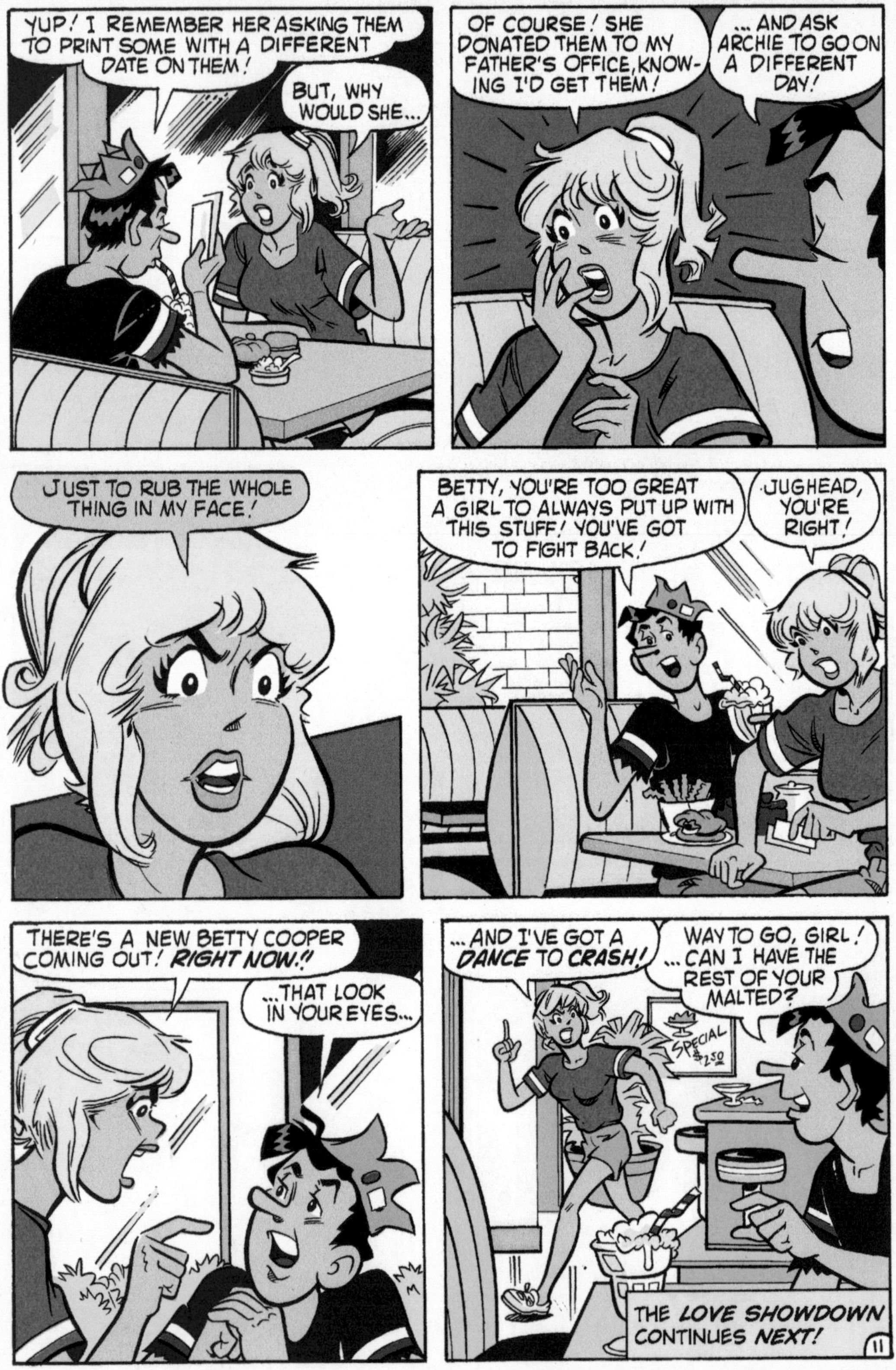
YUP! I REMEMBER HER ASKING THEM TO PRINT SOME WITH A DIFFERENT DATE ON THEM!
BUT, WHY WOULD SHE...
OF COURSE! SHE DONATED THEM TO MY FATHER'S OFFICE, KNOWING I'D GET THEM!
...AND ASK ARCHIE TO GO ON A DIFFERENT DAY!
JUST TO RUB THE WHOLE THING IN MY FACE!
BETTY, YOU'RE TOO GREAT A GIRL TO ALWAYS PUT UP WITH THIS STUFF! YOU'VE GOT TO FIGHT BACK!
JUGHEAD, YOU'RE RIGHT!
THERE'S A NEW BETTY COOPER COMING OUT! RIGHT NOW!!
...THAT LOOK IN YOUR EYES...
...AND I'VE GOT A DANCE TO CRASH!
WAY TO GO, GIRL! ...CAN I HAVE THE REST OF YOUR MALTED?
SPECIAL $2.50
THE LOVE SHOWDOWN CONTINUES NEXT!
11

Chapter Three

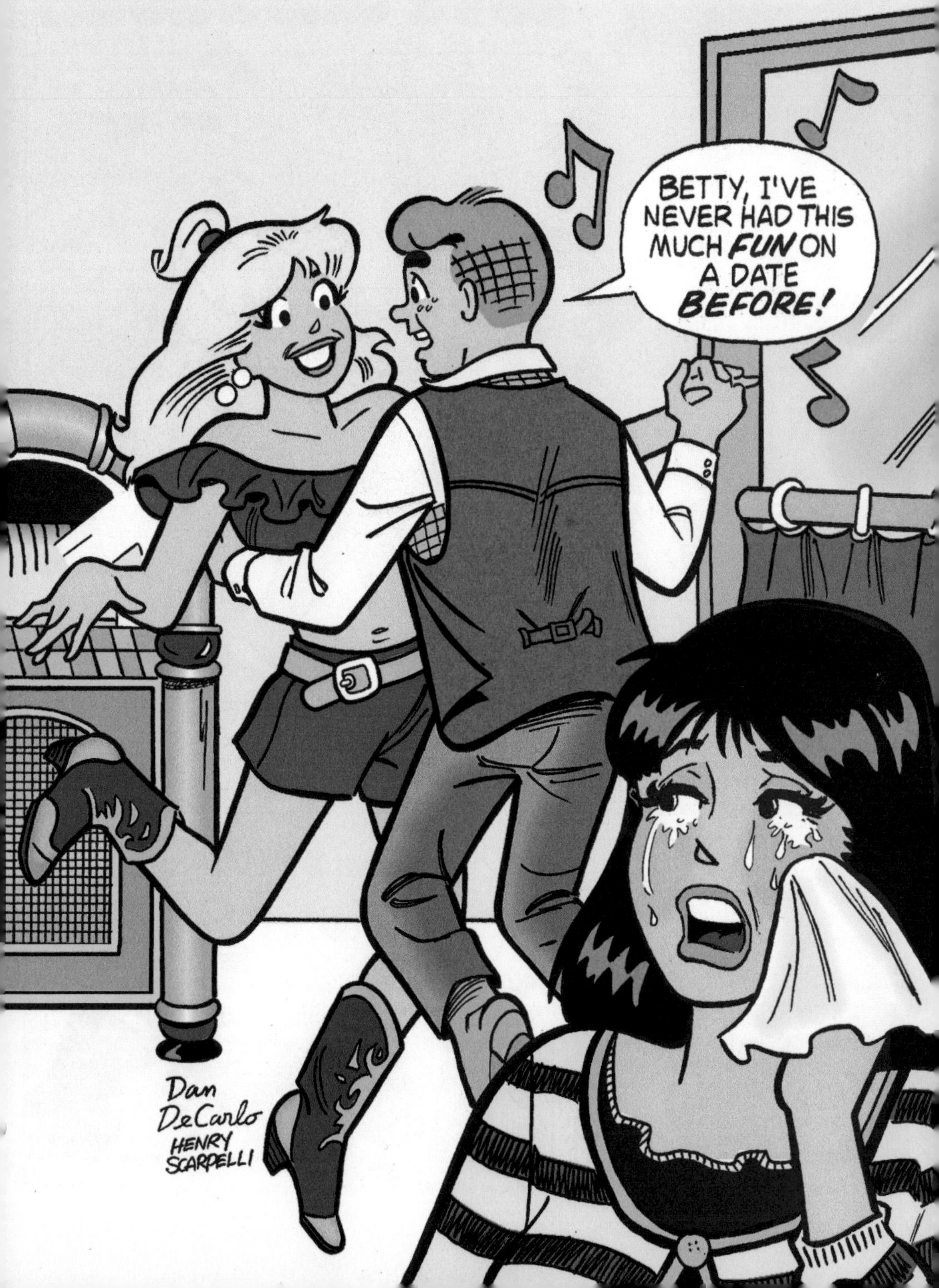
BETTY, I'VE NEVER HAD THIS MUCH FUN ON A DATE BEFORE!
Dan DeCarlo
HENRY SCARPELLI

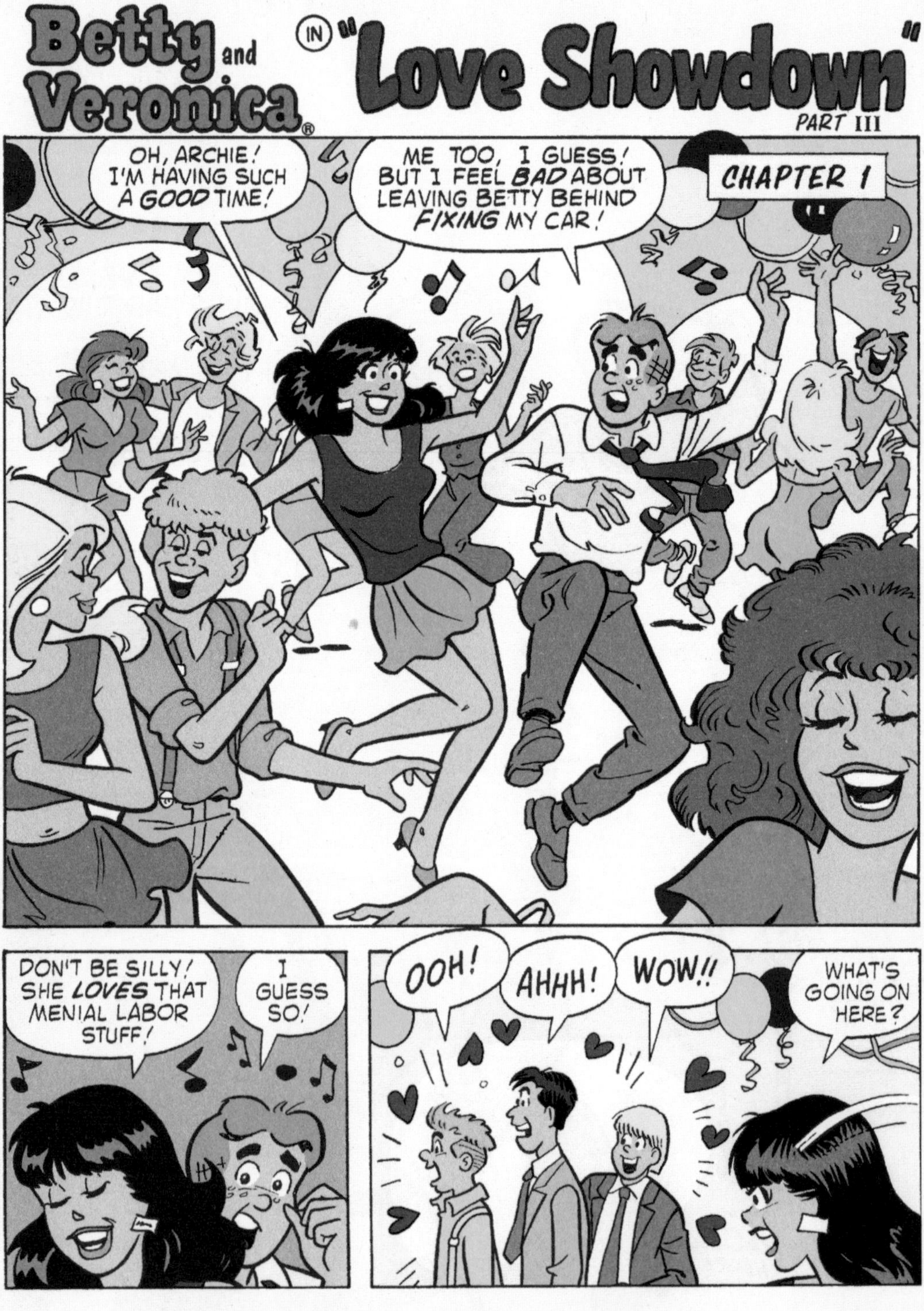
Betty and Veronica
IN "Love Showdown"
PART III
CHAPTER 1
OH, ARCHIE! I'M HAVING SUCH A GOOD TIME!
ME TOO, I GUESS! BUT I FEEL BAD ABOUT LEAVING BETTY BEHIND FIXING MY CAR!
DON'T BE SILLY! SHE LOVES THAT MENIAL LABOR STUFF!
I GUESS SO!
OOH!
AHHH!
WOW!!
WHAT'S GOING ON HERE?

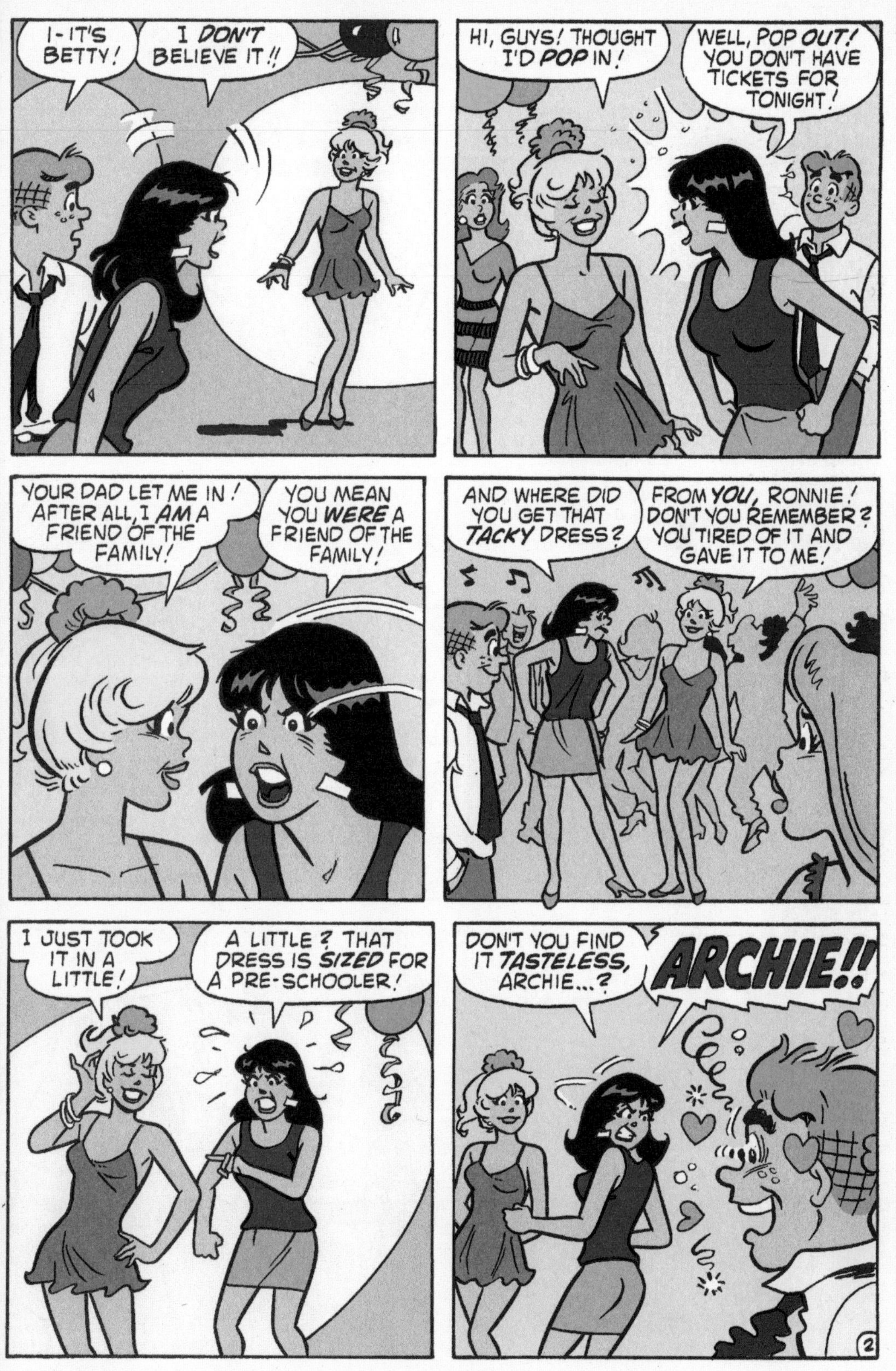
I-IT'S BETTY!
I DON'T BELIEVE IT!!
HI, GUYS! THOUGHT I'D POP IN!
WELL, POP OUT! YOU DON'T HAVE TICKETS FOR TONIGHT!
YOUR DAD LET ME IN! AFTER ALL, I AM A FRIEND OF THE FAMILY!
YOU MEAN YOU WERE A FRIEND OF THE FAMILY!
AND WHERE DID YOU GET THAT TACKY DRESS?
FROM YOU, RONNIE! DON'T YOU REMEMBER? YOU TIRED OF IT AND GAVE IT TO ME!
I JUST TOOK IT IN A LITTLE!
A LITTLE? THAT DRESS IS SIZED FOR A PRE-SCHOOLER!
DON'T YOU FIND IT TASTELESS, ARCHIE...?
ARCHIE!!
2

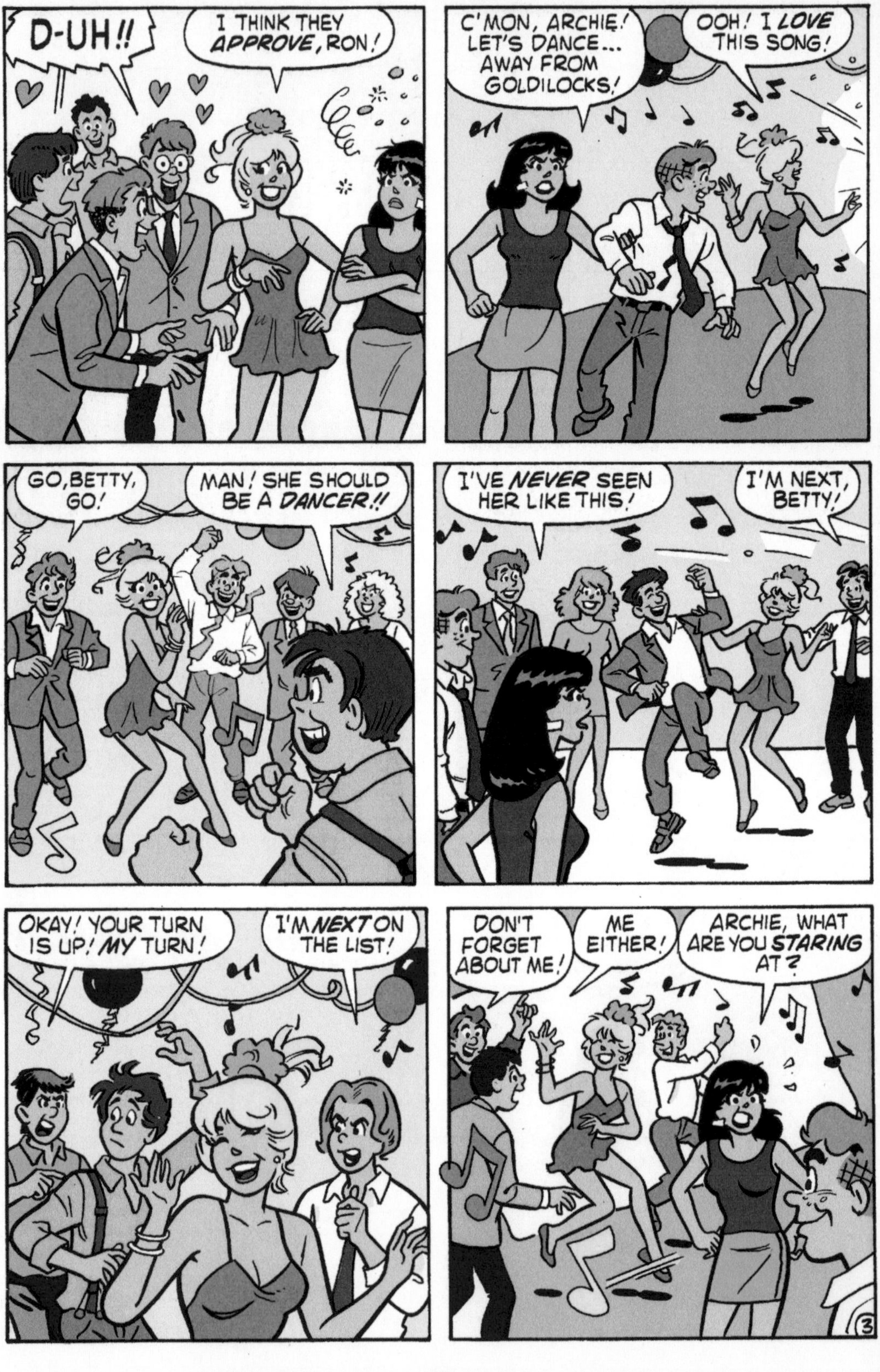
D-UH!!
I THINK THEY APPROVE, RON!
C'MON, ARCHIE! LET'S DANCE... AWAY FROM GOLDILOCKS!
OOH! I LOVE THIS SONG!
GO, BETTY, GO!
MAN! SHE SHOULD BE A DANCER!!
I'VE NEVER SEEN HER LIKE THIS!
I'M NEXT, BETTY!
OKAY! YOUR TURN IS UP! MY TURN!
I'M NEXT ON THE LIST!
DON'T FORGET ABOUT ME!
ME EITHER!
ARCHIE, WHAT ARE YOU STARING AT?
3

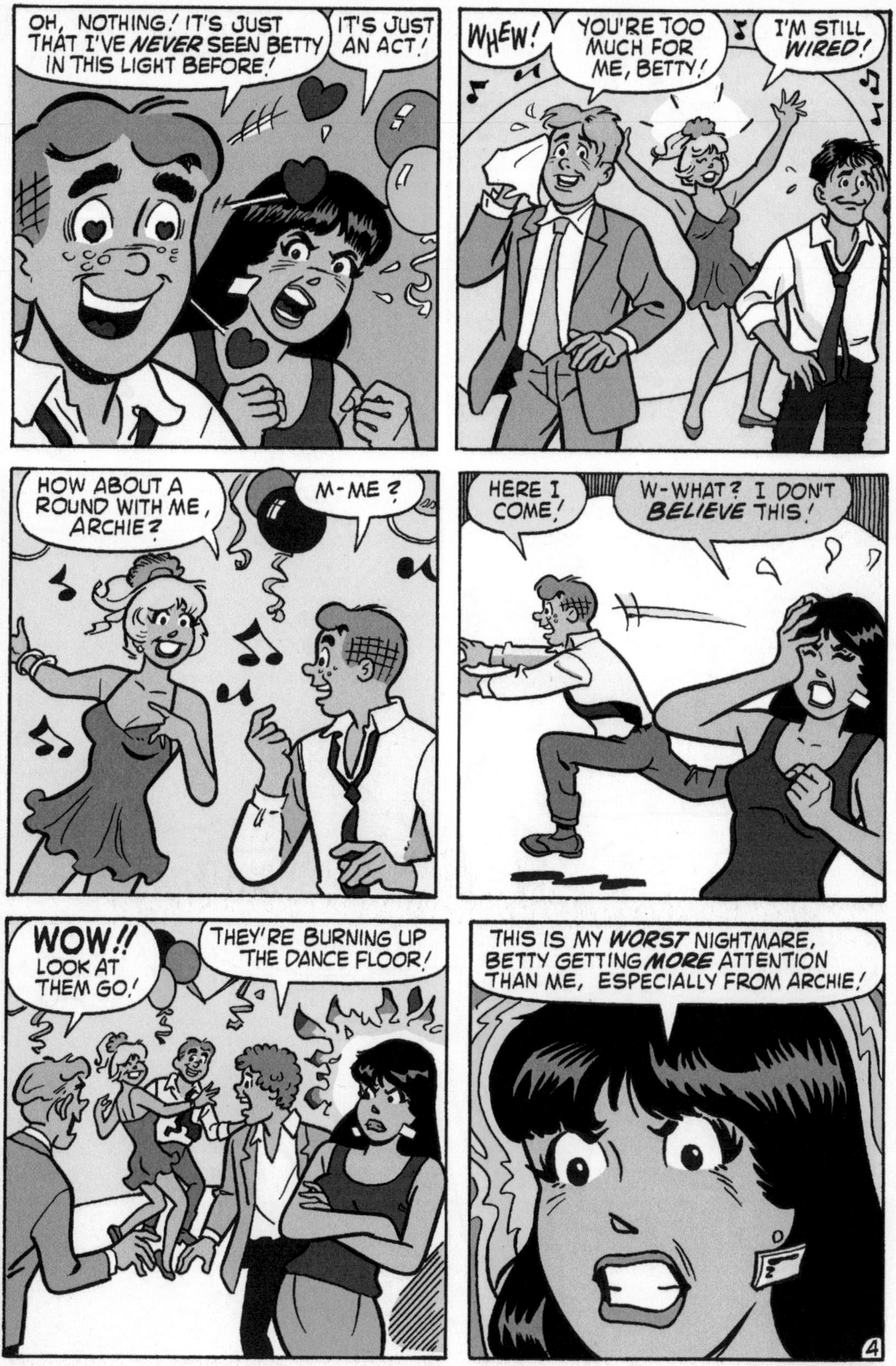
OH, NOTHING! IT'S JUST THAT I'VE NEVER SEEN BETTY IN THIS LIGHT BEFORE!
IT'S JUST AN ACT!
WHEW!
YOU'RE TOO MUCH FOR ME, BETTY!
I'M STILL WIRED!
HOW ABOUT A ROUND WITH ME, ARCHIE?
M-ME?
HERE I COME!
W-WHAT? I DON'T BELIEVE THIS!
WOW!! LOOK AT THEM GO!
THEY'RE BURNING UP THE DANCE FLOOR!
THIS IS MY WORST NIGHTMARE, BETTY GETTING MORE ATTENTION THAN ME, ESPECIALLY FROM ARCHIE!
4

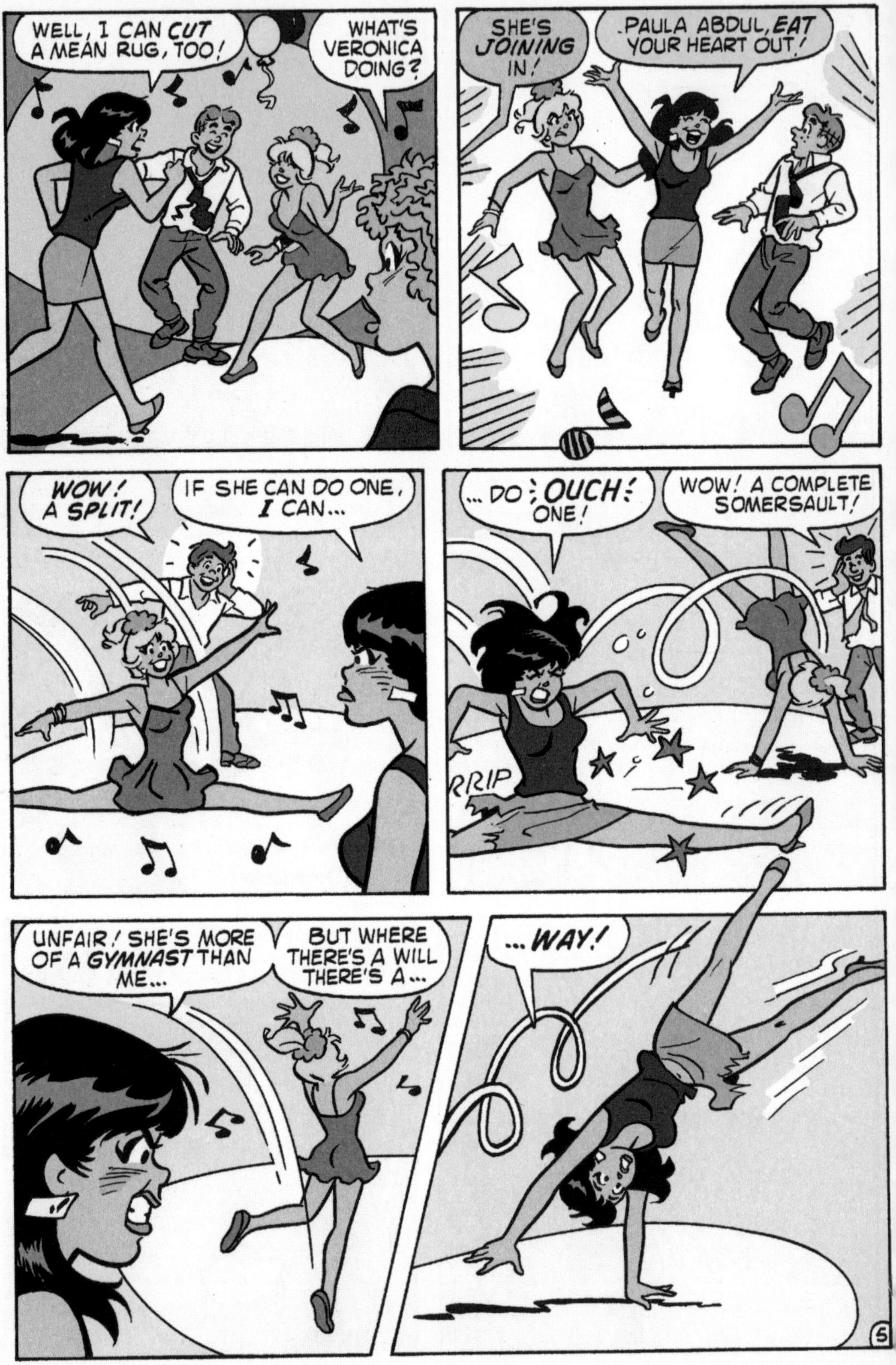
WELL, I CAN CUT A MEAN RUG, TOO!
WHAT'S VERONICA DOING?
SHE'S JOINING IN!
PAULA ABDUL, EAT YOUR HEART OUT!
WOW! A SPLIT!
IF SHE CAN DO ONE, I CAN...
... DO OUCH! ONE!
WOW! A COMPLETE SOMERSAULT!
RRIP
UNFAIR! SHE'S MORE OF A GYMNAST THAN ME...
BUT WHERE THERE'S A WILL THERE'S A...
...WAY!
5

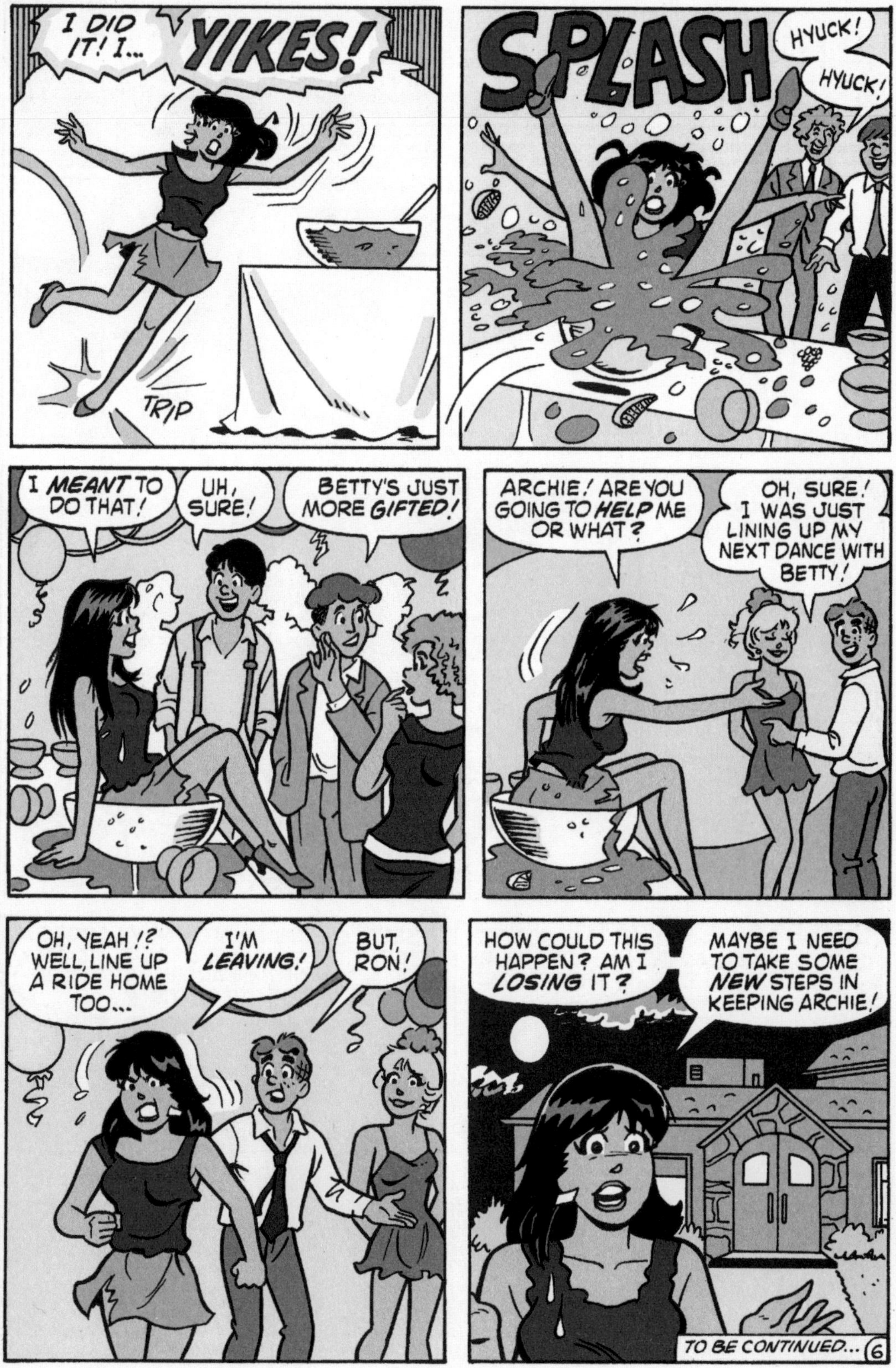
I DID IT! I... YIKES!
TRIP
SPLASH
HYUCK!
HYUCK!
I MEANT TO DO THAT!
UH, SURE!
BETTY'S JUST MORE GIFTED!
ARCHIE! ARE YOU GOING TO HELP ME OR WHAT?
OH, SURE! I WAS JUST LINING UP MY NEXT DANCE WITH BETTY!
OH, YEAH!? WELL, LINE UP A RIDE HOME TOO...
I'M LEAVING!
BUT, RON!
HOW COULD THIS HAPPEN? AM I LOSING IT?
MAYBE I NEED TO TAKE SOME NEW STEPS IN KEEPING ARCHIE!
TO BE CONTINUED... 6

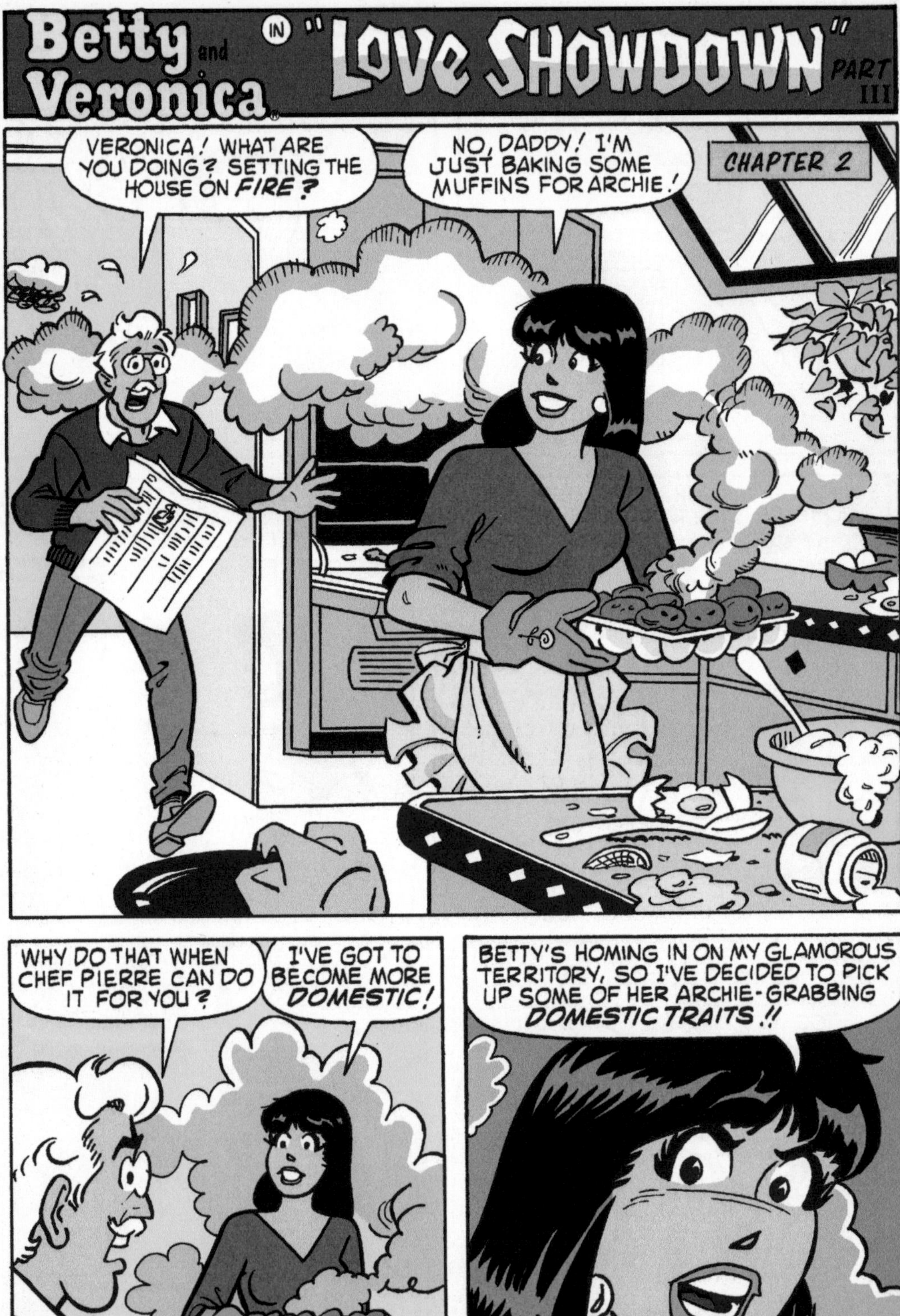
Betty and Veronica
IN "LOVE SHOWDOWN" PART III
VERONICA! WHAT ARE YOU DOING? SETTING THE HOUSE ON FIRE?
NO, DADDY! I'M JUST BAKING SOME MUFFINS FOR ARCHIE!
CHAPTER 2
WHY DO THAT WHEN CHEF PIERRE CAN DO IT FOR YOU?
I'VE GOT TO BECOME MORE DOMESTIC!
BETTY'S HOMING IN ON MY GLAMOROUS TERRITORY, SO I'VE DECIDED TO PICK UP SOME OF HER ARCHIE-GRABBING DOMESTIC TRAITS!!
7

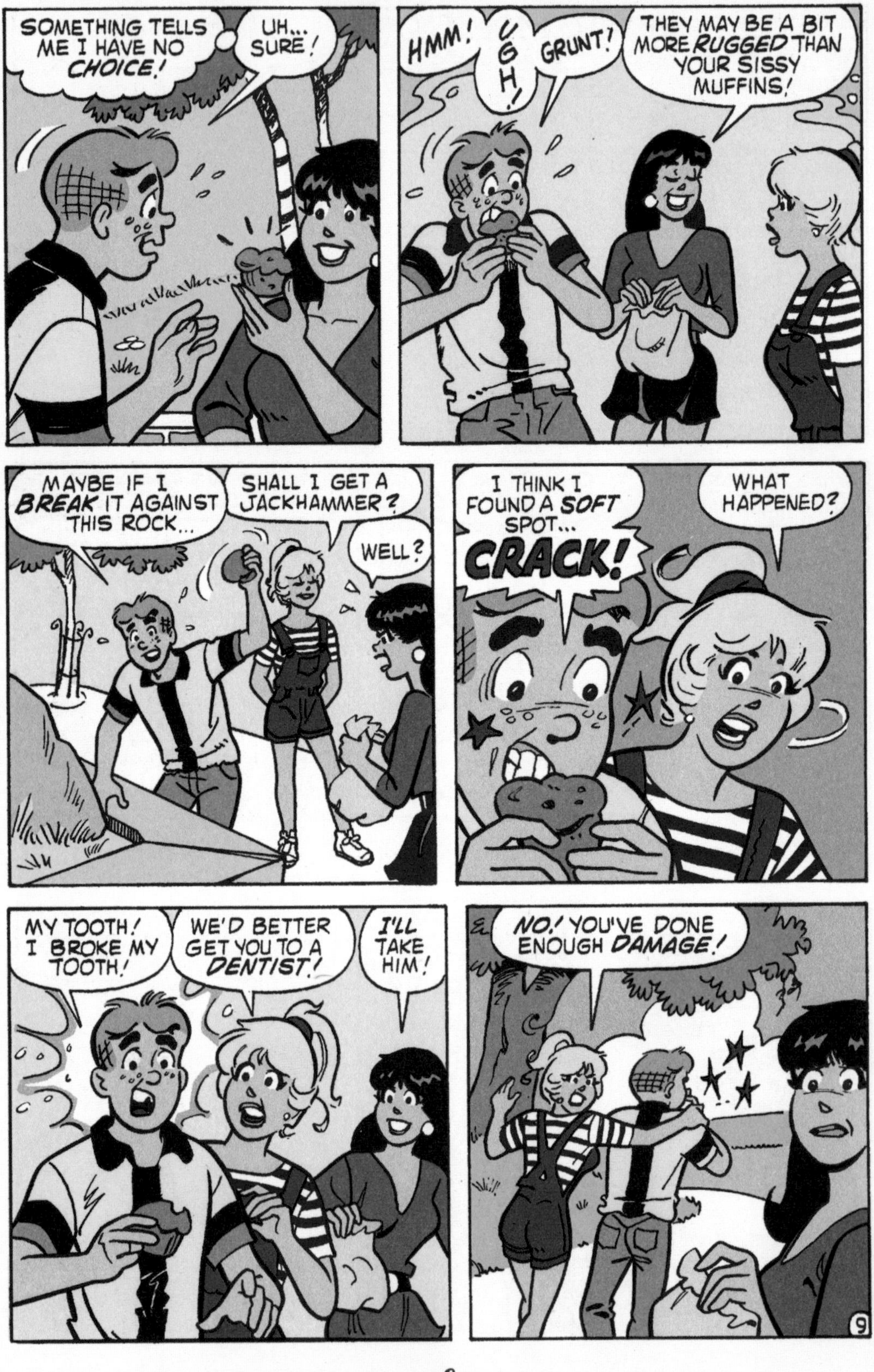
SOMETHING TELLS ME I HAVE NO CHOICE!
UH... SURE!
HMM!
UGH!
GRUNT!
THEY MAY BE A BIT MORE RUGGED THAN YOUR SISSY MUFFINS!
MAYBE IF I BREAK IT AGAINST THIS ROCK...
SHALL I GET A JACKHAMMER?
WELL?
I THINK I FOUND A SOFT SPOT...
CRACK!
WHAT HAPPENED?
MY TOOTH! I BROKE MY TOOTH!
WE'D BETTER GET YOU TO A DENTIST!
I'LL TAKE HIM!
NO! YOU'VE DONE ENOUGH DAMAGE!
9

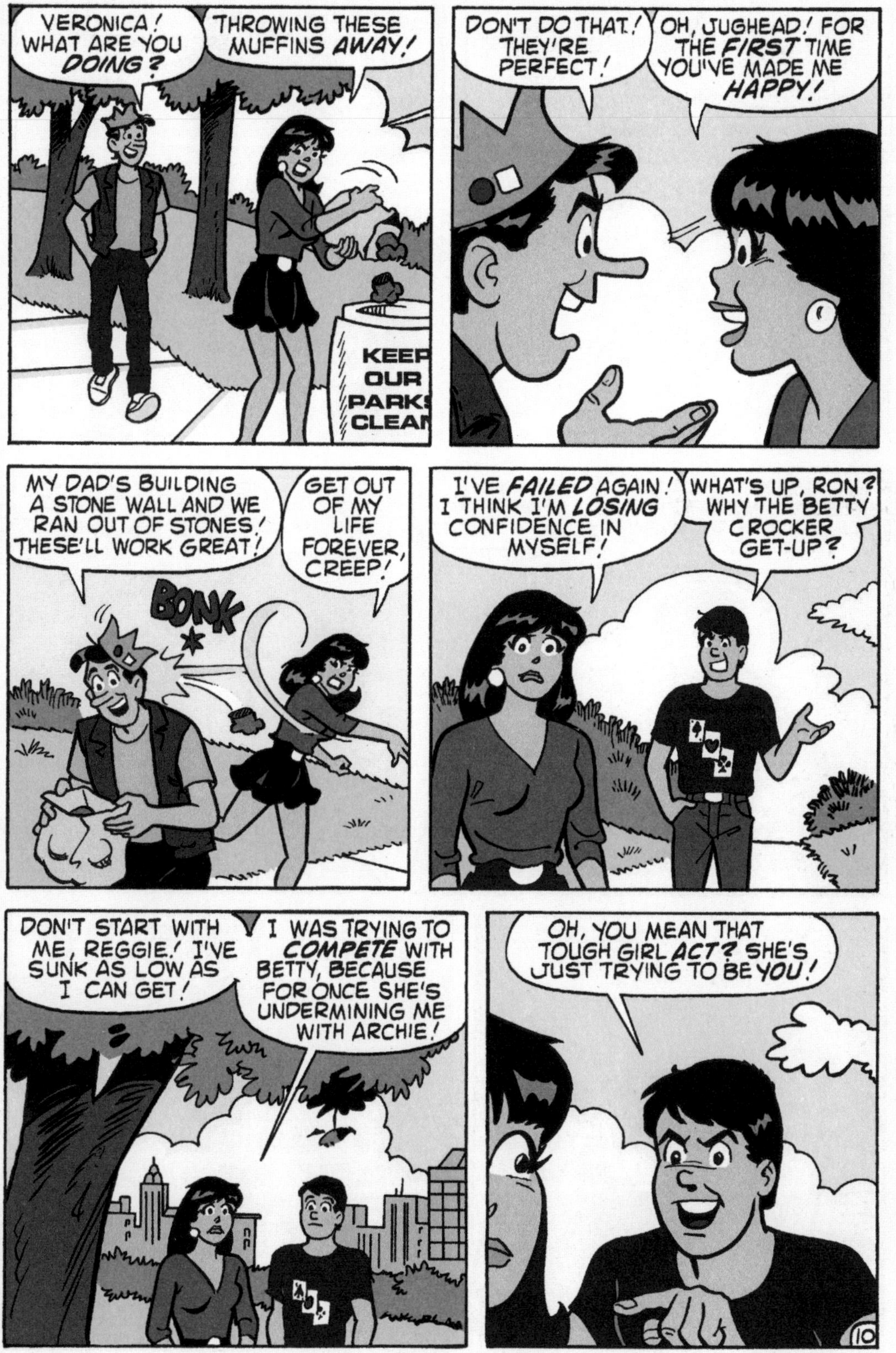
VERONICA! WHAT ARE YOU DOING?
THROWING THESE MUFFINS AWAY!
KEEP OUR PARKS CLEAN
DON'T DO THAT! THEY'RE PERFECT!
OH, JUGHEAD! FOR THE FIRST TIME YOU'VE MADE ME HAPPY!
MY DAD'S BUILDING A STONE WALL AND WE RAN OUT OF STONES! THESE'LL WORK GREAT!
GET OUT OF MY LIFE FOREVER, CREEP!
BONK
I'VE FAILED AGAIN! I THINK I'M LOSING CONFIDENCE IN MYSELF!
WHAT'S UP, RON? WHY THE BETTY CROCKER GET-UP?
DON'T START WITH ME, REGGIE! I'VE SUNK AS LOW AS I CAN GET!
I WAS TRYING TO COMPETE WITH BETTY, BECAUSE FOR ONCE SHE'S UNDERMINING ME WITH ARCHIE!
OH, YOU MEAN THAT TOUGH GIRL ACT? SHE'S JUST TRYING TO BE YOU!
10

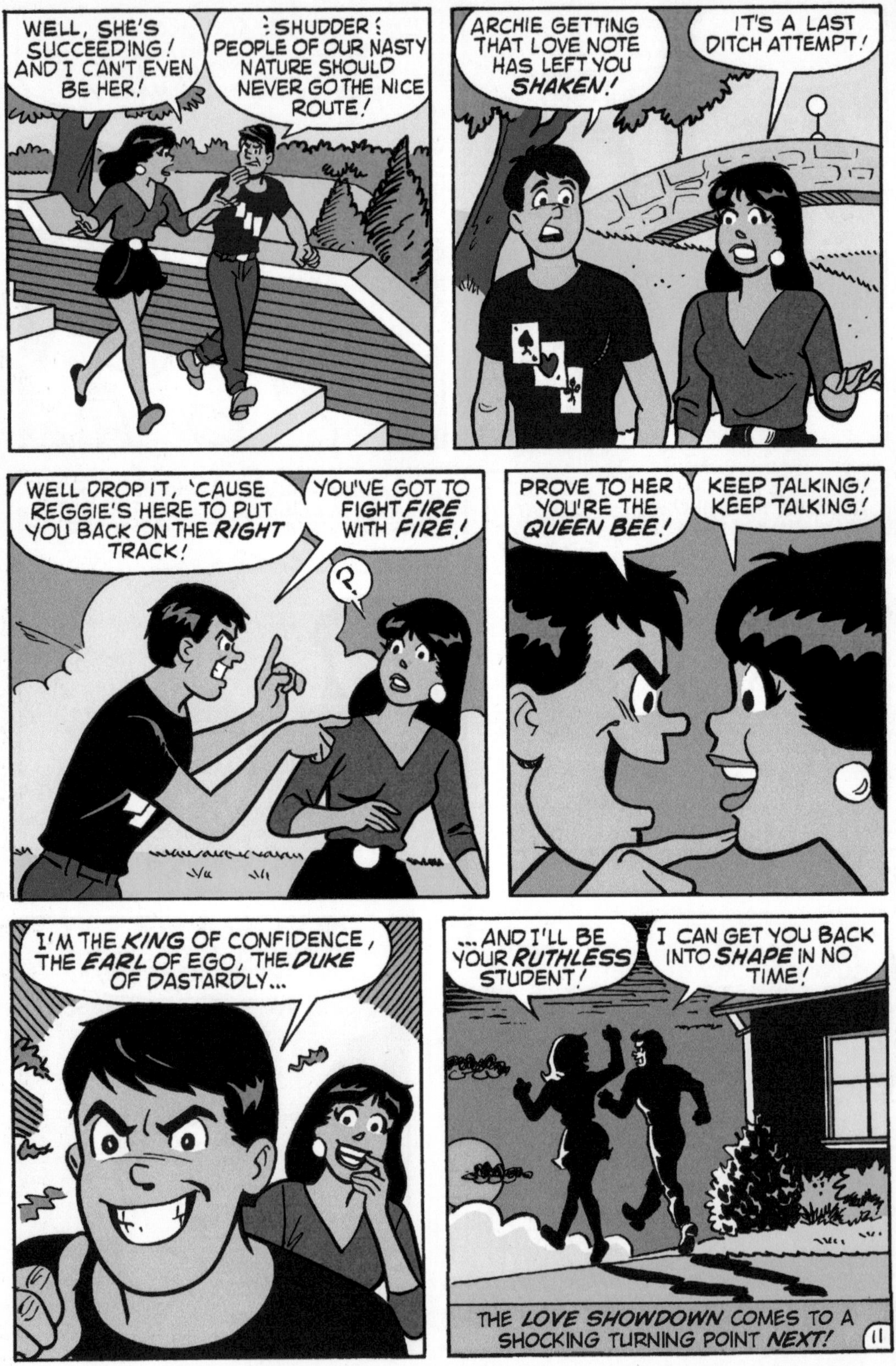
WELL, SHE'S SUCCEEDING! AND I CAN'T EVEN BE HER!
⁝SHUDDER⁝ PEOPLE OF OUR NASTY NATURE SHOULD NEVER GO THE NICE ROUTE!
ARCHIE GETTING THAT LOVE NOTE HAS LEFT YOU SHAKEN!
IT'S A LAST DITCH ATTEMPT!
WELL DROP IT, 'CAUSE REGGIE'S HERE TO PUT YOU BACK ON THE RIGHT TRACK!
YOU'VE GOT TO FIGHT FIRE WITH FIRE!
?
PROVE TO HER YOU'RE THE QUEEN BEE!
KEEP TALKING! KEEP TALKING!
I'M THE KING OF CONFIDENCE, THE EARL OF EGO, THE DUKE OF DASTARDLY...
...AND I'LL BE YOUR RUTHLESS STUDENT!
I CAN GET YOU BACK INTO SHAPE IN NO TIME!
THE LOVE SHOWDOWN COMES TO A SHOCKING TURNING POINT NEXT!
11

Chapter Four

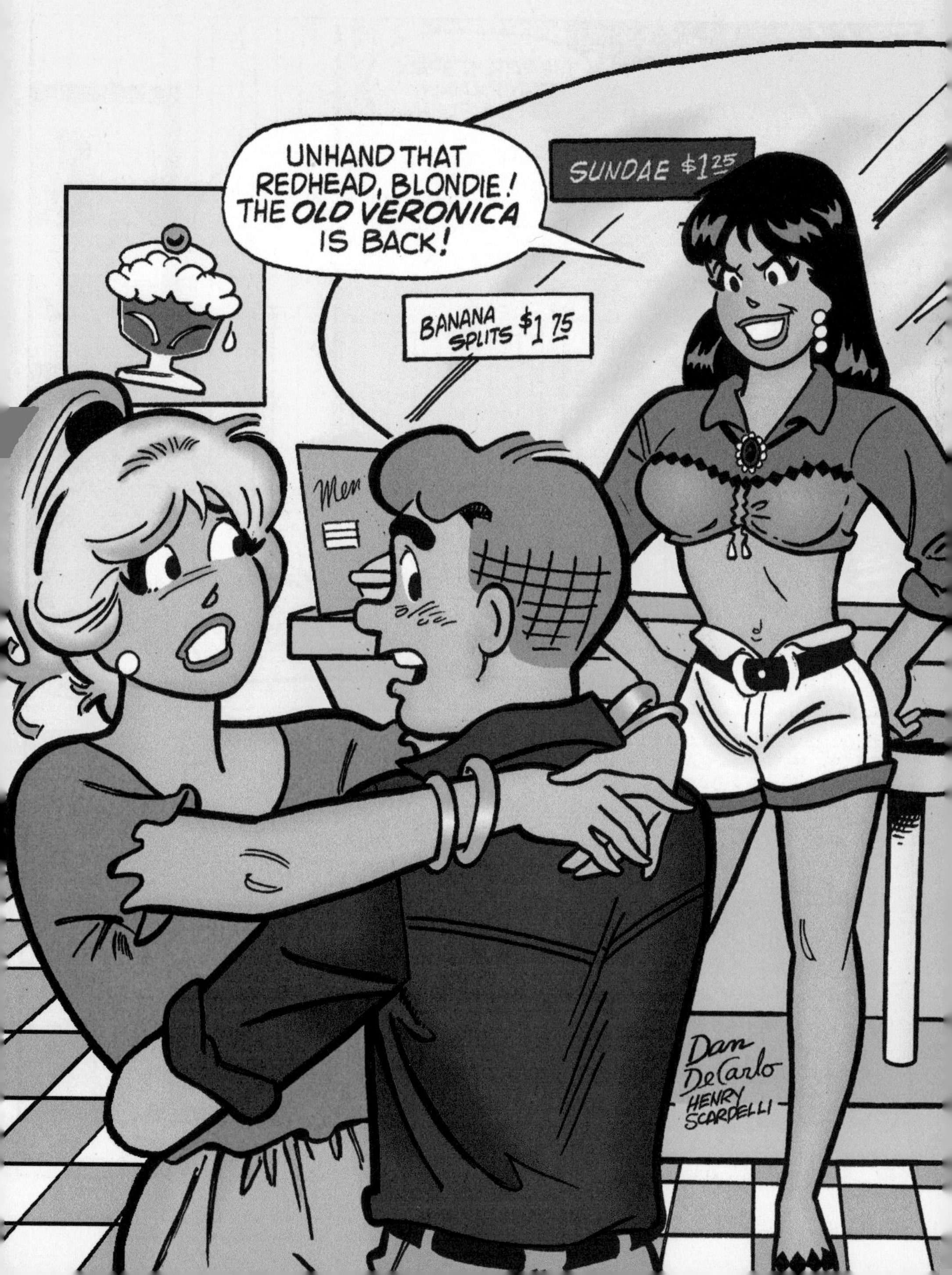

UNHAND THAT REDHEAD, BLONDIE! THE OLD VERONICA IS BACK!
SUNDAE $1.25
BANANA SPLITS $1.75
Men
Dan DeCarlo
HENRY SCARDELLI

Veronica® in "Love Showdown"

THE RAIN IN SPAIN STAYS MAINLY ON THE PLAIN...

THE RAIN IN SPAIN STAYS MAINLY ON THE PLAIN...

KEEP IT UP AND DON'T LET THAT BOOK FALL OFF YOUR HEAD!

REGGIE, IS THIS REALLY GOING TO HELP ME GET BACK TO BEING MY OLD NASTY SELF?

SURE IT IS! JUST DO IT ANOTHER FIVE HUNDRED TIMES WHILE YOU BALANCE THAT BOOK!

FIVE HUNDRED TIMES? WHAT ARE YOU, NUTS? I'M SICK AND TIRED OF REPEATING THAT STUPID PHRASE!

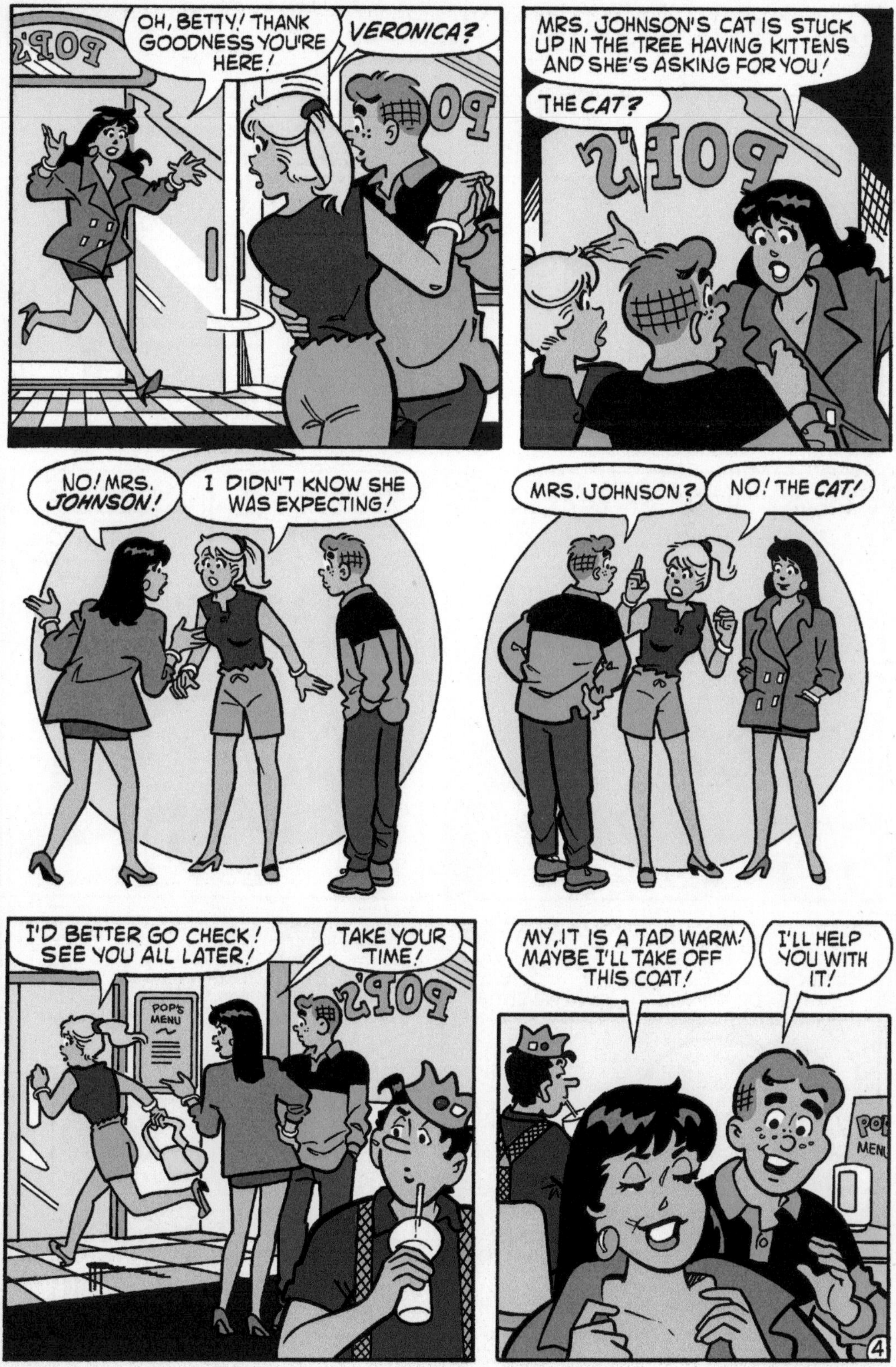
OH, BETTY! THANK GOODNESS YOU'RE HERE!
VERONICA?
MRS. JOHNSON'S CAT IS STUCK UP IN THE TREE HAVING KITTENS AND SHE'S ASKING FOR YOU!
THE CAT?
NO! MRS. JOHNSON!
I DIDN'T KNOW SHE WAS EXPECTING!
MRS. JOHNSON?
NO! THE CAT!
I'D BETTER GO CHECK! SEE YOU ALL LATER!
TAKE YOUR TIME!
MY, IT IS A TAD WARM! MAYBE I'LL TAKE OFF THIS COAT!
I'LL HELP YOU WITH IT!
4

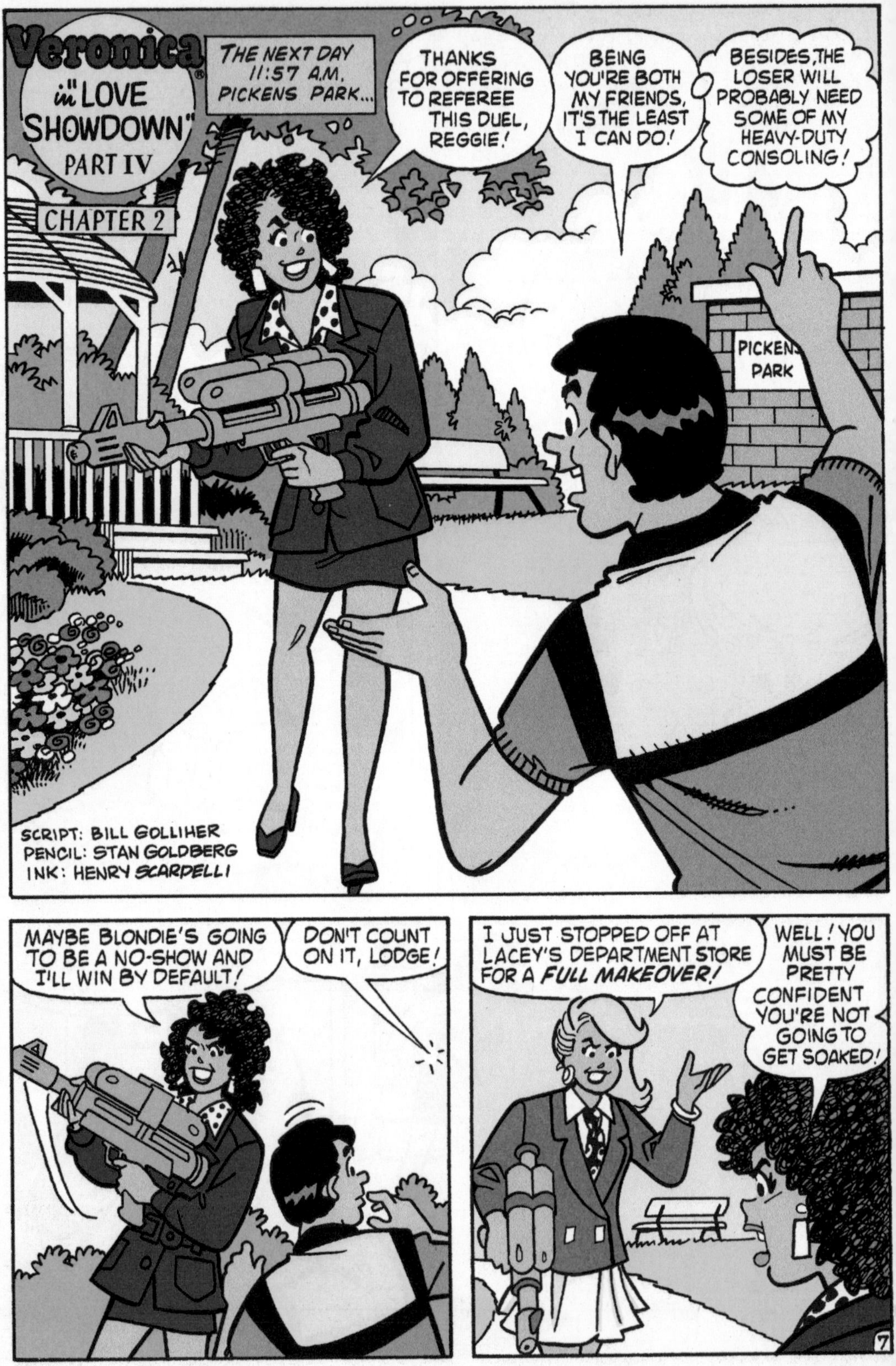
Veronica in "LOVE SHOWDOWN" PART IV
CHAPTER 2
THE NEXT DAY 11:57 A.M. PICKENS PARK...
THANKS FOR OFFERING TO REFEREE THIS DUEL, REGGIE!
BEING YOU'RE BOTH MY FRIENDS, IT'S THE LEAST I CAN DO!
BESIDES, THE LOSER WILL PROBABLY NEED SOME OF MY HEAVY-DUTY CONSOLING!
PICKENS PARK
SCRIPT: BILL GOLLIHER
PENCIL: STAN GOLDBERG
INK: HENRY SCARPELLI
MAYBE BLONDIE'S GOING TO BE A NO-SHOW AND I'LL WIN BY DEFAULT!
DON'T COUNT ON IT, LODGE!
I JUST STOPPED OFF AT LACEY'S DEPARTMENT STORE FOR A FULL MAKEOVER!
WELL! YOU MUST BE PRETTY CONFIDENT YOU'RE NOT GOING TO GET SOAKED!
7

49

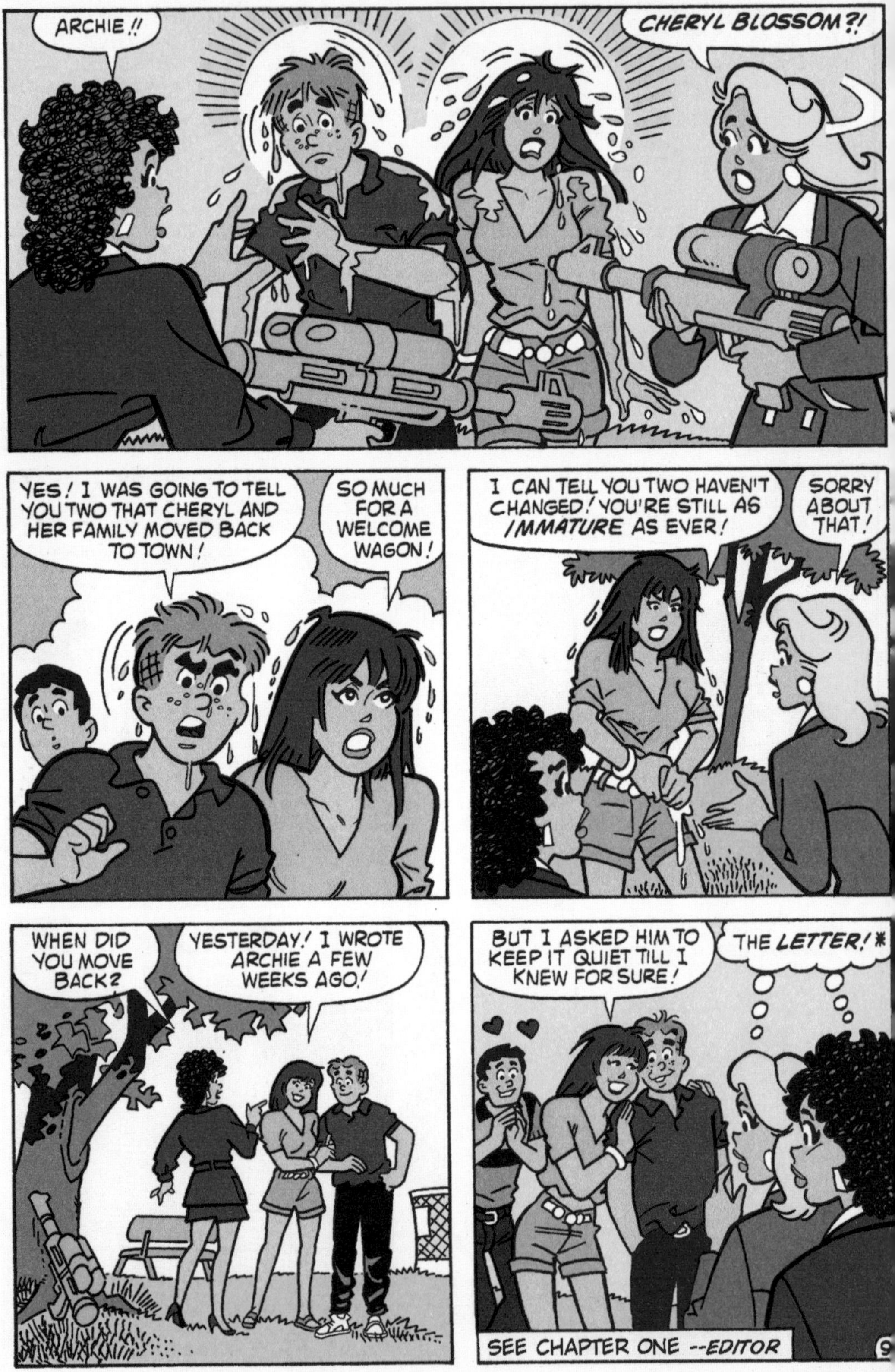

ARCHIE!!
CHERYL BLOSSOM?!
YES! I WAS GOING TO TELL YOU TWO THAT CHERYL AND HER FAMILY MOVED BACK TO TOWN!
SO MUCH FOR A WELCOME WAGON!
I CAN TELL YOU TWO HAVEN'T CHANGED! YOU'RE STILL AS IMMATURE AS EVER!
SORRY ABOUT THAT!
WHEN DID YOU MOVE BACK?
YESTERDAY! I WROTE ARCHIE A FEW WEEKS AGO!
BUT I ASKED HIM TO KEEP IT QUIET TILL I KNEW FOR SURE!
THE LETTER! *
SEE CHAPTER ONE --EDITOR
9

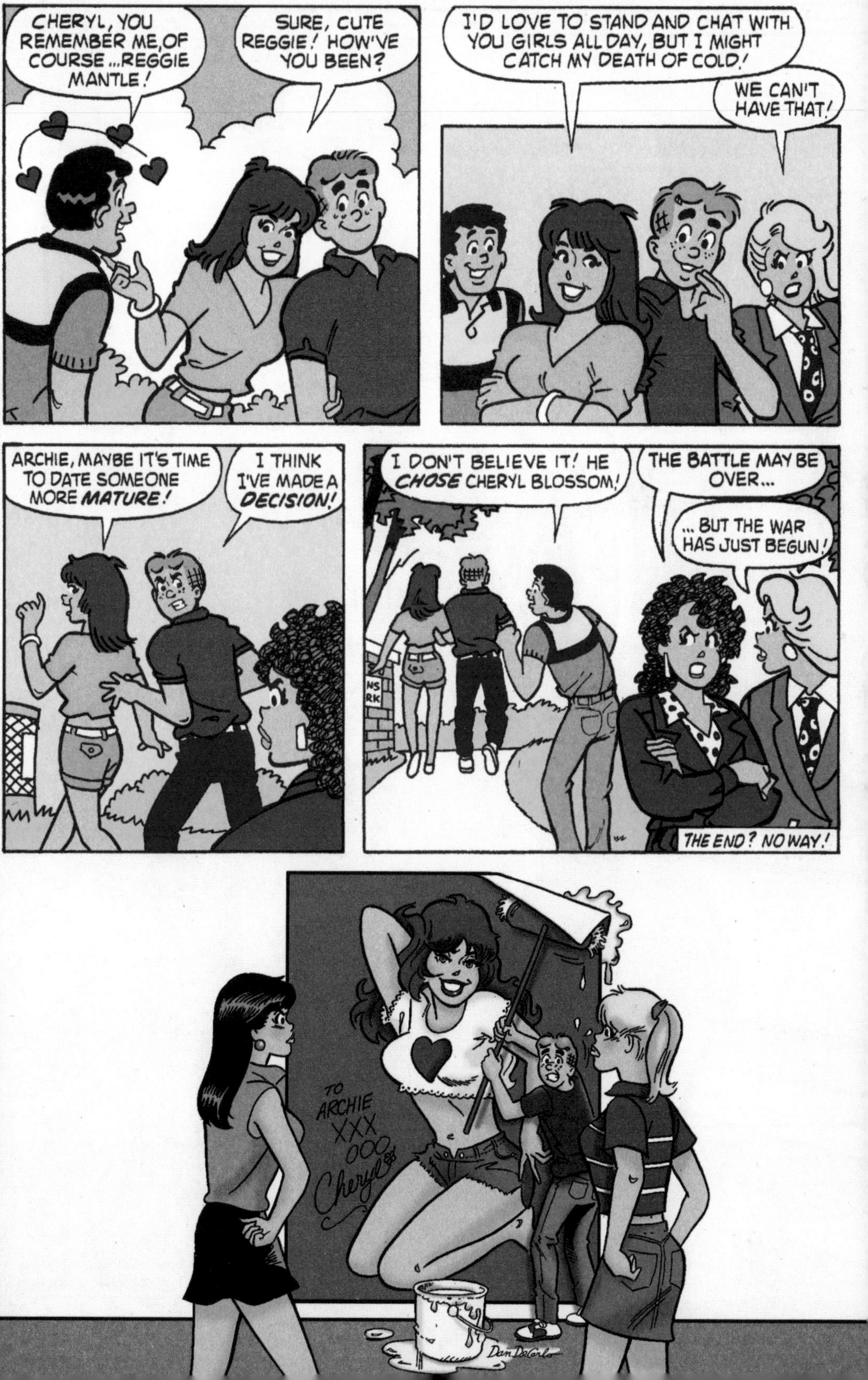
CHERYL, YOU REMEMBER ME, OF COURSE ...REGGIE MANTLE!
SURE, CUTE REGGIE! HOW'VE YOU BEEN?
I'D LOVE TO STAND AND CHAT WITH YOU GIRLS ALL DAY, BUT I MIGHT CATCH MY DEATH OF COLD!
WE CAN'T HAVE THAT!
ARCHIE, MAYBE IT'S TIME TO DATE SOMEONE MORE MATURE!
I THINK I'VE MADE A DECISION!
I DON'T BELIEVE IT! HE CHOSE CHERYL BLOSSOM!
THE BATTLE MAY BE OVER...
... BUT THE WAR HAS JUST BEGUN!
THE END? NO WAY!
TO ARCHIE XXX OOO Cheryl
Dan DeCarlo

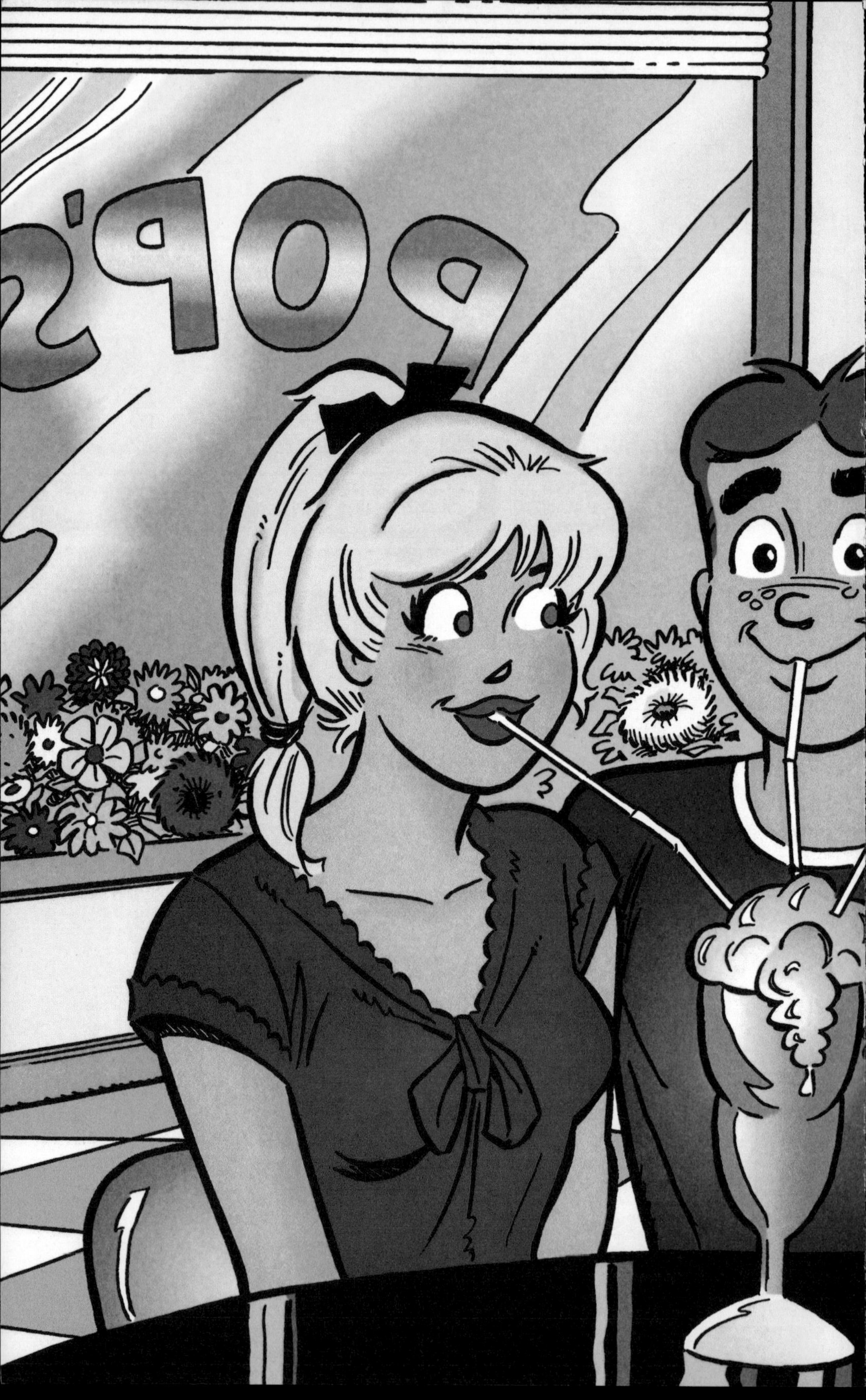
POP'S

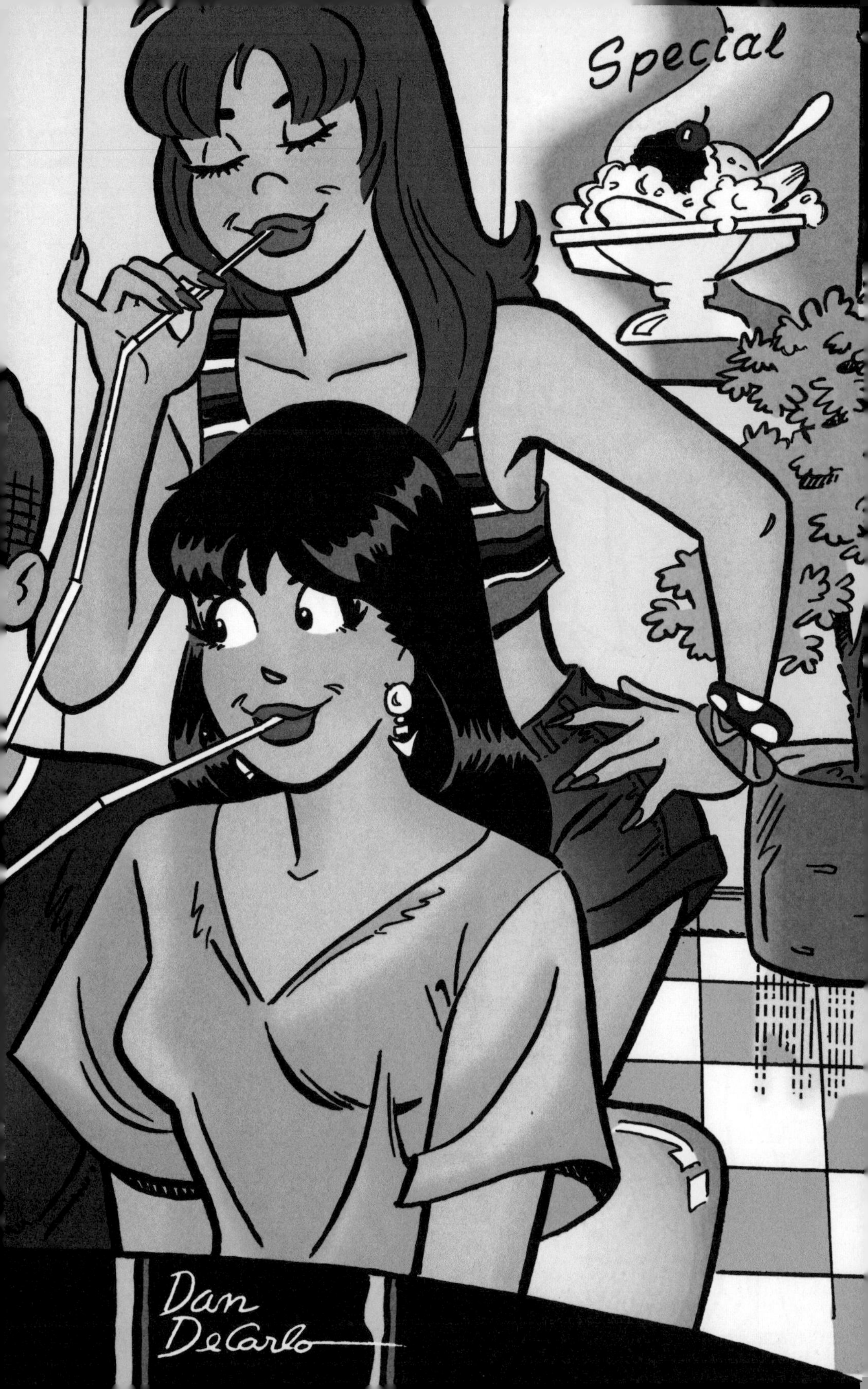
Special
Dan DeCarlo

Chapter Five

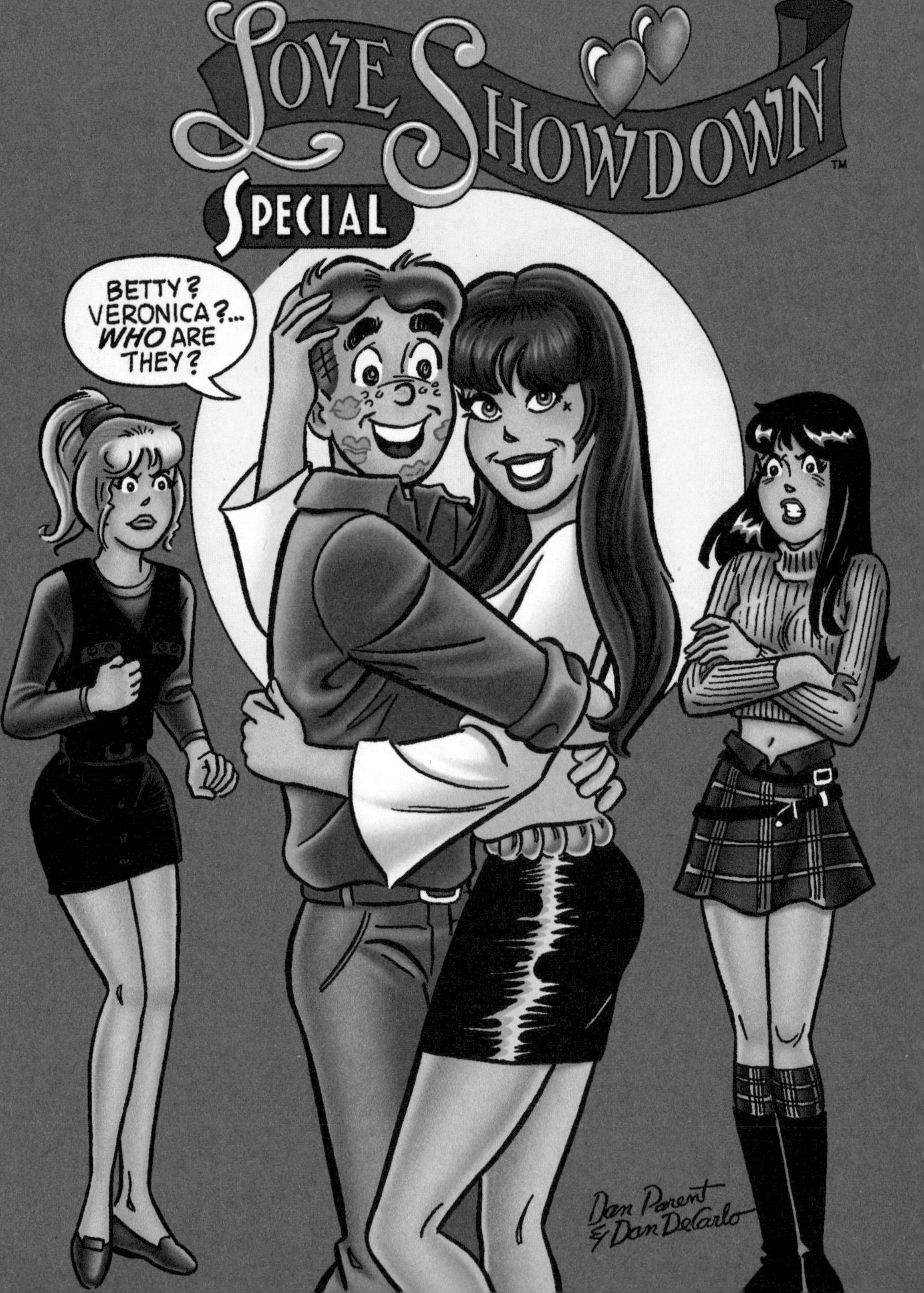
LOVE SHOWDOWN SPECIAL™
BETTY? VERONICA?... WHO ARE THEY?
Dan Parent & Dan DeCarlo

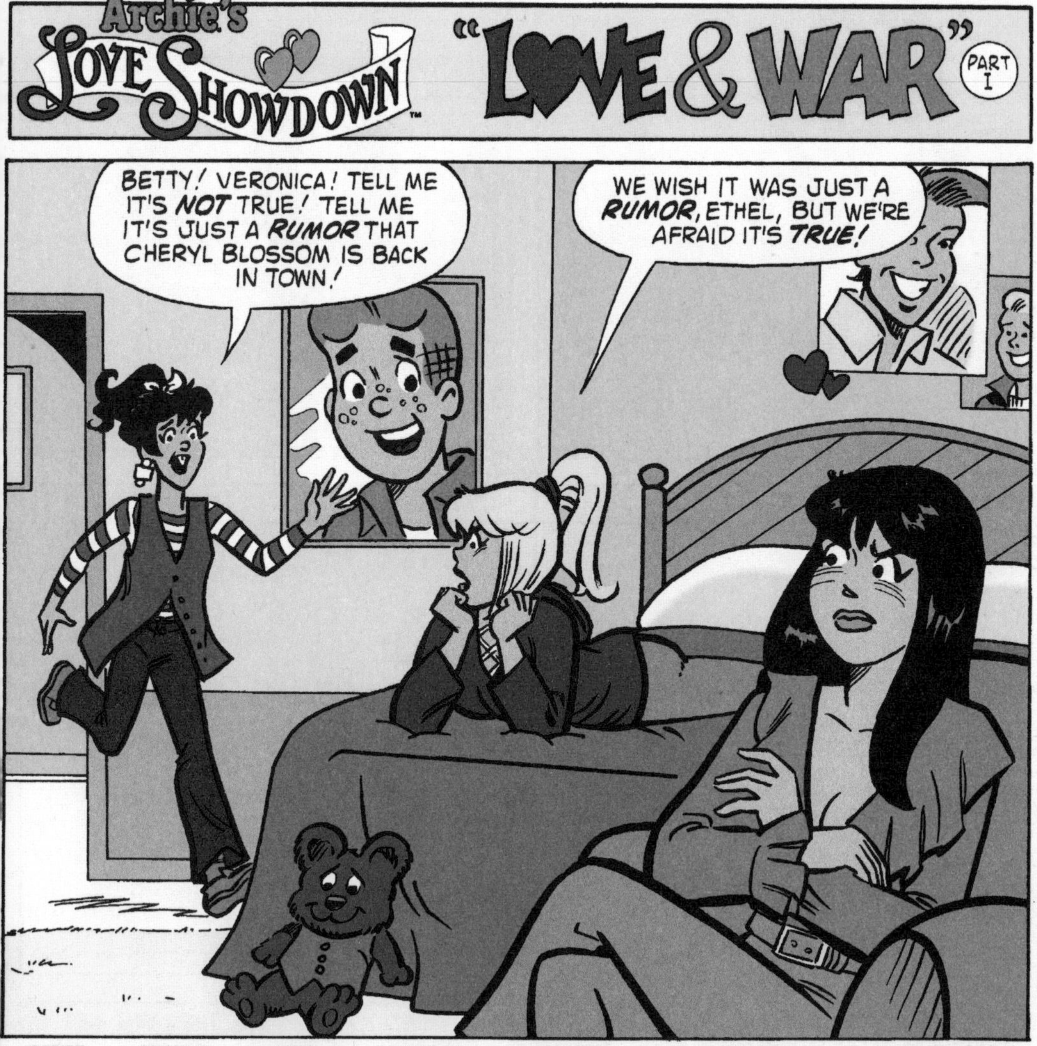
Archie's LOVE SHOWDOWN ™
"LOVE & WAR" PART I
BETTY! VERONICA! TELL ME IT'S NOT TRUE! TELL ME IT'S JUST A RUMOR THAT CHERYL BLOSSOM IS BACK IN TOWN!
WE WISH IT WAS JUST A RUMOR, ETHEL, BUT WE'RE AFRAID IT'S TRUE!

SCRIPT: DAN PARENT PENCILS: DAN PARENT INKS: MIKE ESPOSITO LETTERING: BILL YOSHIDA COLORING: BARRY GROSSMAN EDITORS: S.FULOP & V.GORELICK EDITOR-IN-CHIEF: RICHARD GOLDWATER

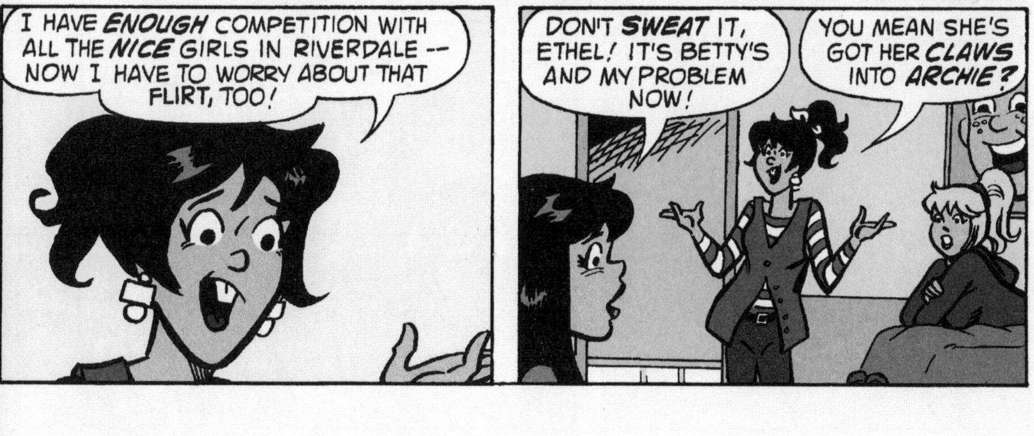
I HAVE ENOUGH COMPETITION WITH ALL THE NICE GIRLS IN RIVERDALE -- NOW I HAVE TO WORRY ABOUT THAT FLIRT, TOO!
YOU MEAN SHE'S GOT HER CLAWS INTO ARCHIE?
DON'T SWEAT IT, ETHEL! IT'S BETTY'S AND MY PROBLEM NOW!

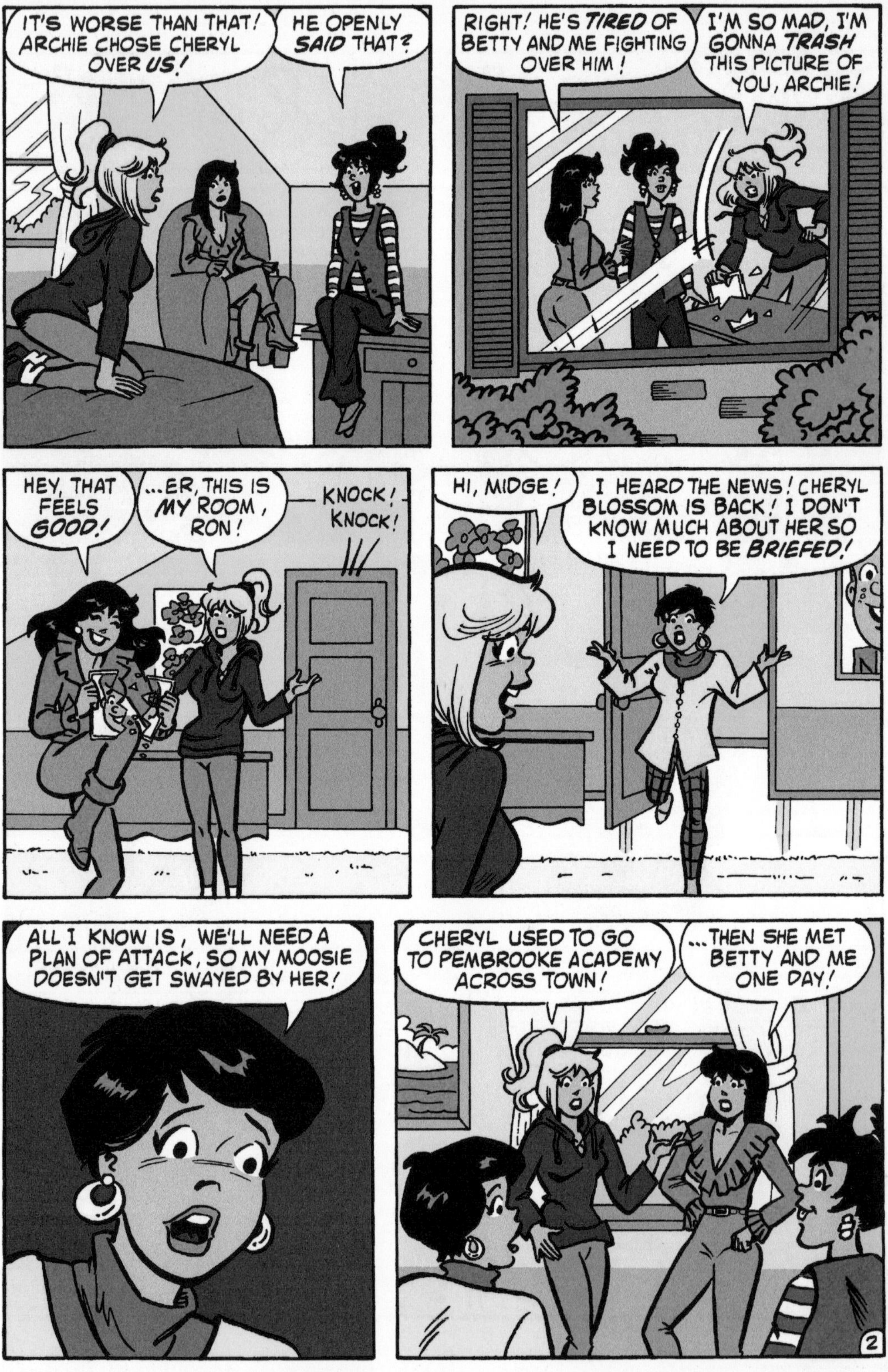

IT'S WORSE THAN THAT! ARCHIE CHOSE CHERYL OVER US!
HE OPENLY SAID THAT?
RIGHT! HE'S TIRED OF BETTY AND ME FIGHTING OVER HIM!
I'M SO MAD, I'M GONNA TRASH THIS PICTURE OF YOU, ARCHIE!
HEY, THAT FEELS GOOD!
...ER, THIS IS MY ROOM, RON!
KNOCK! KNOCK!
HI, MIDGE!
I HEARD THE NEWS! CHERYL BLOSSOM IS BACK! I DON'T KNOW MUCH ABOUT HER SO I NEED TO BE BRIEFED!
ALL I KNOW IS, WE'LL NEED A PLAN OF ATTACK, SO MY MOOSIE DOESN'T GET SWAYED BY HER!
CHERYL USED TO GO TO PEMBROOKE ACADEMY ACROSS TOWN!
...THEN SHE MET BETTY AND ME ONE DAY!
2

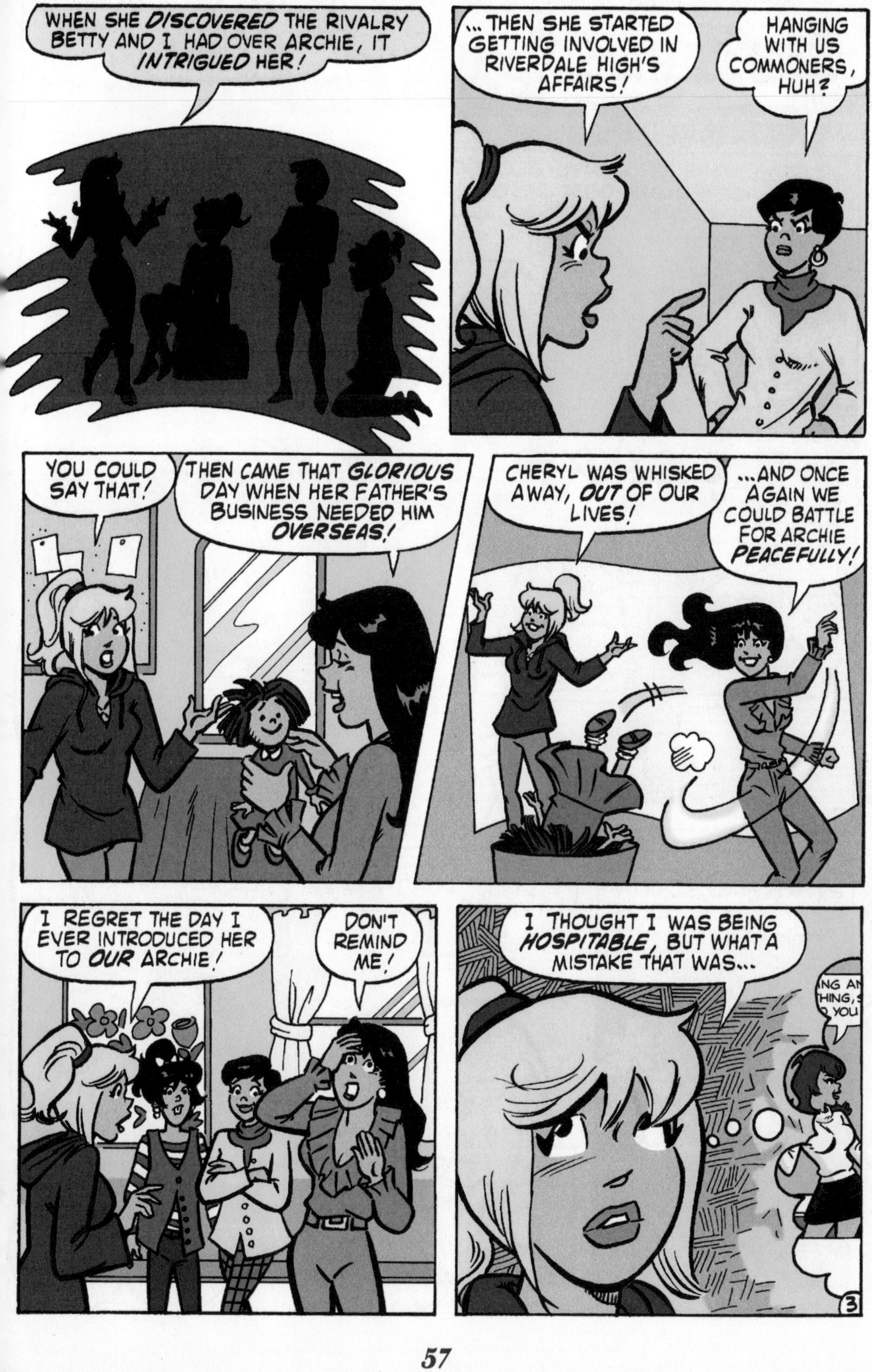
WHEN SHE DISCOVERED THE RIVALRY BETTY AND I HAD OVER ARCHIE, IT INTRIGUED HER!
...THEN SHE STARTED GETTING INVOLVED IN RIVERDALE HIGH'S AFFAIRS!
HANGING WITH US COMMONERS, HUH?
YOU COULD SAY THAT!
THEN CAME THAT GLORIOUS DAY WHEN HER FATHER'S BUSINESS NEEDED HIM OVERSEAS!
CHERYL WAS WHISKED AWAY, OUT OF OUR LIVES!
...AND ONCE AGAIN WE COULD BATTLE FOR ARCHIE PEACEFULLY!
I REGRET THE DAY I EVER INTRODUCED HER TO OUR ARCHIE!
DON'T REMIND ME!
I THOUGHT I WAS BEING HOSPITABLE, BUT WHAT A MISTAKE THAT WAS...
3

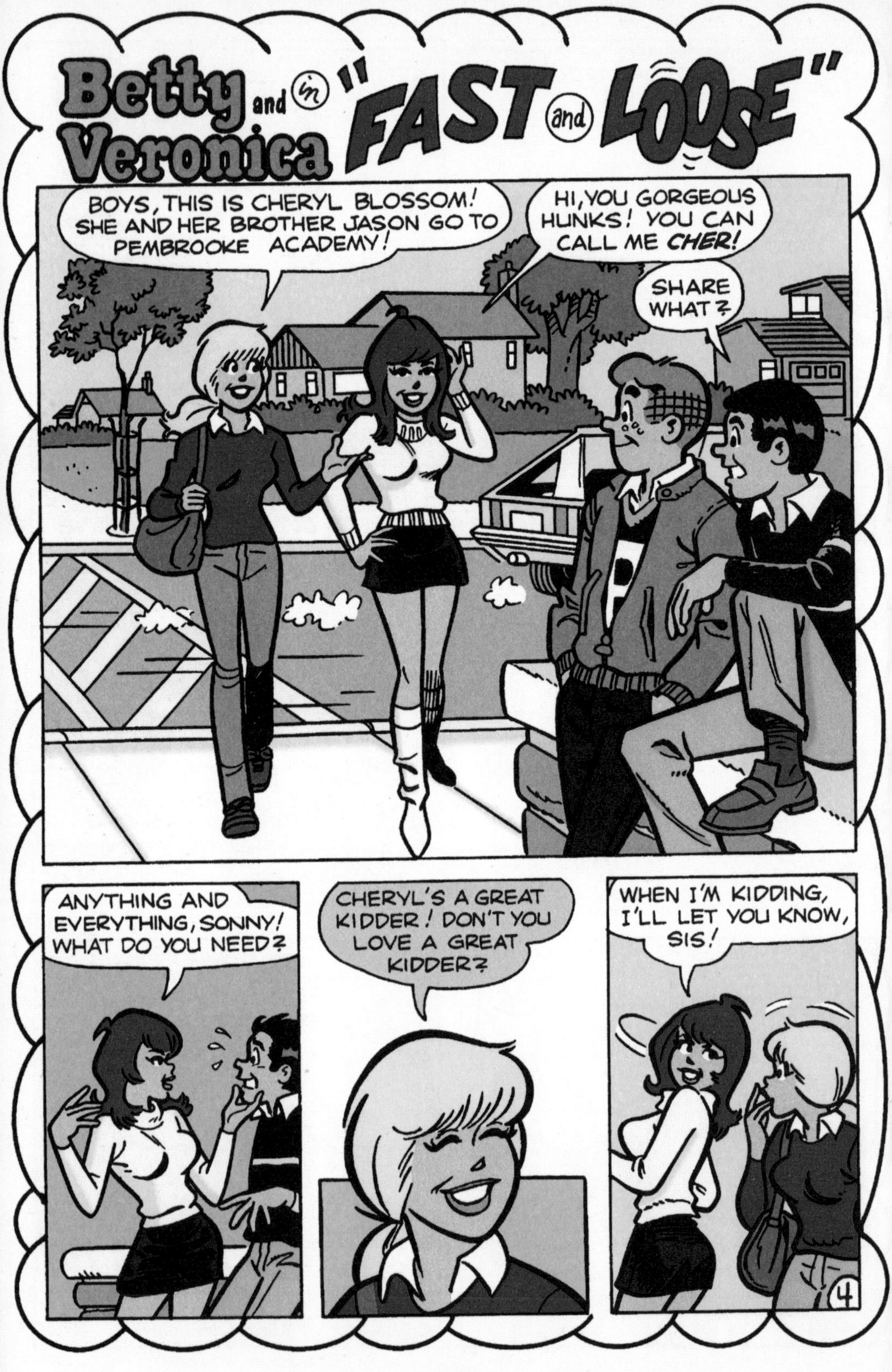
Betty and Veronica in "FAST and LOOSE"
BOYS, THIS IS CHERYL BLOSSOM! SHE AND HER BROTHER JASON GO TO PEMBROOKE ACADEMY!
HI, YOU GORGEOUS HUNKS! YOU CAN CALL ME CHER!
SHARE WHAT?
ANYTHING AND EVERYTHING, SONNY! WHAT DO YOU NEED?
CHERYL'S A GREAT KIDDER! DON'T YOU LOVE A GREAT KIDDER?
WHEN I'M KIDDING, I'LL LET YOU KNOW, SIS!
4

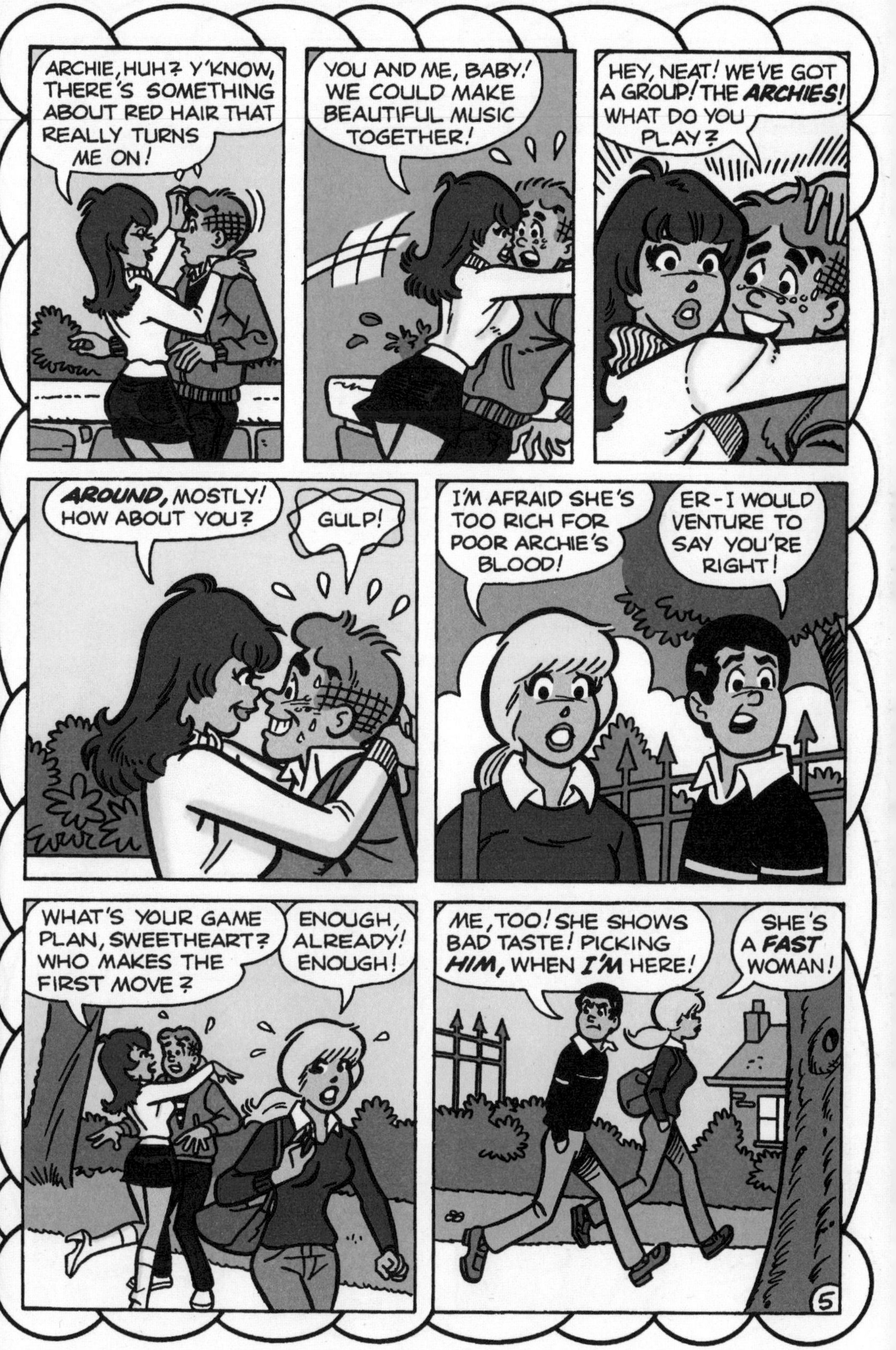
ARCHIE, HUH? Y'KNOW, THERE'S SOMETHING ABOUT RED HAIR THAT REALLY TURNS ME ON!
YOU AND ME, BABY! WE COULD MAKE BEAUTIFUL MUSIC TOGETHER!
HEY, NEAT! WE'VE GOT A GROUP! THE ARCHIES! WHAT DO YOU PLAY?
AROUND, MOSTLY! HOW ABOUT YOU?
GULP!
I'M AFRAID SHE'S TOO RICH FOR POOR ARCHIE'S BLOOD!
ER-I WOULD VENTURE TO SAY YOU'RE RIGHT!
WHAT'S YOUR GAME PLAN, SWEETHEART? WHO MAKES THE FIRST MOVE?
ENOUGH, ALREADY! ENOUGH!
ME, TOO! SHE SHOWS BAD TASTE! PICKING HIM, WHEN I'M HERE!
SHE'S A FAST WOMAN!
5

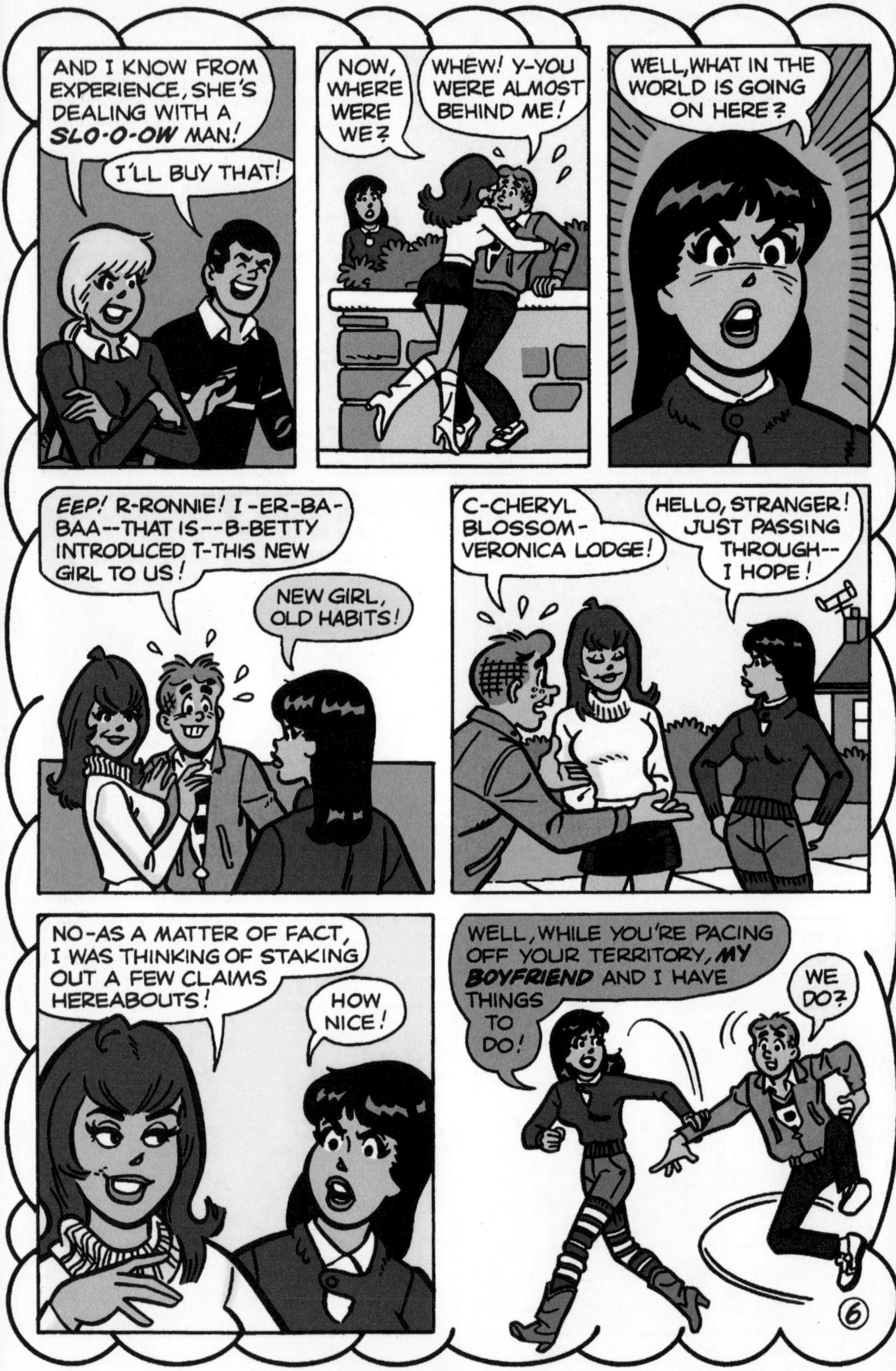
AND I KNOW FROM EXPERIENCE, SHE'S DEALING WITH A SLO-O-OW MAN!
I'LL BUY THAT!
NOW, WHERE WERE WE?
WHEW! Y-YOU WERE ALMOST BEHIND ME!
WELL, WHAT IN THE WORLD IS GOING ON HERE?
EEP! R-RONNIE! I-ER-BA-BAA--THAT IS--B-BETTY INTRODUCED T-THIS NEW GIRL TO US!
NEW GIRL, OLD HABITS!
C-CHERYL BLOSSOM-VERONICA LODGE!
HELLO, STRANGER! JUST PASSING THROUGH--I HOPE!
NO-AS A MATTER OF FACT, I WAS THINKING OF STAKING OUT A FEW CLAIMS HEREABOUTS!
HOW NICE!
WELL, WHILE YOU'RE PACING OFF YOUR TERRITORY, MY BOYFRIEND AND I HAVE THINGS TO DO!
WE DO?
6

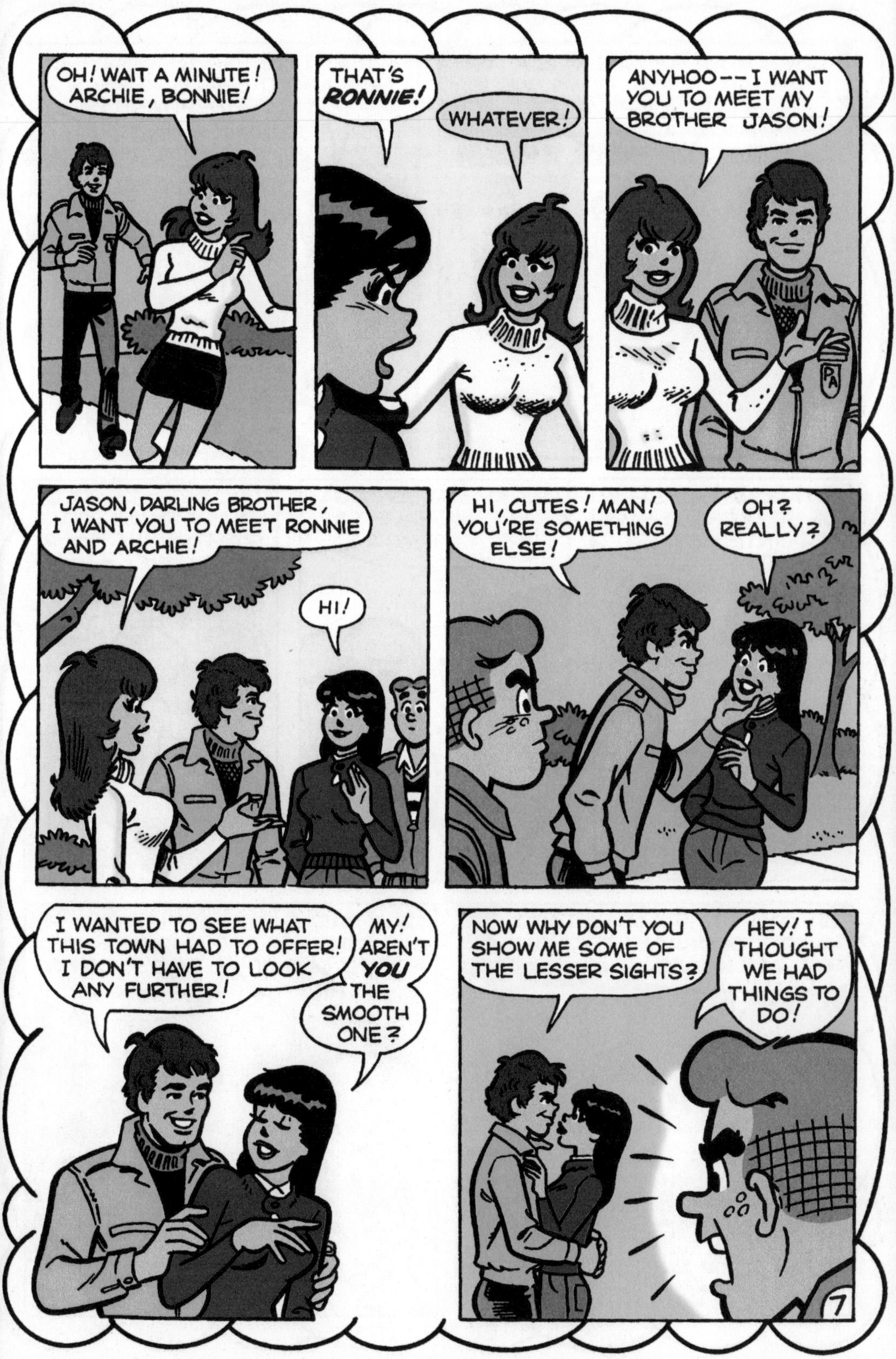
OH! WAIT A MINUTE! ARCHIE, BONNIE!
THAT'S RONNIE!
WHATEVER!
ANYHOO -- I WANT YOU TO MEET MY BROTHER JASON!
JASON, DARLING BROTHER, I WANT YOU TO MEET RONNIE AND ARCHIE!
HI!
HI, CUTES! MAN! YOU'RE SOMETHING ELSE!
OH? REALLY?
I WANTED TO SEE WHAT THIS TOWN HAD TO OFFER! I DON'T HAVE TO LOOK ANY FURTHER!
MY! AREN'T YOU THE SMOOTH ONE?
NOW WHY DON'T YOU SHOW ME SOME OF THE LESSER SIGHTS?
HEY! I THOUGHT WE HAD THINGS TO DO!
7

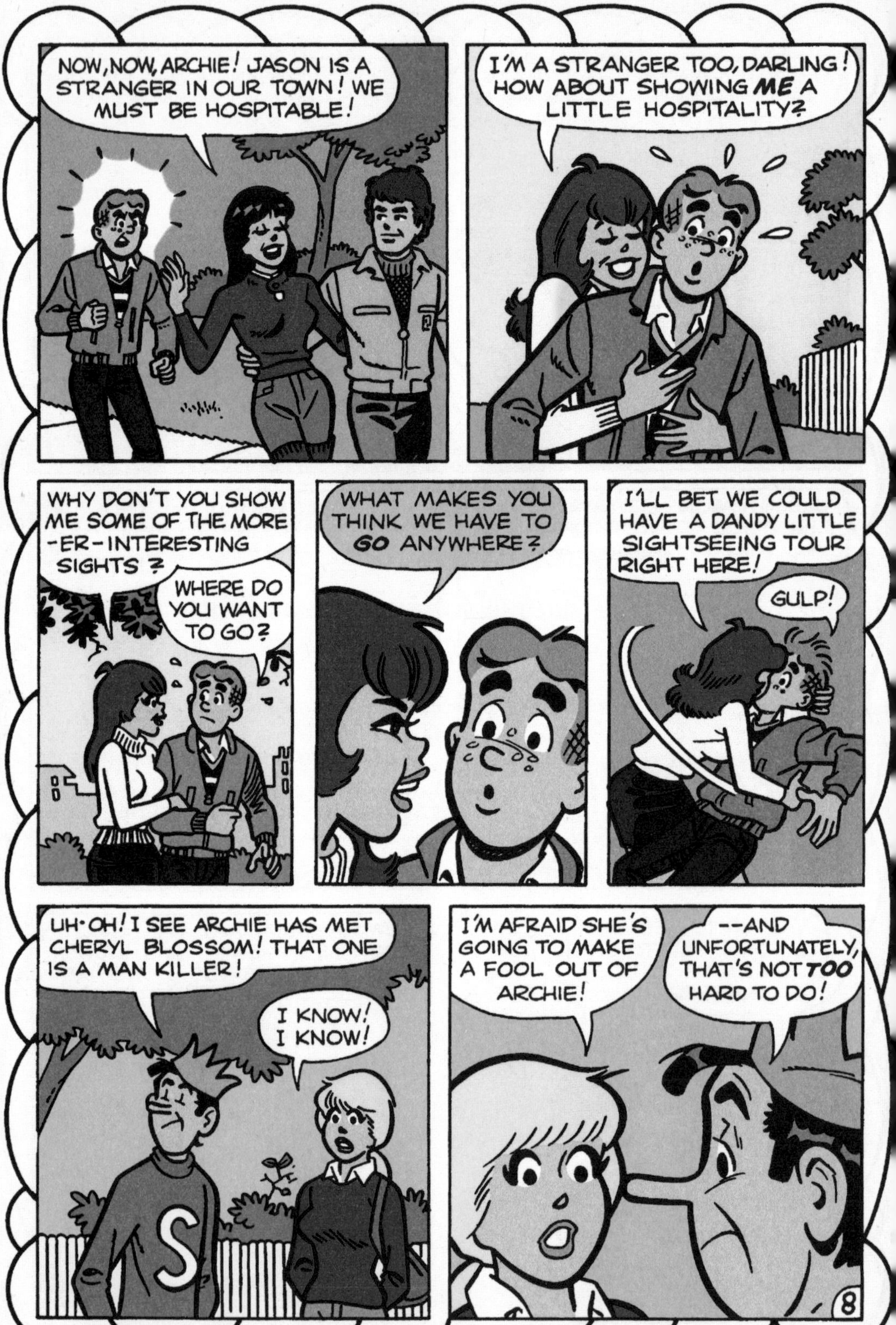
NOW, NOW, ARCHIE! JASON IS A STRANGER IN OUR TOWN! WE MUST BE HOSPITABLE!
I'M A STRANGER TOO, DARLING! HOW ABOUT SHOWING **ME** A LITTLE HOSPITALITY?
WHY DON'T YOU SHOW ME SOME OF THE MORE -ER- INTERESTING SIGHTS?
WHERE DO YOU WANT TO GO?
WHAT MAKES YOU THINK WE HAVE TO **GO** ANYWHERE?
I'LL BET WE COULD HAVE A DANDY LITTLE SIGHTSEEING TOUR RIGHT HERE!
GULP!
UH-OH! I SEE ARCHIE HAS MET CHERYL BLOSSOM! THAT ONE IS A MAN KILLER!
I KNOW! I KNOW!
I'M AFRAID SHE'S GOING TO MAKE A FOOL OUT OF ARCHIE!
--AND UNFORTUNATELY, THAT'S NOT **TOO** HARD TO DO!
8

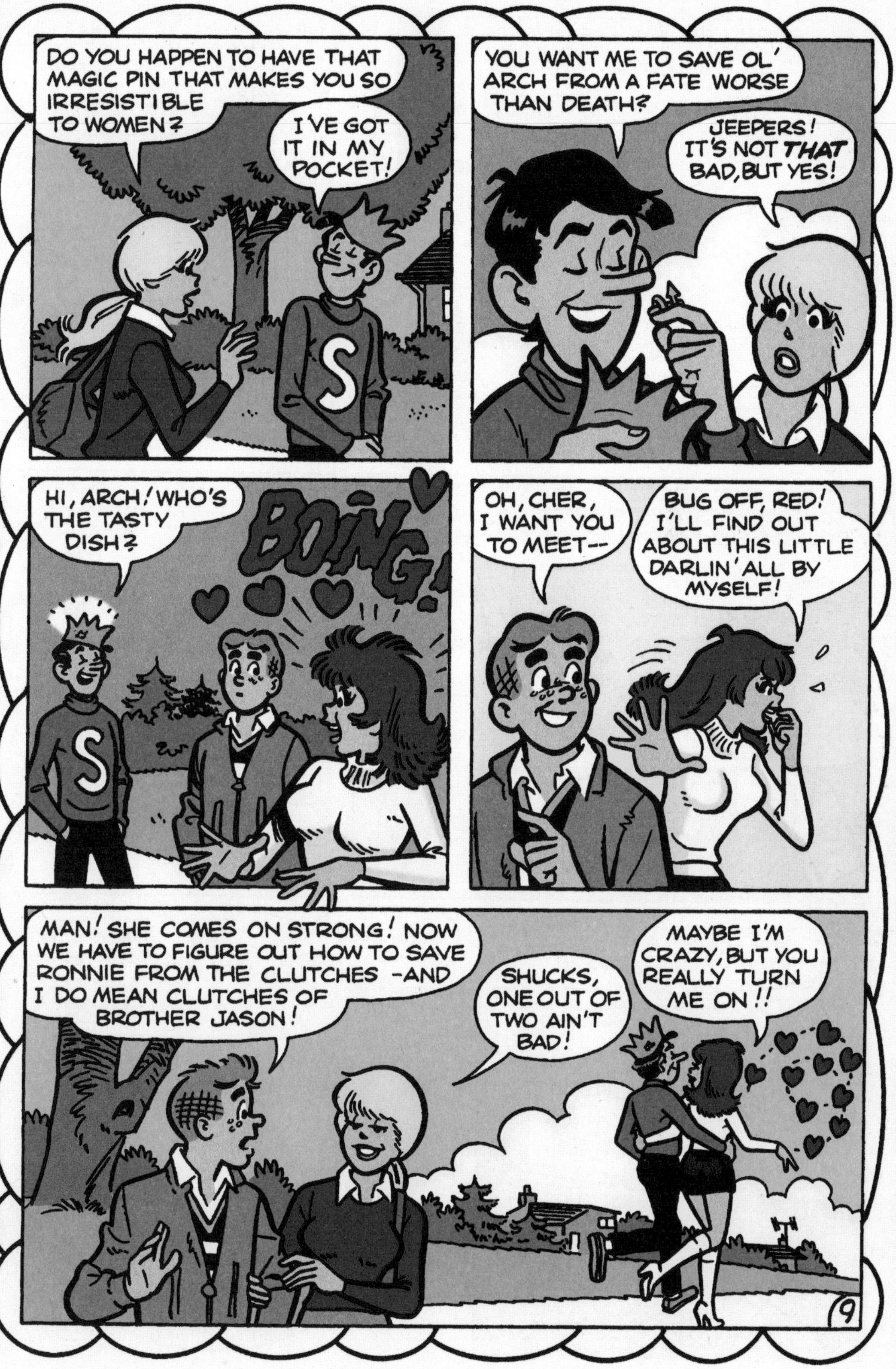
DO YOU HAPPEN TO HAVE THAT MAGIC PIN THAT MAKES YOU SO IRRESISTIBLE TO WOMEN?
I'VE GOT IT IN MY POCKET!
YOU WANT ME TO SAVE OL' ARCH FROM A FATE WORSE THAN DEATH?
JEEPERS! IT'S NOT *THAT* BAD, BUT YES!
HI, ARCH! WHO'S THE TASTY DISH?
BOING!
OH, CHER, I WANT YOU TO MEET--
BUG OFF, RED! I'LL FIND OUT ABOUT THIS LITTLE DARLIN' ALL BY MYSELF!
MAN! SHE COMES ON STRONG! NOW WE HAVE TO FIGURE OUT HOW TO SAVE RONNIE FROM THE CLUTCHES -AND I DO MEAN CLUTCHES OF BROTHER JASON!
SHUCKS, ONE OUT OF TWO AIN'T BAD!
MAYBE I'M CRAZY, BUT YOU REALLY TURN ME ON!!
9

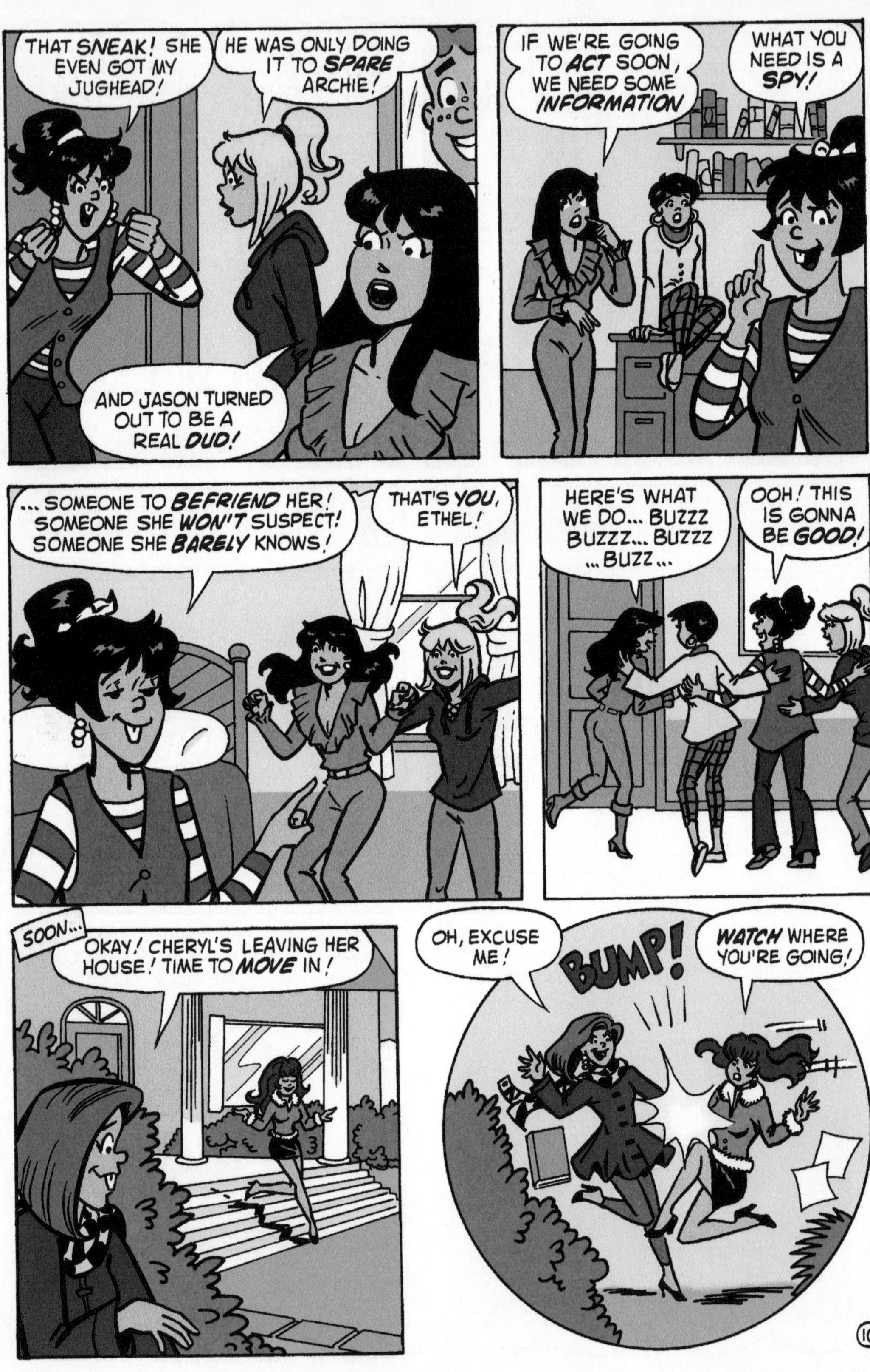
THAT SNEAK! SHE EVEN GOT MY JUGHEAD!
HE WAS ONLY DOING IT TO SPARE ARCHIE!
AND JASON TURNED OUT TO BE A REAL DUD!
IF WE'RE GOING TO ACT SOON, WE NEED SOME INFORMATION
WHAT YOU NEED IS A SPY!
... SOMEONE TO BEFRIEND HER! SOMEONE SHE WON'T SUSPECT! SOMEONE SHE BARELY KNOWS!
THAT'S YOU, ETHEL!
HERE'S WHAT WE DO... BUZZZ BUZZZ... BUZZZ ...BUZZ...
OOH! THIS IS GONNA BE GOOD!
SOON...
OKAY! CHERYL'S LEAVING HER HOUSE! TIME TO MOVE IN!
OH, EXCUSE ME!
BUMP!
WATCH WHERE YOU'RE GOING!
10

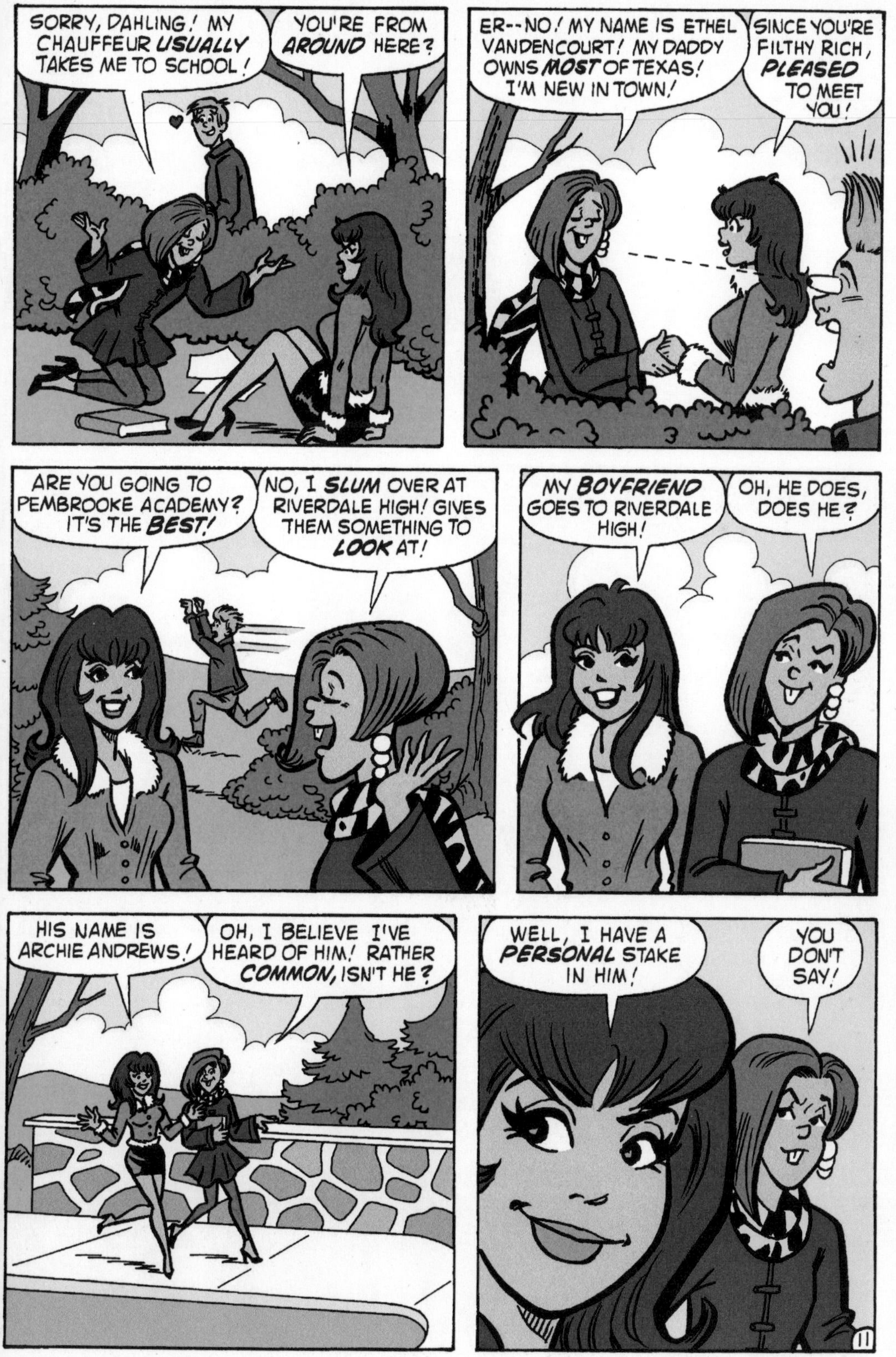
SORRY, DAHLING! MY CHAUFFEUR USUALLY TAKES ME TO SCHOOL!
YOU'RE FROM AROUND HERE?
ER--NO! MY NAME IS ETHEL VANDENCOURT! MY DADDY OWNS MOST OF TEXAS! I'M NEW IN TOWN!
SINCE YOU'RE FILTHY RICH, PLEASED TO MEET YOU!
ARE YOU GOING TO PEMBROOKE ACADEMY? IT'S THE BEST!
NO, I SLUM OVER AT RIVERDALE HIGH! GIVES THEM SOMETHING TO LOOK AT!
MY BOYFRIEND GOES TO RIVERDALE HIGH!
OH, HE DOES, DOES HE?
HIS NAME IS ARCHIE ANDREWS!
OH, I BELIEVE I'VE HEARD OF HIM! RATHER COMMON, ISN'T HE?
WELL, I HAVE A PERSONAL STAKE IN HIM!
YOU DON'T SAY!
11

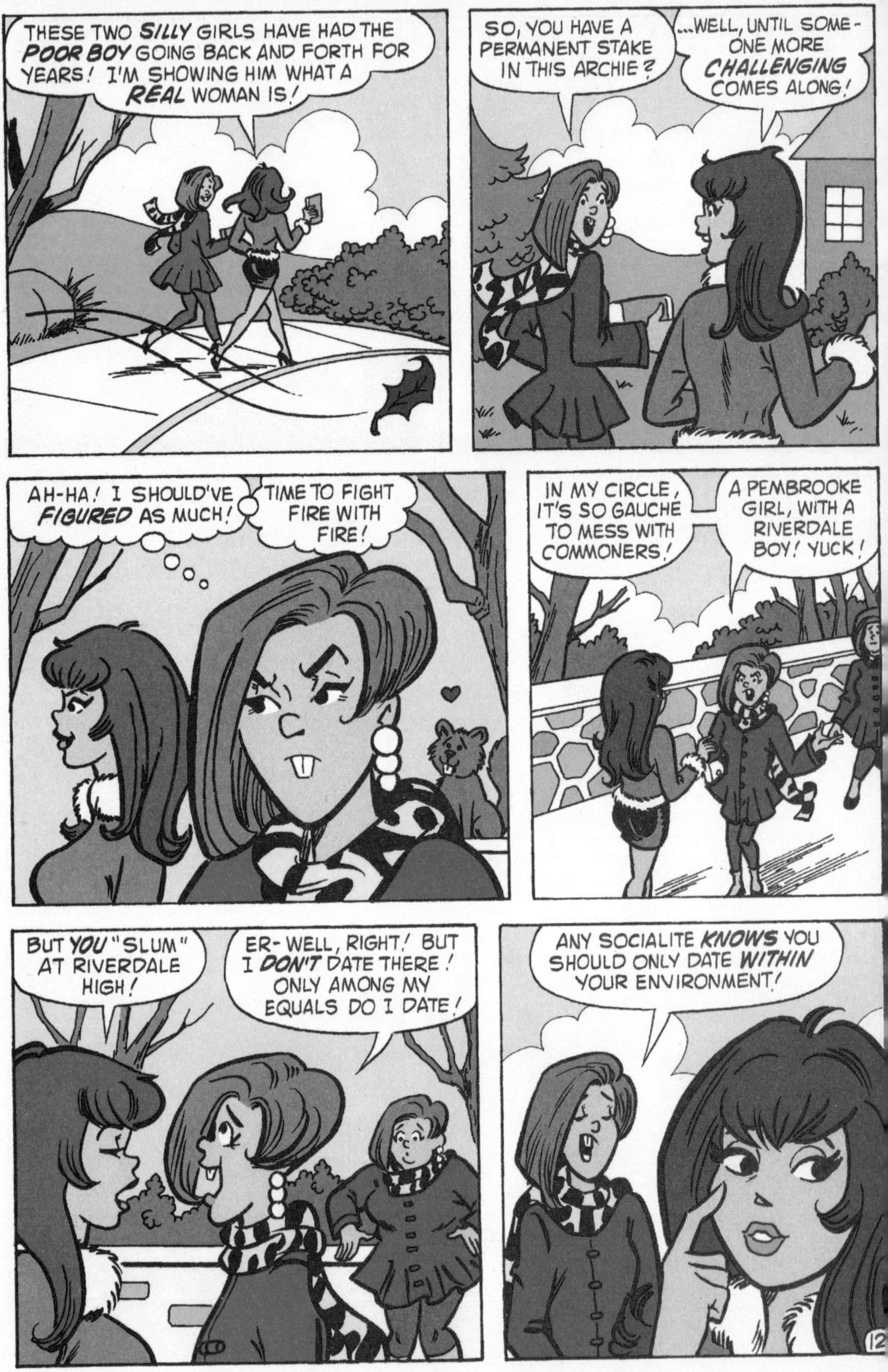
THESE TWO SILLY GIRLS HAVE HAD THE POOR BOY GOING BACK AND FORTH FOR YEARS! I'M SHOWING HIM WHAT A REAL WOMAN IS!
SO, YOU HAVE A PERMANENT STAKE IN THIS ARCHIE?
...WELL, UNTIL SOME-ONE MORE CHALLENGING COMES ALONG!
AH-HA! I SHOULD'VE FIGURED AS MUCH!
TIME TO FIGHT FIRE WITH FIRE!
IN MY CIRCLE, IT'S SO GAUCHE TO MESS WITH COMMONERS!
A PEMBROOKE GIRL, WITH A RIVERDALE BOY! YUCK!
BUT YOU "SLUM" AT RIVERDALE HIGH!
ER-WELL, RIGHT! BUT I DON'T DATE THERE! ONLY AMONG MY EQUALS DO I DATE!
ANY SOCIALITE KNOWS YOU SHOULD ONLY DATE WITHIN YOUR ENVIRONMENT!
12

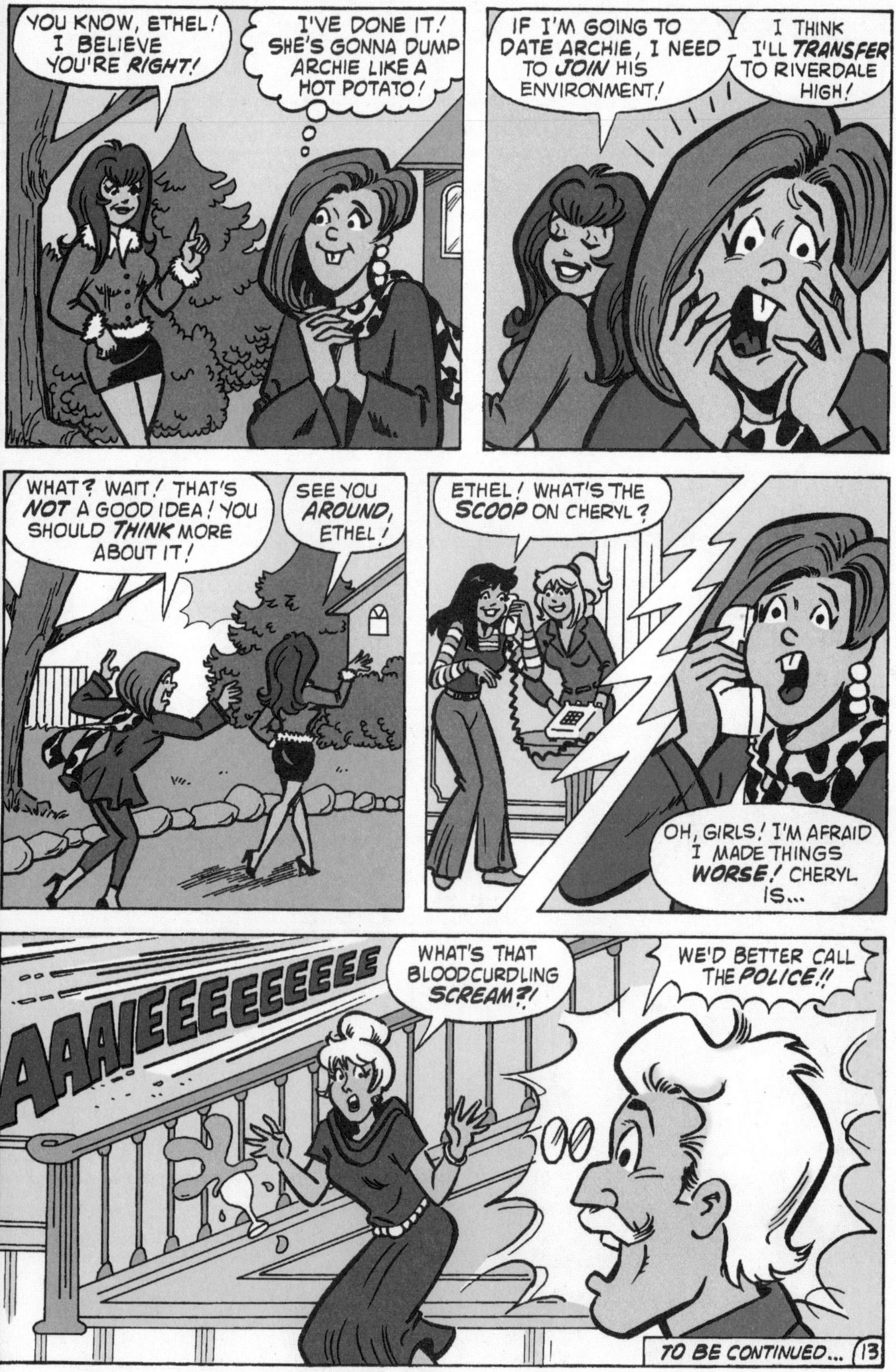
YOU KNOW, ETHEL! I BELIEVE YOU'RE RIGHT!
I'VE DONE IT! SHE'S GONNA DUMP ARCHIE LIKE A HOT POTATO!
IF I'M GOING TO DATE ARCHIE, I NEED TO JOIN HIS ENVIRONMENT!
I THINK I'LL TRANSFER TO RIVERDALE HIGH!
WHAT? WAIT! THAT'S NOT A GOOD IDEA! YOU SHOULD THINK MORE ABOUT IT!
SEE YOU AROUND, ETHEL!
ETHEL! WHAT'S THE SCOOP ON CHERYL?
OH, GIRLS! I'M AFRAID I MADE THINGS WORSE! CHERYL IS...
AAAIEEEEEEEEEE
WHAT'S THAT BLOODCURDLING SCREAM?!
WE'D BETTER CALL THE POLICE!!
TO BE CONTINUED... 13

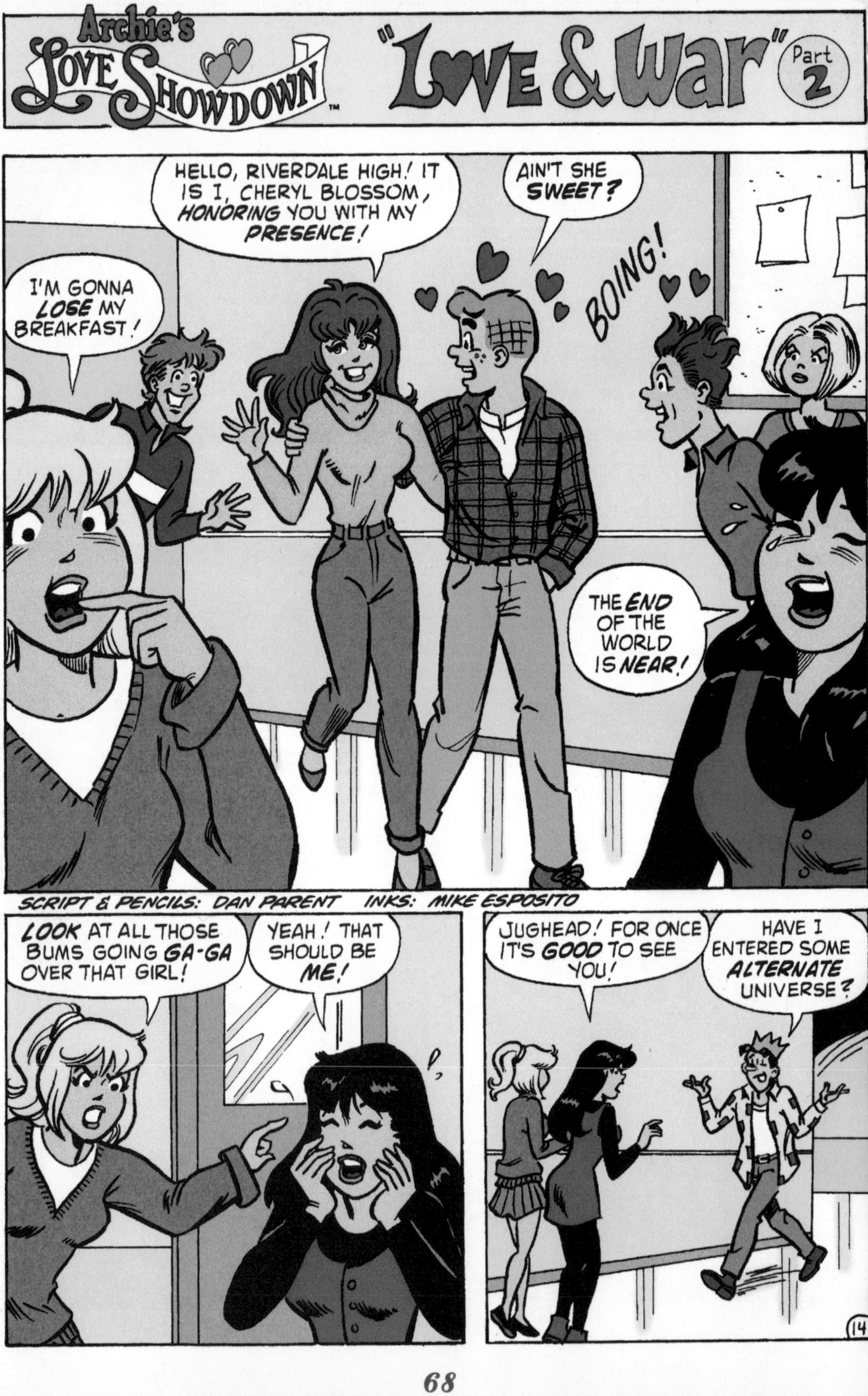
Archie's LOVE SHOWDOWN
"LOVE & WAR" Part 2
HELLO, RIVERDALE HIGH! IT IS I, CHERYL BLOSSOM, HONORING YOU WITH MY PRESENCE!
AIN'T SHE SWEET?
I'M GONNA LOSE MY BREAKFAST!
BOING!
THE END OF THE WORLD IS NEAR!
SCRIPT & PENCILS: DAN PARENT INKS: MIKE ESPOSITO
LOOK AT ALL THOSE BUMS GOING GA-GA OVER THAT GIRL!
YEAH! THAT SHOULD BE ME!
JUGHEAD! FOR ONCE IT'S GOOD TO SEE YOU!
HAVE I ENTERED SOME ALTERNATE UNIVERSE?
14

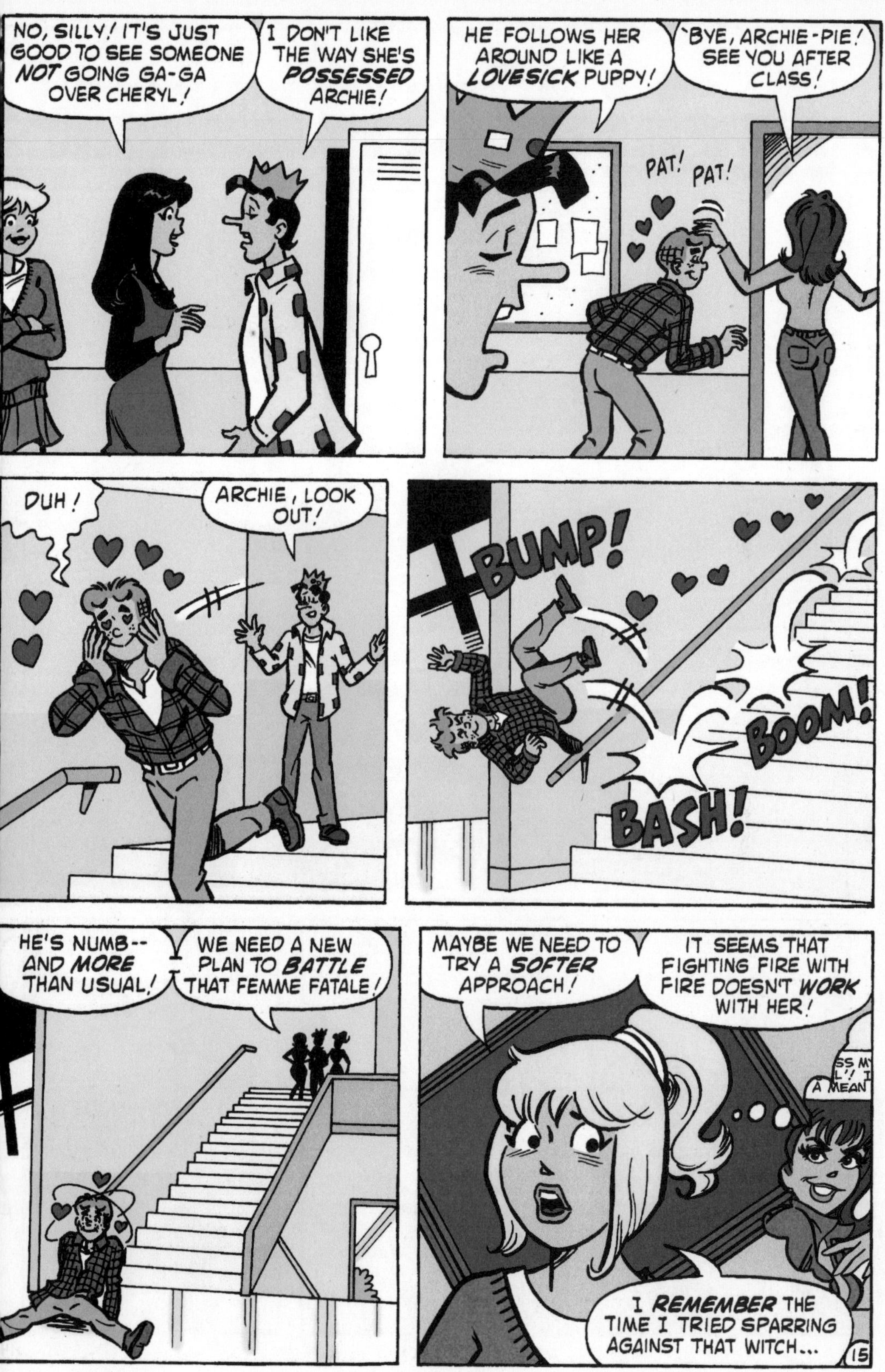
NO, SILLY! IT'S JUST GOOD TO SEE SOMEONE NOT GOING GA-GA OVER CHERYL!
I DON'T LIKE THE WAY SHE'S POSSESSED ARCHIE!
HE FOLLOWS HER AROUND LIKE A LOVESICK PUPPY!
'BYE, ARCHIE-PIE! SEE YOU AFTER CLASS!
PAT! PAT!
DUH!
ARCHIE, LOOK OUT!
BUMP!
BOOM!
BASH!
HE'S NUMB-- AND MORE THAN USUAL!
WE NEED A NEW PLAN TO BATTLE THAT FEMME FATALE!
MAYBE WE NEED TO TRY A SOFTER APPROACH!
IT SEEMS THAT FIGHTING FIRE WITH FIRE DOESN'T WORK WITH HER!
I REMEMBER THE TIME I TRIED SPARRING AGAINST THAT WITCH...
15

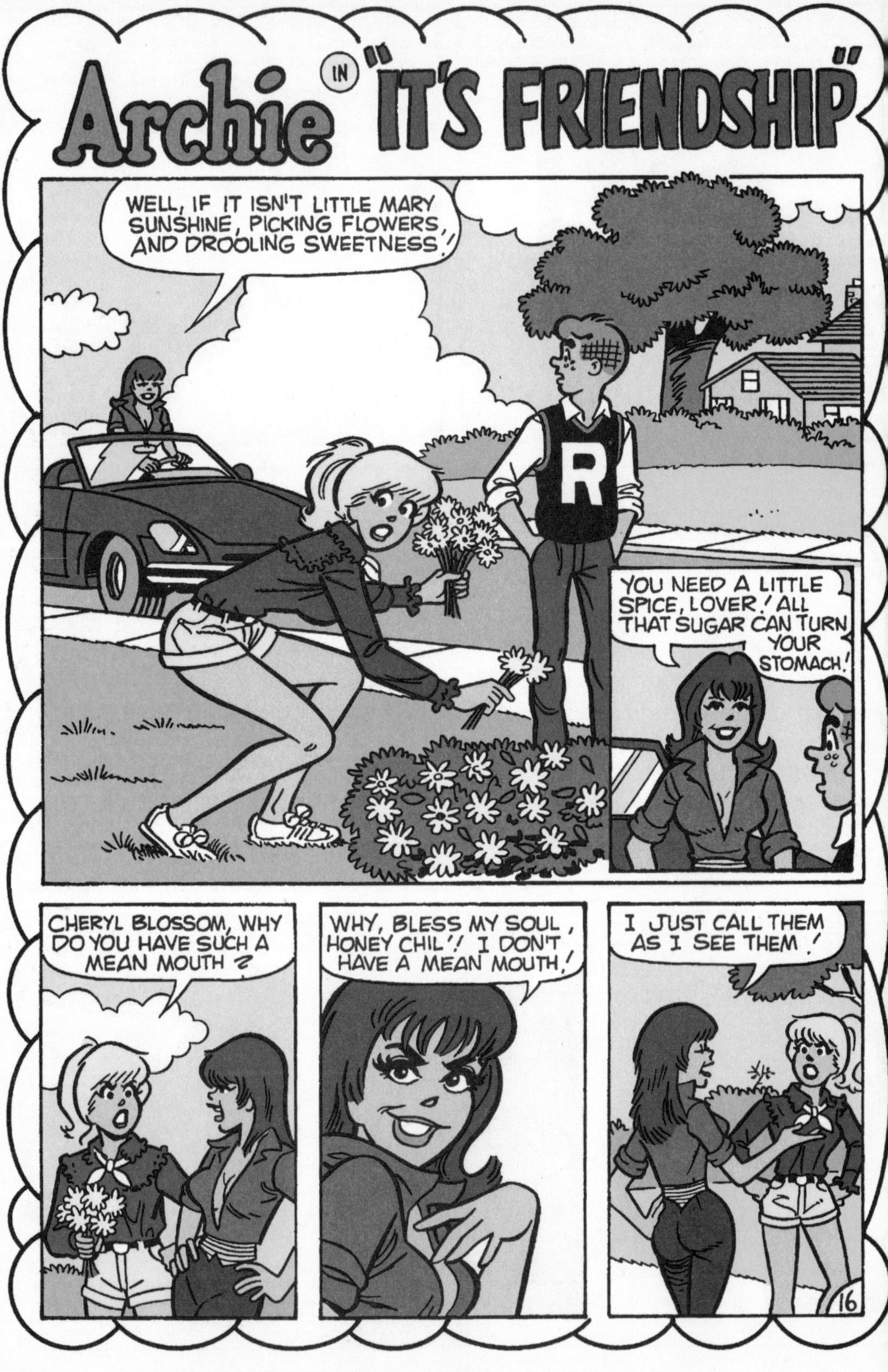

Archie IN "IT'S FRIENDSHIP"
WELL, IF IT ISN'T LITTLE MARY SUNSHINE, PICKING FLOWERS, AND DROOLING SWEETNESS!
R
YOU NEED A LITTLE SPICE, LOVER! ALL THAT SUGAR CAN TURN YOUR STOMACH!
CHERYL BLOSSOM, WHY DO YOU HAVE SUCH A MEAN MOUTH ?
WHY, BLESS MY SOUL, HONEY CHIL'! I DON'T HAVE A MEAN MOUTH!
I JUST CALL THEM AS I SEE THEM!
16

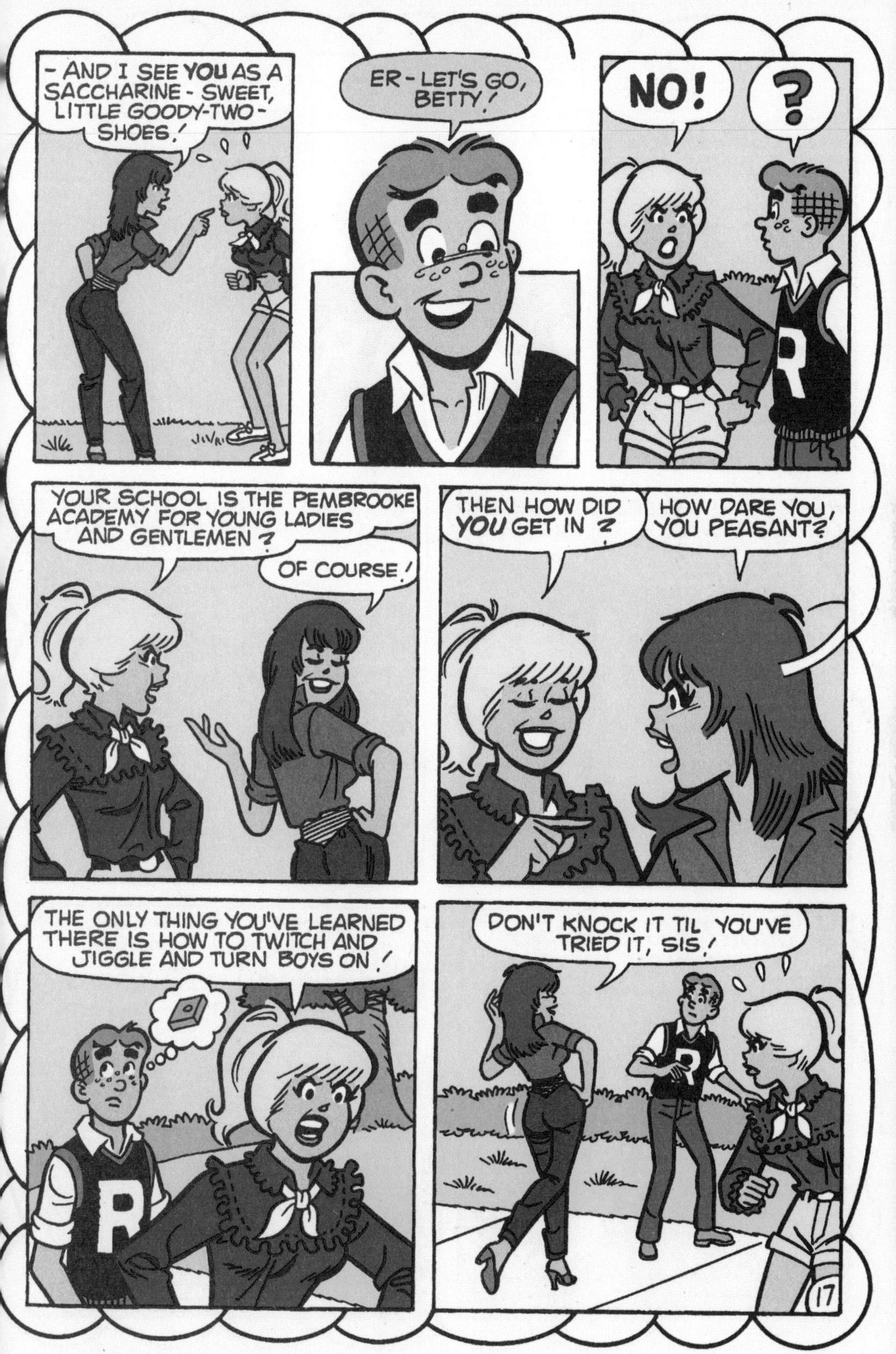
- AND I SEE YOU AS A SACCHARINE - SWEET, LITTLE GOODY-TWO-SHOES!
ER - LET'S GO, BETTY!
NO!
?
YOUR SCHOOL IS THE PEMBROOKE ACADEMY FOR YOUNG LADIES AND GENTLEMEN?
OF COURSE!
THEN HOW DID YOU GET IN?
HOW DARE YOU, YOU PEASANT?
THE ONLY THING YOU'VE LEARNED THERE IS HOW TO TWITCH AND JIGGLE AND TURN BOYS ON!
DON'T KNOCK IT TIL YOU'VE TRIED IT, SIS!
R
R
R
17

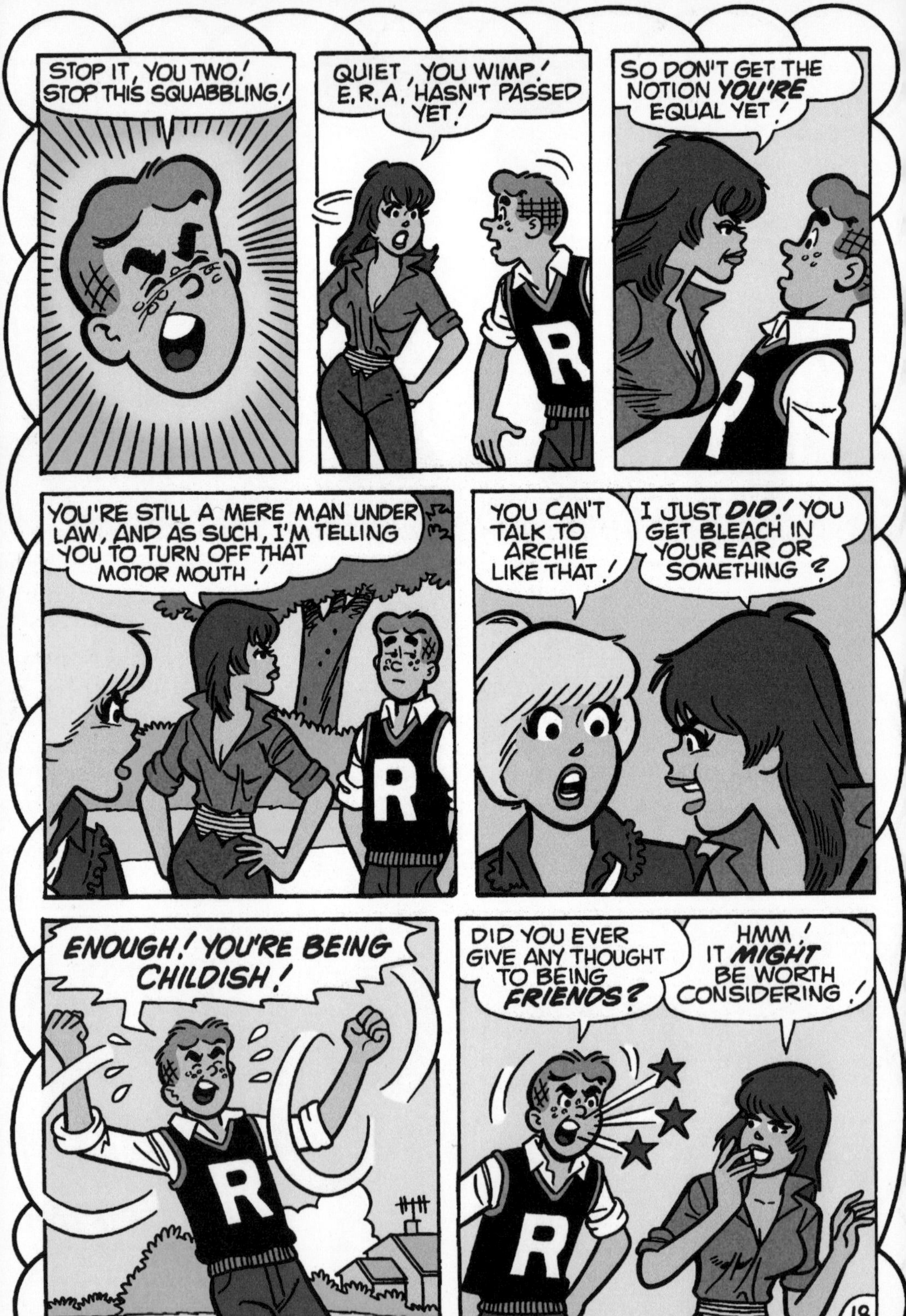
STOP IT, YOU TWO! STOP THIS SQUABBLING!
QUIET, YOU WIMP! E.R.A. HASN'T PASSED YET!
SO DON'T GET THE NOTION YOU'RE EQUAL YET!
YOU'RE STILL A MERE MAN UNDER LAW, AND AS SUCH, I'M TELLING YOU TO TURN OFF THAT MOTOR MOUTH!
YOU CAN'T TALK TO ARCHIE LIKE THAT!
I JUST DID! YOU GET BLEACH IN YOUR EAR OR SOMETHING?
ENOUGH! YOU'RE BEING CHILDISH!
DID YOU EVER GIVE ANY THOUGHT TO BEING FRIENDS?
HMM! IT MIGHT BE WORTH CONSIDERING!
18

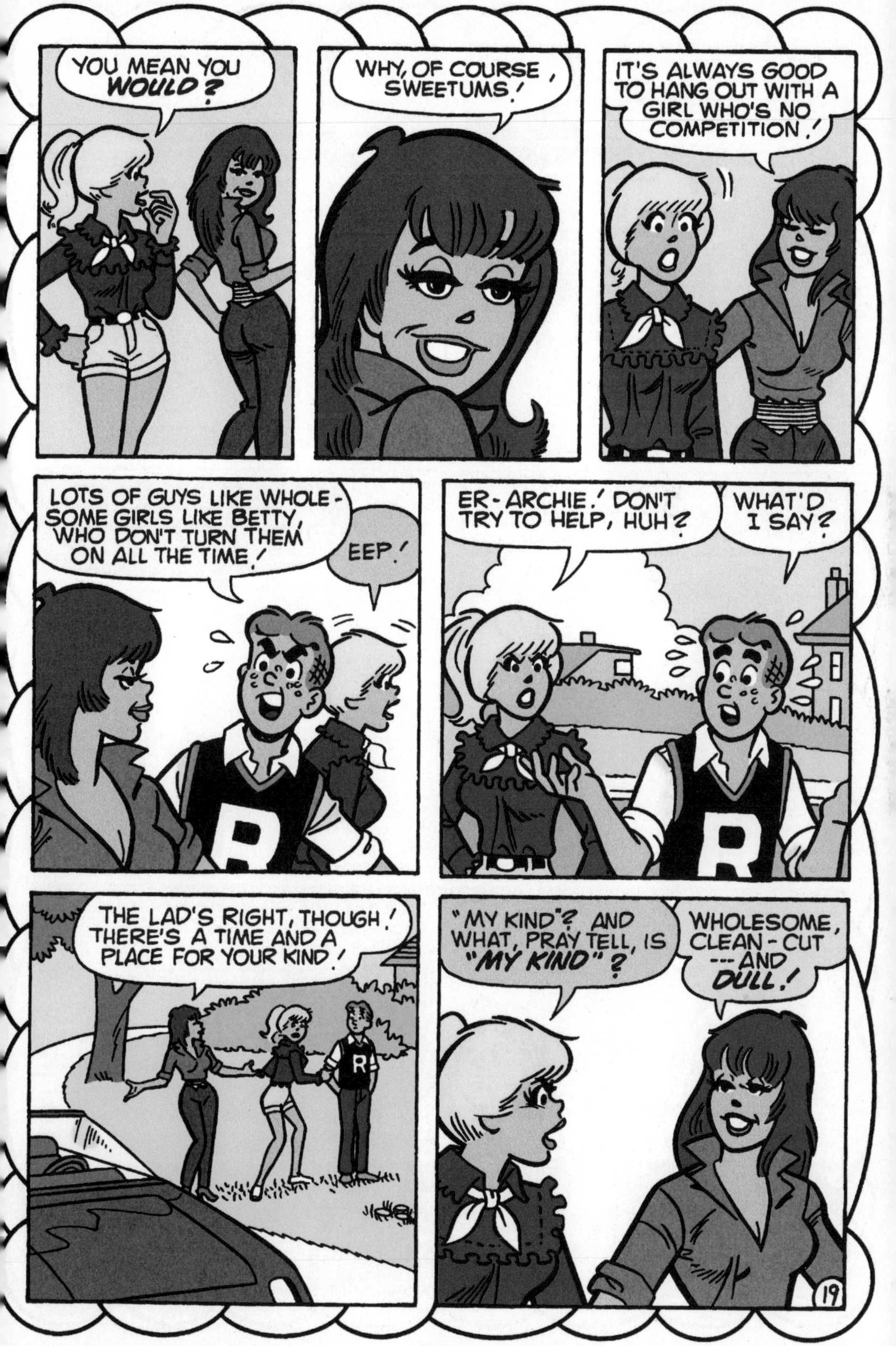
YOU MEAN YOU WOULD?
WHY, OF COURSE, SWEETUMS!
IT'S ALWAYS GOOD TO HANG OUT WITH A GIRL WHO'S NO COMPETITION!
LOTS OF GUYS LIKE WHOLE-SOME GIRLS LIKE BETTY, WHO DON'T TURN THEM ON ALL THE TIME!
EEP!
ER-ARCHIE! DON'T TRY TO HELP, HUH?
WHAT'D I SAY?
THE LAD'S RIGHT, THOUGH! THERE'S A TIME AND A PLACE FOR YOUR KIND!
"MY KIND"? AND WHAT, PRAY TELL, IS "MY KIND"?
WHOLESOME, CLEAN-CUT ---AND DULL!
19

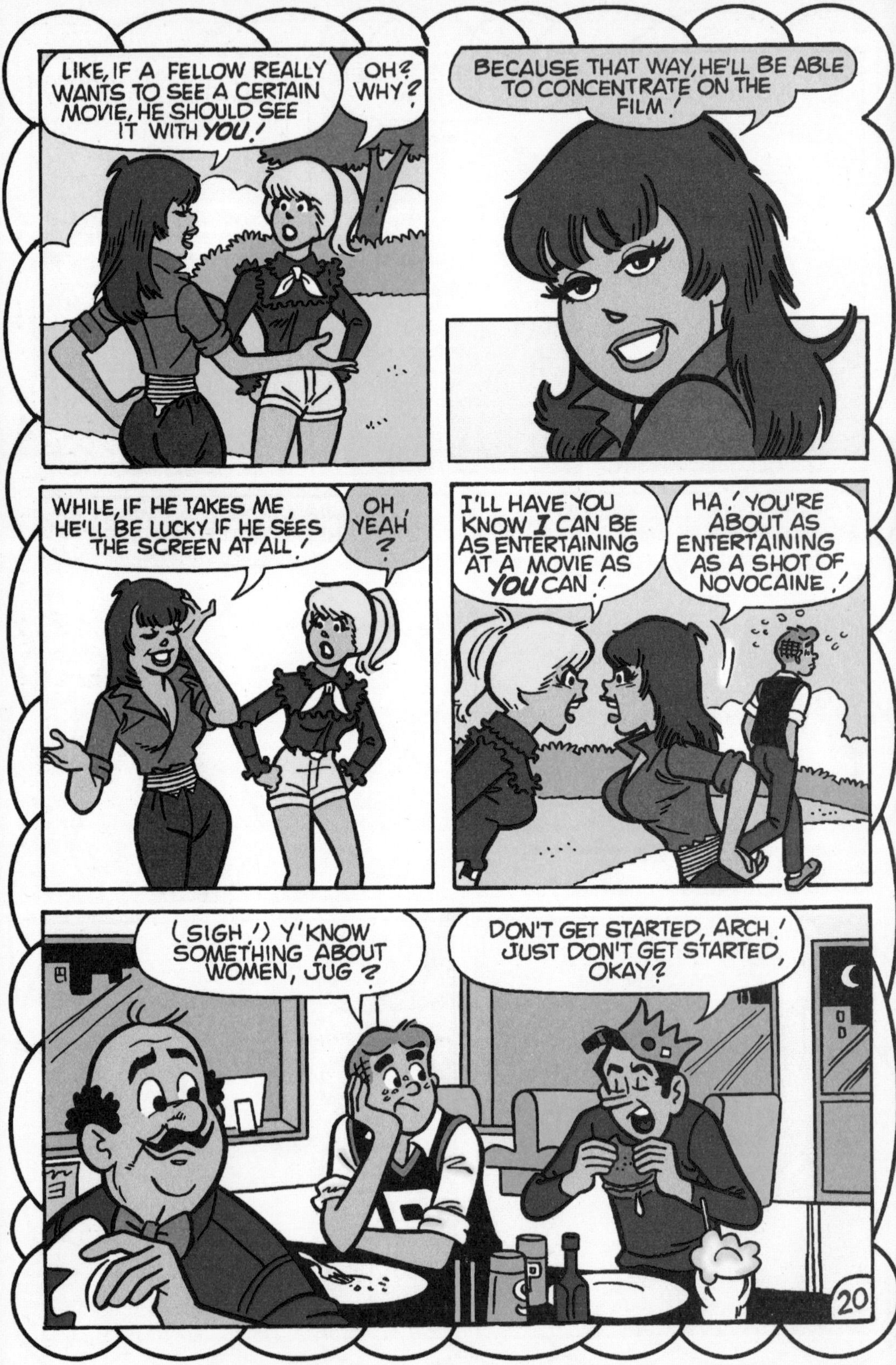
LIKE, IF A FELLOW REALLY WANTS TO SEE A CERTAIN MOVIE, HE SHOULD SEE IT WITH YOU!
OH? WHY?
BECAUSE THAT WAY, HE'LL BE ABLE TO CONCENTRATE ON THE FILM!
WHILE, IF HE TAKES ME, HE'LL BE LUCKY IF HE SEES THE SCREEN AT ALL!
OH, YEAH?
I'LL HAVE YOU KNOW I CAN BE AS ENTERTAINING AT A MOVIE AS YOU CAN!
HA! YOU'RE ABOUT AS ENTERTAINING AS A SHOT OF NOVOCAINE!
(SIGH!) Y'KNOW SOMETHING ABOUT WOMEN, JUG?
DON'T GET STARTED, ARCH! JUST DON'T GET STARTED, OKAY?
20

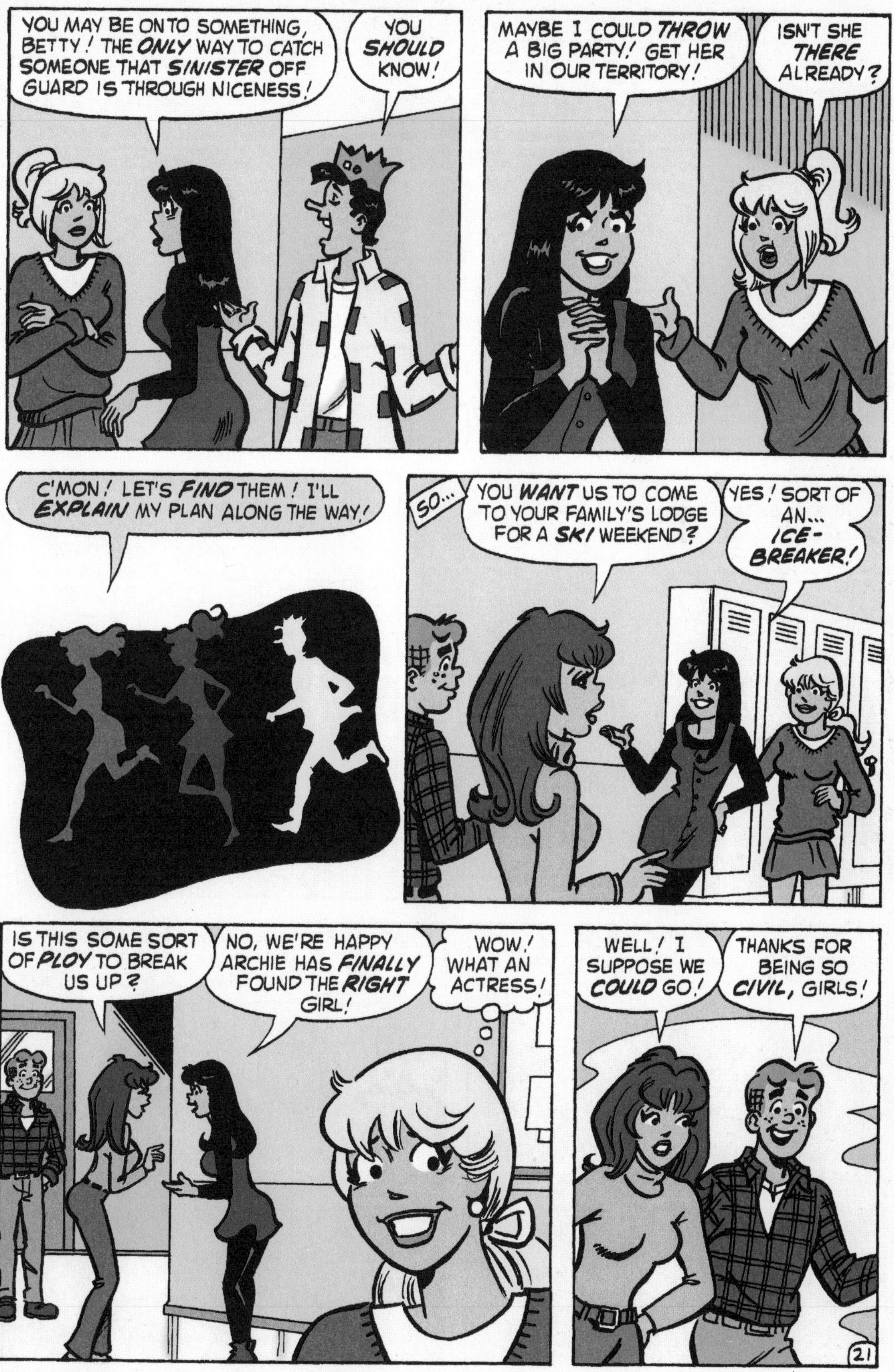
YOU MAY BE ONTO SOMETHING, BETTY! THE ONLY WAY TO CATCH SOMEONE THAT SINISTER OFF GUARD IS THROUGH NICENESS!
YOU SHOULD KNOW!
MAYBE I COULD THROW A BIG PARTY! GET HER IN OUR TERRITORY!
ISN'T SHE THERE ALREADY?
C'MON! LET'S FIND THEM! I'LL EXPLAIN MY PLAN ALONG THE WAY!
SO...
YOU WANT US TO COME TO YOUR FAMILY'S LODGE FOR A SKI WEEKEND?
YES! SORT OF AN... ICE-BREAKER!
IS THIS SOME SORT OF PLOY TO BREAK US UP?
NO, WE'RE HAPPY ARCHIE HAS FINALLY FOUND THE RIGHT GIRL!
WOW! WHAT AN ACTRESS!
WELL! I SUPPOSE WE COULD GO!
THANKS FOR BEING SO CIVIL, GIRLS!
21

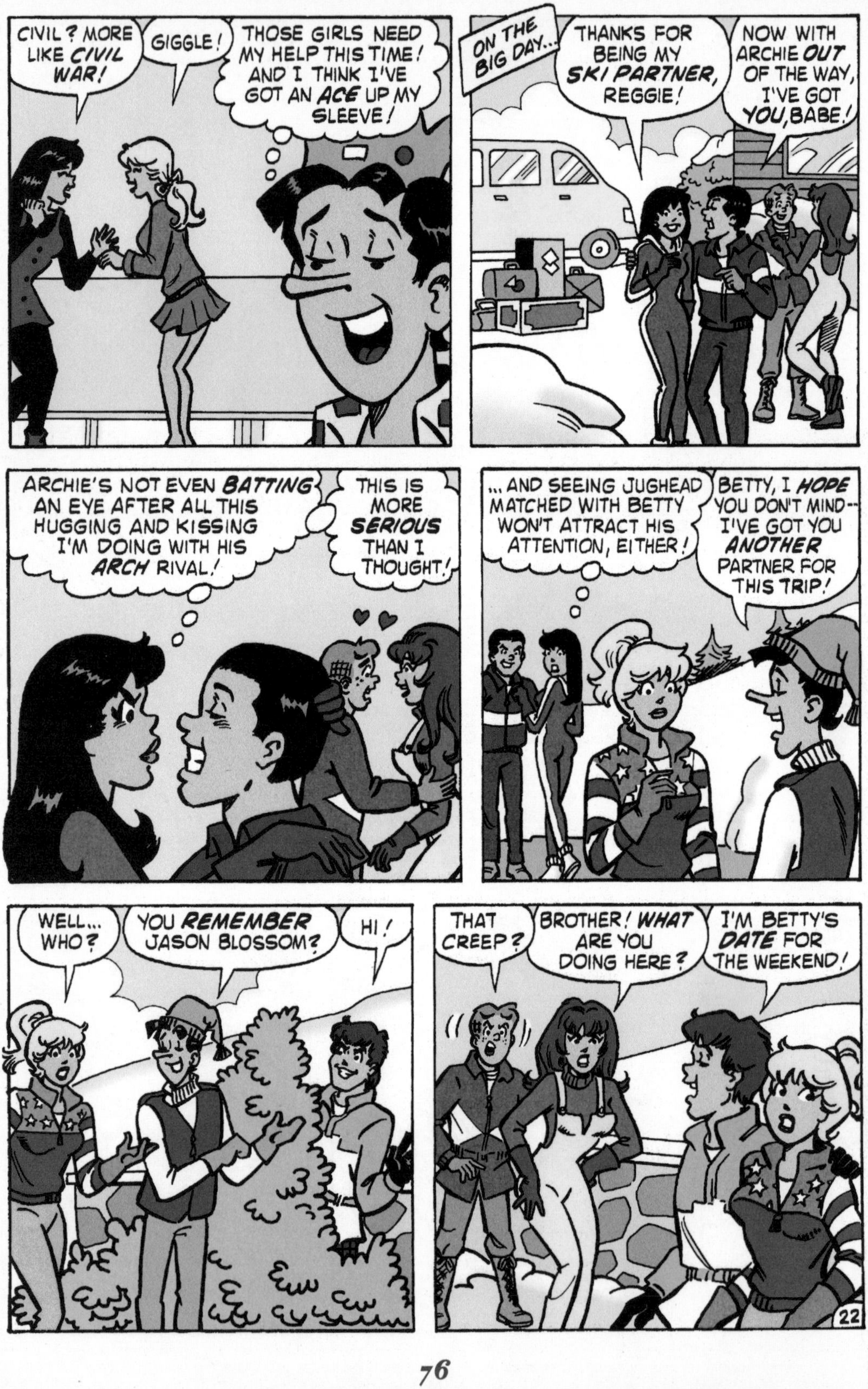
CIVIL? MORE LIKE CIVIL WAR!
GIGGLE!
THOSE GIRLS NEED MY HELP THIS TIME! AND I THINK I'VE GOT AN ACE UP MY SLEEVE!
ON THE BIG DAY...
THANKS FOR BEING MY SKI PARTNER, REGGIE!
NOW WITH ARCHIE OUT OF THE WAY, I'VE GOT YOU, BABE!
ARCHIE'S NOT EVEN BATTING AN EYE AFTER ALL THIS HUGGING AND KISSING I'M DOING WITH HIS ARCH RIVAL!
THIS IS MORE SERIOUS THAN I THOUGHT!
...AND SEEING JUGHEAD MATCHED WITH BETTY WON'T ATTRACT HIS ATTENTION, EITHER!
BETTY, I HOPE YOU DON'T MIND-- I'VE GOT YOU ANOTHER PARTNER FOR THIS TRIP!
WELL... WHO?
YOU REMEMBER JASON BLOSSOM?
HI!
THAT CREEP?
BROTHER! WHAT ARE YOU DOING HERE?
I'M BETTY'S DATE FOR THE WEEKEND!
22

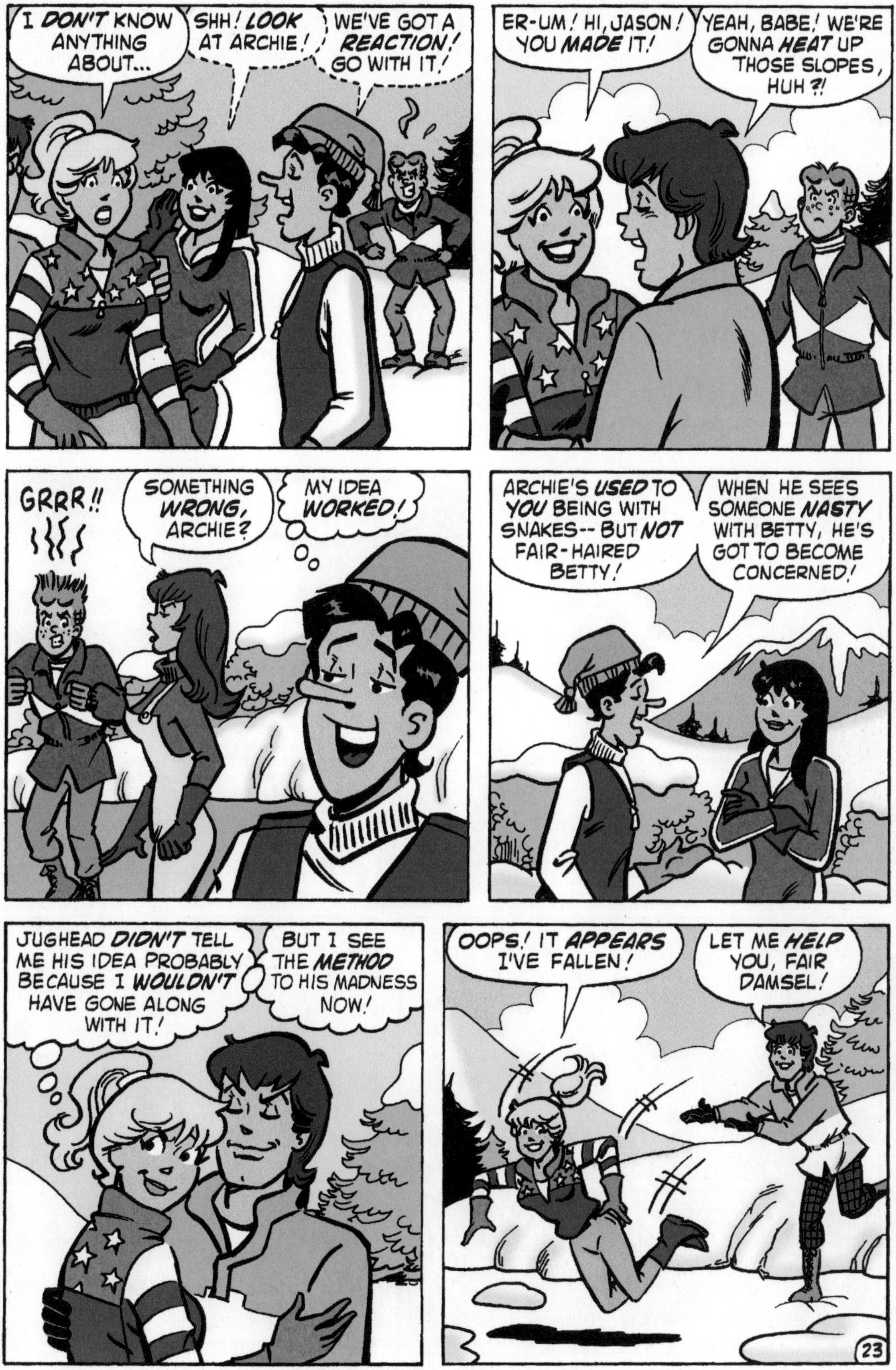
I DON'T KNOW ANYTHING ABOUT...
SHH! LOOK AT ARCHIE!
WE'VE GOT A REACTION! GO WITH IT!
ER-UM! HI, JASON! YOU MADE IT!
YEAH, BABE! WE'RE GONNA HEAT UP THOSE SLOPES, HUH ?!
GRRR!!
SOMETHING WRONG, ARCHIE?
MY IDEA WORKED!
ARCHIE'S USED TO YOU BEING WITH SNAKES-- BUT NOT FAIR-HAIRED BETTY!
WHEN HE SEES SOMEONE NASTY WITH BETTY, HE'S GOT TO BECOME CONCERNED!
JUGHEAD DIDN'T TELL ME HIS IDEA PROBABLY BECAUSE I WOULDN'T HAVE GONE ALONG WITH IT!
BUT I SEE THE METHOD TO HIS MADNESS NOW!
OOPS! IT APPEARS I'VE FALLEN!
LET ME HELP YOU, FAIR DAMSEL!
23

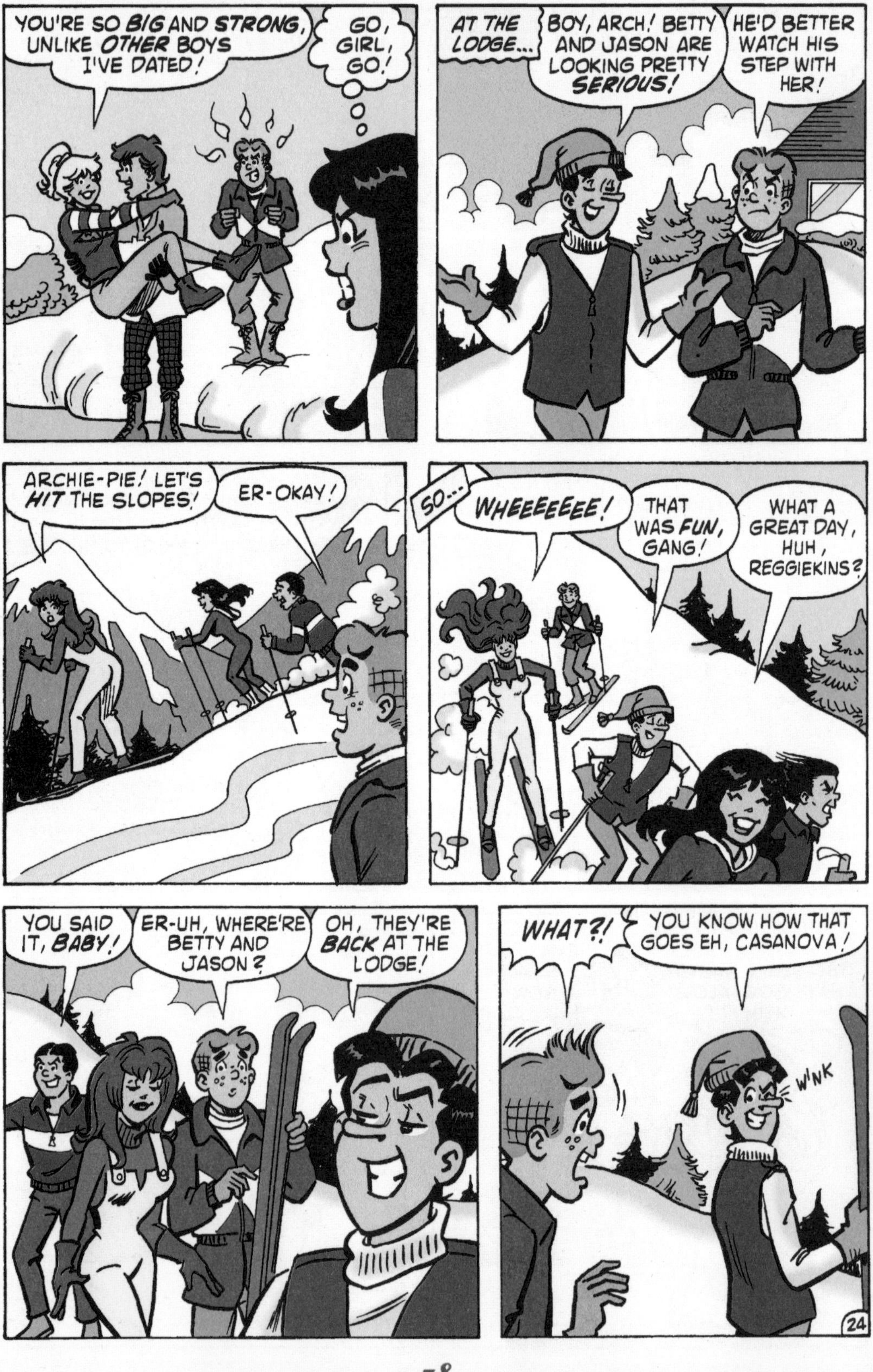

YOU'RE SO BIG AND STRONG, UNLIKE OTHER BOYS I'VE DATED!
GO, GIRL, GO!
AT THE LODGE...
BOY, ARCH! BETTY AND JASON ARE LOOKING PRETTY SERIOUS!
HE'D BETTER WATCH HIS STEP WITH HER!
ARCHIE-PIE! LET'S HIT THE SLOPES!
ER-OKAY!
SO...
WHEEEEEEE!
THAT WAS FUN, GANG!
WHAT A GREAT DAY, HUH, REGGIEKINS?
YOU SAID IT, BABY!
ER-UH, WHERE'RE BETTY AND JASON?
OH, THEY'RE BACK AT THE LODGE!
WHAT?!
YOU KNOW HOW THAT GOES EH, CASANOVA!
W'NK
24

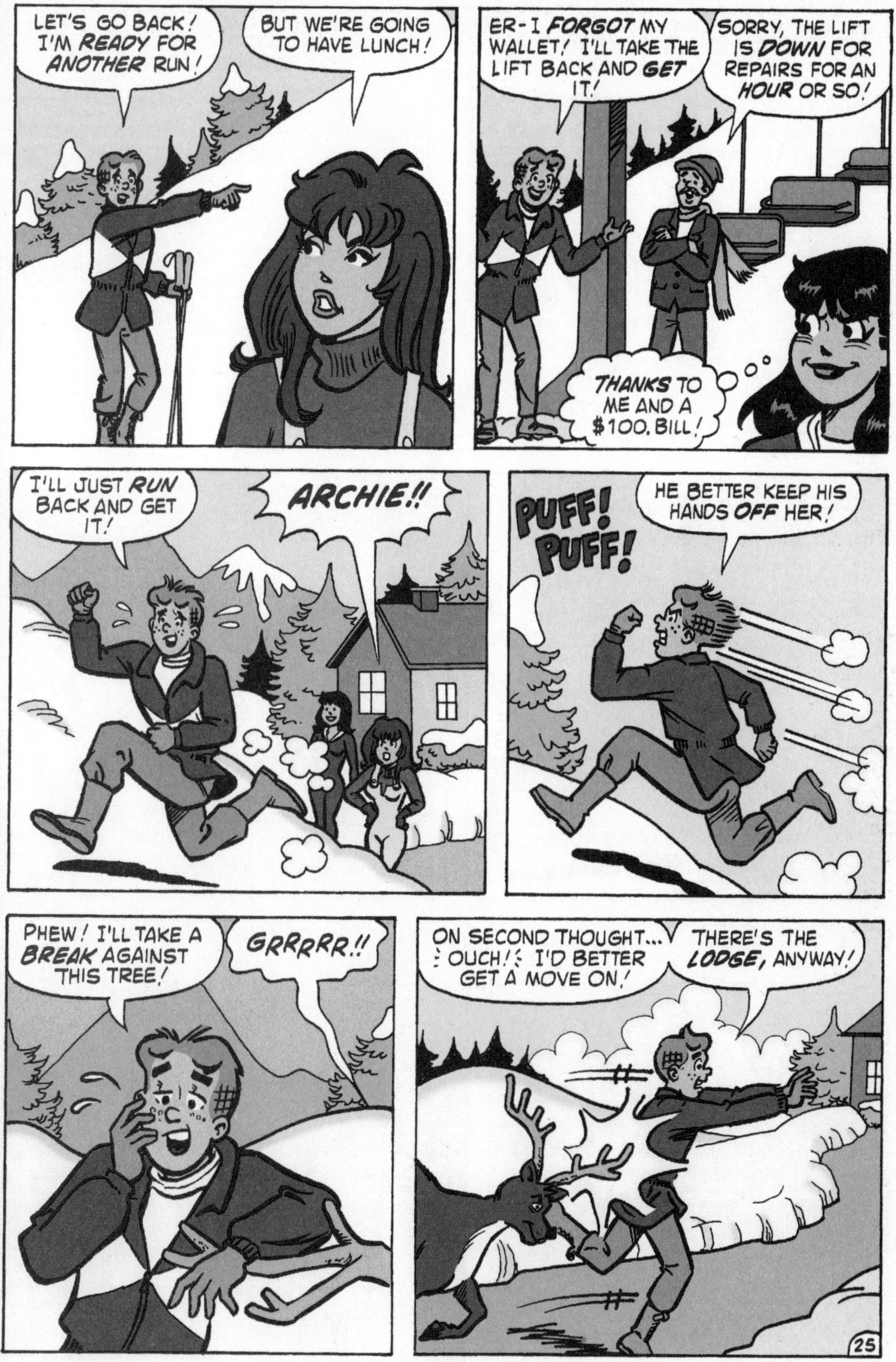
LET'S GO BACK! I'M READY FOR ANOTHER RUN!
BUT WE'RE GOING TO HAVE LUNCH!
ER-I FORGOT MY WALLET! I'LL TAKE THE LIFT BACK AND GET IT!
SORRY, THE LIFT IS DOWN FOR REPAIRS FOR AN HOUR OR SO!
THANKS TO ME AND A $100. BILL!
I'LL JUST RUN BACK AND GET IT!
ARCHIE!!
PUFF! PUFF!
HE BETTER KEEP HIS HANDS OFF HER!
PHEW! I'LL TAKE A BREAK AGAINST THIS TREE!
GRRRRR!!
ON SECOND THOUGHT... OUCH! I'D BETTER GET A MOVE ON!
THERE'S THE LODGE, ANYWAY!
25

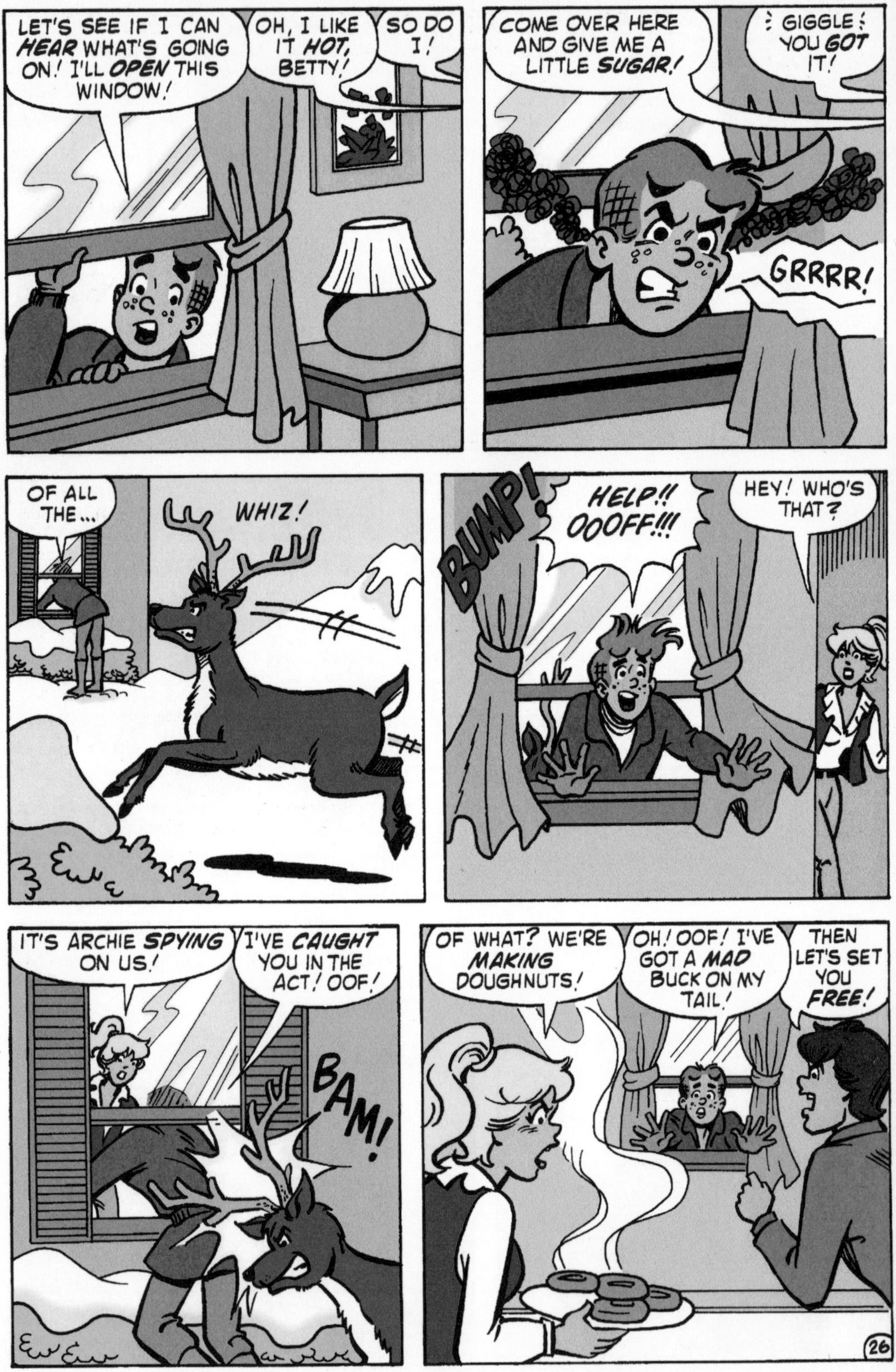
LET'S SEE IF I CAN HEAR WHAT'S GOING ON! I'LL OPEN THIS WINDOW!
OH, I LIKE IT HOT, BETTY!
SO DO I!
COME OVER HERE AND GIVE ME A LITTLE SUGAR!
GIGGLE! YOU GOT IT!
GRRRR!
OF ALL THE...
WHIZ!
BUMP!
HELP!! OOOFF!!!
HEY! WHO'S THAT?
IT'S ARCHIE SPYING ON US!
I'VE CAUGHT YOU IN THE ACT! OOF!
BAM!
OF WHAT? WE'RE MAKING DOUGHNUTS!
OH! OOF! I'VE GOT A MAD BUCK ON MY TAIL!
THEN LET'S SET YOU FREE!
26

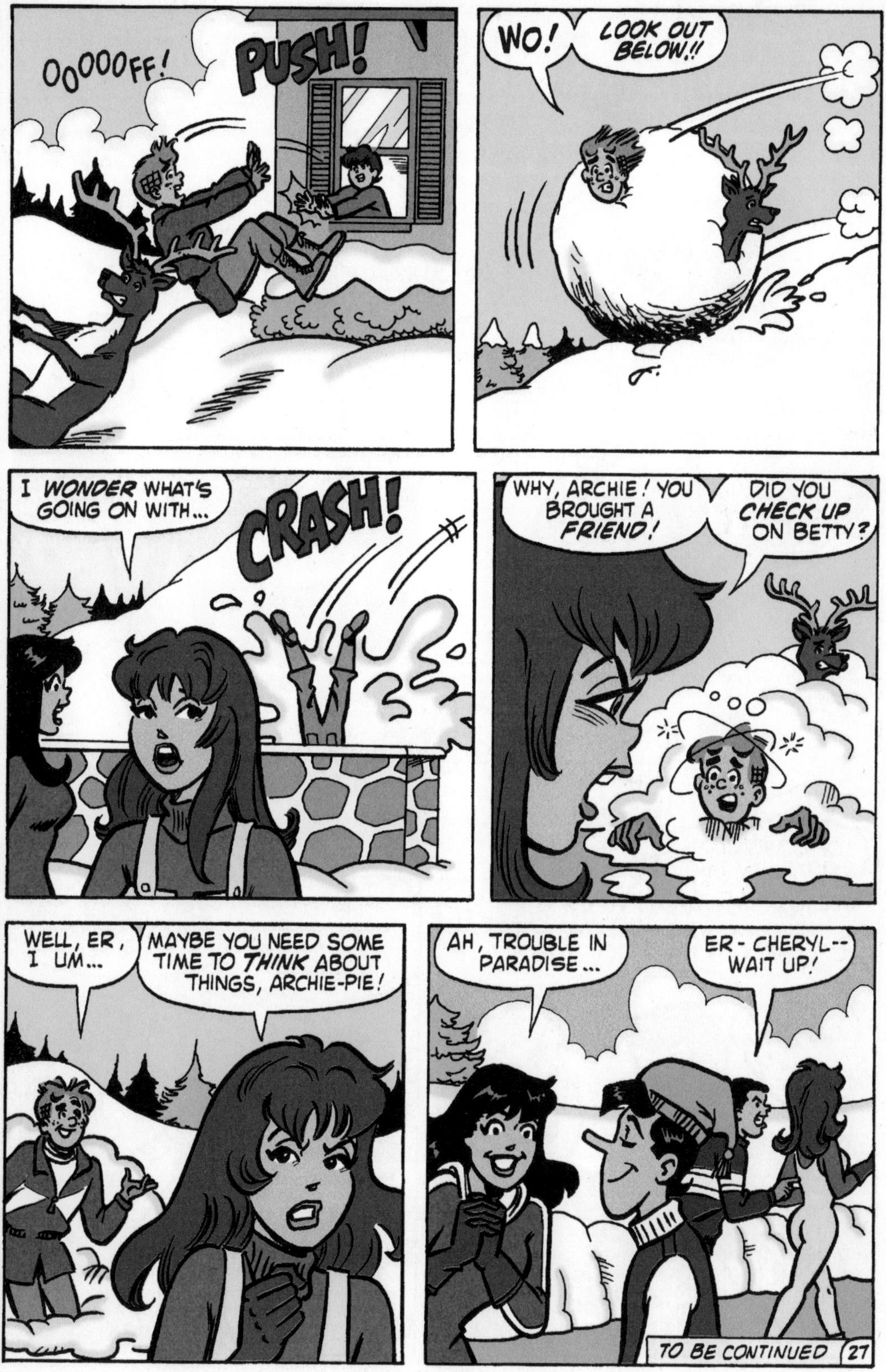
OOOOOFF!
PUSH!
WO!
LOOK OUT BELOW!!
I WONDER WHAT'S GOING ON WITH...
CRASH!
WHY, ARCHIE! YOU BROUGHT A FRIEND!
DID YOU CHECK UP ON BETTY?
WELL, ER, I UM...
MAYBE YOU NEED SOME TIME TO THINK ABOUT THINGS, ARCHIE-PIE!
AH, TROUBLE IN PARADISE...
ER- CHERYL-- WAIT UP!
TO BE CONTINUED
27

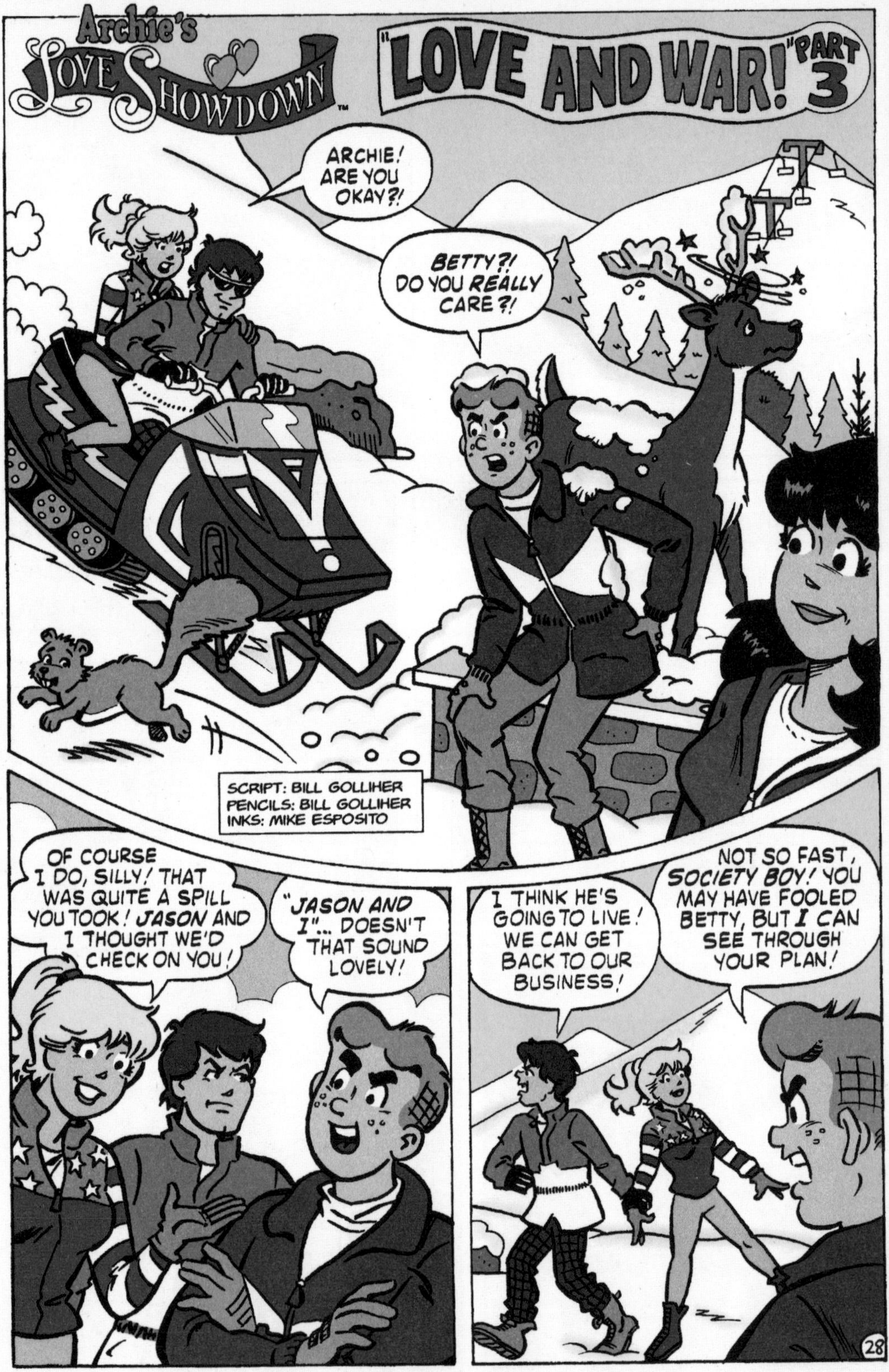
Archie's LOVE SHOWDOWN™
"LOVE AND WAR!" PART 3
ARCHIE! ARE YOU OKAY?!
BETTY?! DO YOU REALLY CARE?!
SCRIPT: BILL GOLLIHER
PENCILS: BILL GOLLIHER
INKS: MIKE ESPOSITO
OF COURSE I DO, SILLY! THAT WAS QUITE A SPILL YOU TOOK! JASON AND I THOUGHT WE'D CHECK ON YOU!
"JASON AND I"... DOESN'T THAT SOUND LOVELY!
I THINK HE'S GOING TO LIVE! WE CAN GET BACK TO OUR BUSINESS!
NOT SO FAST, SOCIETY BOY! YOU MAY HAVE FOOLED BETTY, BUT I CAN SEE THROUGH YOUR PLAN!
28

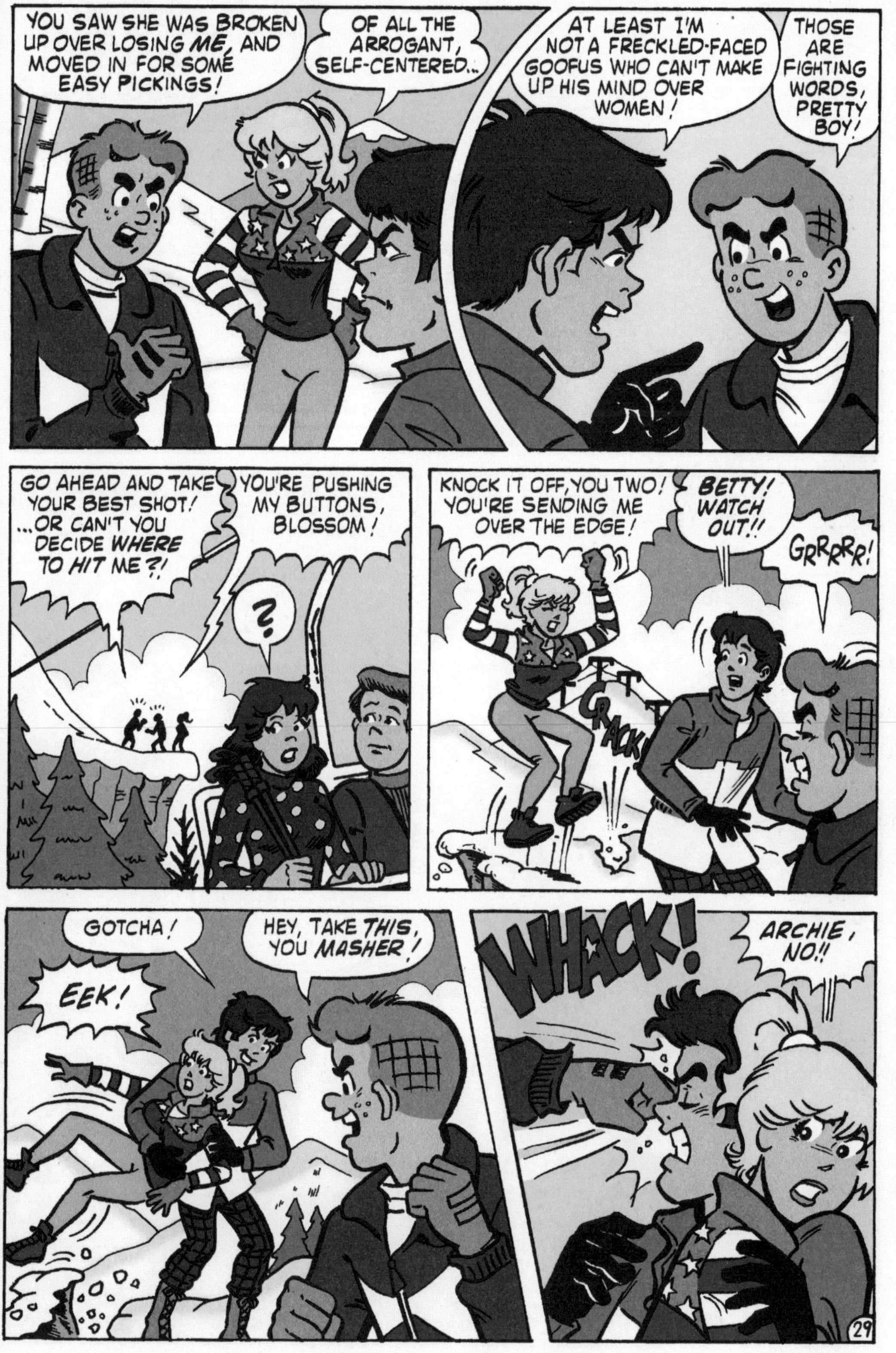
YOU SAW SHE WAS BROKEN UP OVER LOSING ME, AND MOVED IN FOR SOME EASY PICKINGS!
OF ALL THE ARROGANT, SELF-CENTERED...
AT LEAST I'M NOT A FRECKLED-FACED GOOFUS WHO CAN'T MAKE UP HIS MIND OVER WOMEN!
THOSE ARE FIGHTING WORDS, PRETTY BOY!
GO AHEAD AND TAKE YOUR BEST SHOT! ...OR CAN'T YOU DECIDE WHERE TO HIT ME?!
YOU'RE PUSHING MY BUTTONS, BLOSSOM!
?
KNOCK IT OFF, YOU TWO! YOU'RE SENDING ME OVER THE EDGE!
BETTY! WATCH OUT!!
GRRRRR!
CRACK!
GOTCHA!
EEK!
HEY, TAKE THIS, YOU MASHER!
WHACK!
ARCHIE, NO!!
29

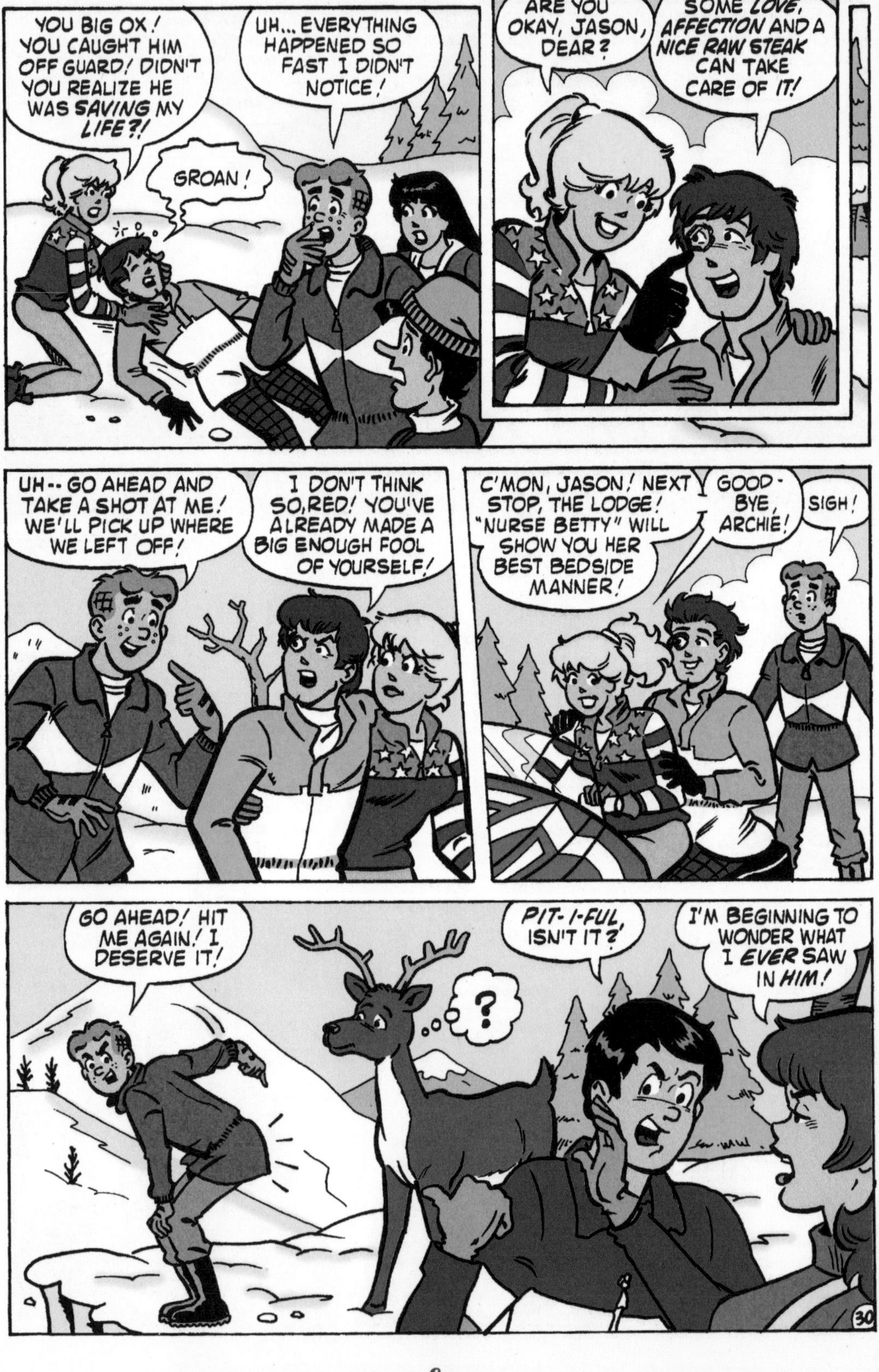

YOU BIG OX! YOU CAUGHT HIM OFF GUARD! DIDN'T YOU REALIZE HE WAS SAVING MY LIFE?!
UH... EVERYTHING HAPPENED SO FAST I DIDN'T NOTICE!
GROAN!
ARE YOU OKAY, JASON, DEAR?
SOME LOVE, AFFECTION AND A NICE RAW STEAK CAN TAKE CARE OF IT!
UH -- GO AHEAD AND TAKE A SHOT AT ME! WE'LL PICK UP WHERE WE LEFT OFF!
I DON'T THINK SO, RED! YOU'VE ALREADY MADE A BIG ENOUGH FOOL OF YOURSELF!
C'MON, JASON! NEXT STOP, THE LODGE! "NURSE BETTY" WILL SHOW YOU HER BEST BEDSIDE MANNER!
GOOD-BYE, ARCHIE!
SIGH!
GO AHEAD! HIT ME AGAIN! I DESERVE IT!
?
PIT-I-FUL, ISN'T IT?
I'M BEGINNING TO WONDER WHAT I EVER SAW IN HIM!
30

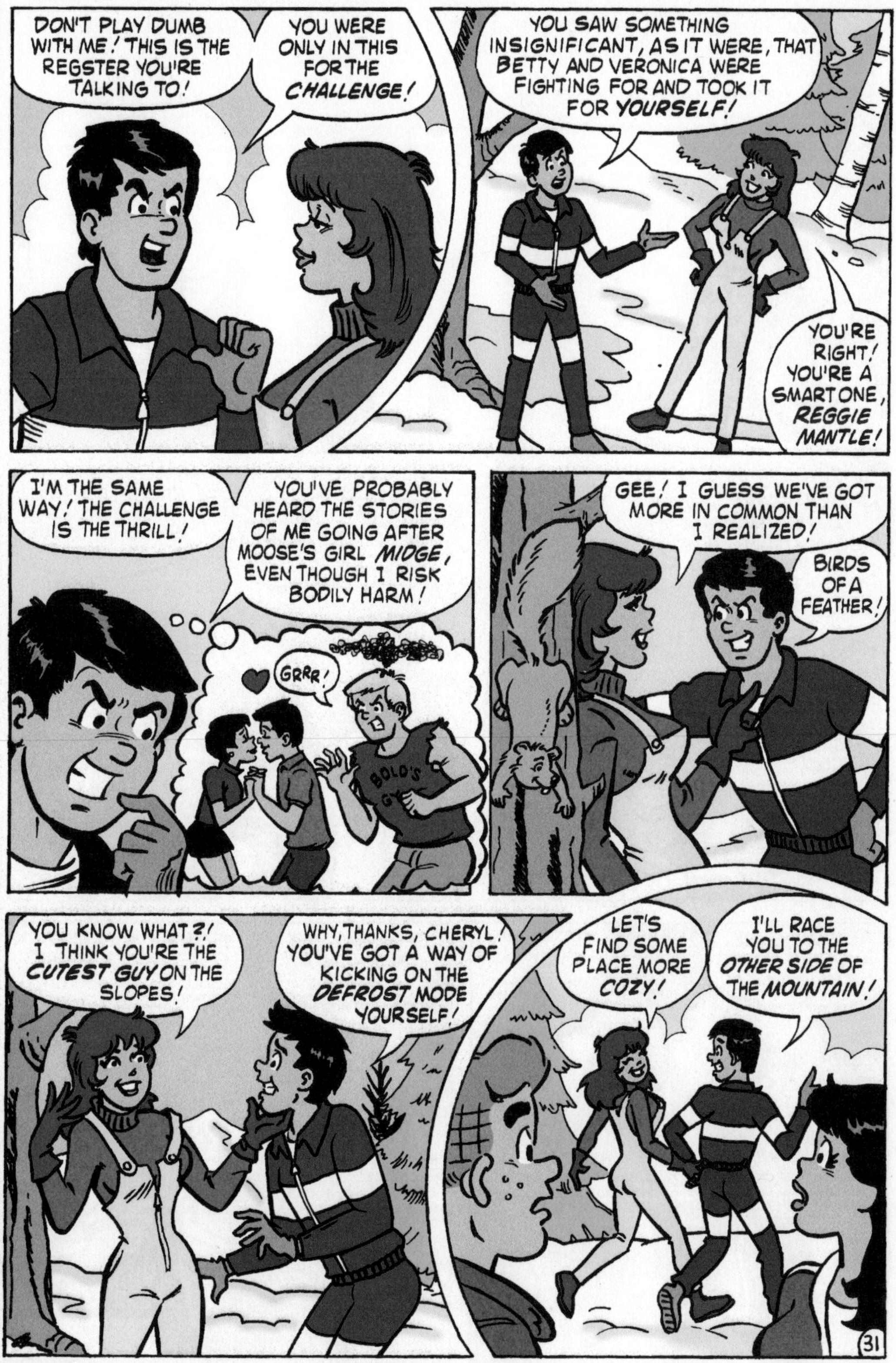
DON'T PLAY DUMB WITH ME! THIS IS THE REGSTER YOU'RE TALKING TO!
YOU WERE ONLY IN THIS FOR THE CHALLENGE!
YOU SAW SOMETHING INSIGNIFICANT, AS IT WERE, THAT BETTY AND VERONICA WERE FIGHTING FOR AND TOOK IT FOR YOURSELF!
YOU'RE RIGHT! YOU'RE A SMART ONE, REGGIE MANTLE!
I'M THE SAME WAY! THE CHALLENGE IS THE THRILL!
YOU'VE PROBABLY HEARD THE STORIES OF ME GOING AFTER MOOSE'S GIRL MIDGE, EVEN THOUGH I RISK BODILY HARM!
GRRR!
GEE! I GUESS WE'VE GOT MORE IN COMMON THAN I REALIZED!
BIRDS OF A FEATHER!
YOU KNOW WHAT?! I THINK YOU'RE THE CUTEST GUY ON THE SLOPES!
WHY, THANKS, CHERYL! YOU'VE GOT A WAY OF KICKING ON THE DEFROST MODE YOURSELF!
LET'S FIND SOME PLACE MORE COZY!
I'LL RACE YOU TO THE OTHER SIDE OF THE MOUNTAIN!
31

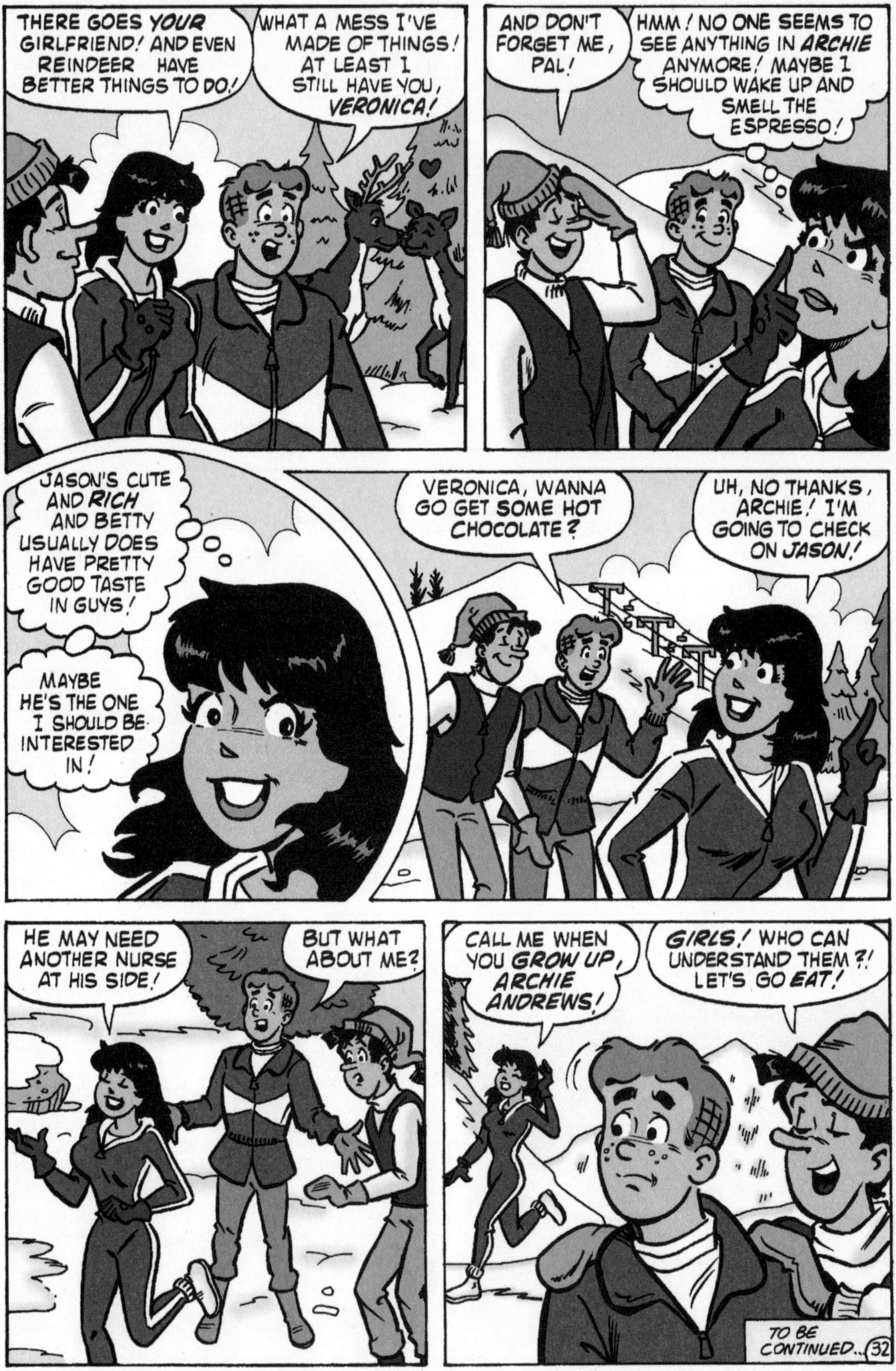
THERE GOES YOUR GIRLFRIEND! AND EVEN REINDEER HAVE BETTER THINGS TO DO!
WHAT A MESS I'VE MADE OF THINGS! AT LEAST I STILL HAVE YOU, VERONICA!
AND DON'T FORGET ME, PAL!
HMM! NO ONE SEEMS TO SEE ANYTHING IN ARCHIE ANYMORE! MAYBE I SHOULD WAKE UP AND SMELL THE ESPRESSO!
JASON'S CUTE AND RICH AND BETTY USUALLY DOES HAVE PRETTY GOOD TASTE IN GUYS!
MAYBE HE'S THE ONE I SHOULD BE INTERESTED IN!
VERONICA, WANNA GO GET SOME HOT CHOCOLATE?
UH, NO THANKS, ARCHIE! I'M GOING TO CHECK ON JASON!
HE MAY NEED ANOTHER NURSE AT HIS SIDE!
BUT WHAT ABOUT ME?
CALL ME WHEN YOU GROW UP, ARCHIE ANDREWS!
GIRLS! WHO CAN UNDERSTAND THEM?! LET'S GO EAT!
TO BE CONTINUED... 32

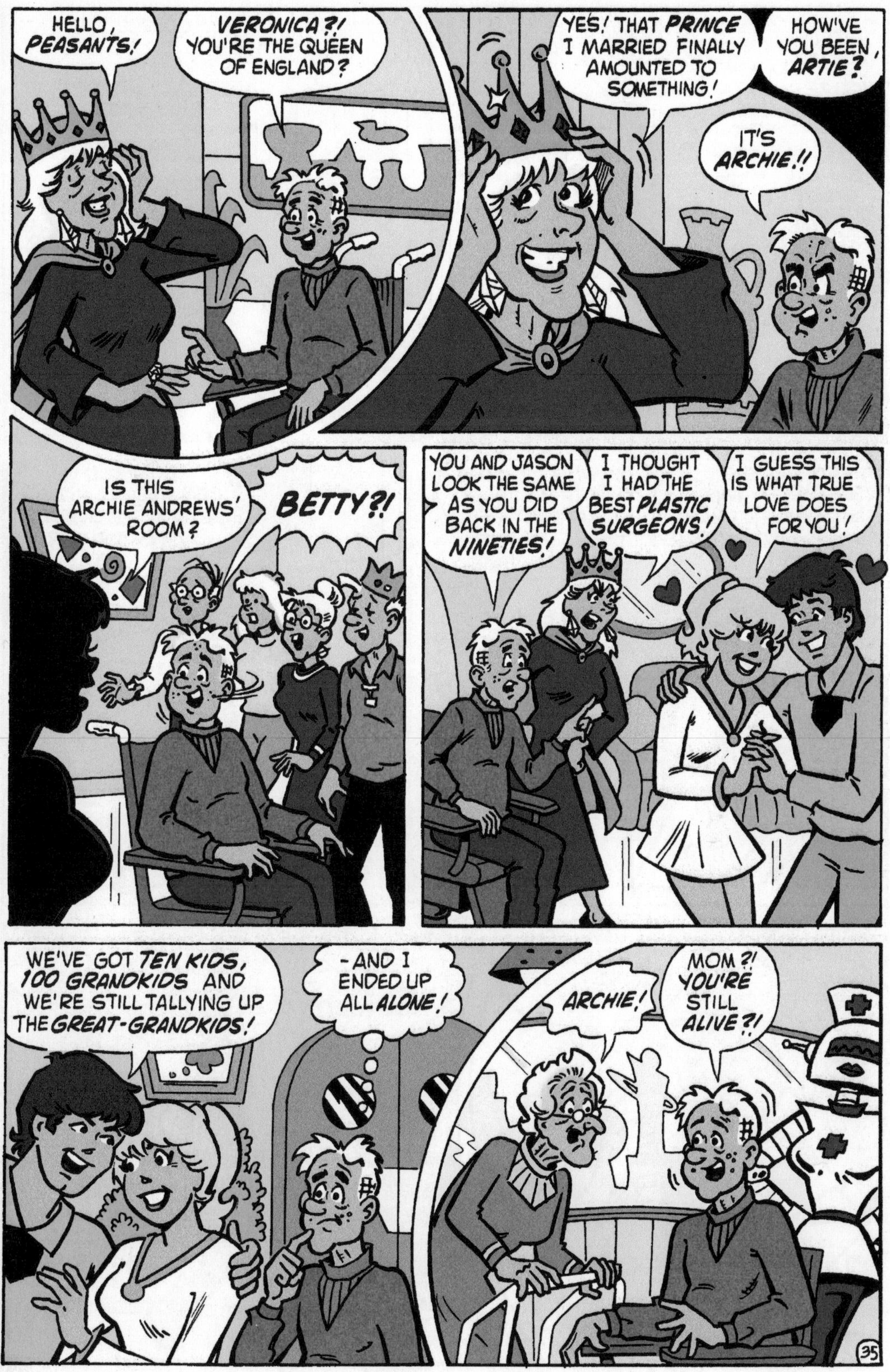
HELLO, PEASANTS!
VERONICA?! YOU'RE THE QUEEN OF ENGLAND?
YES! THAT PRINCE I MARRIED FINALLY AMOUNTED TO SOMETHING!
HOW'VE YOU BEEN, ARTIE?
IT'S ARCHIE!!
IS THIS ARCHIE ANDREWS' ROOM?
BETTY?!
YOU AND JASON LOOK THE SAME AS YOU DID BACK IN THE NINETIES!
I THOUGHT I HAD THE BEST PLASTIC SURGEONS!
I GUESS THIS IS WHAT TRUE LOVE DOES FOR YOU!
WE'VE GOT TEN KIDS, 100 GRANDKIDS AND WE'RE STILL TALLYING UP THE GREAT-GRANDKIDS!
-AND I ENDED UP ALL ALONE!
ARCHIE!
MOM?! YOU'RE STILL ALIVE?!
35

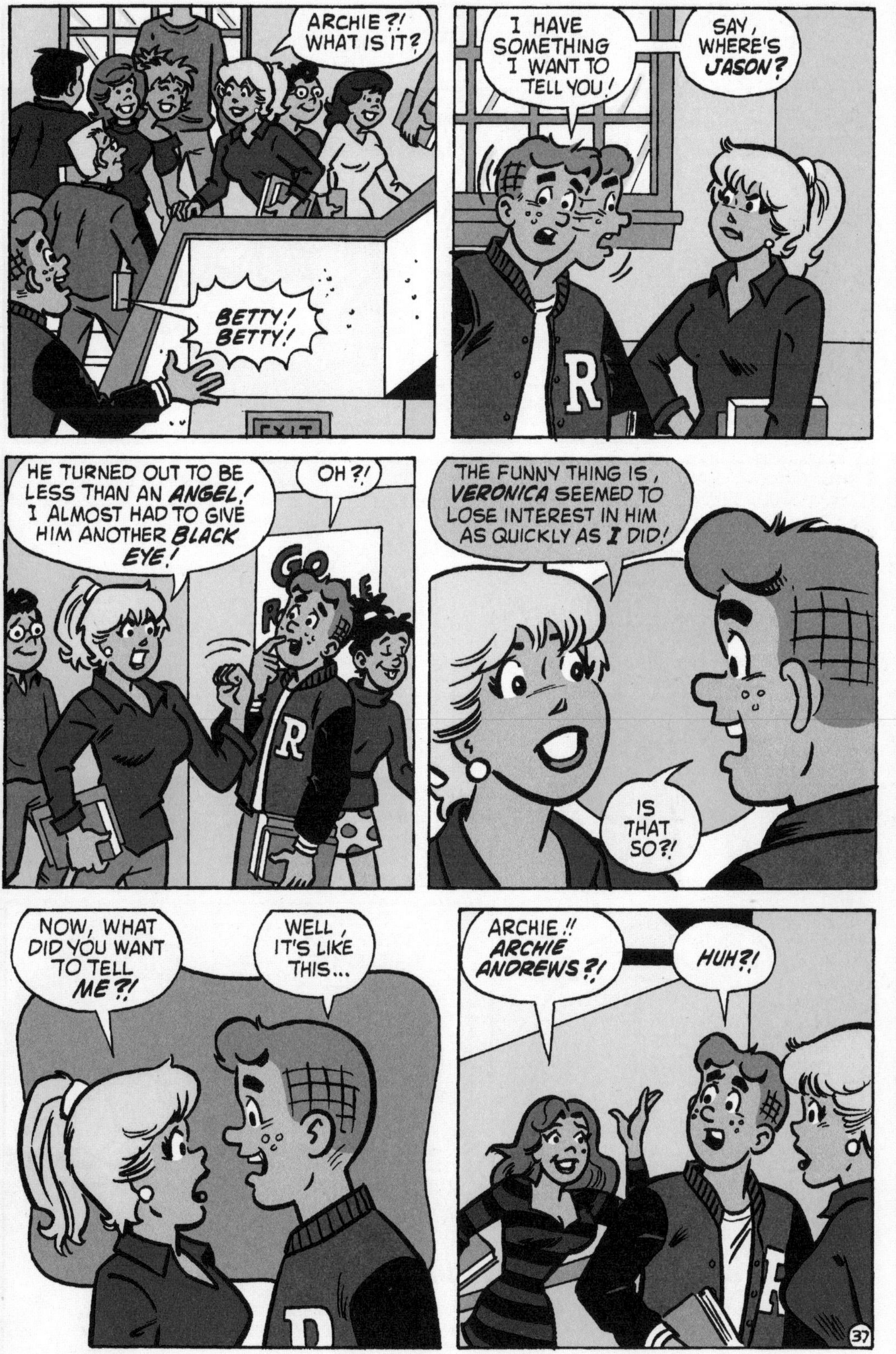
BETTY! BETTY!
ARCHIE?! WHAT IS IT?
I HAVE SOMETHING I WANT TO TELL YOU!
SAY, WHERE'S JASON?
HE TURNED OUT TO BE LESS THAN AN ANGEL! I ALMOST HAD TO GIVE HIM ANOTHER BLACK EYE!
OH?!
THE FUNNY THING IS, VERONICA SEEMED TO LOSE INTEREST IN HIM AS QUICKLY AS I DID!
IS THAT SO?!
NOW, WHAT DID YOU WANT TO TELL ME?!
WELL, IT'S LIKE THIS...
ARCHIE!! ARCHIE ANDREWS?!
HUH?!
37

Bonus Pin-up

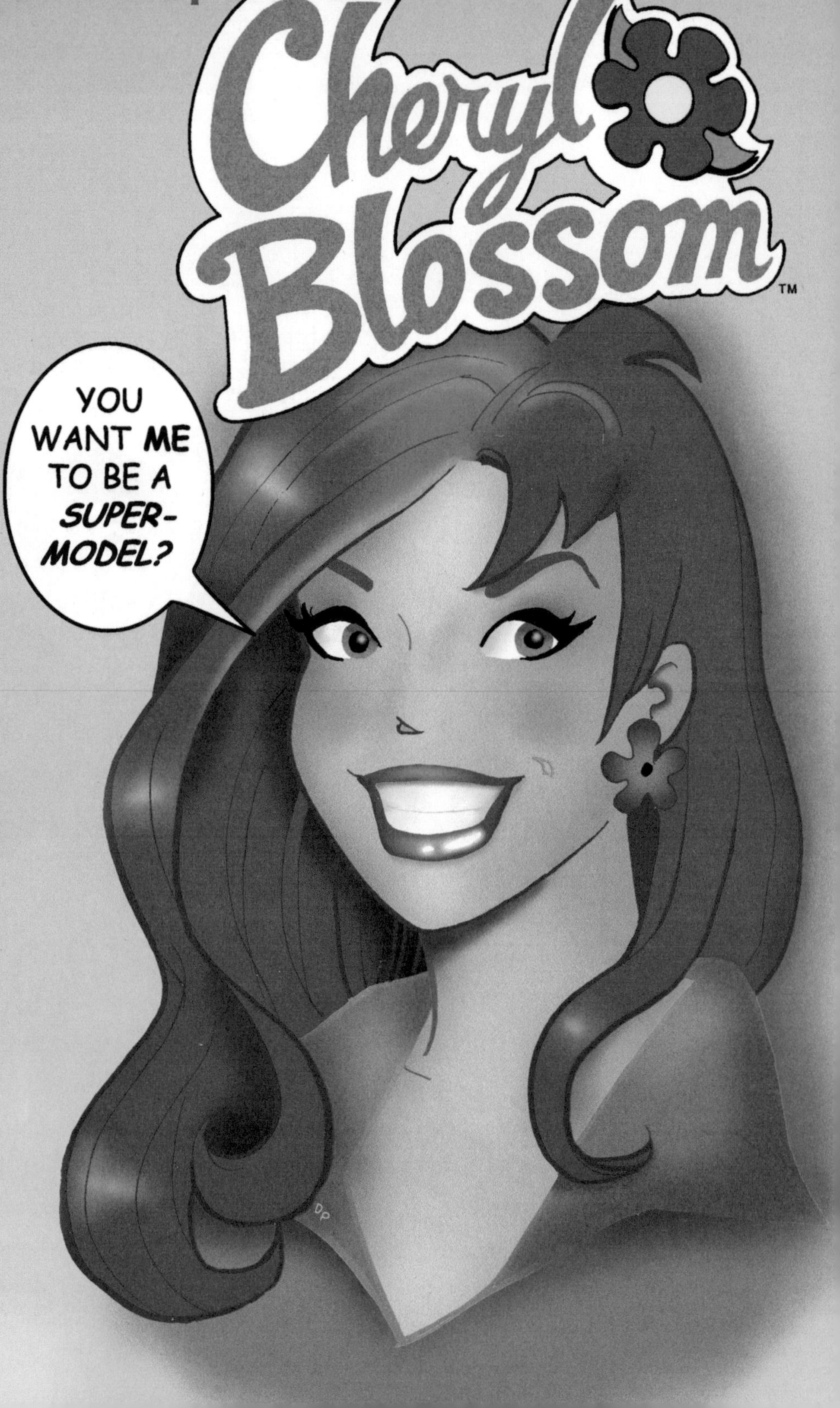
Cheryl Blossom™
YOU WANT ME TO BE A SUPER-MODEL?
DP

Chapter Six

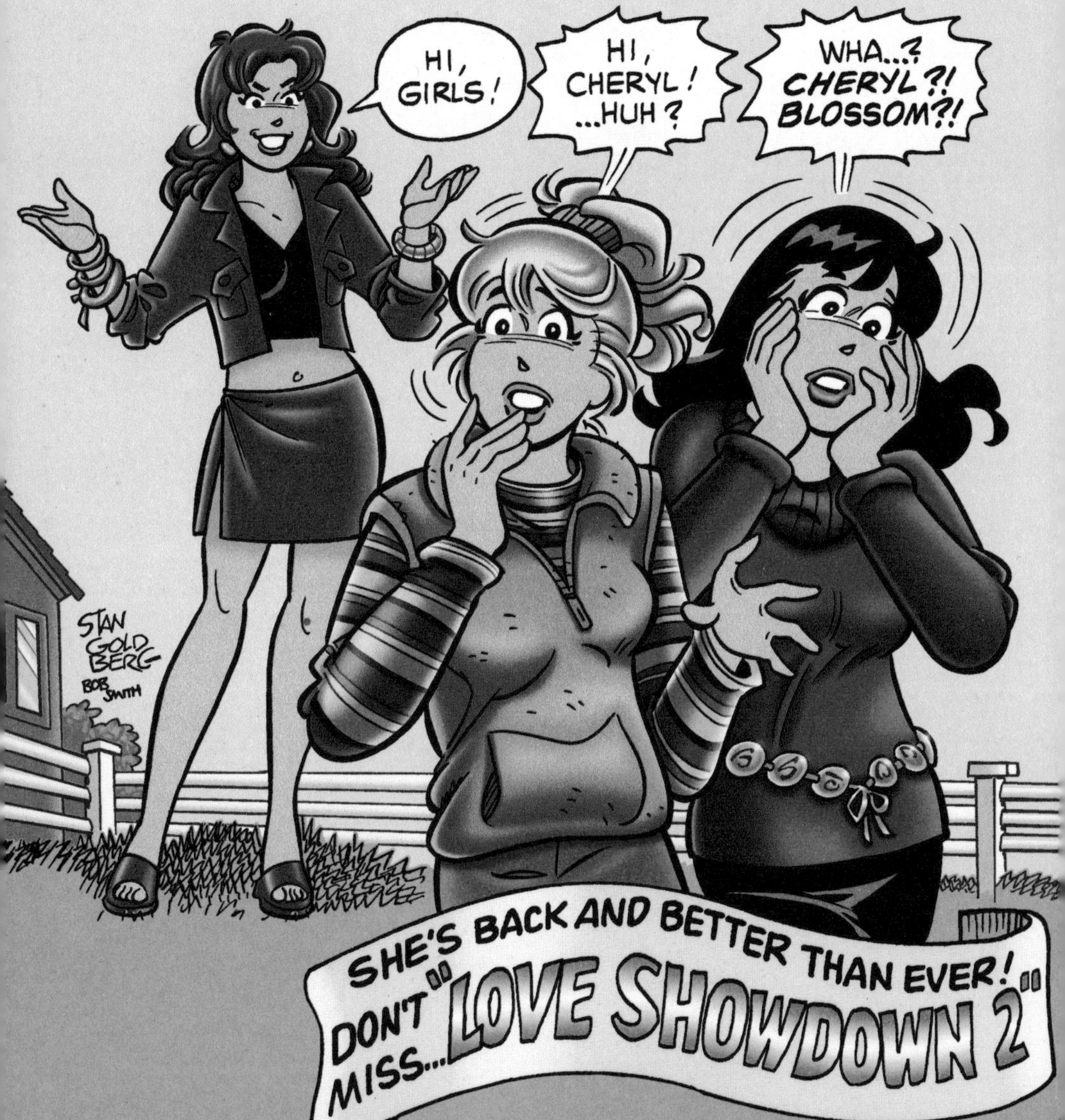
HI, GIRLS!
HI, CHERYL! ...HUH?
WHA...? CHERYL?! BLOSSOM?!
STAN GOLDBERG
BOB SMITH
SHE'S BACK AND BETTER THAN EVER!
DON'T MISS... "LOVE SHOWDOWN 2"

Betty and Veronica in "SHE'S BA-A-ACK!"

LOVE SHOWDOWN II

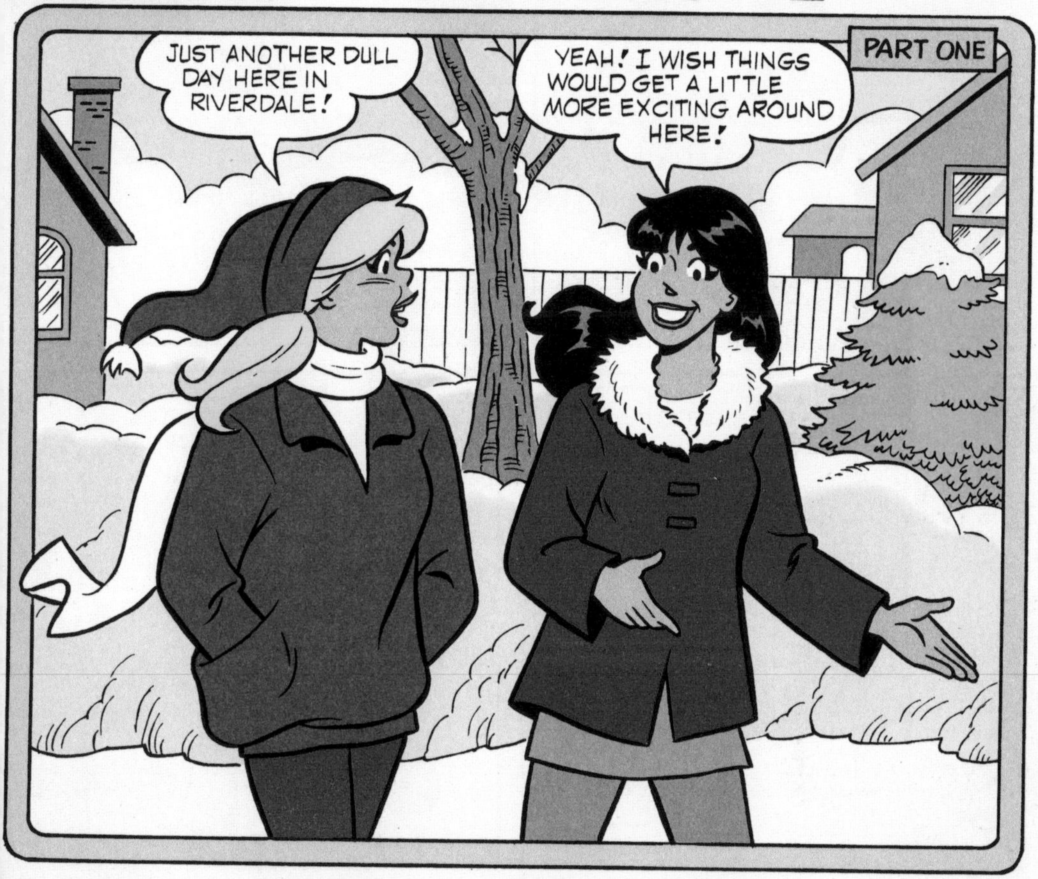
PART ONE
JUST ANOTHER DULL DAY HERE IN RIVERDALE!
YEAH! I WISH THINGS WOULD GET A LITTLE MORE EXCITING AROUND HERE!

SCRIPT AND PENCILS: DAN PARENT **INKING AND LETTERING:** JON D'AGOSTINO **COLORING:** BARRY GROSSMAN **EDITOR:** VICTOR GORELICK **EDITOR-IN-CHIEF:** RICHARD GOLDWATER

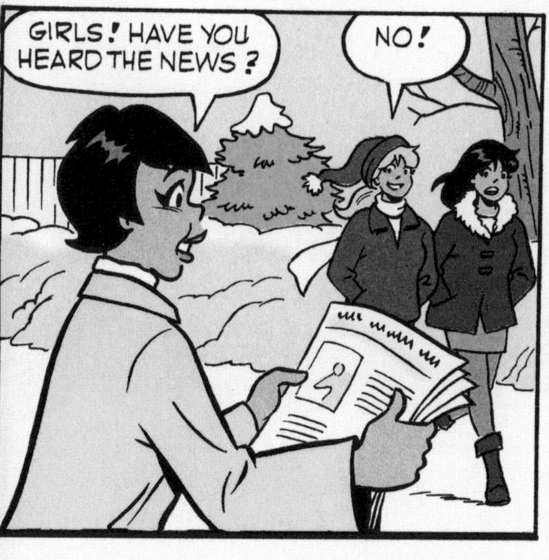
GIRLS! HAVE YOU HEARD THE NEWS?
NO!

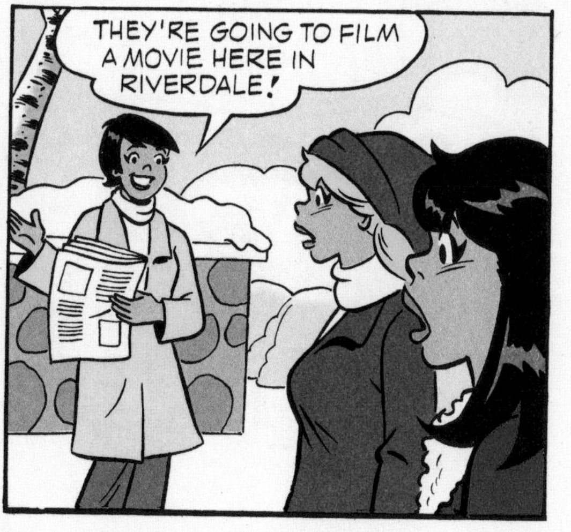
THEY'RE GOING TO FILM A MOVIE HERE IN RIVERDALE!

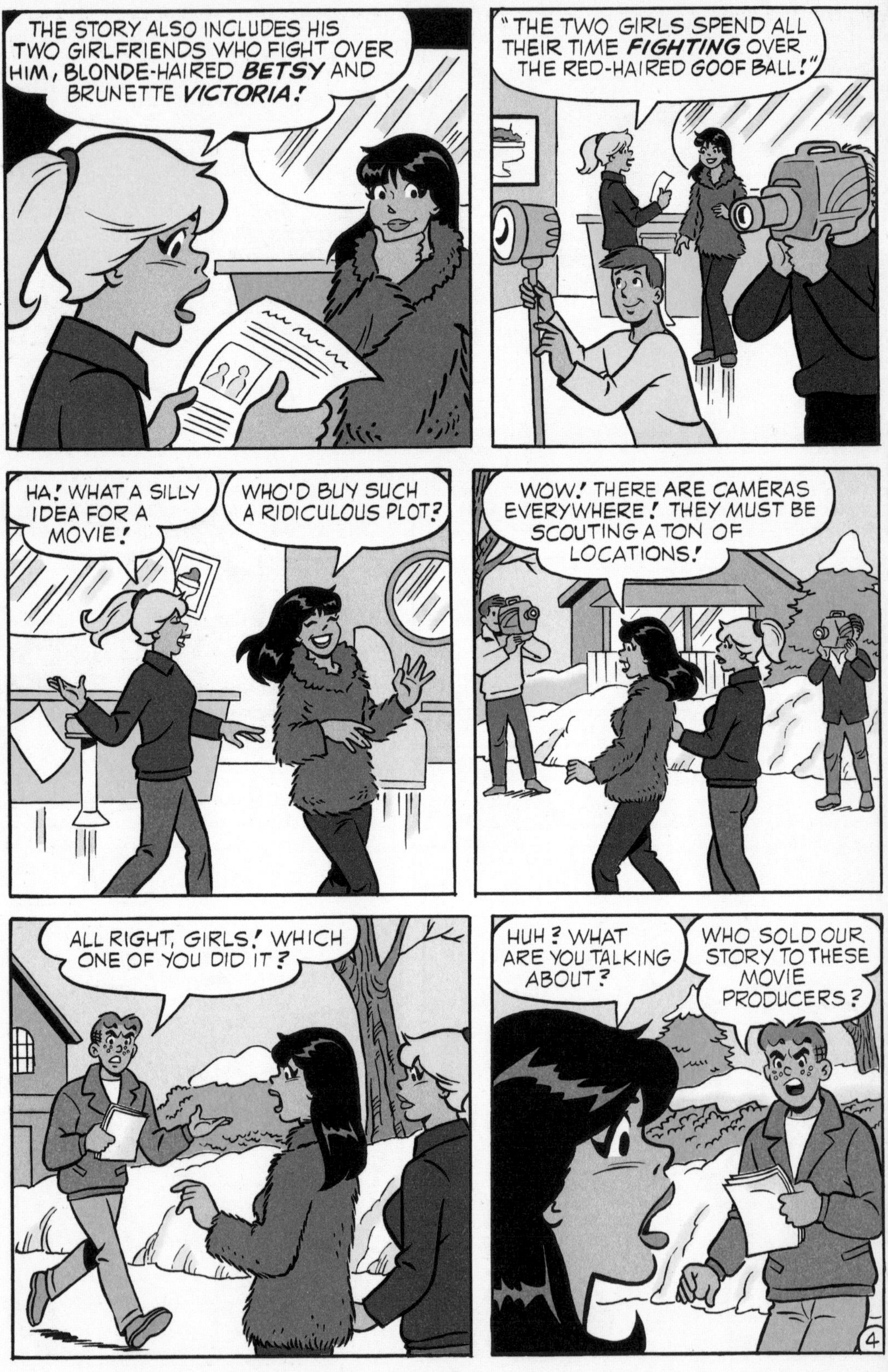
THE STORY ALSO INCLUDES HIS TWO GIRLFRIENDS WHO FIGHT OVER HIM, BLONDE-HAIRED BETSY AND BRUNETTE VICTORIA!
"THE TWO GIRLS SPEND ALL THEIR TIME FIGHTING OVER THE RED-HAIRED GOOF BALL!"
HA! WHAT A SILLY IDEA FOR A MOVIE!
WHO'D BUY SUCH A RIDICULOUS PLOT?
WOW! THERE ARE CAMERAS EVERYWHERE! THEY MUST BE SCOUTING A TON OF LOCATIONS!
ALL RIGHT, GIRLS! WHICH ONE OF YOU DID IT?
HUH? WHAT ARE YOU TALKING ABOUT?
WHO SOLD OUR STORY TO THESE MOVIE PRODUCERS?
4

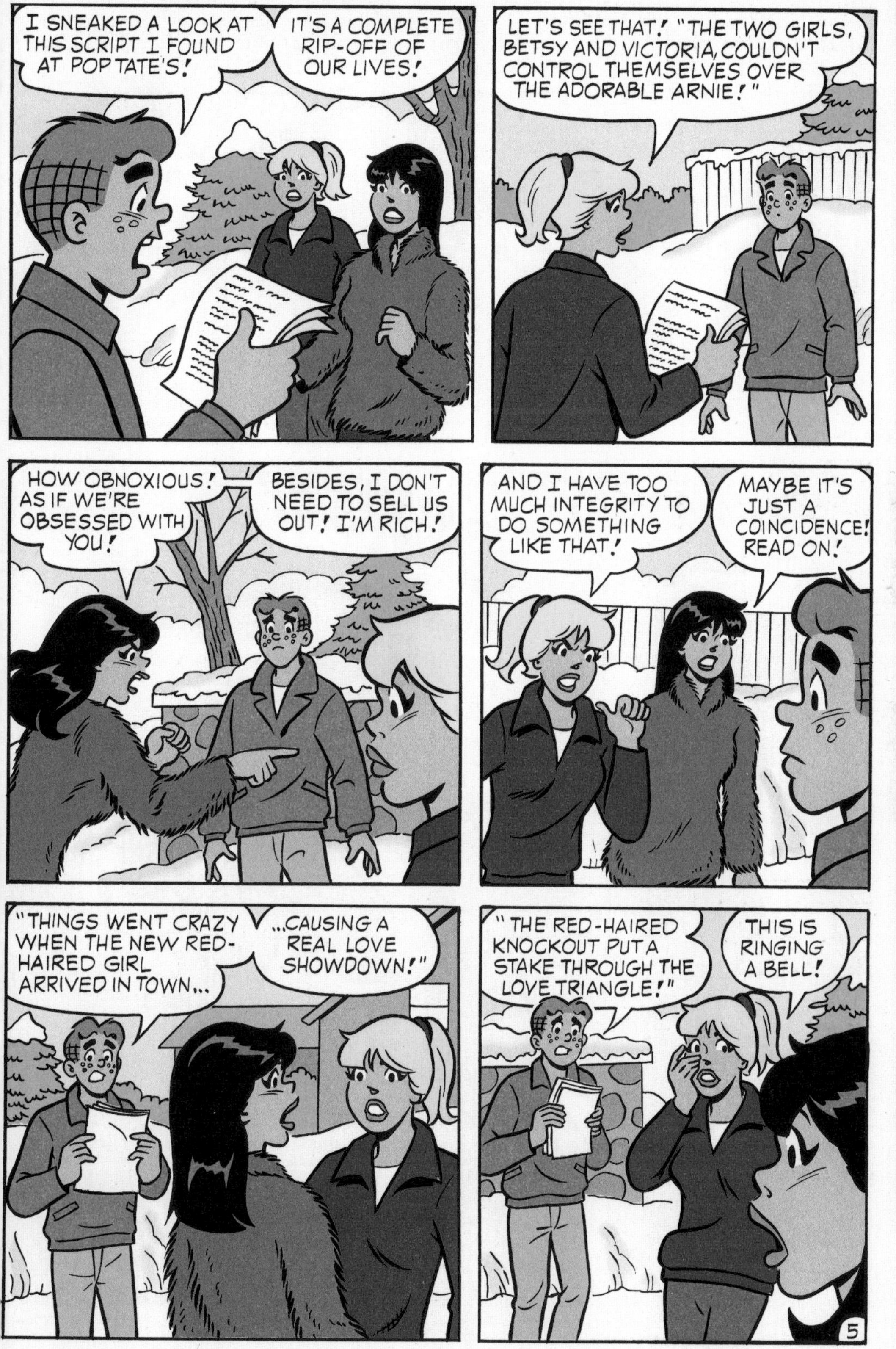
I SNEAKED A LOOK AT THIS SCRIPT I FOUND AT POP TATE'S!
IT'S A COMPLETE RIP-OFF OF OUR LIVES!
LET'S SEE THAT! "THE TWO GIRLS, BETSY AND VICTORIA, COULDN'T CONTROL THEMSELVES OVER THE ADORABLE ARNIE!"
HOW OBNOXIOUS! AS IF WE'RE OBSESSED WITH YOU!
BESIDES, I DON'T NEED TO SELL US OUT! I'M RICH!
AND I HAVE TOO MUCH INTEGRITY TO DO SOMETHING LIKE THAT!
MAYBE IT'S JUST A COINCIDENCE! READ ON!
"THINGS WENT CRAZY WHEN THE NEW RED-HAIRED GIRL ARRIVED IN TOWN...
...CAUSING A REAL LOVE SHOWDOWN!"
"THE RED-HAIRED KNOCKOUT PUT A STAKE THROUGH THE LOVE TRIANGLE!"
THIS IS RINGING A BELL!
5

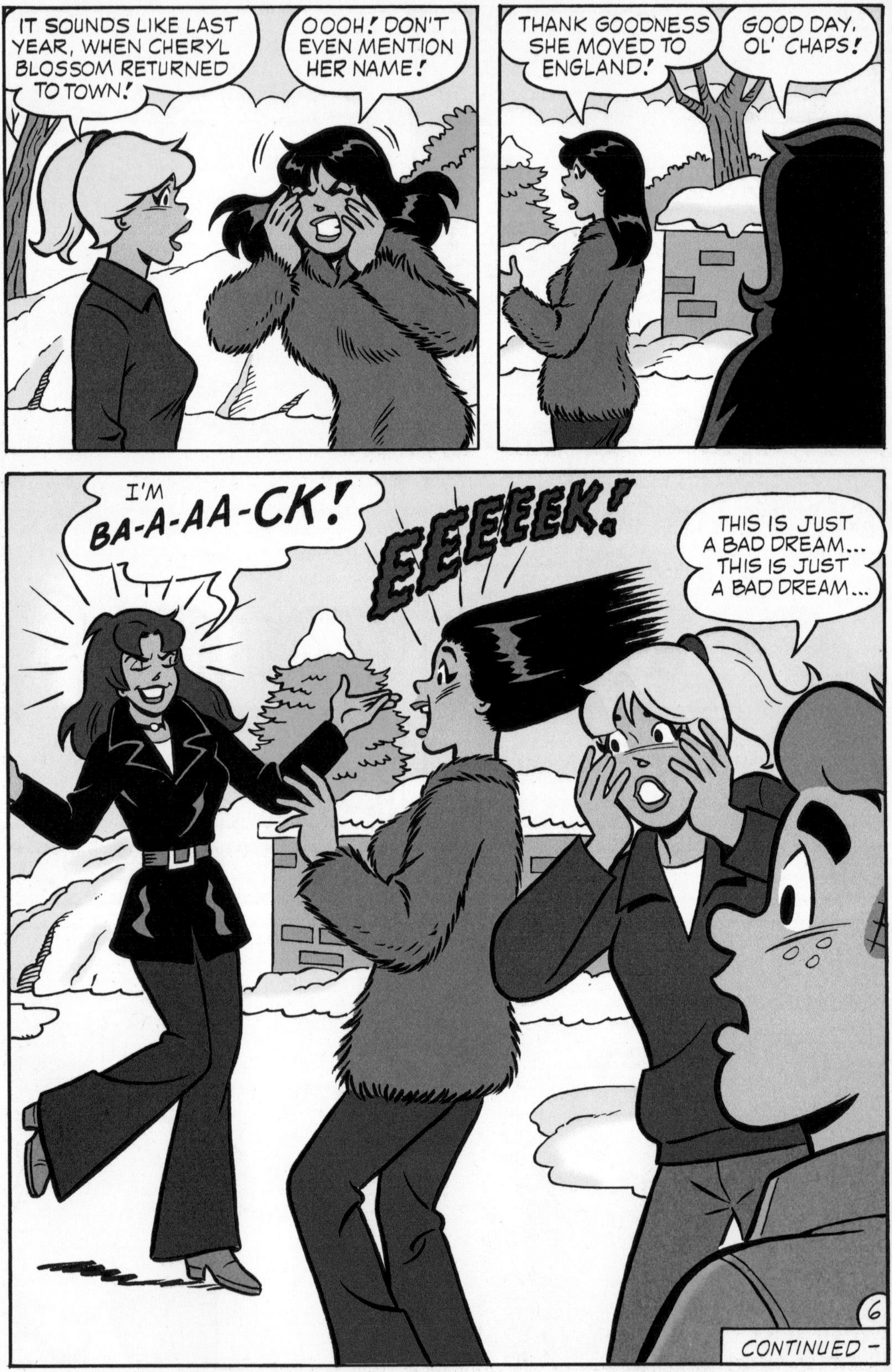
IT SOUNDS LIKE LAST YEAR, WHEN CHERYL BLOSSOM RETURNED TO TOWN!
OOOH! DON'T EVEN MENTION HER NAME!
THANK GOODNESS SHE MOVED TO ENGLAND!
GOOD DAY, OL' CHAPS!
I'M BA-A-AA-CK!
EEEEEK!
THIS IS JUST A BAD DREAM... THIS IS JUST A BAD DREAM...
6
CONTINUED -

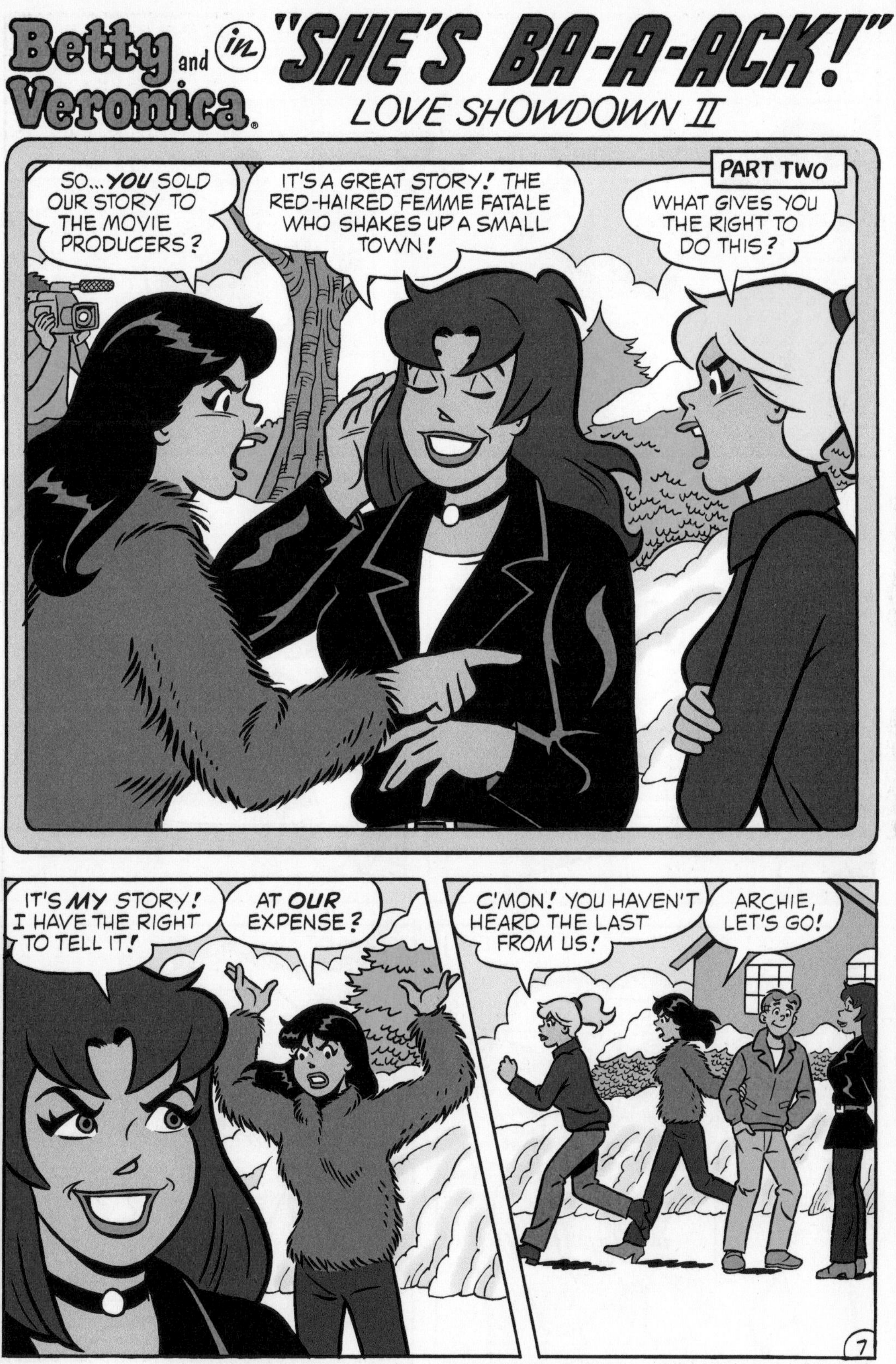
Betty and Veronica in
"SHE'S BA-A-ACK!"
LOVE SHOWDOWN II
PART TWO
SO... YOU SOLD OUR STORY TO THE MOVIE PRODUCERS?
IT'S A GREAT STORY! THE RED-HAIRED FEMME FATALE WHO SHAKES UP A SMALL TOWN!
WHAT GIVES YOU THE RIGHT TO DO THIS?
IT'S MY STORY! I HAVE THE RIGHT TO TELL IT!
AT OUR EXPENSE?
C'MON! YOU HAVEN'T HEARD THE LAST FROM US!
ARCHIE, LET'S GO!
7

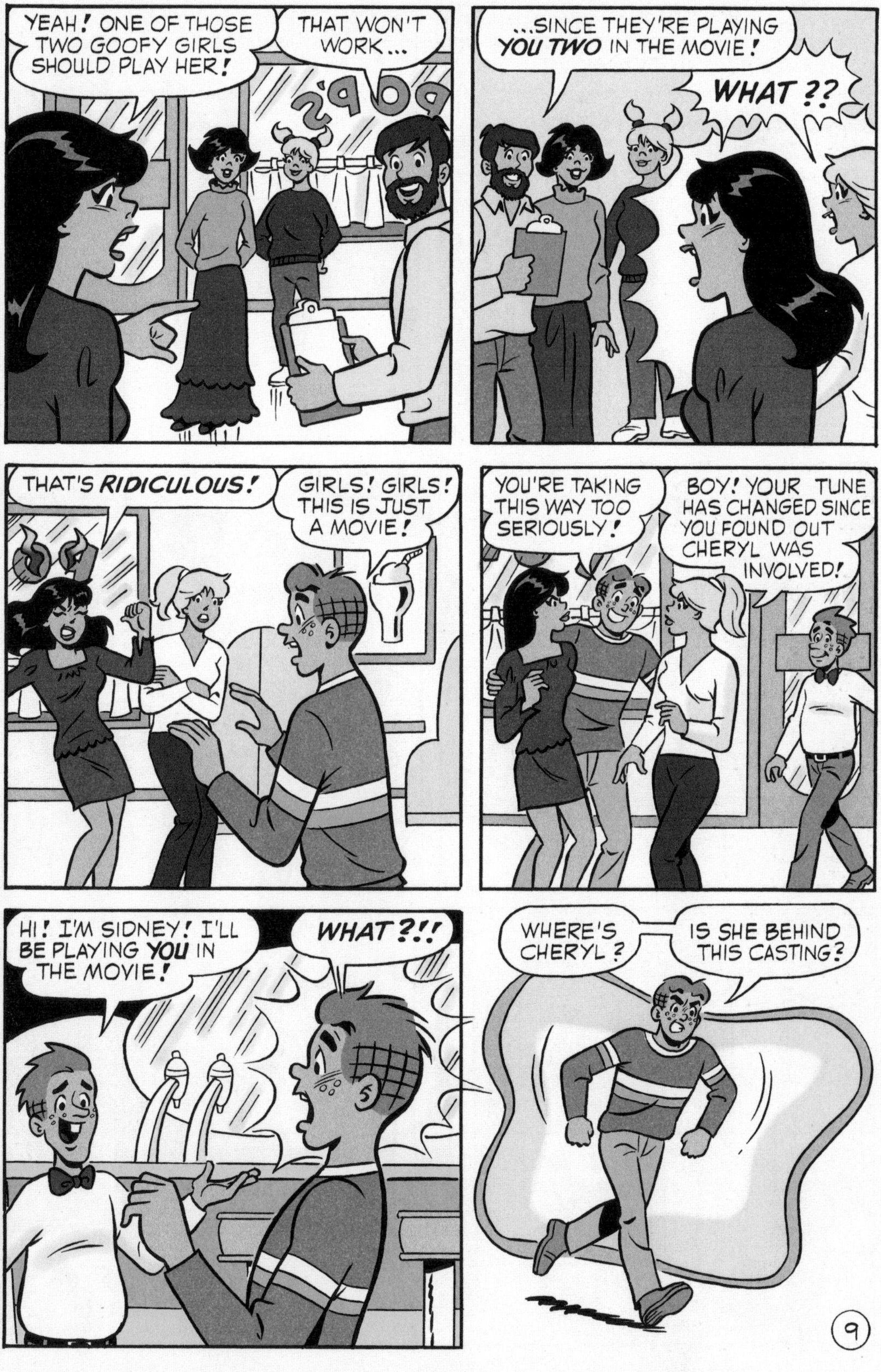

YEAH! ONE OF THOSE TWO GOOFY GIRLS SHOULD PLAY HER!
THAT WON'T WORK...
POP'S
...SINCE THEY'RE PLAYING **YOU TWO** IN THE MOVIE!
WHAT ??
THAT'S **RIDICULOUS!**
GIRLS! GIRLS! THIS IS JUST A MOVIE!
YOU'RE TAKING THIS WAY TOO SERIOUSLY!
BOY! YOUR TUNE HAS CHANGED SINCE YOU FOUND OUT CHERYL WAS INVOLVED!
HI! I'M SIDNEY! I'LL BE PLAYING **YOU** IN THE MOVIE!
WHAT ?!!
WHERE'S CHERYL?
IS SHE BEHIND THIS CASTING?
9

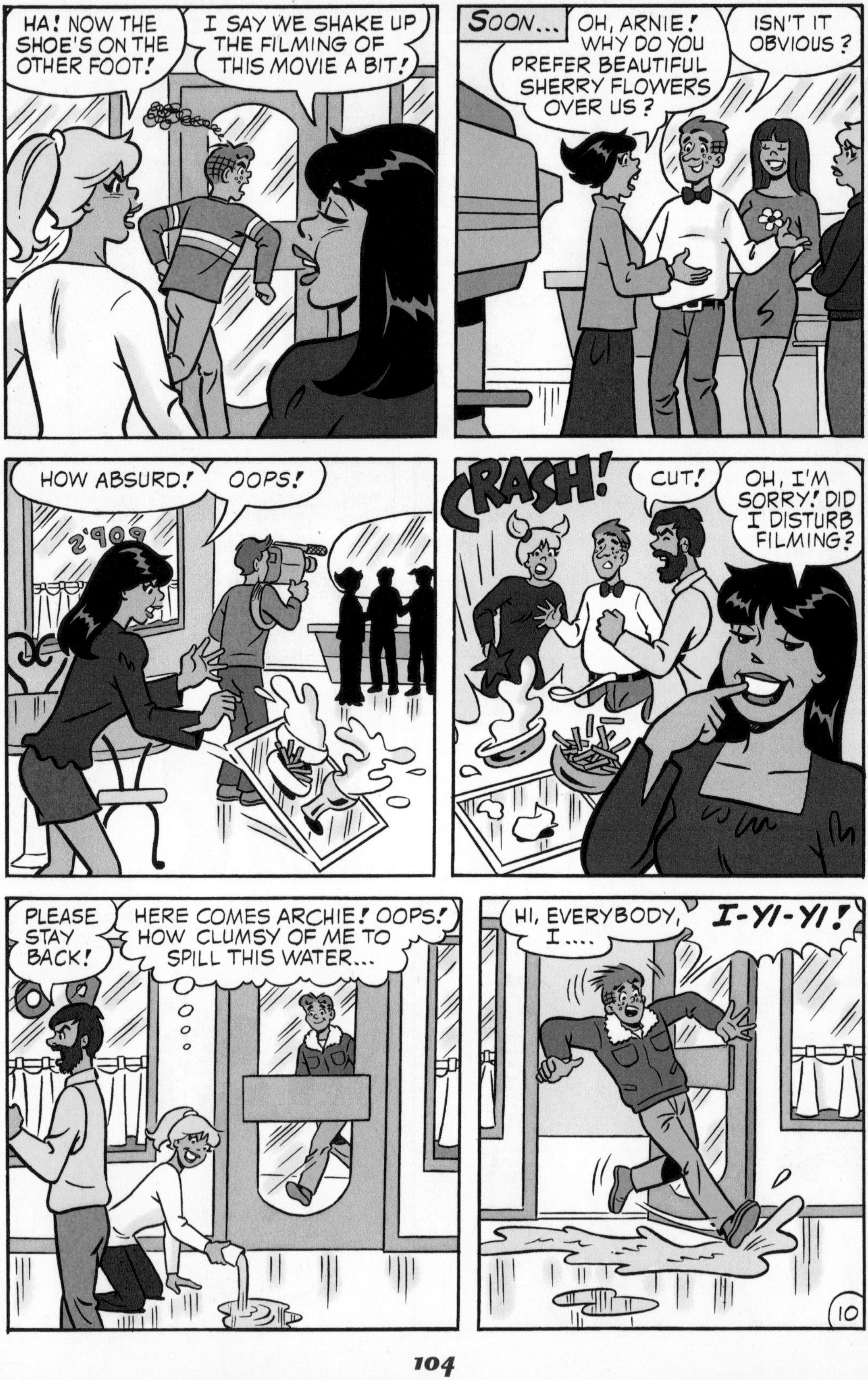
HA! NOW THE SHOE'S ON THE OTHER FOOT!
I SAY WE SHAKE UP THE FILMING OF THIS MOVIE A BIT!
SOON...
OH, ARNIE! WHY DO YOU PREFER BEAUTIFUL SHERRY FLOWERS OVER US?
ISN'T IT OBVIOUS?
HOW ABSURD!
OOPS!
POP'S
CRASH!
CUT!
OH, I'M SORRY! DID I DISTURB FILMING?
PLEASE STAY BACK!
HERE COMES ARCHIE! OOPS! HOW CLUMSY OF ME TO SPILL THIS WATER...
HI, EVERYBODY, I....
I-YI-YI!
10

Chapter Seven

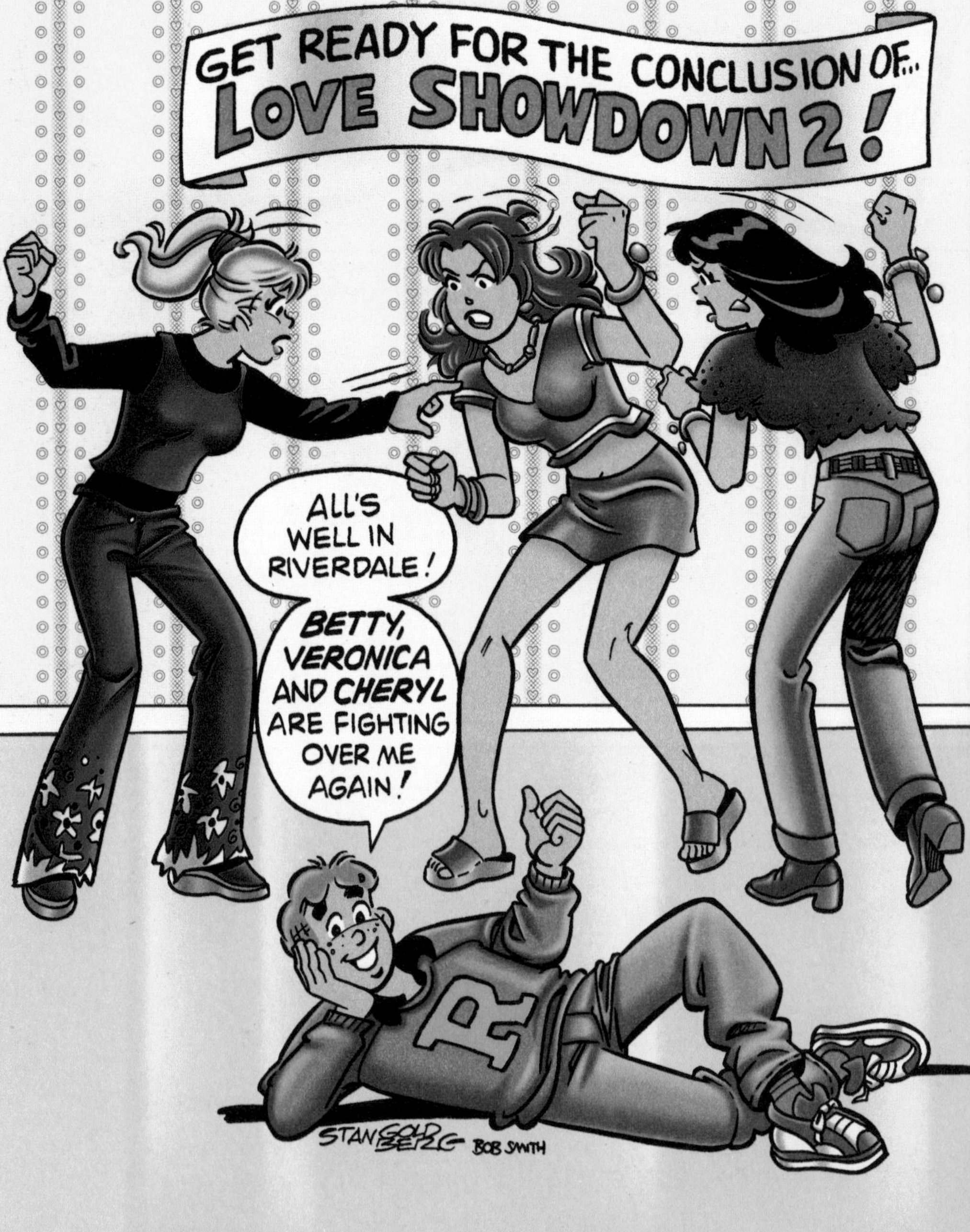
GET READY FOR THE CONCLUSION OF... LOVE SHOWDOWN 2!
ALL'S WELL IN RIVERDALE!
BETTY, VERONICA AND CHERYL ARE FIGHTING OVER ME AGAIN!
STAN GOLDBERG
BOB SMITH

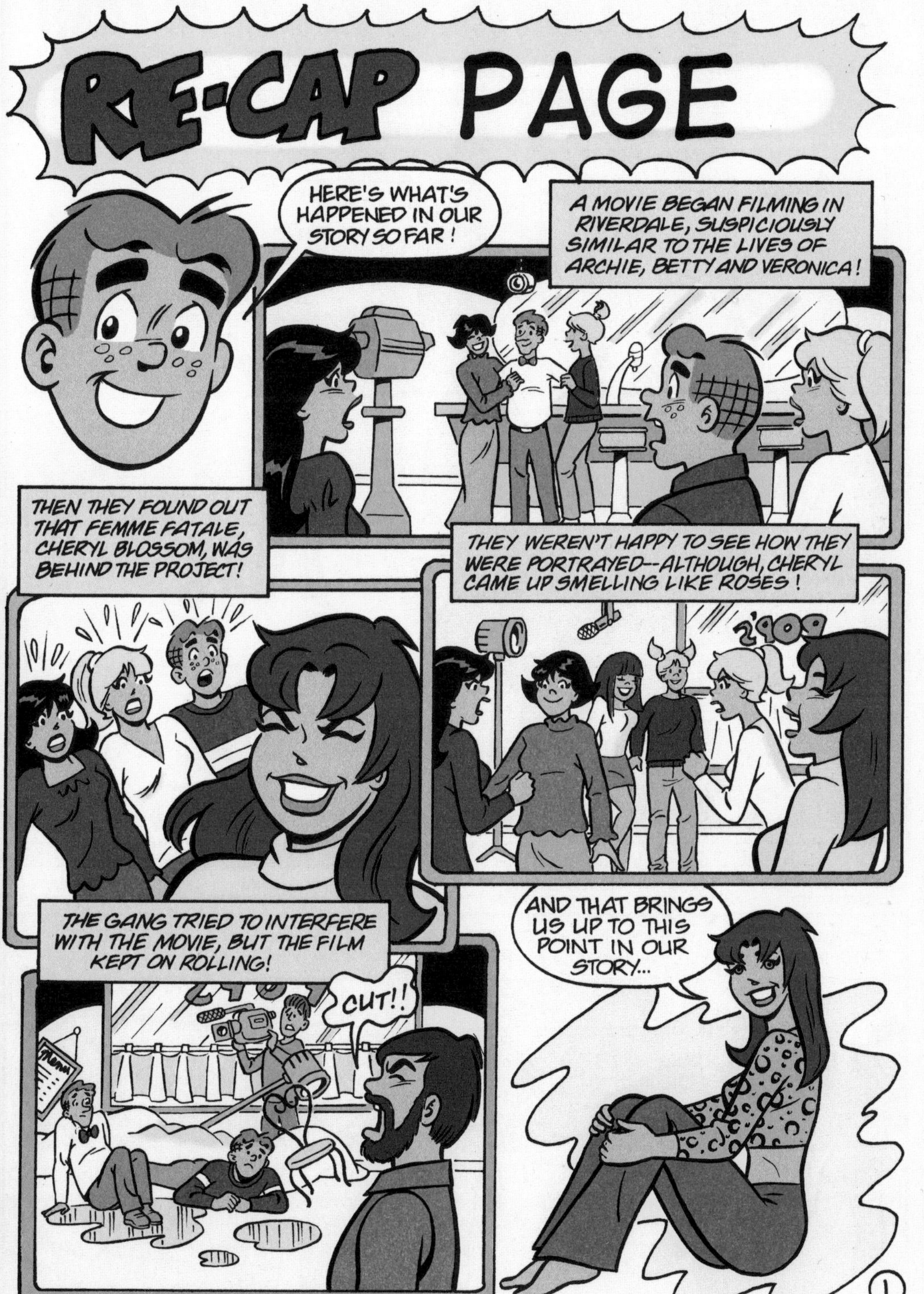
RE-CAP PAGE
HERE'S WHAT'S HAPPENED IN OUR STORY SO FAR!
A MOVIE BEGAN FILMING IN RIVERDALE, SUSPICIOUSLY SIMILAR TO THE LIVES OF ARCHIE, BETTY AND VERONICA!
THEN THEY FOUND OUT THAT FEMME FATALE, CHERYL BLOSSOM, WAS BEHIND THE PROJECT!
THEY WEREN'T HAPPY TO SEE HOW THEY WERE PORTRAYED--ALTHOUGH, CHERYL CAME UP SMELLING LIKE ROSES!
THE GANG TRIED TO INTERFERE WITH THE MOVIE, BUT THE FILM KEPT ON ROLLING!
CUT!!
AND THAT BRINGS US UP TO THIS POINT IN OUR STORY...
1

Archie & FRIENDS in "LIGHTS, CAMERA, ACTION!"

Love Showdown II (PART 3)

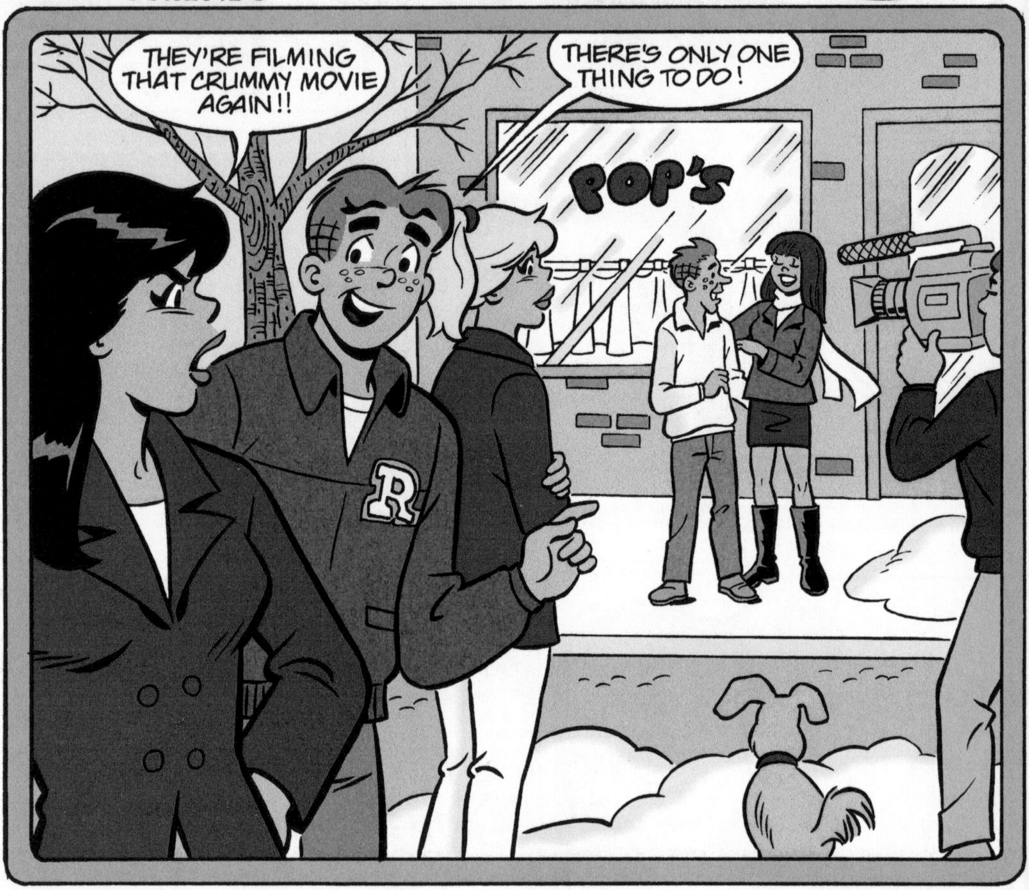

THEY'RE FILMING THAT CRUMMY MOVIE AGAIN!!
THERE'S ONLY ONE THING TO DO!
POP'S

SCRIPT AND PENCILS: DAN PARENT | INKING: JON D'AGOSTINO | LETTERING: VICKIE WILLIAMS | COLORING: BARRY GROSSMAN | EDITOR: VICTOR GORELICK | EDITOR-IN-CHIEF: RICHARD GOLDWATER

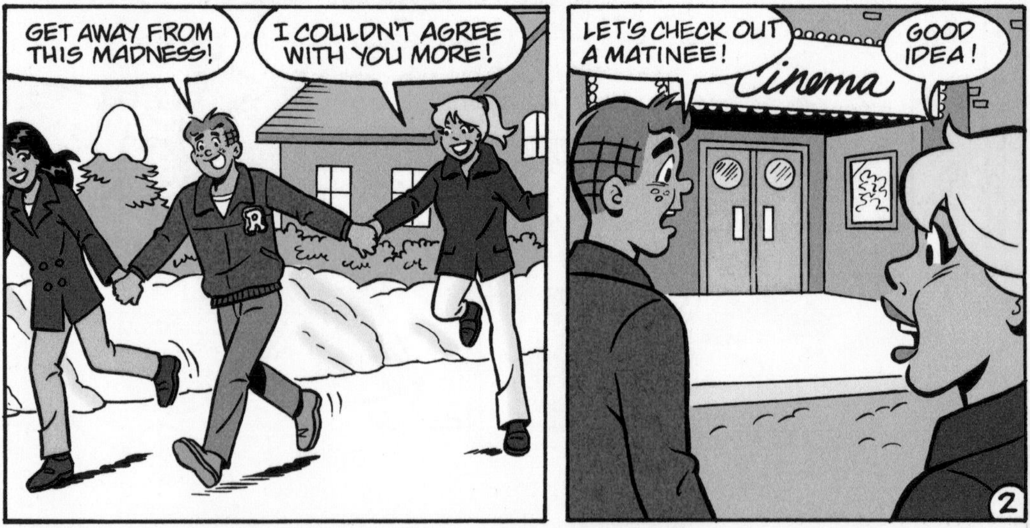

GET AWAY FROM THIS MADNESS!
I COULDN'T AGREE WITH YOU MORE!
LET'S CHECK OUT A MATINEE!
GOOD IDEA!
Cinema
2

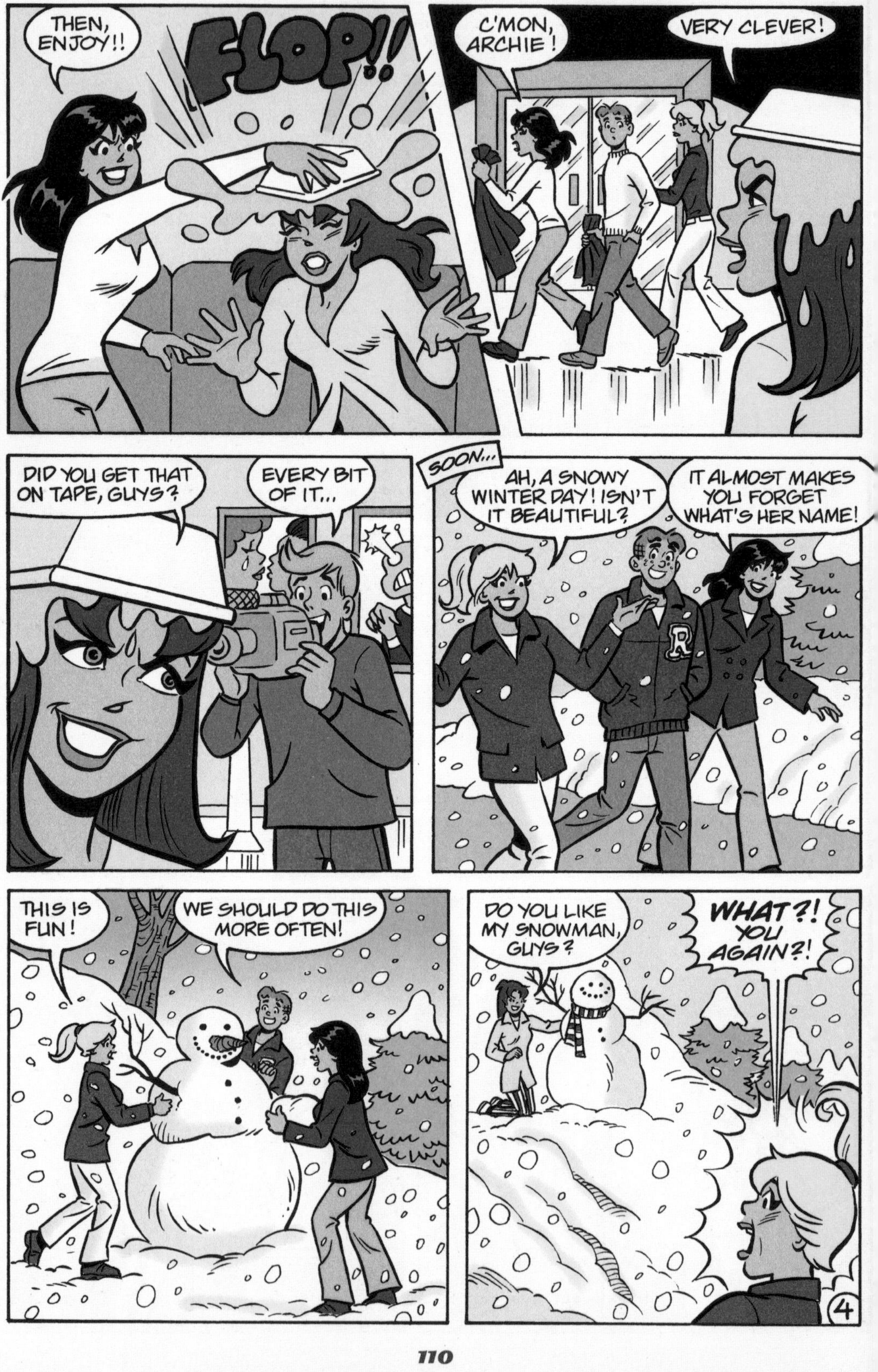
THEN, ENJOY!!
FLOP!!
C'MON, ARCHIE!
VERY CLEVER!
DID YOU GET THAT ON TAPE, GUYS?
EVERY BIT OF IT...
SOON...
AH, A SNOWY WINTER DAY! ISN'T IT BEAUTIFUL?
IT ALMOST MAKES YOU FORGET WHAT'S HER NAME!
R
THIS IS FUN!
WE SHOULD DO THIS MORE OFTEN!
DO YOU LIKE MY SNOWMAN, GUYS?
WHAT?! YOU AGAIN?!
4

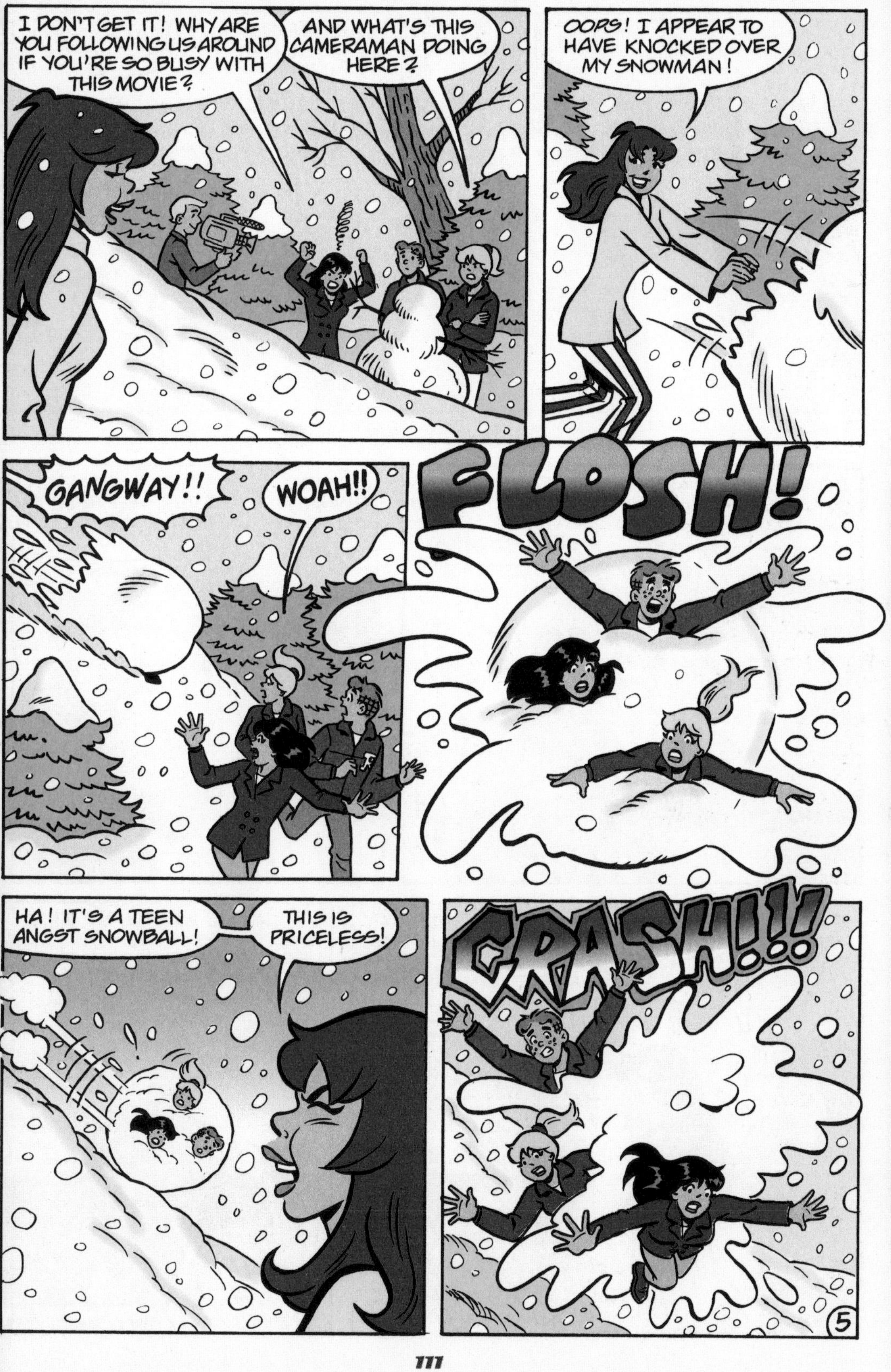
I DON'T GET IT! WHY ARE YOU FOLLOWING US AROUND IF YOU'RE SO BUSY WITH THIS MOVIE?
AND WHAT'S THIS CAMERAMAN DOING HERE?
OOPS! I APPEAR TO HAVE KNOCKED OVER MY SNOWMAN!
GANGWAY!!
WOAH!!
FLOSH!
HA! IT'S A TEEN ANGST SNOWBALL!
THIS IS PRICELESS!
!
CRASH!!!!
5

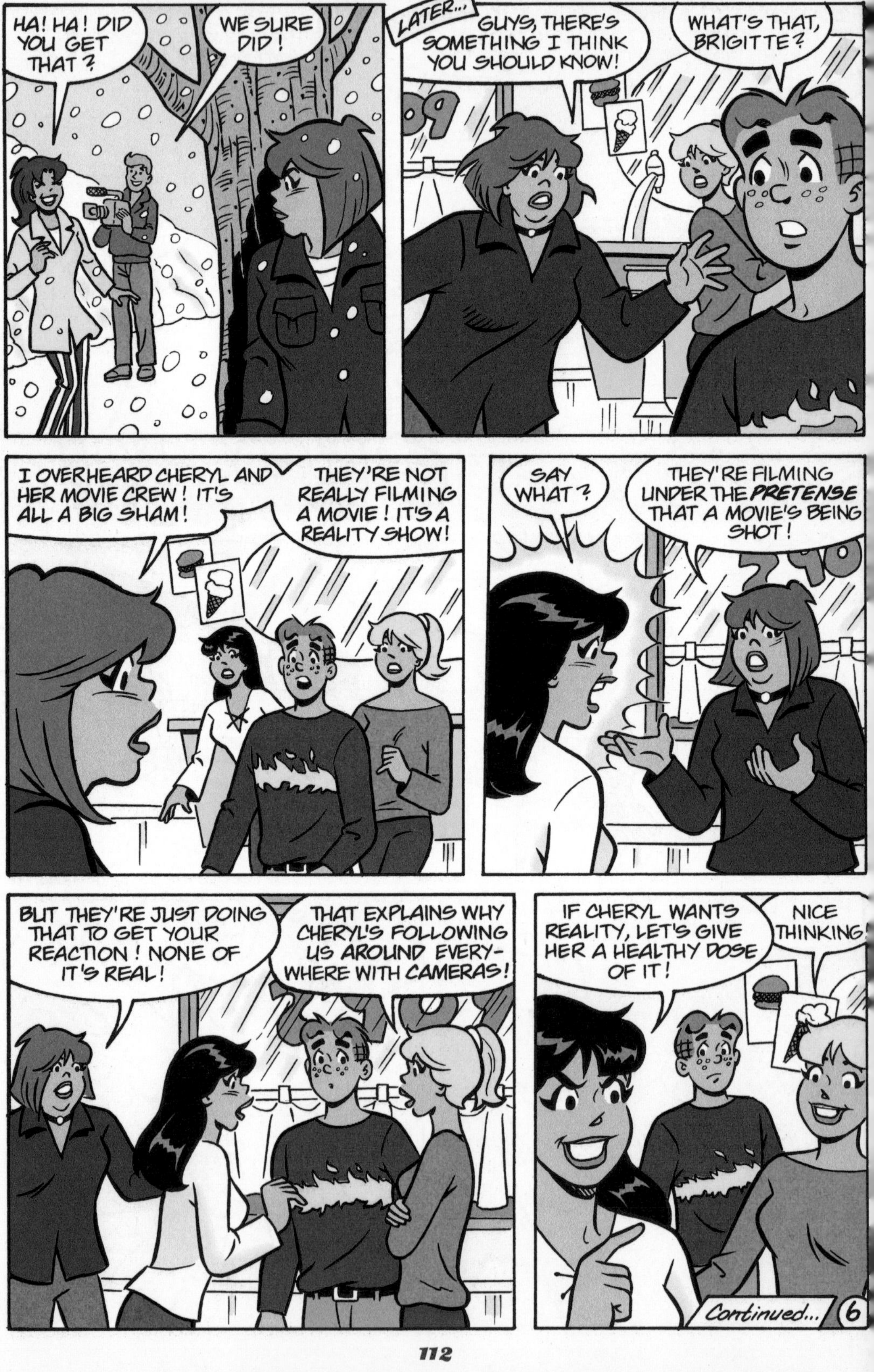
HA! HA! DID YOU GET THAT?
WE SURE DID!
LATER...
GUYS, THERE'S SOMETHING I THINK YOU SHOULD KNOW!
WHAT'S THAT, BRIGITTE?
I OVERHEARD CHERYL AND HER MOVIE CREW! IT'S ALL A BIG SHAM!
THEY'RE NOT REALLY FILMING A MOVIE! IT'S A REALITY SHOW!
SAY WHAT?
THEY'RE FILMING UNDER THE PRETENSE THAT A MOVIE'S BEING SHOT!
BUT THEY'RE JUST DOING THAT TO GET YOUR REACTION! NONE OF IT'S REAL!
THAT EXPLAINS WHY CHERYL'S FOLLOWING US AROUND EVERY-WHERE WITH CAMERAS!
IF CHERYL WANTS REALITY, LET'S GIVE HER A HEALTHY DOSE OF IT!
NICE THINKING
Continued...
6

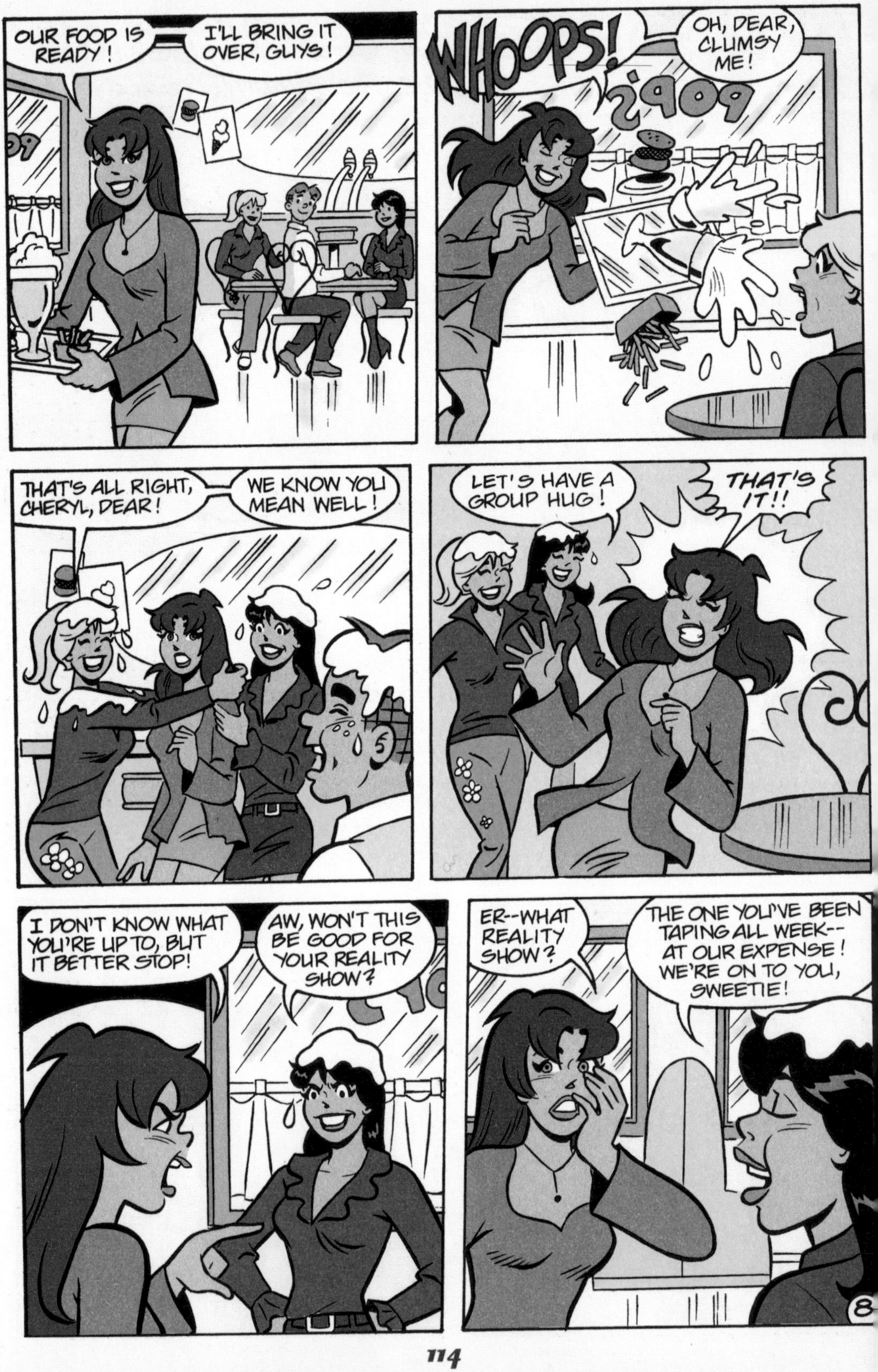
OUR FOOD IS READY!
I'LL BRING IT OVER, GUYS!
WHOOPS!
OH, DEAR, CLUMSY ME!
POP'S
THAT'S ALL RIGHT, CHERYL, DEAR!
WE KNOW YOU MEAN WELL!
LET'S HAVE A GROUP HUG!
THAT'S IT!!
I DON'T KNOW WHAT YOU'RE UP TO, BUT IT BETTER STOP!
AW, WON'T THIS BE GOOD FOR YOUR REALITY SHOW?
ER--WHAT REALITY SHOW?
THE ONE YOU'VE BEEN TAPING ALL WEEK-- AT OUR EXPENSE! WE'RE ON TO YOU, SWEETIE!
8

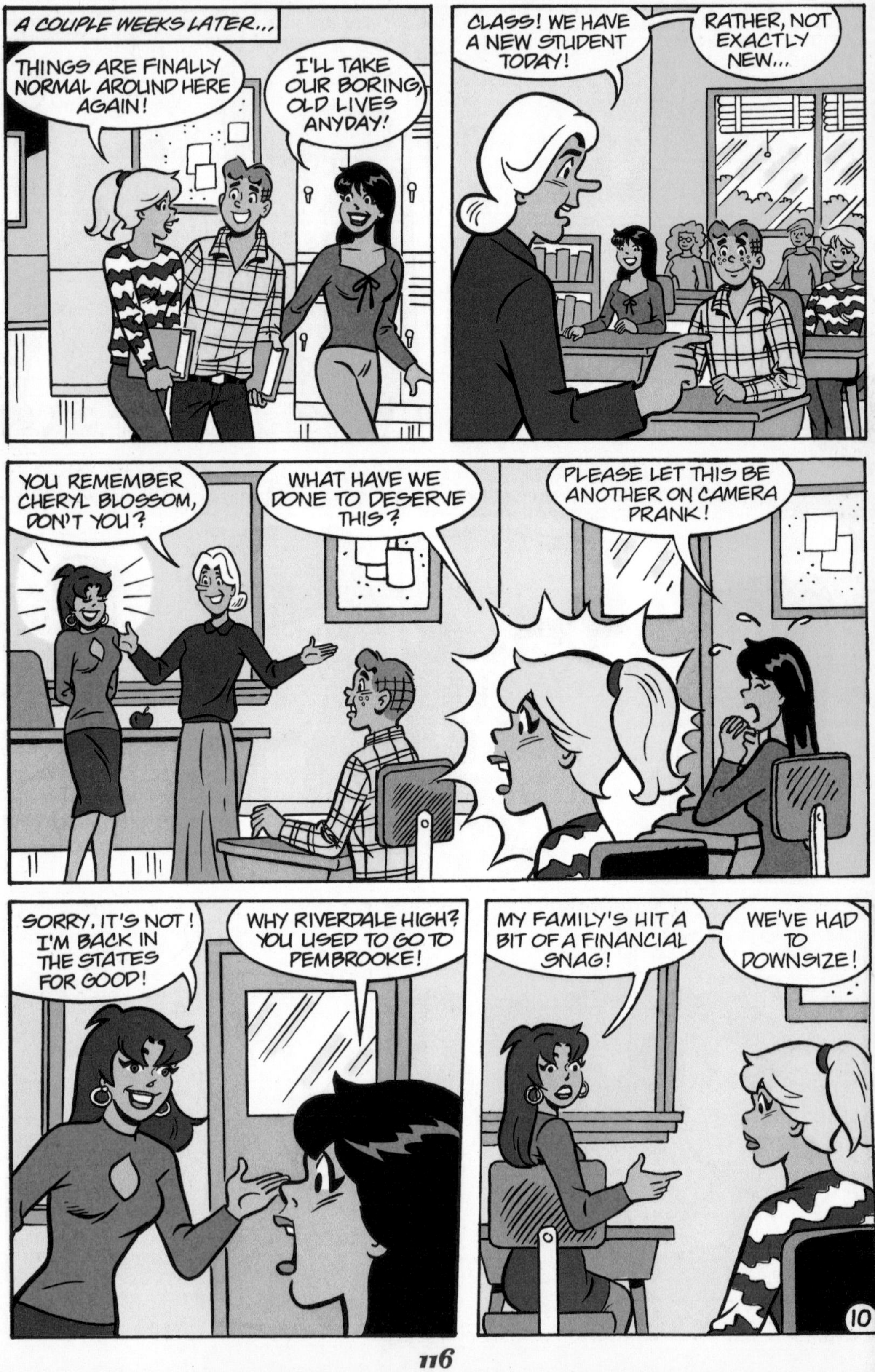
A COUPLE WEEKS LATER...
THINGS ARE FINALLY NORMAL AROUND HERE AGAIN!
I'LL TAKE OUR BORING, OLD LIVES ANYDAY!
CLASS! WE HAVE A NEW STUDENT TODAY!
RATHER, NOT EXACTLY NEW...
YOU REMEMBER CHERYL BLOSSOM, DON'T YOU?
WHAT HAVE WE DONE TO DESERVE THIS?
PLEASE LET THIS BE ANOTHER ON CAMERA PRANK!
SORRY, IT'S NOT! I'M BACK IN THE STATES FOR GOOD!
WHY RIVERDALE HIGH? YOU USED TO GO TO PEMBROOKE!
MY FAMILY'S HIT A BIT OF A FINANCIAL SNAG!
WE'VE HAD TO DOWNSIZE!
10

Afterword

By Dan Parent

What can you say about the classic "Love Showdown" storyline that hasn't already been said? Plenty! Since the theme of the story is timeless (young love and those everlasting love triangles), both new fans and past generations of readers can appreciate it. It boils down to one thing: we all care about these characters.

Of course, I'm biased—I wrote the story along with Bill Golliher. But I'm an Archie fan too, having grown up on the comics, so I had a vested interest in these characters for sure! And when Victor Gorelick, editor extraordinaire, said to come up with a big storyline, I knew where to go—right to the heart of the love triangle... but now it would be expanded to a love quadrilateral!

Bringing in a threat to the love triangle was easy. It arrived in the form of Cheryl Blossom. I was a huge fan of the early Cheryl stories—they were some of the best stories ever done, really pushing the envelope as far as where Archie could go. Cheryl was such a sexy femme fatale, with that beautiful DeCarlo art and Frank Doyle's sharp writing, that she made the perfect threat to the love triangle.

The "Love Showdown" story got huge media exposure, making it one of the most—if not THE most—nationally covered Archie events of all time. People wanted to know who Archie was leaving Betty and Veronica for, and stuck around to see that it was Cheryl. In fact, she became a major player in the Archie universe again, and remains a prominent character to this day. I'd like to take all the credit for this, but I can't. It's all about these characters—characters that had been around long before me, and will be around long after.

The word "character" sums it all up. People care about these characters, which is why you'll see new editions of "Love Showdown" and other stories introduced year after year. Archie, Betty , Veronica, Jughead, Reggie, Cheryl Blossom and the rest— they're part of Americana, pop culture, whatever you want to call it. They're our childhood friends, and friends we want to introduce to our children, grandchildren, etc... and like the way we come back to our friends and family year after year, we'll always come back to characters we care about. I know I will!

Dan Parent

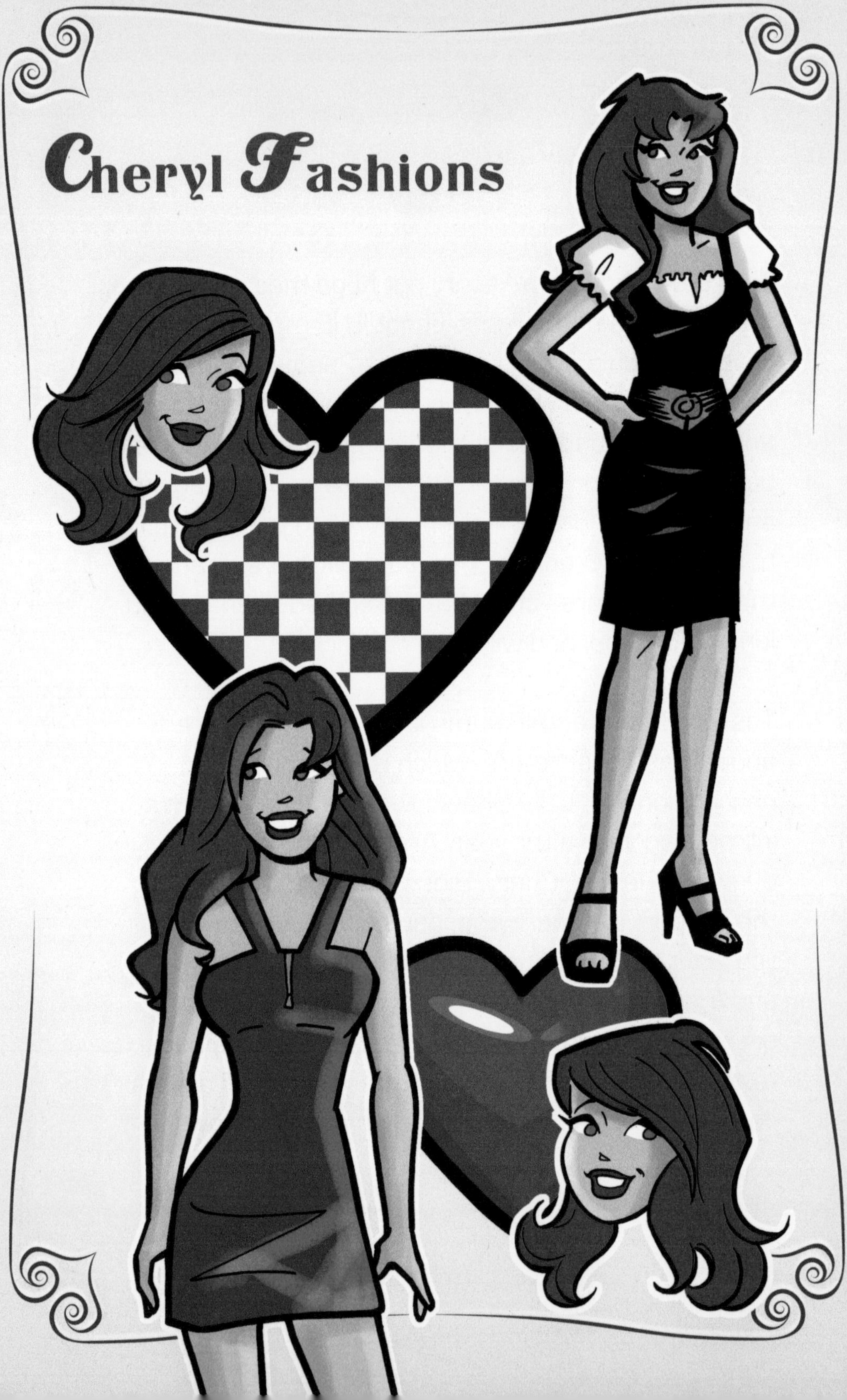
Cheryl Fashions

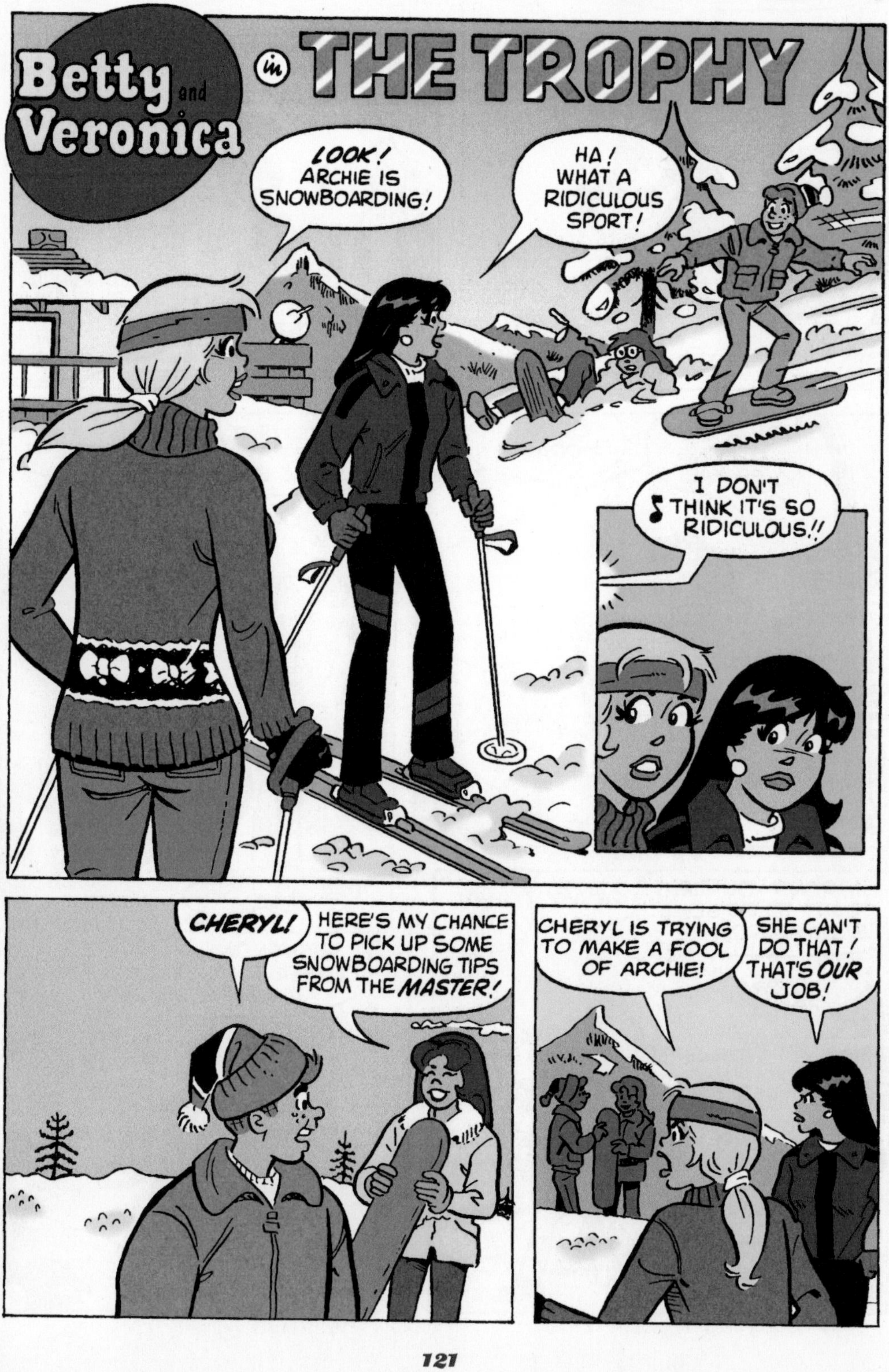
Betty and Veronica
in
THE TROPHY
LOOK! ARCHIE IS SNOWBOARDING!
HA! WHAT A RIDICULOUS SPORT!
I DON'T THINK IT'S SO RIDICULOUS!!
CHERYL!
HERE'S MY CHANCE TO PICK UP SOME SNOWBOARDING TIPS FROM THE MASTER!
CHERYL IS TRYING TO MAKE A FOOL OF ARCHIE!
SHE CAN'T DO THAT! THAT'S OUR JOB!

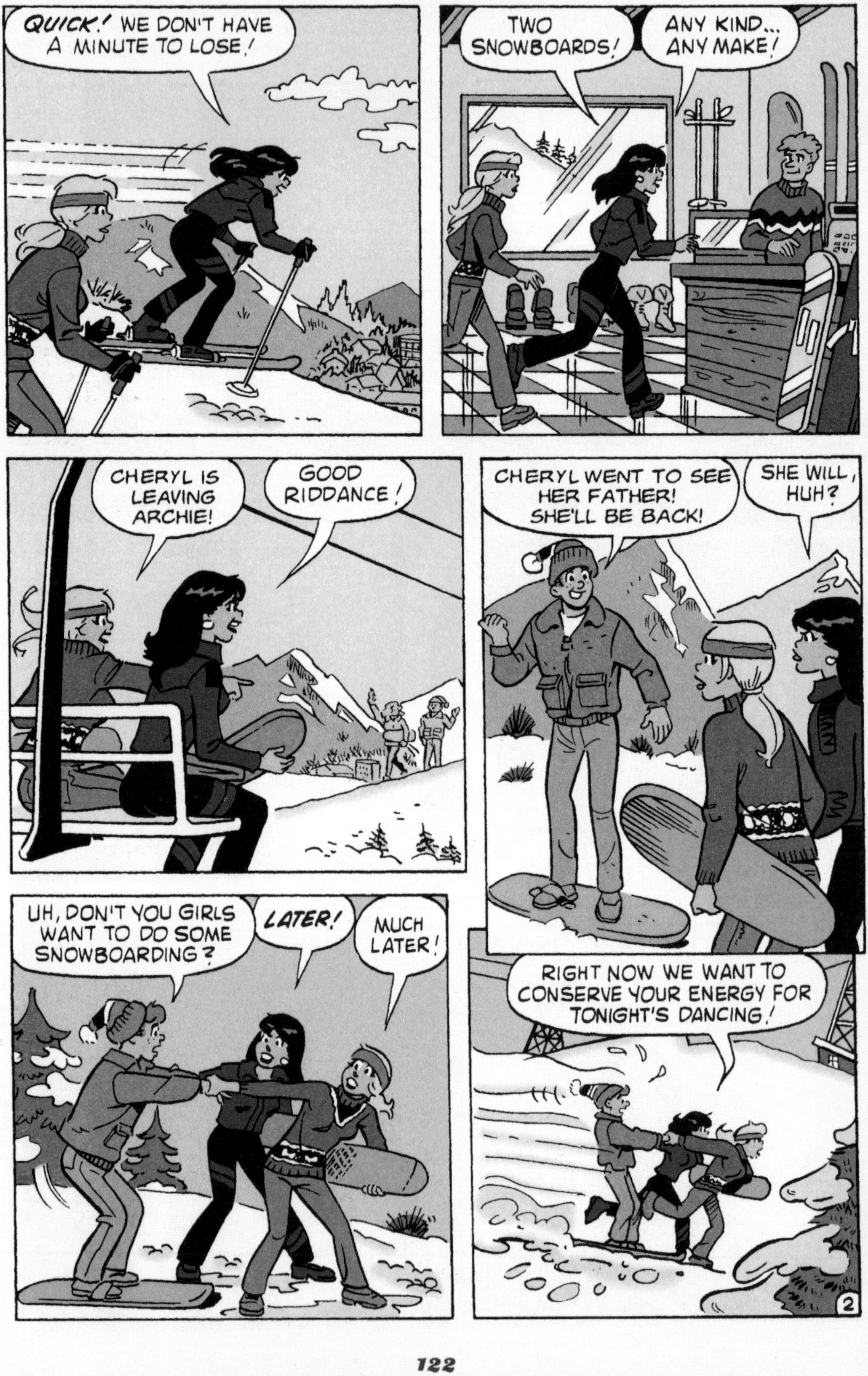
QUICK! WE DON'T HAVE A MINUTE TO LOSE!
TWO SNOWBOARDS!
ANY KIND... ANY MAKE!
CHERYL IS LEAVING ARCHIE!
GOOD RIDDANCE!
CHERYL WENT TO SEE HER FATHER! SHE'LL BE BACK!
SHE WILL, HUH?
UH, DON'T YOU GIRLS WANT TO DO SOME SNOWBOARDING?
LATER!
MUCH LATER!
RIGHT NOW WE WANT TO CONSERVE YOUR ENERGY FOR TONIGHT'S DANCING!
2

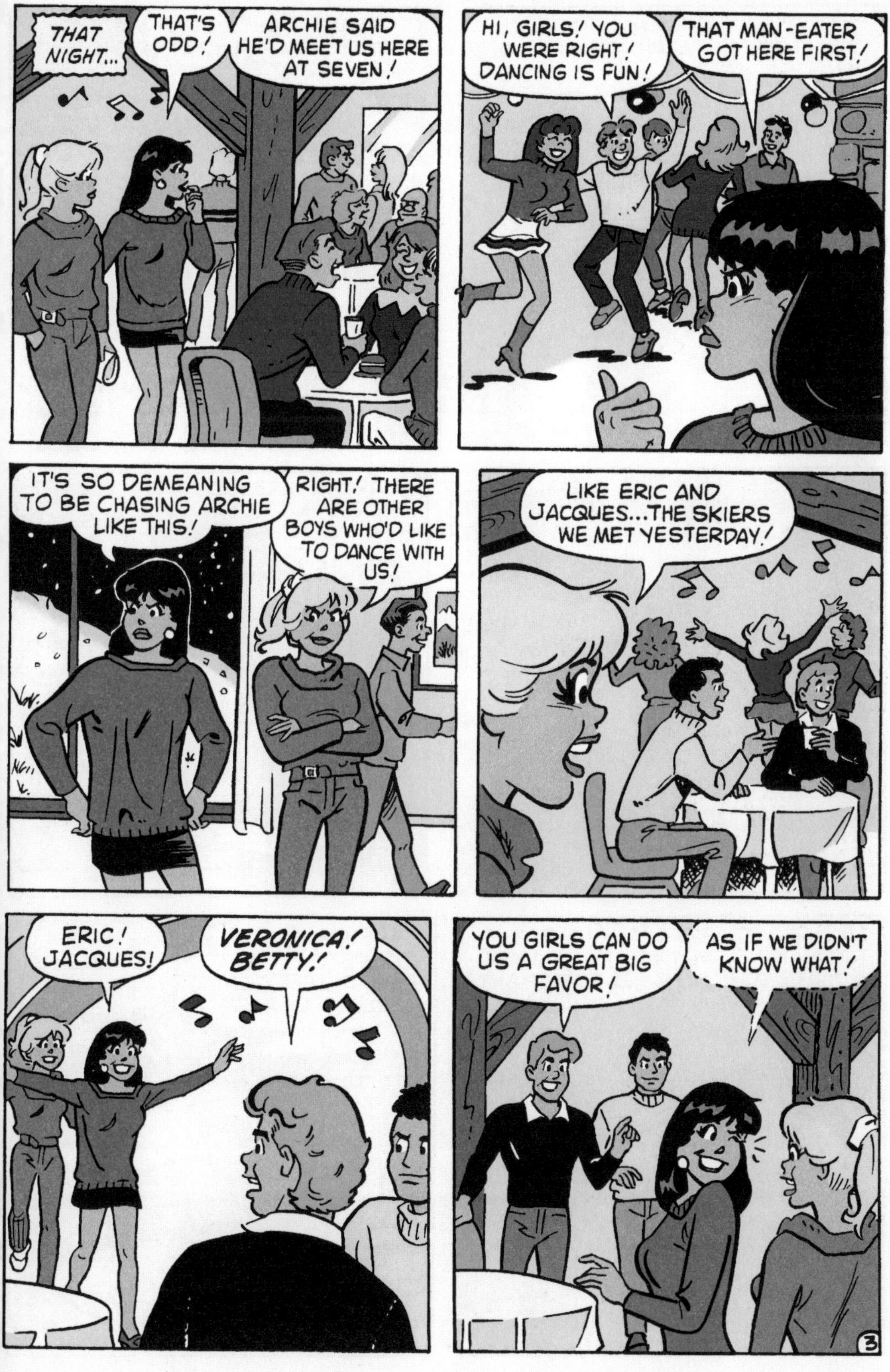
THAT NIGHT...
THAT'S ODD!
ARCHIE SAID HE'D MEET US HERE AT SEVEN!
HI, GIRLS! YOU WERE RIGHT! DANCING IS FUN!
THAT MAN-EATER GOT HERE FIRST!
IT'S SO DEMEANING TO BE CHASING ARCHIE LIKE THIS!
RIGHT! THERE ARE OTHER BOYS WHO'D LIKE TO DANCE WITH US!
LIKE ERIC AND JACQUES...THE SKIERS WE MET YESTERDAY!
ERIC! JACQUES!
VERONICA! BETTY!
YOU GIRLS CAN DO US A GREAT BIG FAVOR!
AS IF WE DIDN'T KNOW WHAT!
3

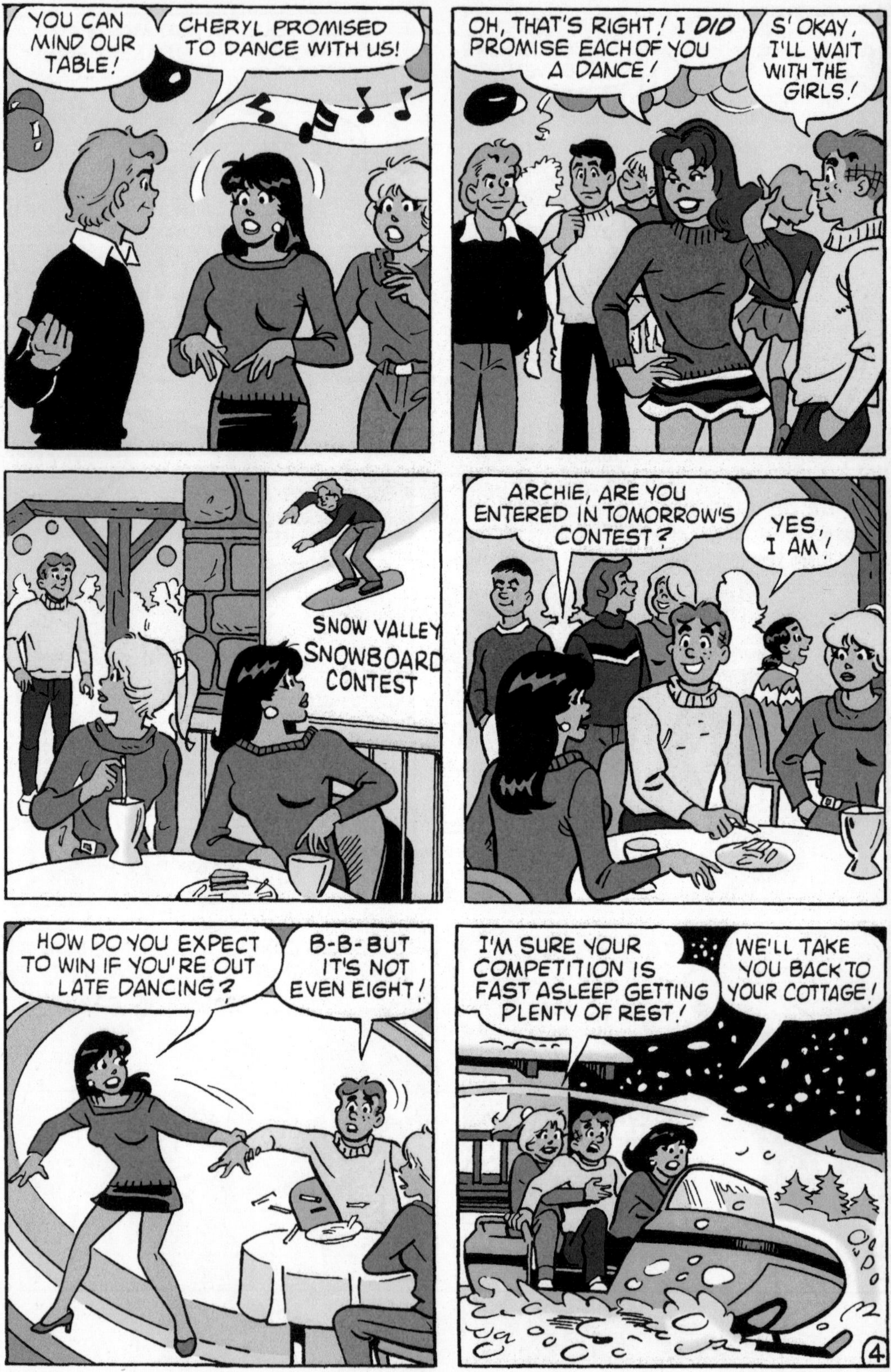
YOU CAN MIND OUR TABLE!
CHERYL PROMISED TO DANCE WITH US!
OH, THAT'S RIGHT! I DID PROMISE EACH OF YOU A DANCE!
S' OKAY, I'LL WAIT WITH THE GIRLS!
SNOW VALLEY SNOWBOARD CONTEST
ARCHIE, ARE YOU ENTERED IN TOMORROW'S CONTEST?
YES, I AM!
HOW DO YOU EXPECT TO WIN IF YOU'RE OUT LATE DANCING?
B-B-BUT IT'S NOT EVEN EIGHT!
I'M SURE YOUR COMPETITION IS FAST ASLEEP GETTING PLENTY OF REST!
WE'LL TAKE YOU BACK TO YOUR COTTAGE!
4

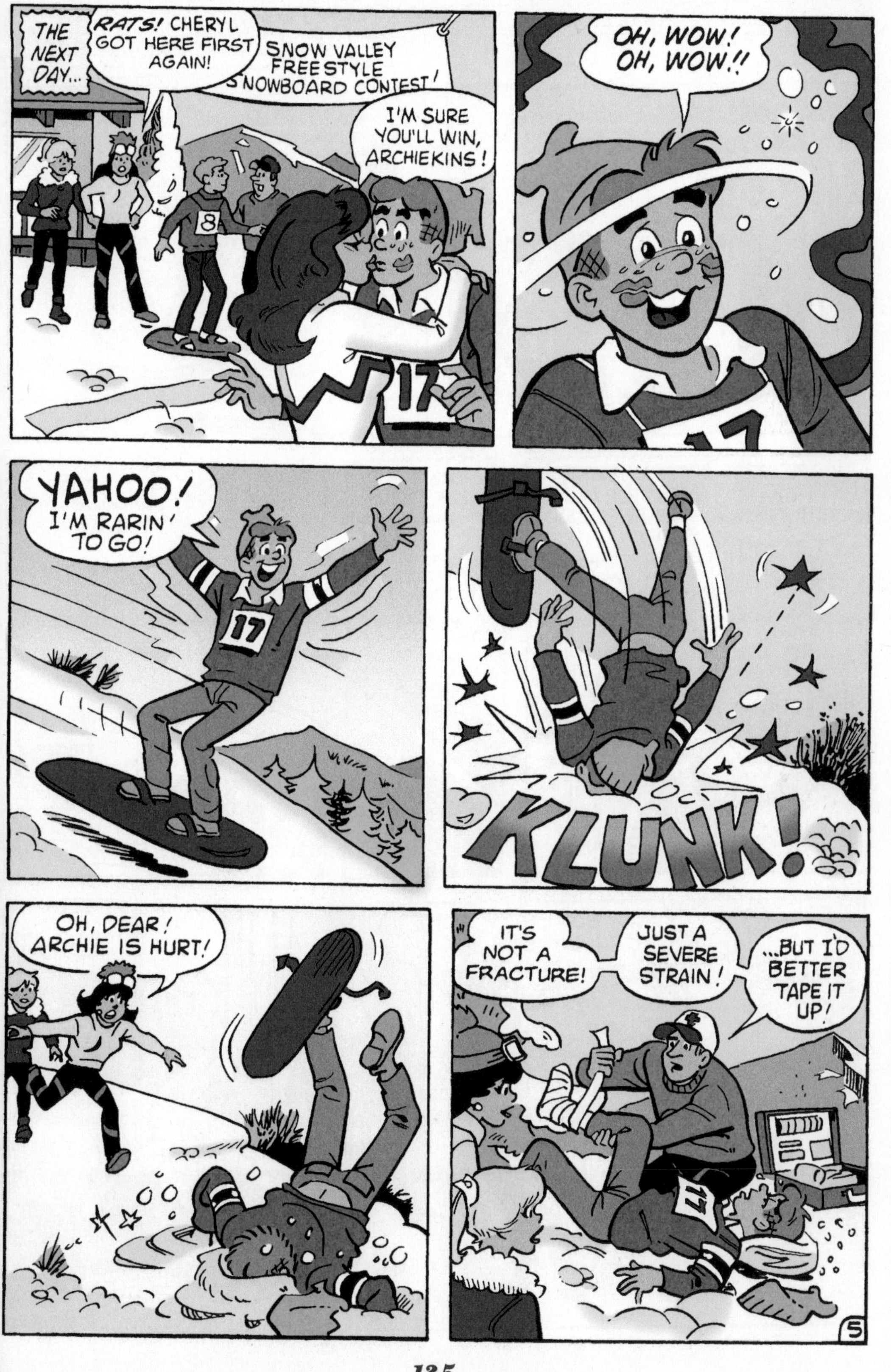
THE NEXT DAY...
RATS! CHERYL GOT HERE FIRST AGAIN!
SNOW VALLEY FREESTYLE SNOWBOARD CONTEST!
I'M SURE YOU'LL WIN, ARCHIEKINS!
OH, WOW! OH, WOW!!
YAHOO! I'M RARIN' TO GO!
KLUNK!
OH, DEAR! ARCHIE IS HURT!
IT'S NOT A FRACTURE!
JUST A SEVERE STRAIN!
...BUT I'D BETTER TAPE IT UP!
5

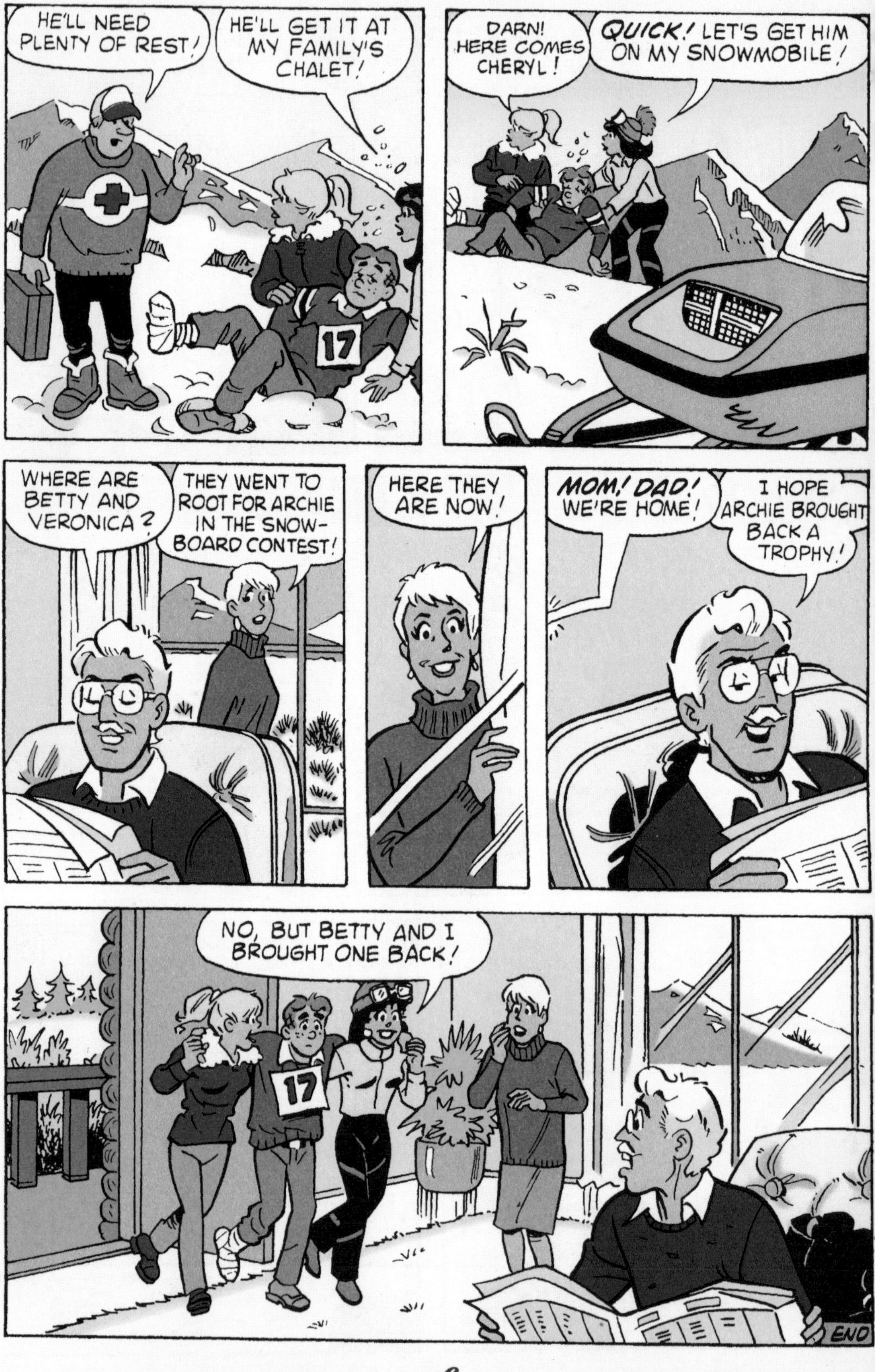
HE'LL NEED PLENTY OF REST!
HE'LL GET IT AT MY FAMILY'S CHALET!
DARN! HERE COMES CHERYL!
QUICK! LET'S GET HIM ON MY SNOWMOBILE!
WHERE ARE BETTY AND VERONICA?
THEY WENT TO ROOT FOR ARCHIE IN THE SNOW-BOARD CONTEST!
HERE THEY ARE NOW!
MOM! DAD! WE'RE HOME!
I HOPE ARCHIE BROUGHT BACK A TROPHY!
NO, BUT BETTY AND I BROUGHT ONE BACK!
17
ENO